Handsome and Hideous

HANDSOME

AND

HIDEOUS

MARIA FOX

Bird in Hand Publishing

Handsome and Hideous

Content and Trigger Warnings

This story contains the following situations:

- Rejection by a parent

- Serious illness of a parent

- Suicidal ideation (remembered briefly)

- Magic-induced physical pain and loss of mobility (not permanent)

- Loss of a child (remembered)

To Jamie,
Nick, Luke, and Frances Walker,
with love

CONTENTS

Part I

Hidden

Chapter One   3

Chapter Two   13

Chapter Three   23

Chapter Four   31

Chapter Five   43

Chapter Six   53

Chapter Seven   65

Chapter Eight   69

Chapter Nine   75

Chapter Ten   79

Chapter Eleven   85

Chapter Twelve   91

Chapter Thirteen   95

Chapter Fourteen   101

Chapter Fifteen   111

Chapter Sixteen   117

Chapter Seventeen   121

Chapter Eighteen   133

Chapter Nineteen   137

Part II
Scion

Chapter Twenty   143

Chapter Twenty-One   151

Chapter Twenty-Two   161

Chapter Twenty-Three   167

Chapter Twenty-Four   171

Chapter Twenty-Five   177

Chapter Twenty-Six   183

Chapter Twenty-Seven   205

Chapter Twenty-Eight   217

Chapter Twenty-Nine   225

Chapter Thirty   231

Chapter Thirty-One   241

Chapter Thirty-Two   249

Chapter Thirty-Three   261

Chapter Thirty-Four   265

Chapter Thirty-Five   275

Chapter Thirty-Six   283

Chapter Thirty-Seven   287

Chapter Thirty-Eight 299

Chapter Thirty-Nine 311

Chapter Forty 317

Chapter Forty-One 325

Chapter Forty-Two 333

Chapter Forty-Three 337

Chapter Forty-Four 341

Part III

Flame

Chapter Forty-Five 347

Chapter Forty-Six 357

Chapter Forty-Seven 373

Chapter Forty-Eight 393

Chapter Forty-Nine 413

Chapter Fifty 419

Chapter Fifty-One 427

Chapter Fifty-Two 433

Chapter Fifty-Three 441

Chapter Fifty-Four 445

Chapter Fifty-Five 459

Chapter Fifty-Six 481

Chapter Fifty-Seven 487

Chapter Fifty-Eight 489

Chapter Fifty-Nine 495

Chapter Sixty 501

Chapter Sixty-One 509

Chapter Sixty-Two 519

Chapter Sixty-Three 525

Chapter Sixty-Four 533

Chapter Sixty-Five 537

Chapter Sixty-Six 541

Chapter Sixty-Seven 545

Chapter Sixty-Eight 551

Chapter Sixty-Nine 557

Chapter Seventy 563

Epilogue 567

Acknowledgments 571

About the Author 573

PART I

HIDDEN

Chapter One

It was hard to scrub with the screams of the woman in labor winding their way through the halls and stairs of the tower. Rue's own heart was heavy with the death of her baby not two days ago. *Dulsan.* The hard stone of the step abraded her knees as she worked, even through the coarse fabric of her skirts. She paused on the fifth step, the wooden bucket of warm water and crushed soaproot two steps above her, and sat back on her heels. Rubbing the back of one wrist over her eyes did nothing to stop the leak of tears. Her swollen breasts hurt with the milk her baby no longer needed. Another scream shredded the air and Rue bent to her work, scrubbing with the worn brush, but lost in her own memories.

She had not screamed as much when birthing Dulsan a few months earlier. But then, she had not had the same store of rage and hatred to expel, either. Rue had come to Reavinstoft, the tower of Besserdech of the Ice Raven Clan, less than a year ago. The year before that, the other servants said, Master Besserdech, a powerful mage, had gone on a raid. There, in a distant land, he had destroyed the tower and vale of a family of sorcerers who looked to the Fire Bird. He killed adults and children alike, all except for one girl—the woman now straining in childbirth. Amarrasal had been barely twenty and though strong in raw power, she was no match for the cunning and the skill of a mage twice her age.

He had brought her, draped in cold chains that glittered like adamant, to Reavinstoft, his lair. Besserdech spoke before witnesses the words of power that would bind him to the girl, soul to soul, and managed to stun her long enough with a spell to get her to speak her own part. When she recovered her senses, she found herself married to the man who had murdered her family and raped her. When she tried to use her power to free herself, Amarrasal discovered to her horror that he had opened a magical conduit between them, so that her own strength was at his disposal. Her husband, or rather, master, saw her as nothing but a means of breeding a child for him: a son strong in power and trained from infancy in loyalty and submission.

For a time, or so said the scullery girl to Rue, the mistress had tried to win the aid of the servants. But Amarrasal was a visible sign of her lord's power: since their binding rite, she was always enveloped in a cold blue glow. No one asked about it, but everyone knew that the glow was the result of the spells Besserdech had laid on her. And if he could do that to a daughter of the only mage bloodline that rivaled his own in power, what could he do to a plain mortal?

When Amarrasal realized she was pregnant, she withdrew from the life of Reavinstoft completely. She ignored the servants who cleaned her room and tended the fire. Food was brought and the dishes removed after the food was eaten without a word or a glance from the still form sitting by the window, shrouded always in the blue glow that never wavered or faded. Yet the very stones of the tower seemed to echo with her bitterness, grief, and rage.

For his part, Besserdech had no dealings with his captive wife once she was with child. He had all he needed from her: a direct channel to her reservoir of power and the promise of a son. If Amarrasal wanted to sit and brood, it made no difference to him or to the plans he laid when he shut himself up in his study in the highest chamber of the keep.

Rue was at the midpoint of the main stair that wound up the center of the tower when the tenor of Amarrasal's cries changed, so close to the birthing room that she could hear the murmur of the midwife speaking to the laboring woman. Suddenly, Amarrasal shrieked. Rue clapped her hands over her ears, one fist still clutching the scrub brush; the wet bristles pricked her flesh and dripped water into one ear. A blue light pulsed inside the room and there was a flash as if of fire. Rue stood so quickly on the step that she nearly lost her footing. The blue light retreated; the laboring woman fell silent. The midwife crooned. Then Rue heard the thin, lost cry of a baby. Her milk-heavy breasts began leaking in response to its wail. Rue turned and sat down hard on the still-damp step, grinding the heels of her hands into her eyes as she tried to contain the tears.

She had stopped crying but had not yet returned to scrubbing when the hard, sure steps of the master sounded on the stairs. Besserdech had realized that the birthing was over and he had come to inspect his son. He strode into his wife's room and Rue heard him demanding something of the midwife. Her voice was muffled, but his rang out, full of outrage.

"A *girl*? Let me see!" There was a sound of movement from within the room. Rue started scrubbing the next step and tried to shut out the voices. There were more angry words from Besserdech and pleading ones from the midwife. Rue heard *scrawny* and *weakling* in the master's harsh tones and *healthy* and *beautiful* from the low-voiced midwife. She did not see the step that she had now scrubbed well past cleanliness; the memory of Dulsan as a newborn, red-faced and wrinkled, filled her mind's eye. She moved the bucket again. Now she was scouring the landing outside the door of the birthing room.

"That hideous creature is no child of mine," hissed Besserdech.

A croaking, horrible laugh interrupted the midwife's protest. The sound of it was so disturbing, Rue froze on her hands and knees outside the door, her scrub brush still. Then the mistress's rasping voice, hoarse from screaming, spoke slowly, every word as sharp-edged as carved rock: "*No joy, nor success, nor freedom for thee, while Hideous unloved by husband be.*" Another crack of bleak laughter that ended in a kind of sigh, and then silence.

"Y—your lady wife—she's—she's dead!" whispered the midwife, shocked.

"Yes," said the cold voice of the baby's father. "Good riddance, if all she could produce was this powerless runt." Rue heard him approaching the door and she moved herself and the bucket against the wall, out of his way.

"But what of the babe?" the midwife asked.

"Find someone to keep it alive until I decide whether it's worth anything," snapped Besserdech. He did not even glance in Rue's direction as he swept out of the room and up the stairs, his dark robes billowing after him. Rue watched his tall form vanish around the curve of the staircase, the dark head bent in thought. This was a man whose wife had died mere moments ago? Whose child had just been born?

The midwife stood at the door with the swaddled baby in her arms. She looked about and saw Rue. The baby started crying; Rue crossed her arms against her chest, trying to suppress the reflexive letdown of milk. The midwife's eyes narrowed.

"Are you nursing?" she asked.

"I was, but—but my baby died," Rue answered.

"You still have milk?"

"Yes," said Rue.

"Take the child then," said the midwife, stepping out of the room. "Your mistress is dead and the babe needs you." She held the baby out to Rue.

Rue slowly put down her brush and wiped her rough, wet hands on her skirts. She thought of her own Dulsan, and a flash of resentment burned through her. This child lived while hers was dead. Then the little face twisted and the seeking mouth opened and closed on nothing. The baby howled her indignation, her eyes squeezed shut and her brows knit. Rue had the baby in her arms before she had made the decision to take her. She stood and nudged aside the bucket and the brush with her foot, rocking the baby against her.

"Shh, little one," she whispered. "Soon."

She walked down the stairs she had just scrubbed, hearing the midwife calling in the distance for another servant to help wash the dead woman and clean up the birthing room.

Rue found a quiet corner in the kitchen and slid to the floor with her back to the wall. She opened her dress and guided the small mouth to her breast. As she looked upon the little face, so intent in its desire for sustenance, for life, Rue knew this baby was no replacement for Dulsan, just as she was not the child's blood mother. But maybe they could be candles for each other in the ocean-darkness of grief and loss.

A week after the master's wife had died, he demanded to see the baby, whom he called Hideous. Rue climbed the stairs to the highest floor where Besserdech had his study. Holding the infant carefully in one arm, she knocked at the door, waited for the barked order to enter, and walked in.

She had never been inside the master's workroom before. No one was allowed to clean it; she had never taken him food there. She looked around as she hovered by the door, reluctant to come in farther without an explicit command. The single, large, octagonal room had glazed windows at the four cardinal points of the compass. Two large worktables were piled with books, papers, and instruments of glass and metal. Shelves on three of the walls between the windows held scrolls and other papers, as well as vials, jars, and pots of clay, iron, and copper. In the wall to the right of the door was a large fireplace with a fire burning. A huge chair of jet-black stone streaked with silver dominated the center of the room. Rising from the chairback with its wings outspread was a carved raven, its beak open, and one diamond eye fixed on the doorway. It seemed made of the same kind of stone as the chair, but of a blindingly white color instead, veined with black and ice-blue. Rue's gaze stopped at the sight of the stone bird, and she hesitated under its staring eye.

"Come here, girl," commanded the master, and she saw him then, a tall, thin, dark shape at the eastern window. "Let me see the creature."

Rue crossed the room and stopped before him. She was reluctant to expose the baby to this man's cold gaze, but she nevertheless folded back the blanket so that he could view his daughter. Besserdech stared down at Hideous in silence for a moment.

"Lay her down," he said, pointing to one of the long tables. Rue took her to the table, and after the sorcerer had pushed aside some papers, laid the baby down. He then unwrapped the baby completely and began poking and prodding her. The baby started crying and her father's lips tightened, but he continued his examination. Rue wondered what he was trying to discover. He held his hand above the child and Rue cried out at the flash of blue light. She tried to grab the baby, but Besserdech slapped her hands aside.

"That bitch," he snarled, and turned away. He returned to the window and stared out of it, his hands knotting themselves behind his back, his mouth an angry twist.

Rue meanwhile had picked up the baby and soothed her cries. The child did not seem to be hurt, but Rue carefully swaddled her once more and waited for further orders, not daring to leave until she was dismissed.

Besserdech swung around and looked at Rue, who held his daughter close. To Rue it seemed as if he were being forced into a decision, and that he resented it with all his considerable will.

"Do you know where the Spinoz Forest is, girl?"

Rue nodded. It was a large wood to the east. The trees there did not provide good timber for building or furniture, but a few villages on its edges harvested firewood and made charcoal for selling. No road led through it, besides woodcutters' paths, for it was too thick and tangled.

"There is a cottage in the heart of it. Take Hideous and go live there. Return when she is married." Besserdech turned back to the window.

Beyond him snow was beginning to fall. In shock from the abrupt orders, Rue said, "Today, master? It is—" Her words dried up as he whirled and strode toward her. He did not stop until he was almost on her; Rue leaned back from his looming, furious form, her body turned and curled protectively around the baby, who started crying once more. His daughter's wailing seemed to make Besserdech even larger and more frightening.

"Yes," he hissed, his voice no less terrible for being so soft that Rue could barely hear him. "Take Hideous and go, today. If you are not gone by sundown, I will throw you from this tower and find someone who can obey simple commands."

"Yes, master," Rue said. But she did not move, wondering if she dared... She felt his rage expanding, like a cloud of freezing air emanating from his body. Rue dropped to her knees, her forehead almost to the floor, holding the screaming child close to her chest.

"Master, I will go! Only...may I give her another name?"

The cold air retreated, and Besserdech laughed with a bitterness that felt like a slap in the face.

"You are welcome to try," he sneered, and turned away.

Rue scrambled to her feet and ran out the door.

An hour before sunset on that day of deep winter, a girl swathed in a coarse woolen cloak that bulged over the pack on her back shut the door at the foot of the tower behind her. In her arms she held a well-wrapped bundle. The snow fell thinly as she trudged away from Reavinstoft.

Twenty years later

She stilled, disturbed from her study of A Compendium of Malice: Body-Bindings and Soul-Snares. *The faint, feathery ink marks on the page eluded her weak eyes if she did not concentrate, but she had felt...yes, an intruder into her woods. She smothered the useless anger that flared up and focused on the stranger's presence. A bright crackle on the edge of her awareness, for he was just entering her domain; a scraping along her skin, as though she had been brushed by a thin-thorned branch. This one used a firebrand to burn a path. Bespelled fire, of course, that he was controlling with...?*

She picked up a penknife from its groove in the desk surface and pricked the tip of her finger. One, two, three drops of dark blood dripped into a small gold bowl. Enough. Leaving behind her unwieldy, pain-racked body as an anchor, she spun out her shadow-self, slipping unperceived through the tenebrous trees. Ah, fire controlled by a spell linked to the amulet he wore. She heard the crooning of the spell, soft and persistent as a banked ember.

Sitting at her study table, her gritty eyes closed, she rewound the impalpable, blood-powered cord that tethered body and shadow. She panted a moment, absorbing the pain of the spell. As the acid receded from her veins and her cramping muscles eased, she wondered about this one's quest. Usually intruders and seekers needed some token or rune to take away, a prized snippet of her power that would mend a local evil and win them glory. She was the monster they sought to overcome and yet the unrecognized source of their relief. Anger rose again, tightening hot wires all through her bones, searing her vision with flames. She gritted her teeth and damped it down, calling up ice-cool self-discipline. Anger increased her suffering: she had learned that long ago. She listened to her breath whistle in and out until it was even and under control.

Well. Tomorrow she would meet this quester, and discover his need, and bear his horror, and ask every day, until he left, the question she must ask. Perhaps he would accomplish his task. Perhaps this one would have the knowledge or the luck or the heart to undo the last words of her mother, the final curse of her father.

He did not.

Chapter Two

In the year of the Lady's Gift 1382, on the thirtieth day of Menavet, Queen Gladna of the small but prosperous kingdom of Tamtir fell ill. King Arkost, the palace, and all the royal city of Zolatar thought of nothing but the failing health of the queen. It did not take many weeks before it became clear that this was a mortal illness. She had no symptoms but weakness and fatigue. There were no fevers, no rashes, no lesions, no lumps. She was simply fading before the horrified eyes of her husband and people.

Then the reports began to come in from the edges of the kingdom: the salt curse that had hesitated for years on the hem of the realm had crossed the border. The curse had been cast, it was said, by the sorcerer Besserdech, master of the Griefstone; no one knew why or how. The salt had crept into Tamtir the very day Queen Gladna had said to her husband with a little laugh, "My dear, I cannot think why, but I am quite tired. I must lie down."

Now the kingdom found itself in the quandary of so many others, beset by a curse it did not know how to turn back or undo. None of the sages and scholars, the priests and priestesses, the wisewomen and weather watchers summoned by King Arkost and his son, Prince Radvyed, knew of any remedy for either the salt or the queen's illness.

There was a deaf gardener in the royal household. She spent all her time with the roses, so it was some while before she learned of the troubles afflicting the kingdom. One day an undergardener told her about the silence and sorrow inhabiting the palace. The queen grew worse every day. No one could help her. Strangest of all, the beginning of her illness coincided with the first forays of the devastating salt into Tamtir. Forgetting the climbing vine she had been inspecting, the gardener stilled, eyes dark and intent as he signed the news again. She stepped back, swiped at her eyes with a rough sleeve, and stared off toward the distant trees. Then she took a deep breath, turned back to him, and signed that she must go to the king at once.

King Arkost now spent all the time he could in the bedchamber of his frail wife. As the gardener stepped through the door, she could see that everything had been arranged to give the queen what pleasure and comfort she could receive: the cheerful flowers by her bed, which was situated to allow for gazing out the window into the gardens; a harp in a corner where a musician might play at the queen's request; two or three books on a table, open to delicate and brilliant illuminations. By the bed, holding her hand gently, sat the burly and graying king, his look tender and sad as he watched his sleeping wife.

He did not move his head to see who had entered, but after a short silence, he bade the gardener to come around to face him. When she stood before him, he raised weary eyes to her face. His brow wrinkled as he took a moment to pull his thoughts from his wife, but then he said, shaping his words clearly, "Ah yes. Dris Rose Gardener. Well. What news of the roses do you bring me this day?" He made a brief circling sign with his hand, inviting her response.

Dris knew that the king's knowledge of sign language was limited, so she pulled out a small slate and a piece of chalk from one of her many pockets. She replied, *I know what is ailing the queen and how to cure it.*

Arkost closed his eyes and did not speak. Then he opened them and, looking at Dris, said, "Good Dris, I know you come to me out of true concern for the queen." As he spoke, he placed one hand on his heart and pointed at Dris. Then he shook his head, sadly but decisively. "But this is an illness beyond herbs and tisanes. She is dying." He moved one hand in front of his eyes as if gently closing the lids.

Dris gave a sharp nod, erased the slate with a small cloth, and wrote again, her hand firm and steady. To the king's eyes she seemed certain and purposeful. She was not offering a wisp of hope to grasp—no old remedy, no faintly remembered rune. She knew of what she spoke.

I know where salt comes from, why queen ill, what to do. Prince must find house of hideous, bring back inner rose. The terse sentences filled the cramped surface of the slate.

Arkost looked at Dris's dark eyes, bright with intelligence and authority, and studied her weathered face. His gaze dropped to the thick-knuckled hands resting at her sides. Those hands coaxed roses from brambles even in hard years. He turned back to his wife, so colorless, her hand drooping in his grasp like a faded petal. Her eyelids were purpled with fatigue, her lips pale. He could barely discern the rising and falling of her chest as her breath slipped in and out. One day the life that lingered in this dearly loved body would ebb away, leaving skin, bone, and sorrow. He rubbed his thumb gently over the papery skin on the back of her hand. How many remedies had been tried? How many scholars, healers, and holy ones had stood by this bed, baffled and perplexed? How many woodswomen, herbalists, and even midwives? And he the most pitiful and powerless of all, the king who could do nothing for his own wife, the love of his heart. Hopelessness stooped his shoulders and bowed his chin to his chest. He absorbed its relentless weight. Then he set his teeth, straightened, and raised his head. There was, it seemed, still a stone unturned. The king turned to Dris and nodded. Then, his eyes on the sleeping queen, he spoke.

"Send for the prince."

Prince Radvyed came quickly, fearing some new decline in his mother's condition. Dris turned as he entered his mother's chamber.

The gardener blinked a few times. The prince was known to be handsome, even beautiful, and from the distant glimpses she had seen of him about the palace and grounds, so he had seemed to be. But standing in the same room with him was like finding oneself in a star-cloud or a sunburst: dazzling and disorienting. Prince Radvyed's face arrested the eye and scattered all thought. Light and shadow played over his features, each shift revealing new aspects of grace. His body, a perfectly proportioned balance of strength and form, moved with lithe, easy energy.

Dris shook her head, as if clearing her vision, and was relieved to realize that once the first shock of his appearance was absorbed, she could regain her wits, although the prince seemed a bronze statue come to life from the temple of the Master. *He is but a man*, Dris told herself, *though I see why the people call him the Jewel of the House of Mirkamen*.

The prince strode to the bed and saw that his mother was still living, seemingly in no worse case than earlier in the day. He knelt on one knee before the king.

"You sent for me, Father?"

Arkost turned his eyes to his son, although his hand still held his wife's. "Yes, my son. Dris here, our Rose Gardener, knows what to do."

The prince's shoulders fell and he pressed his forehead to his father's free hand. "Father..."

"Radvyed, listen to me. I admit that I am desperate, but I hope I am not yet foolish. Dris speaks with authority. She was not born here in Tamtir. It may be she knows something our loremasters do not."

Radvyed, his forehead still pressed to his father's hand, said nothing, although he breathed more harshly. Finally, he spoke, and there was no missing the despair and the anger in his whisper. "Father. I do not doubt that she knows of a remedy for many things. But this...*How* can she know? Why has she not spoken before?"

"How she knows I do not know. Yet speak with her and see what you think. And why she has not spoken before now...I believe that she did not know the severity of your mother's illness, nor of the salt curse. It seems she learned of it today—and she insisted on seeing me immediately. But question her yourself. If you think I am only a desperate man..."

At this the prince choked a denial against Arkost's hand. Radvyed took a moment to compose himself, and then he released his father's hand, rose, and turned to face the silent woman who had been watching his conversation with his father. He said, beckoning, "Come apart with me."

They stepped away from the bed. The prince sat in a carved wooden chair, as if at judgment. "Tell me," he said, and signed, *Speak*.

Dris held out her slate with the message she had shown the king. The prince read the brief sentences and frowned. He tapped the word *hideous* and flicked his fingers, signing *What?* in a request for clarification. Dris replied, *girl*, and tapped *hideous* in her turn. Radvyed stared at her, then stood and walked back to the bed. "Father."

"Yes, son."

"You want me to leave you, leave Mother, at this time? To search for a hideous girl and her rose garden?"

"Yes, son."

Silence. Radvyed did not ask why. He knew that if there was a chance that somewhere a hideous girl possessed a healing flower, his father wanted him to find that flower and bring it back. And if he, Radvyed, thought such a thing existed, he would gladly go. But to abandon his parents for a ridiculous quest was more than he could bear to think of. He turned away so his father would not see his face. How could he obey? How could he disobey?

"Son. If someone had told me when I was a prince that all the lands beyond our borders would be devastated by a plague of salt, I would have listened politely and changed the subject. If they had said that the laughing girl I made my princess would be brought low by a nameless illness the day the salt breached our borders, I would have had the speaker checked for fever. But these things have come to pass. So if this woman tells me there is a rose in the garden of a hideous girl that can bring relief to my wife, I listen. Perhaps she is mistaken. Perhaps she is not. But I do not know what else we can do."

Radvyed nodded, still unable to look at his father. He walked to the window. The shutters were half closed so that the sunlight would not fall into his mother's eyes. From here he could see the gardens she loved and the gravel pathways she had walked. Radvyed lifted his gaze and saw the dark green smudge that was the edge of the Lady's Forest, where he had played at being a knight as a boy and had learned to hunt as a youth. He thought of the salt creeping across farmlands and villages and market towns, woods and pastures, spoiling lakes, ponds, and rivers, creating misery and want wherever it went. And he thought of his mother, who lay joyless and frail, giving all her strength to the beating of her heart and the movement of her lungs. The Lady's Return was but five days off, but there would be no merriment to mark the winter solstice this year. His eyes were wet. *No more salt!* he thought angrily, wiping his face with his sleeve. Radvyed turned from the window and looked at his father.

"I will go."

The prince spent some time with Dris, desiring to obtain as much information about the girl, the flower, and their location as he could. The thought came to Radvyed that Dris knew more than she could or would say, but though he pressed her for more details, he could not breach her reticence. And yet when he looked up from contemplating the map on the table before them, he was surprised to see the gardener's gaze was watchful and her posture taut. Her hand brushed vaguely over the map. His course was set for an unknown road. A direction could be given—Dris indicated west, over the mountains—but no definite route. He must find or make his way.

Yet she did not leave him empty-handed. Dris gave Radvyed a small trowel, wrapped carefully in soft, oiled leather, and a pouch, about the size of his palm, made of similar leather. In the pouch was a gray-green powder, from the leaves of a plant called *orlach*.

Dig for food and water, for you and your horse, Dris wrote pithily on her slate. Radvyed was not fluent enough in Tikrek, the hand speech, to converse solely by signs. *Use trowel. Put pinch of powder on food and in water.* She watched as the prince tucked both items securely in his packs.

Dris then gave him another object, also wrapped in oiled leather. The prince uncovered a pruning hook—for gathering the flower, he assumed. Radvyed put the tool away with her other gifts, then bowed his thanks and farewell to the gardener.

Radvyed went to say good-bye to his mother. He had already bid farewell to his father, who was occupied with business of the kingdom, for the realm needed the king even if the queen lay dying. A lady-in-waiting sat near her, working on embroidery. When he entered, the attendant rose and moved to another seat, far enough away to give mother and son privacy.

Queen Gladna had not moved since he had last seen her. Radvyed's heart was filled with sorrow and anger as he looked down at her. He knelt by the bed. To think that his once-vibrant mother lay here fighting to breathe, and he himself helpless to give her the smallest measure of his strength. Radvyed did not allow himself to weep more salt tears, but he folded his lips, and pressed his cheek to her hand. At the faint movement of her fingers he raised his head. She had half lifted her eyelids and was looking at him. He swallowed, unable to speak.

"Who's my...handsome boy?" Gladna whispered.

"I am, Mother," he answered now as he always did, despite the tightness of his throat. It was an old game with them, from his earliest years. *Who's my handsome, who's my clever, who's my good-hearted boy?* the queen would ask, as if trying to remember. *I am, I am!* he would shriek, giggling as he hugged his laughing mother.

There was silence as she closed her eyes, gathering her strength. Then she half opened them again.

"Love goes with you...Radvyed." He forced his grip to loosen so that he would not hurt her and nodded. He did not think he could speak.

Another silence. This time when she opened her eyes, he could see a trace of the sparkle they once held.

"Curious flower."

"I will bring it to you. I swear I will." It hurt to get the words through his throat, as if they were rough-edged rocks that he coughed onto the coverlet. She gazed at him a moment longer, then the sparkle was gone, and her eyes closed. All her attention returned inward, towards enduring the weakness and the pain. He carefully laid her hand back down, stood, and took a step back. After a swift bow to the queen's honor, Radvyed turned and left the room.

The lady-in-waiting heard his hasty steps running down the stairs as she moved back to her post. The queen, lost in her suffering, heard nothing.

Chapter Three

Radvyed took little with him on his journey, for he needed speed. He rode alone, because he and the king wanted as few to know of his errand as possible: it was not the sort of journey that would be made more fruitful by a cavalcade or curious well-wishers. He rode west, as advised by Dris, towards the border where the salt had advanced the farthest. With his back to the rising sun, the sky still dark, and his hooded cloak wrapped around him, not many early travelers on the road from the royal city knew him for anyone but a well-mounted man of rank or substance—a land-holding *mirena*'s nephew, perhaps, or a merchant's son. His signet ring was under his clothing on a chain around his neck, and his astonishing, handsome face, itself both signet and charm, was obscured by the folds of his hood. No one would remark on him keeping his head covered as the day drew on, for the breeze was sharp.

After a week of travel, he reached the salt's edge at dusk. A few miles ahead lay the last inn before the border, which was marked by a line of wooded mountains. He pulled up his horse and dismounted. The salt reached into the kingdom like a rising tide. Irregular fingers stretched forth and claimed more land, then were themselves crusted over with another slow, relentless layer. What the Griefstone itself must be like he could not imagine. No one knew why the sorcerer in his tower had cursed the world with salt. No one, he thought, except perhaps Dris. He stooped and touched the edge of the salt with an ungloved hand; it was fine-grained, but gritty and hard-edged. He lifted his fingers to his nose and sniffed, then cautiously touched a few grains with the tip of his tongue. Salt. It did not seem magic or menacing, except that it was rendering entire realms wastelands of dead earth. He remounted and rode on.

The next day Radvyed crossed the border through a rocky gap. Belikon, his horse, came to a stop, seemingly as astonished as the prince at the view laid out before them. The thicker crust of salt, yes, Radvyed, at least, had expected that. But the shriveled trees, the grit-covered lumps of what might be shrubs, the silence of no animal or human moving about on the sterile soil: those he had not thought to imagine. As he traveled farther west, he encountered here and there a thin beast digging for insects, perhaps, or a gaunt deer pawing at the roots of some blighted tree. He saw no people abroad. Radvyed wondered whether they had fled, or died, or had found some means of wresting sustenance from the accursed land. Recalling the desperation of the envoys of other realms as they had begged to know what power protected his own kingdom, Radvyed once again felt pity and helplessness. Soon this would be the fate of his own country. He rode on, ever more determined.

The first evening, Radvyed made a simple camp: a bedroll and a small fire. He tied Belikon to one of the sad little trees and then looked around. There was no water around for the horse to drink as he usually did while his rider tended him, nor any green grass or other likely forage.

"Soon," the prince said, rubbing Belikon's forehead. "We will see what Dris's gifts may do." Belikon flicked an ear back and pawed once, but stayed quiet as his rider removed bridle and saddle. He relaxed under the good brushing Radvyed gave him, but became impatient as the prince checked his hooves.

"Yes, water, soon," promised Radvyed, hoping that he would find something. They had crossed only a single stream as they had descended from the mountain gap, and man and horse were both thirsty.

Radvyed pulled some provisions from one of the saddle bags: hard bread and a little dried meat and fruit. There was also a feed mix that the royal couriers gave their horses when traveling longer distances. He would give some of that to Belikon—probably not as much as the horse would like—but Radvyed wanted to conserve their supplies as he could, because he did not know how long their journey would be or what they would find.

Before eating the food he had brought, however, the prince unwrapped the trowel Dris had given him and grasped the tool somewhat awkwardly, for he had rarely dug in the dirt except as a child, to play. Belikon was snuffling and pawing, purposefully, Radvyed thought, at a spot on the ground. The prince scraped away the layered salt until the earth itself was exposed. He had scooped a largish hole when he grazed something: not rock, nor a clod of dirt. It was some kind of large tuber, about the length of his forearm. The prince excavated it, sniffed at it, brushed the soil off, and considered it. Then taking a pinch of powder from Dris's pouch, he sprinkled it on the tuber, and bit it. It was not particularly tasty, but neither was it disgusting. He fed the rest of the tuber to Belikon, who accepted it without enthusiasm. The horse wanted water.

After some more digging, the prince found a few more tubers and gave them to Belikon. Radvyed then considered the hole, which was no longer shallow. Was it damp at the bottom? He dug a little more, but to no avail. He sat back on his heels and, shrugging, tossed a pinch of powder in. When Belikon put his nose into the hole, Radvyed realized that water had risen in it. The water was brackish, but it rose steadily in the hole he had dug. Belikon and then the prince drank their fill. Radvyed thought of Dris with gratitude and tucked away the pouch of *orlach* powder with care.

That night he lay awake by the fire, staring up at the field of stars, a distant reflection of the salt's glitter. Usually the Master's stars comforted him with an order that no earthly troubles could disconcert, but that solace eluded him now. He felt small and lonely and absurd. With a sigh, he shut his eyes and willed himself to sleep.

Time slipped by, featureless as the country Radvyed and Belikon passed through. He found he could not mark the days of travel through the eerie, empty, salt-rimed landscape. After that first night, the sky was overcast: weak sunlight, dim moonlight, no starlight. When he tried to count back or keep track of days, his mind blurred, and he stared confused at the notches he had made on a stick he had broken off a stunted tree. Yet Radvyed pushed on, in a half stupor but still obstinate, until there rose in their way a dark wood.

There was salt here, too, but the thorny trees and thick brambles had their own power, and were not completely covered by salt, merely dusted with it. Belikon slowed as they drew near, then stopped. Radvyed looked left and right, but the wood did not thin or curve back: in fact, it seemed its distant arms reached out to draw him in. To pursue his way he must make a path through the dense growth. He dismounted and walked nearer, but could see nothing:

the pale sun did not penetrate the forest canopy, and the trees and the brambles were so thick Radvyed was not sure he would see his hand if he thrust his arm ahead of him.

He stepped back and considered. How could anyone, much less a horse, enter the wood? He remounted and rode up and down along the edge of the trees, looking for any kind of path or thinning of growth, but found none. Radvyed had not thought to bring an axe, only his sword, but there was no room either to swing the sword he had or the axe he did not. After dismounting once more, he unhooked his saddlebags. In the watery morning light he laid out what he had brought: clothes, tools, weapons, and Dris's gifts. The powder and the trowel could do him no good in making a way, but he picked up the last gift, the pruning hook. He unwrapped it and held it in his hand, trying to hold it as Dris had shown him. He had thought that the hook was for gathering the flower, but perhaps... Radvyed looked at the woods. It would be a day's work, surely, just to make a space for his horse to step into that dense growth. Yet there seemed to be no other way.

Radvyed packed everything up except the hook, fastened the saddlebags once more to Belikon's saddle, and approached the woods. He hesitated a moment, then with an awkward swipe cut at a bramble. It fell neatly and easily at his feet. Startled, he stared at it a moment, then, with more confidence, attempted a second one. The hook was quite sharp, or perhaps it possessed some further virtue, for it bit deeply and cut cleanly into vine and branch. Radvyed cleared a path just large enough for himself and Belikon.

At first he wondered whether he would manage to stay on course or wander the dark wood forever, but shortly after Belikon's tail swished across the forest's threshold, Radvyed's eye caught a dot of light ahead in the gloom. He stood and watched it. It did not move, so it was not some flying insect. It lay straight ahead into the woods. Perhaps that dot of light came from the other side of the thornwood and marked its end. Radvyed decided to use it as his orientation point, since he lacked any other reference. What sunlight reached him was too scattered for him to determine direction by its aid.

Hours later, the prince was sweaty with effort and his arms and back ached, but the tool had not lost its edge and seemed not to resent his inexperience. Radvyed stood, panting, wiping the sweat out of his eyes with his sleeve. The dot of light had grown into a line. What was it? He set to work again and almost fell a few moments later when his tired arm reached to cut a branch that was not there. In the dusk and his fatigue, Radvyed had not noticed that he had cut his way through the woods and now stood in a small clearing. Belikon pushed him from behind and Radvyed stumbled a few steps, then turned to lean against his horse. Looking back at the wood, he saw the path he had just made disappear. *We are like a stone thrown into water*, he thought. *Even as it sinks, the way closes behind it.*

Radvyed shut his eyes and leaned his forehead against Belikon's neck. Then he turned from the point where the path had been and looked at the light on the other side of the clearing. A pale, yellow glow escaped through the crack of a shuttered window. Its weak light suggested the indistinct form of a tumbledown shack. He stared at it, head heavy and thoughts sluggish, as they had been for all the days of travel across the salt. His back and arms burned from hours spent cutting a path through the thornwood; his hands were cramped and sore. Radvyed decided, after some time of no perceptible movement or sound from the hovel, to camp this night. Tomorrow he would knock on the door and find out who or what lay within.

He noticed that his horse was finding grass to eat here, so he unsaddled his mount, dug for water, and rubbed Belikon down as the horse drank. The prince was too tired to do more, so he rolled himself into his blankets, sword within reach, and slept.

Another one. She thudded the mug of tea onto the table and splashed a few drops. She fingered the coolness of the looped handle, ignoring the spilled liquid. Perhaps...

But what was the use of hoping? Years of disappointment had hollowed out the heart of her, leaving nothing but bitterness and self-mockery.

She did not spy anymore with her shadow-self when a newcomer trespassed. The recoil had grown too harsh; it was not worth the pain. With the years her thornwood defenses had strengthened, anyway.

Let him come. Let them perform the charade of his labored flattery and her futile attempts to please. Let him snatch his token or talisman and flee. Then she could resume her peace.

She should tell...but not yet. She needed a moment to swallow the lump of despair. The handle of the mug broke off in her tense fingers. She opened her hand and let it fall to the tabletop. She would mend it, but not now, not yet.

Let him come. Let him go.

She sat by the open window and watched, with blurred eyes, the light of day die.

Chapter Four

R advyed woke at morning light to the cold touch of dew; he sat up and looked about. The dense, daunting wood crouched around the clearing. The shack still stood, looking like it might collapse if he but coughed. Yet it not only stood, but provided someone shelter, if the light from its window last night had been neither dream nor phantom. He sat for a moment more, pondering it, then rose and broke camp.

The prince led Belikon up to the hut and circled it until they found a decayed wooden door. Radvyed hesitated, wondering if a knock would tip it off its remaining hinge, then rapped on the door. He heard movement and imagined someone coming through darkness, dust, and cobwebs to answer his summons. The footsteps drew nearer and the door eased open.

"Good rising. I am Prince Radvyed of Tamtir," Radvyed said. He could not see anyone, for the door blocked his view.

"Come in," invited a woman's low voice. Radvyed still could not see the speaker.

"I have my horse, mistress. Is there somewhere—"

"Come in," repeated the voice, "and bring your mount with you. There is room."

Radvyed doubted that, but he obeyed. After all, some country people kept their beasts in their homes in the coldest nights of winter. He ducked, for the doorway was low, and leading Belikon, stepped into the darkness of the shack.

Except it was not a shack and it was not dark. He blinked and heard the door shut behind them. Radvyed looked over his shoulder and saw a woman with graying hair in a plain but neat brown dress turning away from the door. A door that was high, wide, and well-set on its hinges; it was of wood, yes, but beautifully carved with flowers, leaves, and birds. Radvyed stared around what should have been the inside of the hut. They were in a spacious courtyard with evenly set, pinkish-gray stones. Around it ran a shaded walkway. Flowering trees in carved planters and trailing greenery drifting down the walls softened the lines of the stone building that enclosed the yard. A fountain, in the shape of a girl pouring water from a large jar, stood in the center, catching the sunlight in the falling water and adding a pleasant burble to the scene. A youth, dressed in breeches and boots and a leather vest, ran up and waited until the prince recalled himself enough to hand over Belikon's reins. Radvyed watched his horse being led off. The youth seemed to know what he was about and Belikon was eager for better rations than he had been getting recently. Radvyed could glimpse a stone stable and well-swept stableyard through an archway. He turned back to look around the courtyard in which he stood and realized that it was but the entrance to a large house or manor, perhaps even a palace. The sunlit air breathed of spring. Yet he knew he had entered the door of a shack on a chill winter morning.

Apparently deciding that Radvyed had had enough time to adjust to the light and the space, the woman in brown moved.

"Come," she said, "I will show you to your rooms. You may then roam the house and the grounds as you like. But you must come to dinner, which is at the third bell." She stepped past him and led him to the staircase that swept in a graceful curve to the second floor. He could not stop looking around as they made their way to his rooms. He was a prince and had lived all his life in the royal palace, but the beautiful things—paintings, rugs, statues, furniture—that he saw displayed in this place were unlike anything he had seen or known before: rich wood of varied shades; gleaming, glitter-veined stonework; huge, deep-hued tapestries; gossamer-delicate carvings. At last they reached a suite of apartments. The brown-clad woman looked around, as if making sure that everything was as it should be. She lifted the cover from a large tray on the sideboard and began placing the various dishes on a table set for one.

"Did you know I was coming?" asked Radvyed, suddenly wondering at the untroubled hospitality he had been shown.

She paused, a pitcher of some iced drink in one hand and a crystal goblet in the other, and turned to look at him gravely. "Yes. You have been expected." She finished her task.

There was a pause, while the prince thought about that, remembered a few tales of credulous heroes who did not fare well, and worried for Belikon. The woman adjusted a flower stem in the arrangement on the table, then moved to the door. Radvyed shook his head as if to clear it, and spoke to her.

"Pardon, lady, but who are you? How should I address you? What is this place?" She stopped, her hand on the door handle. Looking over her shoulder, she answered him.

"I am the keeper of this house. You may call me Rue. And this place," she said, her eyes never wavering from his face, "is the house of the sorceress Hideous, with whom you will dine." With that, she opened the door and left the room, shutting the door behind her.

Radvyed took a few steps about the room. The sorceress Hideous. The house of the sorceress Hideous. Not a hideous girl, but a woman, a sorceress, named Hideous. That explained the sun-drenched palace hidden inside a neglected shack. And from this Hideous he was to procure the flower that, if his mother was not dead already—his heart seized at the thought—might cure the queen. He put out his hand and leaned on the bedpost, which was carved with myrtle trees and roses. On a low chest at the foot of the bed were his travel-worn saddlebags. Radvyed unpacked them, using the task to calm his fear for his mother. Nothing seemed to have been taken or disarranged. His gifts from Dris were there, safe in their wrappings. He put his things away in the chest.

Looking out one of the large windows, Radvyed saw gardens and grounds laid out in intricate, flowing designs. He decided that after washing he would explore the house. He might learn something about his hostess. At least he could find the stables and see that Belikon was happy and well cared for.

At the third bell, Radvyed was ready to be escorted to the dining room, which he had not found in his earlier explorations. There was a knock on the door. He opened it; Rue waited on the other side. She nodded a greeting then silently turned and started down the hallway. The prince followed.

Radvyed had spent a good deal of time that afternoon thinking about his upcoming encounter with the sorceress. As a prince, he had been trained to converse with a wide array of people, both ordinary and powerful, even young women hoping to become the next queen, and their families, too. But he could not recall lessons in dinner conversation with a mysterious sorceress. There was no powerful magic in his kingdom, nor did any foreign adepts attend the royal court. Could the sorceress use magic to entrance him, or to compel his will, or to perhaps transform him into a beast or statue? Which tales of magic were legend, and which might be true report? Why and how had he been expected? What would the sorceress require in exchange for the flower, if indeed she had or would admit to having such a thing?

They stopped in front of huge bronze doors. Like so much in the house, they were adorned with figures, here rendered in bas-relief. As he stared at them, he realized they represented famous tales of young women gruesomely dying for love: Swan Girl, Lady Butterfly, Weeping Tree. Rue pushed open one door.

She gestured for him to enter the room, which was dimly candlelit. Although it was not particularly chilly, there was a small fire in the hearth. A pleasantly bright scent, overlaid with smoky spice, drifted through the room.

"Prince Radvyed of Tamtir, my lady," announced Rue, then withdrew and pulled the door closed.

The prince let his eyes adjust to the obscurity of the cavernous, windowless room. Before him was a table with two places set, perpendicular to each other. But where was his hostess? He ventured farther into the room. Another odor, this one a fetid, spoiled-meat stench, stung his nose. Radvyed stopped. He heard a regular, raspy noise, like that of a small bellows. Then he saw her.

Pressed back into the shadows of the far wall, leaning with her hand upon a tabletop, was the lady with whom he was to dine. His hostess was large, but in a shapeless, off-putting way. Uncanny bumps and rolls pushed under her clothes, seeming neither appurtenance nor flesh. Her eyes were small and piggish. Her nose was a formless lump; her lips were slack and wet, imperfectly concealing uneven yellow teeth. Her hair, what there was of it, was stringy and dull. Her skin was a dirty, yellowish gray; the flickering light seemed to throw strange stripes of shadow across it. They streaked her face and neck and twined around her wrists and hands. The raspy noise he had heard was her breath laboring in and out of her overworked lungs. She was the ugliest, most repulsive creature he had ever seen.

Hideous.

The prince swallowed. Then his royal training came to his rescue. Composing his features into an expression of affable interest, Radvyed made a low bow to his hostess, then said, "Thank you for your hospitality, my lady. I have been enjoying all day the beauties and the graces of your house."

A pause, filled only by the sound of Hideous's breathing. Then she said, in a voice that grated unbearably against the ear, "Welcome."

Another pause. Again, the irritating voice. "We dine?" She started towards the table. He saw that movement for her was either painful or awkward or both. Radvyed stepped forward.

"My lady?" He held out his arm. She stared at it for a moment and even raised her hand as if to take it. But it seemed the sight of her own misshapen, shadow-striped fingers changed her mind, and she lowered it.

"No, thank you...Prince," she half croaked, half screeched.

Radvyed watched her half waddle, half shuffle to her place. As she entered the circle of light thrown by the candelabrum on the table, Radvyed discerned what seemed like swollen cords underneath her skin, winding about the puffy wrists, across the backs of her hands, tapering to thick strands that curled about some of her fingers. There was something wrong about the angle of the arms, as if they had an extra joint. Tightening the muscles of one thigh to help him maintain his calm expression, he lifted his eyes to her face. Some kind of coil seemed to wrap her thick throat under the dull gray skin, and spread dark filaments across her face, pushing against the skin. Not shadows, for she was in full candlelight now, neither on her face nor hands, but traceries of—what? Blood vessels? Surely not, given that the one around her neck was as thick as two of his fingers held together.

A chair smoothly drew back from the table, although he could see no one moving it. Hideous lowered herself slowly into her seat. Radvyed waited until she was settled, then also sat. His gaze lingered on the strange coiling lines under the skin of the hand nearest to him, trembling as it rested on the table. The vein, or growth, or whatever it was, showed darker than any normal vein. This close he could see dark red lines branching off from it, reminding him of the hair-thin roots he'd turned up as a boy, digging for treasure in a forest. And there, where the dark coil pushed closest to the surface—

Something brushed his shoulder, and he almost jumped in surprise. He looked up and around, embarrassed to have been staring like a lout at his hostess's hand.

Platters and tureens floated to the table, seemingly borne by no servant's hands, setting a sumptuous dinner before them. Forks and ladles rose and served them food. The prince sat very still, watching the utensils and serving pieces move about. Was this a deliberate display of power, a move to throw him off-balance? An unseen arm brushed his shoulder, and Radvyed started. A breadbasket wafted to the table. He controlled his surprise at once, but Hideous had noticed.

"Not worry...Prince. No ghosts...no evil...spells." Her scratchy voice paused as she took a few raspy breaths. "Invisibility...spell." Another breath sawed in and out of her lungs. "Ease my people." This was how she spoke: the briefest sentences possible, and even those brief phrases broken with strain.

Radvyed was uncertain of her exact meaning—how could an invisibility spell ease someone?—but understood they were being attended by people of the house, not spirits or fey creatures. He smiled at her to show he was not disturbed by the way a decanter hovered over his goblet, pouring out wine. She blinked vacantly at him and he felt his smile fade.

Radvyed noticed that she ate very little, despite the excellence of the dishes. The good smells of yeasty bread, braised meat, and roasted vegetables mingled with the spicy-smoky scent that had first greeted him. Yet under it all crept the putrid smell of spoiled meat. Radvyed could not tell from where it emanated, and he remained on edge and ill at ease.

In the candlelight, he could see more of her unloveliness, although he forced himself not to stare: the gray-yellow color of her dark-streaked skin, covered in a thin film of sweat, or perhaps oiliness; her eyes, not merely small, but almost lashless and red-rimmed, dull and rheumy. He had been taught that every woman, however plain, had her own particular grace. His part was to notice and appreciate it, whether it be shapely hands, an unusual hair color, a melodious voice, a regal carriage. . . Radvyed looked upon Hideous and could not find one charm of person or manner. He was repulsed and moved by pity at the same time.

It was a silent meal, for Hideous spoke very little and Radvyed followed his hostess's lead. The dessert things were cleared away and small goblets of wine were poured. A lamp of scented oil was set on the table and lit; the noxious smell retreated somewhat.

Radvyed tasted his wine: sweet, but not cloying. He took a deep breath and broke the heavy silence.

"My lady, I believe you know why I am here."

"Know why"—she wheezed in a breath—"Think you are." Another whistling gasp. "Tell me."

Radvyed told her of his mother's illness and of his journey. "I am here to ask you: do you know of this flower? Will you give it to me?"

"Know of it. Cannot...give it."

"Cannot, my lady, or will not?"

A long silence, long enough for him to consider the foolishness of offending a sorceress. He had opened his mouth to form an apology when her ear-grating voice spoke again.

"Cannot. Flower here. You find. You pluck." They sat in silence. A log collapsed in the hearth. Hideous said, "Not fear food...Prince?"

"Should I? Do you wish my death?"

"No." A pause. "Not fear spell?" Radvyed took a moment to think what kind of spell she might have in mind. His memory flickered with tales of beautiful youths ensnared by witches and never seen again. But what could Hideous want of him?

"What use would I be as a captive? What ransom could you desire, you who are mistress of this house?"

"No ransom." Another pause. She spoke again, her gaze fixed on the tablecloth. "Marry me, Prince?"

"No!" And then realizing his swift answer was hardly politic, Radvyed spoke more gently. "No, I thank you, Lady. Unfortunately, I—" What was the phrase one of his cousins had told him her sister had used when rejecting a marriage proposal? "I believe we would not—suit."

Hideous nodded, then turned her face away, a twisted, swollen hand over her eyes. It may have been a trick of the shadows, or because his eyes bleared at a sudden whiff of the spoiled-meat smell, but it seemed that her puffy hand had...prickles?...protruding from it where the streaks were darkest.

"Good night...Prince."

A dismissal. Radvyed stood, bowed, and withdrew. As the door shut, he thought he heard a harsh but muffled sound. He breathed deep the clean air on this side of the door and blinked his eyes clear.

Rue was in the passageway, waiting for him, somber and quiet. She led him back to his rooms. Alone, he stripped off his clothes, thinking about the dinner, unsure what to make of the conversation. Hideous could not give the flower? Was he, or was he not, a captive? And then the proposal of marriage. He regretted the hastiness and manner of his refusal, but the thought of being husband to the creature he had dined with made him feel ill. The uncanny coils under the sallow gray skin, the vacuous eyes and ear-flinching voice, the stench of rotting meat that had filled the room...

He found a velvet robe in the large, ornate wardrobe. Radvyed wandered to the window and gazed at the gardens, illuminated by starlight and colored lanterns. After a time, he turned away, got into bed, and fell into a restless sleep.

She had lost her breath when she beheld him standing by the door, so tall and easy and beautiful. The candlelight threw its glow on him like a tribute of glory, haloing him against the shadows; the light caressed the high forehead, the line of cheekbone, the straight nose, the curved lip. The thick hair, the fierce brows balanced by the disarming cleft in his chin, the eyes, bright, curious, thick-lashed... He turned his head, searching the room for his hostess, perhaps. Even that mild movement—the youthful strength of his throat, the angle of his jaw—was imbued with god-like grace. So handsome was he, it seemed impossible that he was a real man.

Maybe her own longing had conjured up this phantom, to torture and tantalize her.

And then she saw, because she was staring at him, rapt as a worshipper before a shrine, the slightest flaring of the elegant nostrils. Yes, he was flesh and bone, and she disgusted him.

She allowed herself a moment to absorb the cramp of shame that gripped her stomach. Then she shuffled forward, despite the humiliation and the pain. His gaze found her, and he smiled. She welcomed the sweetness of his greeting even as it deepened her despair.

Later, when he left her alone, she did not allow anyone into the room, not even Rue. Of course, he had rejected her; it was stupid to weep. She watched the fire shrink and grow cold, and clutched the fresh memory to her, of the most beautiful man she had ever seen or ever would see, sitting at her table, softly radiant in the candlelight, gentle-voiced, kind, his whole being focused for those few hours on her.

Chapter Five

When Radvyed woke in the morning, he was in a bed and a room he did not recognize. He sat up and looked around. The bed-curtains, which yesterday had been sky blue, were today a dark red, almost black. The bed itself was made of a different wood, in a heavier style, carved with—he turned and leaned close to one of the posts at the head of the bed—ravens and poppy flowers? And if the room's window was in the same place, then the bed had been moved. He got up, noticing that the previous day's alabaster figures of forest animals and dancing country couples had vanished, replaced by empty bowls and vases shaped of thick boiled leather studded with brass. The wall hangings were darker, as well: the one near his bed that had featured a comely maiden taming a unicorn had been replaced by a tapestry depicting the moment of the kill at a boar hunt. He went to the window and looked out. Low gray clouds hung over the gardens, which seemed tangled, weary, and lifeless. There was no smell of rain.

It took a little while to discover where his clothes were stored, but eventually Radvyed opened a heavy ironwood chest against the far wall and found them. He had not been dressed for more than a few minutes when there came a knock on the door. Rue entered after his reply. She bore a tray with breakfast and set about arranging a table for it. She seemed neither surprised nor disoriented by the changed room.

"Does it change every day?" asked Radvyed. She looked at him, then paused before casting a glance about the room. It seemed to him that she refocused her eyes somehow.

"No." She poured tea into a teacup for him, then stood back. "You are made free of the house and grounds. You will dine at the third bell again tonight." She gave no hint of her opinion of him nor of his meeting with Hideous the previous evening. Before Radvyed could collect his thoughts to ask her anything else, Rue had left the room with her swift, quiet step.

He sat and addressed himself to the meal of bread, fruit, cheese, and honey set before him. Clearly the house formed part of a *mirenzem*, or some other kind of manor holding, that could provide its needs and even luxuries. As he ate, Radvyed thought about Rue's words. Did she mean that he could not leave? But of course he could not leave without the flower to cure his mother, the whole reason for his journey. So he was free to search for the flower that he must find for himself. Well, he would explore the gardens and grounds, then. Radvyed had no idea how he would recognize the flower if he did come upon it, but he surely would not recognize it if he did not look for it. He would also stop by the stables and make sure Belikon was well and happy. Radvyed wiped his mouth on the ample white napkin provided, swallowed a last gulp of tea, and left his chamber.

And found himself baffled. His room was not the only one that had changed shape and décor. How would he get out to the gardens? But he found, through trial and error, that if he consistently thought about where he wanted to go in a specific way (*the gardens on the east side of the house*) the passages and doors seemed to lead him there willingly, as if some helpful sylph were heeding him. At last Radvyed came to the door that led to those gardens and he stepped outside. The sky was still low and heavy and the gardens still sad and bleak. He watched as a flock of starlings lifted from the far trees and drifted together until they settled upon a different spot. Immediately before him gravel paths led out to the gardens, which opened with overgrown designs of low boxwood hedges. They reminded Radvyed of the knot-gardens of the palace in Tamtir, except these hedges were not well tended. Beyond them were planted shrubs and flowers, taller but also a bit shabby. Farther on he saw a stand of deciduous trees, too distant to identify.

Radvyed had wandered among the strangely wan flowers for half an hour before it had occurred to him to try the method he had used inside the house. He stopped, cleared his mind, and then thought, *The flower that can cure my mother*. Repeating this phrase over and over in his mind, he began to walk again, following the path where it led him, and trying not to think ahead where it might go. He had found in the house that he opened a door to a storage room or some such dead end if he did not allow himself to be led. Yet perhaps he had not been as single-minded as required, because after not quite an hour the prince found himself staring at a high wall, covered with a relative of the dark and formidable thorn brambles he had pruned to get to the clearing. He looked about. There was only one path in view: the path that had brought him to the wall. The house was far off. Today it was of gray stone dully echoing the overcast sky.

Thinking perhaps a door was hidden behind the leafless thorns, Radvyed gingerly pushed his hand through them. The thorns on these vines were finer and longer than the ones of the wood, and they had slightly hooked tips. He ignored as best he could the long scratches they gave him and reached farther until his hand pressed against a rough stone wall. His arm was into the brambles up to his shoulder. He could not distinguish much with the tips of his fingers, but what he did feel did not seem to be any kind of door. Carefully he pulled his arm out; the sleeve was sliced to rags, and his arm and hand were bleeding from several thorn wounds. He picked out what thorns he could.

Leaving the path, Radvyed followed the wall, hoping that some other entry would present itself. None did, but he learned that although the enclosed space was small, the wall was forbiddingly high, perhaps three times his own height. When he had circled round to his original point, the pathway still stubbornly running directly into the thorns, he decided to scale the wall. The thick vines would support his weight and provide foot- and handholds. Radvyed looked at his bloody arm and paused. Yet would the path bring him back here again another time? He took off his shirt, tore it in half, and wrapped each half about a palm. His hands somewhat protected, he stood in the center of the path facing the wall, then reached up, grasped two handfuls of vines, thrust a booted toe into the brambles, and heaved himself up.

An instant later, Radvyed sprawled on his back on the gravel path, the rags wrapped around each hand shredded and useless. He was not sure what had happened: the wall had shrugged him off, or the thorny vines had turned slick and he had slipped, or maybe the thorns had cut through his wraps and so freed themselves from his grip. And now, if he was not mistaken, he had a back full of gravel.

Radvyed sat up and looped his arms around his raised knees, considering. It seemed the flower was inside a closed and guarded garden. The magic of the place was willing to lead him to the garden, but not to grant him entry. Yet the mistress of the house had not forbidden him the flower. She had said only that she could not give it to him. He himself must find the way. Radvyed stared at the thorny wall, discouraged. His mother's life was seeping away, and he, in no wise skilled or gifted in the ways of magic, must overcome the strong enchantments that kept the cure out of his hands. For it seemed plain that force would not work. Could the spell or spells be outwitted? Could they be outwitted by *him*?

Finally, wincing with his hurts, Radvyed got to his feet. If nothing else, he should return to his room and repair his bloody and ragged state. The prince inspected his limbs and pulled out a few more long thorns from his scratches. He rolled his shoulders experimentally: painful, but not unbearable. He turned his back to the wall and took a few steps down the path. He was gathering himself to hold in his mind the thought, *Back to my bedroom*, when he heard voices floating on the air.

Radvyed turned his head, following the sound, and saw before him, past unfamiliar gardens laid out with rosemary hedges and weeping flowering shrubs, an orchard, and in the orchard, people gathering fruit. Although the day had been overcast and heavy, now sunlight fell through the leaves and dappled the figures with green, gold, and shadow. Men, women, children, and youths were working, the elder more steadily than the younger, gathering—apricots? What season was it? The smaller children were running about, darting among the trees, ladders, and baskets. Someone was singing. An adult called out to a child.

Radvyed stood for a moment watching this scene of happy labor. Who were they? They did not seem to be people attached to the house or holding: something about their loose, white-embroidered clothes, or perhaps their gaiety, suggested they looked upon this harvest as an unexpected blessing rather than as a yearly chore. His hurts throbbed and the high sun's heat made him sweat. The salt of his perspiration stung his cuts and scrapes. Radvyed began to turn, but some curious child had wandered away from the orchard and ventured into the gardens. She caught sight of him, her mouth dropped open, and she ran back to her parents, yelling something he did not understand.

Embarrassed, for he was bloodied and bare-chested, he tried following a path in the other direction, but the garden path was now arranged for meandering rather than striding. Soon two men were behind him, calling him. He moved more quickly, but one touched his arm from behind while the other blocked his way.

The man in front of him stared for a moment, blinking. Radvyed waited, knowing it was not only the scrapes and rags that gave the other man pause. He was used to this reaction when someone first saw his face. It had taken Radvyed some years before he understood that people rarely paused in that way before addressing others. As a child he had done the same, until he realized that when he stared silently before speaking, other people either thought he was slow-witted or offering insult. Rue had been the exception, now that he thought of it; she had not seemed affected. Even the stable youth had gasped when he had first run up to take Belikon's reins.

"Ho, stranger, my daughter was right," said the man in front of him. "You need to go to the Help Gate."

Radvyed did not know what to reply. *The Help Gate?* The other man, younger, looked at him, blinked, shook his head, and asked, "What happened to you?"

"I was trying to get into the walled garden," said Radvyed. They looked at him, puzzled. "It is guarded by thorns," he explained, holding up his scratched hands. Then, realizing how that might appear, he added, "I am not a thief. I am a guest."

Both men looked around. "What walled, thorn-guarded garden?" asked the first. "And we know you are no thief. Thieves cannot step on the Lady Generous's lands. But there is no walled garden here, for she is gracious, and opens her lands to all in need."

Radvyed wondered whether they were playing some sort of joke on him. He turned his whole body around, expecting to see the thorn-enclosed garden a few steps away. It was not there. But he could see the house from this angle, and now it was a comfortable, sprawling structure of warm, yellow stone, with pretty ivy trailing up its walls and curling about its windows. He took a deep breath, then turned back to the men.

"Forgive me, I have lost my bearings." Suddenly, he was very tired. He felt like an idiot standing there, bloody, bare of shirt, and babbling. "What is the Help Gate?"

"Many come to the Lady in need...the poor, the sick, vagrants, unlucky ones," replied the first man. His wary look said Radvyed belonged in all four categories. "The Help Gate is where aid is given. Come, we will lead you there."

Radvyed nodded. If nothing else, perhaps there would be someone who could help him back to his room. One man walked in front, one behind, not as guards, Radvyed thought, but as herders not wishing to lose their charge. As they passed by the orchard, the men answered the calls of the others still gathering fruit.

"Are you the Lady's people?" Radvyed asked, noticing that the gravel of the path had given way to bricks set in spirals and loops, and that they walked in the rich scent of bedstraw, the many-petalled white flowers brushing their arms as they passed.

"No, we are Wanderers. We have been in recent years driven by the salt, moving not as the wind calls but as the curse pursued us. Lands that had once been friendly turned suspicious and angry. Then one morning, after a night of fog, we woke here, where the Lady rules. She has not asked us to go, so we linger."

"Have you seen the Lady?" asked Radvyed. He wondered what they thought of the sorceress Hideous.

"Yes, a very quiet woman, always dressed in simple brown. You would not think her the mistress of so much land and power."

Radvyed said nothing. They walked through an arbor paved with slate. Small yellow and pink flowers grew up between the stones. They released a fresh and pungent smell when crushed underfoot. He listened to the men talk, telling him of the bounty and care the Lady provided to every petitioner at the Gate. He was surprised that while they found the Lady's generosity to strangers remarkable and her power to shield her land from the salt curse mysterious and impressive, they did not speak of shifting paths or buildings that changed or any of the phenomena that made the Lady's house difficult for him to navigate. They were untroubled by or oblivious to this aspect of her power.

The arbor ended, and they arrived at a wrought iron gate that led to a white gravel drive for conveyances and horses. The drive swept in a curve close to the house. There was no courtyard. A half-open gate for those on foot, set in the gray fieldstone wall, stood to the side of the larger gate. It was simply made of oak and iron. Beyond he saw a gatekeeper's lodge. The older man knocked on the half-open gate. It was pulled back, and there stood Rue, in her brown dress. She said nothing, but looked at Radvyed.

"Lady," said the older man, touching Radvyed on the shoulder, "this man needs care, of your grace."

"Indeed, so I see," she answered. Radvyed could not tell what she thought of his appearance. He bowed, biting his inner cheek at the pain of stretching the skin of his gravel-pocked back.

"I beg your ladyship to have mercy on an imprudent guest."

Her eyelids flickered, but otherwise her expression did not change. "Better imprudent than impudent," Rue replied, then looked to the two men. "Thank you, sirs. I will take this man into my care." They bowed and turned to walk back to their friends and family.

Rue said, "May I show you to your room, Prince? And perhaps send up a bath?"

"I would be most grateful," Radvyed said.

Chapter Six

His room, Radvyed was relieved to see, was as it had been when he had awakened that same morning. Rue had made no comment nor asked any questions as she escorted him back to it. She departed in silence. The prince could not determine whether she thought well or ill of him.

She was waiting to see what he would do or not do, Radvyed realized as he peeled off the remains of his ragged shirt from his hands and wrists. *Well, today I have shredded my back and arms and hands trying to scale a walled garden that either vanishes or moves about. And I have had to be led back to the house, like a lost child returned to its mother.* He sighed and turned. A large bath, steaming hot, sat on the wool carpet. On a stool next to it were neatly folded white towels topped with a cake of soap and a large flannel square.

He sank slowly into the hot water, hissing as his scratches and cuts became wet. Radvyed tried for a moment to identify the herbal infusions that had been added to the bathwater. Then he relaxed, laid back his head, and cleared his mind to think.

The flower must be in the garden, but the garden was well guarded. He could not scale the wall by mere bodily strength or skill. The wall either had no door or was not willing to reveal it to him. The prince snorted at the idea of a wall with will, but the objects in this sorcerous place seemed unusually lively and changeable. So. If brawn did not work, then perhaps brains would. How are defenses or resistance overcome, other than by brute force? Here his royal training could be of some use. His father daily dealt with people in the kingdom or abroad who did not see eye to eye with him on one matter or another, and his mother in her spheres of authority had similar difficulties. They relied on persuasion and charm more than force. Persuasion and charm. His eyes opened. How did one persuade a wall or charm a thorn?

That evening, Radvyed was once again escorted to dinner with Hideous. He noticed, before the doors were opened, that this evening they were figured with briars remarkably like the ones he had encountered that day, but he was given no time to study them. The dining room was much the same as it had been the night before, only darker, as if everything, textiles, furnishings, even the walls and floors, had been overdyed with a gray wash. The spice scent hung heavily, but did not quite smother the fetor of rotting meat. Radvyed still could not precisely locate the origin of either odor, which made the shadows seem sinister, somehow. Hideous stood obscured in her corner. The table was again laid for two. Once again, they shared a meal in silence; once again, she asked him in her jaw-clenchingly irritating voice to marry her. Once again, he declined, was dismissed, and departed.

And so the pattern of their daily time together was set. Every evening Radvyed dined with Hideous, enveloped in firelight, spice, and the lingering stench. Every evening she asked him, in a voice distorted, he came to believe, by the strange, heavy vein wrapped around her neck, whether he would marry her. Every evening he said no, as gently as he knew how. Every evening there would be silence as they sat, each separately contemplating what they were compelled to pursue but unable to obtain for themselves or give to the other: a flower of healing for a dying queen, a hand in marriage to a hideous woman. The silence between them would grow heavier and heavier, even the flames of the fire seeming subdued by its weight, until at last Hideous would ask her dreaded question. Radvyed would answer, never able to find a way to make the refusal less harsh. Hideous would then wave her hand with a graceless jerk and the prince would rise, bow to her, and depart.

Convinced that the curative flower was within the secluded garden, Radvyed made several more attempts to breach its walls. He tried cutting the thorny vines with Dris's hook; the tool did not break, but the bramble did not yield. Next, he tried his sword and then, a pair of shears left behind by a gardener, to no avail. Radvyed then purloined a ladder from the stables, only to have it splinter to pieces when his foot rested upon the first rung. Stacking furniture dragged from his room produced only bruises when the wall repulsed the tower of small tables and splat-back chairs. He even tried to set fire to the vines with a candle from his chamber; the resultant smelly, oily smoke soon died. The thorny vine remained as robust as ever.

Radvyed's frustration and anxiety grew, until it was all he could do to master himself sufficiently to be civil to Rue. He spent hours sitting outside the garden guarded by thorns, hating his uselessness and its imperviousness, staring at the brambles as if by the power of his eye alone he could bore a hole to the space within. He paced around it again and again, and tore more than one shirt seeking for an entrance. But there was no opening for him, and he began to feel the chill grip of despair.

The house every day took new shapes, but now darker, harder, the carvings more troubled, the figures anguished and the furnishings providing more disturbance of mind than comfort of body. The gardens seemed scarcely navigable mazes. Now when Radvyed forced the paths to bend to his desire and take him to the thorn-walled garden, they led him there swiftly, with an almost scornful insolence. For he had no desire now to see anything in the house or grounds, except the wall that so obstinately resisted and repelled him.

The days passed, blurring into a markless mist until Radvyed could not reckon how many weeks he had lingered. Sometimes he believed the very air rendered him stupid and slow: always he felt that between dawn and dusk he accomplished nothing but sinking more deeply into failure. Also, he was lonely. Rue, never expansive, had her own responsibilities and occupations. The people of the place, working in house, stable, and grounds, avoided him. When Radvyed managed to corner someone—a gardener staking a plant, a *damash* bearing a laundry basket—they would slip away after a hasty, "I couldn't say, sir." Never had his looks and charm been so futile; even attempts at small talk were rebuffed. By Rue's orders or those of her mistress? Or were the household staff captives as well, imprisoned here either by dark magic or some desperate necessity, as he was chained by his need for the healing flower?

His only friend was Belikon, whom he visited daily in the stables. The horse seemed to be well looked after, with bright eyes, pink gums, smooth hooves, and plenty of water available. Belikon's coat gleamed, but sometimes Radvyed brushed him anyway. The horse did not paw restlessly in his stall, although the prince never saw open pastures or fields when he looked out from the stables, hoping to ride. He thought to take Belikon on the paths he himself walked about the grounds, but when his horse was with him no ways opened from the stables and they were firmly turned back. So Radvyed simply visited, and spoke to his animal friend, and at times just rested his forehead on Belikon's neck and waited for the steady, familiar warmth and smell of the horse to bring him a measure of calm.

One dreary day, after visiting Belikon, Radvyed entered the house. Without warning, the dark clouds that had been looming all afternoon let loose their burden of water amid whips of lightning and bone-jarring thunder. The ferocious release of the sky's pent-up power eased him a little. Radvyed wandered to a window and, staring out, took satisfaction in the wildness of the storm. It became so dark he could no longer perceive the flattened shrubs and battered flowers through the almost horizontal, wind-driven sheets of rain. The very house creaked and shook.

As he moved his gaze from the storm outside the window, one of the figures worked into the heavy curtain caught his eye. A bird in a cage, with its long, drooping tail protruding through the bars, its wings partially opened and its beak parted in an anguished cry. The whole curtain, as Radvyed peered at it by the uncertain light of the fireplace and the sconces, held a design of unpleasant writhing vines and various captive, struggling birds: some in cages, like the one that had first caught his attention, and some ensnared by the vines themselves. Radvyed looked around the room he was in. Each ironwork sconce was in the form of a snarling, chained dog. The carpet beneath his feet also presented a theme of captivity, for it seemed to narrate the story of an enslaved people who were being driven from one barren rock to another, flogged by guards. He crouched down and with a finger touched the form of a man, naked to the waist, who was lamenting as he twisted to avoid the lash.

Radvyed rose to his feet. The walls were patterned in dark, close-set vertical bars. The decorative objects, if they could be called such, all depicted or suggested tormented imprisonment. The tables and chests were heavy and too big for the space. The chairs were spindly and hard. Nothing in the room spoke of poverty, but everything suggested unease, despair, and helplessness. He stood in the middle of the room and wondered whether it was intended to reflect his own situation and bring home to him his powerlessness, or, and he was surprised at the thought that arose quietly in his mind in that dark and cheerless room, whether it was an expression of the anguish of the house's mistress. *But how can that be?* Radvyed thought, unwilling to surrender his resentment against the ridiculous and humiliating position he found himself in. *I am the captive here.* A lightning bolt cracked, followed by a teeth-rattling boom of thunder, and then he heard the bell for dinner.

That evening the prince found that despite himself his thoughts had been given a new turn. He looked at his hostess, considering her noisome repulsiveness that never seemed to fade or to disgust less. For the first time, he wondered at the loneliness of being so hideous, so abhorrent in every way, that neither time nor familiarity seemed to soften the effect of her presence. Radvyed forced himself to hold his gaze on her, longer than bare courtesy demanded, yet briefer than insult. Somehow tonight he saw her with eyes unblurred by resentment or his own humiliation.

All during dinner he was able to look fully at her, for she, as always, kept her eyes averted. His gaze traced the thick dark twining lines about her throat, her wrists, her misshapen fingers; he noted the livid coils that raised ridges on her face, making the shape of cheek, chin, and nose unsettlingly repulsive. The coils and cords were punctuated by darker marks, the skin about them putty gray and streaked with angry red. There was something strange—then at last, the niggling sense of bizarre familiarity evoked by the cords twisting under her skin clarified into understanding.

The cords, the coils, they were kin to the thornwood he had fought through and the vines that guarded the garden. The darker marks were not stains or moles, they were holes the underlying thorns had punctured through her skin from the inside. The odd appearance of prickles on her skin was not some skin disease, but the points of the thorns thrusting up. Radvyed's mind reeled as he understood that the visible twists and tendrils might only be the surface branches of a thorned vine that wrapped around her bones and pierced her organs. Perhaps that even broke her bones and poisoned her blood.

He must have gasped with the realization, or made some other noise or movement, for Hideous's gaze slid toward him. Radvyed covered his momentary loss of composure with a reassuring smile, but it failed to convince, for Hideous hunched her rounded shoulders and drew her elbows closer to her body. The movement pressed a thorn—how was it possible he had not seen what it was before?—in her neck farther out from her flesh. A whiff of the spoiled meat odor hit his nose. He blinked, realizing that the protruding thorns were the source of the noxious smell. Radvyed's gaze fell to the table, and he noticed the trembling of one clammy, misshapen hand—misshapen because the bones within had been broken and regrown awry? It came to him that this trembling was not from pain or weakness, but from tension.

She is trying to control the repellent force of her body and she knows she cannot, and yet she is so desperate that she cannot help but try. He saw the humiliation of a person, who, although powerful in many ways, was unable to be a pleasant companion at dinner, a simple skill of many more ordinary folk. But evening after evening, she set herself to try. The prince had pitied her before, but now his pity was different, for it held admiration, even tenderness, for her valiant effort.

When she asked, he answered her bleak proposal gently, regretting his refusal more than ever.

That night Radvyed dreamed of a young woman bound to a dragon and locked in a tower that was covered with thorn and salt.

He awoke confused by elusive images from the dream. A blind-folded young woman...chained to the breast of a horrible, terrifying dragon...isolated by grief and thorn and loneliness in a high tower. Radvyed shook his head, as though to settle the dream pictures into order, but they vanished, leaving only rags of memory. His bed was of cherry wood today, a lighter wood than of late. No one seemed to be writhing in agony in the carving of it.

When the prince came to the door letting him out of the house and into the gardens, he hesitated. His habit had been to direct the path to the walled garden that held the needed flower. But how much good had this plan of action, if such it could be called, done him or his mother? So instead Radvyed said aloud, "Take me where you will." He stepped onto the path and gave himself to wandering.

The graveled way led him first among the more formal gardens that seemed to keep close to the house. He admired a shrubbery filled with every kind of white blossom, all glowing against greens from palest lime to deep pine. Turning a corner, he passed through a cool arbor heavy with grapevines. He stepped out of the arbor into a wide meadow of knee-high grasses, blooming with flowers of every shade of blue and red. Butterflies, bees, and tiny jewel-like birds hovered and dipped in the sunlight. Here the path was made of large flagstones of slate, and it meandered to a wide shallow birdbath, kept fresh by a small fountain, shaped like one of the hovering birds. The creatures took no notice of him as he strolled and looked at them and the flowers. Wherever the path led him, new delights opened, whether of scent or sound or color. All gave him pleasure, but nothing seemed as though it strove to please him, and he neither alarmed nor disturbed any creature.

At last, entering a leafy grove, Radvyed crossed an arched bridge made of river stones. He stopped in the middle to enjoy the burble and flow of the narrow stream it spanned. He looked down at the clear water running over the rocks below, making the green moss on them wave and dance. He watched a few tiny darting fish, then lifted his head at the sound of a birdcall. Turning, he saw that on the other side of the bridge, set back from the path and partially screened by some ferns, was a stone bench. Rue sat on it, staring into the water that eddied below the bank. The prince did not like to disturb her solitude; he had begun to turn away when she said, "Join me, Prince."

He walked slowly over the bridge to the bench and sat next to her. They both looked at the water.

"You have not come this way before," said Rue.

"No," Radvyed answered. "But I found I could not spend another day looking at that wall."

She did not respond.

He turned to face her. "Why will your mistress not give me the flower? Why will you not tell me what I must do? Why will no one help or even speak to me? Sun Lady and Dark Master, do you not understand that my mother is dying?" He heard his voice rising, and swallowed. The calm he had found this day evaporated, leaving him adrift. Clenching his fists on his thighs, he struggled to master his bafflement and grief.

Rue's face remained still, but her eyes cooled. "This task is your own, Prince. You have all that is necessary. Anything else may risk—" She stopped.

"What? Risk what?" he said, driven to his feet. She kept her stony silence as he walked a few paces away.

Radvyed grasped his head in both hands, regretting his loss of control. Nothing would be gained by alienating Rue. He straightened, took several deep breaths, and returned to the bench where she still sat.

"Please forgive my rudeness," he said, as evenly as he could. She nodded.

Another silence. He watched the play of dappling light on the rushing water. What season was it? Neither gardens nor clime seemed to follow the usual rules of order any more than the house did. Then Radvyed remembered that Rue did not seem to notice the changes in the house, unless he drew her attention to them. He sighed. Direct questioning had failed. Perhaps he could learn something from an oblique approach.

"What do you see?" he asked.

She allowed the faintest smile to touch her lips. "Why, what is there. What do you see?"

"A small stream rushing over moss-covered stones. Leafy trees. The sun on the water."

She said nothing, but the faint smile remained.

He tried again. "Who are you to the Lady Hideous?"

The smile faded, and he felt the deep sadness of her, although her expression changed little.

"I was her wet nurse and have been with her ever since."

Radvyed tried to imagine Hideous as a baby, tried to imagine Rue nursing her, teaching her to walk, to speak. Was the vine present even then, piercing and binding her small child's body?

"Has she always been...as she is?"

Rue looked at him. "Have you?"

Radvyed flushed. Trying to be tactful was only making him appear stupid. "Was she, even as a baby, was she…"

"A sorceress? Generous? Lonely?" Rue asked, her voice hard. She turned her face away from him. He opened his mouth, hoping that this time the right words would form, when she said, still not looking at him, "She was born a sorceress. It is in her blood. Her father cursed her and sent her away, with only me to care for her, to the cottage in the wood that you entered."

"Her father cursed her?"

"He was displeased with her, and in disowning her, cursed her with the name of Hideous."

Radvyed waited, but she said no more. He knotted his fingers. *Very well.* If Rue wished to say no more, he would refrain from prying. He was not here to make sense of Hideous's troubles; he was here to find the cure for his dying mother.

Radvyed looked at his empty hands. He had failed, was failing still. Rue's silence pushed at him, steady and unrelenting.

"What is it you want of me?" he demanded at last. "What is it that you think I can do that a Lady who wields so much power cannot do for herself? Why do you, why does *she*, need me here?" Radvyed dropped his head into his hands, his elbows on his knees. "Do you not know that I cannot open a garden gate, even though the flower within might save my mother's life? What power do you think I have?"

"You can marry Hideous."

The water's burble faded into silence; the leafy branches stilled; the sunlight dimmed. The prince lifted his face and stared straight ahead into nothing.

"Is that the price of the flower?"

"No," said Rue. Radvyed looked at her, surprised. "You asked what it is you can do that she cannot. You can be her husband. You have other powers, too, to which you are so accustomed you no longer think of them as powers."

"Failing my mother? Being beaten by a wall?"

"Your beauty. Your charm."

He snorted and returned his gaze to the rushing water.

"You underestimate them because they are yours, much as a rich woman might say that money matters little or a king might say that all his power is nothing, because they desire something beyond what money or authority can bring them."

Radvyed turned to look at her. "That is what my father says about my mother's illness. And it is true."

Rue gazed back at the water. "And yet he was able to command and equip his son to search for a flower known only to a royal advisor."

The prince said nothing.

"You have other powers, of course, besides being handsome and charming. You are honorable and persistent. You have some strength of mind and body. You love your mother and your father. But you will need all your virtues to obtain your desire."

A pause. Still she waited for him to do, to say...what?

"Why does Lady Hideous ask me to marry her?"

Rue stood abruptly and shook the leaves and dirt from the hem of her skirt. She turned and looked down at him, her hands clenched in the folds of her dress, her mouth a thin line.

"Why do you think?"

With that, she stepped around him and away. Her footsteps faded. Radvyed sat alone, staring at the water, the sunlight, the leaves. He wondered what he did not see.

Chapter Seven

Later that day in his room as he prepared for dinner, Radvyed thought about the meal he and the sorceress shared every evening. Clearly Lady Hideous did not need his strength or his brains: even he had found both useless with regard to the wall. She desired, it seemed, his looks and his charm. It seemed too little, too simple, even too ordinary. Her estate was not deserted: why not appoint a good-looking man to wait on her at table, to sing to her accompanied by some sweet-strumming instrument, to dance, to converse, to serve at her pleasure?

And yet. His father liked to say that he loved his wife, Radvyed's mother, because she would laugh at his jokes even if he were not king. But he knew other couples, for whom the plentiful money or high status of one was held by both parties to be an equal trade for the obliging beauty or amusing company of the other. Lady Hideous did not want a companion whose attention and presence she must command. Her loneliness was too harsh for such flimsy substitutes: they would make her isolation more painful, not less.

Radvyed went to dinner, escorted as always by a silent and expressionless Rue. After greeting and being greeted, he sat down at table. He remembered what Rue had said: *I was her wet nurse...only me to care for her*. No mother nor father, no sisters, no brothers, no cousins, no playmates. No friends.

He had been silent at meals because Hideous had spoken very little. But perhaps she had no experience of light talk. Rue loved her nursling, but she was a somber woman.

Radvyed tried to catch Hideous's eye, forcing himself to ignore the flare of strong disgust he felt at the sight and smell of her, despite his pity. He would draw on his royal training in self-control and his lessons in defusing tensions in fraught company. But Hideous was too focused on containing her body's grotesqueness to notice that her guest sought to engage her in conversation. *Very well.*

Radvyed took a sip of wine and said, "Do you have favorite stories you like to read or hear told? Often I see carved figures in your furnishings, but I have rarely recognized what tales they belong to, if indeed they belong to any." He kept his face turned to her, his expression courteously interested. *Pretend she is a normal young woman*, he said to himself. *Do not be distracted by the smell, the binding thorns.*

His unexpected speech surprised Hideous into looking at him and their gazes met. He felt there was a change in the quality of her attention, but the distortion of her face and the dullness of her eye gave him no clues. Was she looking him over? Was she considering his words? *I will pretend that she is simply shy*, Radvyed thought. *That she is a border* mirena*'s daughter at her first formal court dinner. She has been spoken to by a prince; now she must gather her thoughts.*

After a moment, Hideous turned away and stared at her twisted, clammy hand on the table. Her screechy voice spoke, as low and as soft as he had ever heard it, the words punctuated by choked gasps. "Wanderers' tales...Ash Girl...Jack Came Back...Lost Swan...Brave Beggar Boy...Lionheart."

"We have those stories in my country as well. I always loved to hear of Jack and his adventures in outwitting the giant. But Lionheart was the role I preferred in games with my friends. Do you have a favorite tale?" Radvyed made his manner gentle, coaxing, but unthreatening, as though Hideous were a girl of twelve seated with the grown-ups at the royal table for the first time.

A pause. She was not used to this. "Yes." Another pause. Then a whisper. "Tower."

"Ah! One I do not know," said the prince. "Would you tell me it, Lady?"

"No good," she wheezed "at stories." She fixed her rheumy eyes on him. *So I have distracted her at least for a moment from her own repulsiveness and pain.*

Radvyed smiled at her. "I am sure you are better than you think. But perhaps you will allow me to share with you a tale or two?"

Hideous hesitated. "Friends playing...Lionheart?" she asked, the voice grating so irritatingly that it took conscious effort for him to discern her words.

He grinned, remembering. "But of course. I must warn you, however, that they would most likely tell you a very different tale. Now before we played, we drew lots for who would be Lionheart, who the Ogre, and who the Mouse..."

Radvyed understood after a few minutes that she cared less for the story or the game and more for hearing about childhood friends. After telling of his Lionheart adventures, he told her about his first time on a full-sized horse, about the hunting dogs kept at the palace, about the ships that went in and out of the kingdom's largest seaport, Grozgaven. He shaped his talk so that she could make only brief replies, if she wished, carrying the conversation himself, but speaking about what he hoped would amuse and interest her. The candles guttered. Radvyed smiled into his wineglass, thinking of the first time he had seen the horizon delineating sea from sky, and at the same time providing an undemanding pause in which she might choose to speak.

Hideous shifted in her seat, releasing a puff of the rotten-meat stench. He took a shallow breath and looked at her. *She is a normal young woman, a little shy, a little quiet,* he reminded himself as he was assaulted by her ugliness again.

"Prince, marry me?" A choked whisper, as if she were forced, night after night, into accepting the blow of his rejection.

His throat tightened. What was compelling her? Her face was already turned away: she knew his answer. Her gnarled and clammy hands with their long, cracked, yellow nails and black-thorned vines pushing against the skin over her knuckles trembled where they lay on the table.

"I deeply regret," Radvyed said, "that I must decline the honor."

One hand jerked, and at once the prince stood, bowed, and left the room.

Chapter Eight

That night Radvyed dreamed again. He was wandering in a dark wood when he came upon a stone tower, covered in thorn. He entered and ascended the staircase. In the room at the top of the tower was the horrible dragon. There was no sign of the young woman. The dragon was hideous. The prince had imagined dragons to be as magnificent as they were terrible, but this one was horrible without inspiring respect or awe. It wallowed in filth and moaned endlessly, although he could see no injury. As Radvyed turned away, for the beast was not worth the effort of destroying, it shrieked. He spun to face it. It had lurched to its feet and now he could see the dirty chains wound about its limbs and the dragging of its broken wings. "Marry me!" it cried. "Marry me! Marry me, prince! Marry me!" He groped for the doorway behind him. He would not stoop to kill such a miserable creature, but neither would he keep it company. He was out and away. He looked over his shoulder at the tower. It was gone, but in its place was the walled garden that guarded the flower. He stopped and ran back. But the garden had no door and he could not get in.

Radvyed awoke, confused. The bed canopy overhead this morning was a deep green, with some sort of fanciful botanical pattern embroidered in an even darker green. He closed his eyes, trying to remember and understand. These dreams seemed significant. *The Tower*. Was that not her favorite tale? It seemed somehow the key to the garden. He leapt out of bed and hastily dressed, eager to find Rue and ask her about the story.

But Rue, it seemed, was not to be found, not even by asking to be led to her. Radvyed sat on a bench outside that day's main back entrance, leaned his head back against the wall, and considered whether Hideous's house, so full of precious things, might have a library... He heard voices carrying through the air. The Wanderers. *The Wanderers!* Radvyed sat up. The Wanderers who told the tale of the Tower. He went in search of them.

Today they were not gathering apricots, but blueberries. On a sunny slope they picked and ate, sang and played. As he approached, they became quiet and watchful. He was met at the edge of the group by one of the men who had taken him to the Help Gate.

"Lost again, lordling?" he asked pleasantly. Radvyed could see that the girls and women were eyeing him in a friendly and curious way. They had gathered in small groups and were staring at him and obviously making comments that their menfolk did not like. He kept his hands relaxed and in view and did not look at the women directly. *If beauty and charm are my powers, they are not always under my command,* he thought ruefully.

"Not lost, but in search of a little company," Radvyed replied and pretended he did not hear the low buzz that answer generated among the women.

"We are but picking berries here, nothing to amuse one such as yourself." The man spoke a bit less pleasantly.

"I do not seek to be entertained, only...my mother is in a far country and I have not seen her for many days. Is there some kind lady here who would allow me to hold her basket as she works? I do not wish to disturb you." The looks he was getting from several men said that he had already disturbed them and not in a welcome way. Some quiet skirmishing seemed to be going on among the women.

"Yes, young man, you can hold my basket," said a commanding voice. "And you can pick berries for me, too. Come here." He turned toward the voice and saw an old woman sitting on a wooden chair by a large bush. The deference accorded her by the rest of the Wanderers indicated that this was the matriarch of the group. The men stepped back and returned to their work; the women gave last glances but then turned away, calling to their children or picking up a song again.

The old woman waited, watching him as he walked over to her. Her dark blue blouse was elaborately embroidered with white flowers and birds. "Yes, you're a handsome one, aren't you?" she said when he stood before her. "And after our little talk, you'll stay away from us. You bring trouble among us." She thrust her basket at him. It was half full. "You can pick from that bush." She indicated the one near her chair that she had apparently been working on.

Radvyed did not move, startled by her frank desire to have him away. He had not encountered such a reaction before. "I bring no trouble or ill intent, mistress. I wish no harm—"

"No, of course you don't," she interrupted him. The prince was not accustomed to being interrupted, either. "But you bring trouble all the same. The women start looking at you and thinking and talking, and the men start growling and snapping and shouting, and then who knows where it ends? I've seen murder committed a week after a comely girl smiled at a man. Those berries won't fall off the bush, young man, you must *pick* them."

He began picking. "But I do nothing—"

"You don't need to do anything. Now, why have you sought us out? Don't crush the berries."

Radvyed picked berries carefully for a moment. "I wonder if you know the tale of the Tower." He paused and looked at her.

The old woman quieted, setting aside her irritable manner. She did not look at him, but gave her attention to the grass at her feet. Then she raised her gaze to his face, considered him, and asked, "You are a prince in your own land, young man?"

"Yes." Radvyed began picking blueberries again. She watched the motion of his hands for a moment.

"And you have never heard the tale of the Tower?"

"No. The Lady...Generous mentioned it last night."

Silence, as though the old woman were reflecting upon a course of action. He shifted to another spot and continued picking berries.

"The Tower is a strange tale, because no one knows how it ends," she said at last, "although many endings exist." She paused. "There is a dragon in the topmost room of a tower that is guarded by thickest thorn." The prince stilled. "It is a pitiful creature, living in filth and chained to the floor." His hands gripped the basket painfully. "One day, a handsome young prince finds the tower and goes inside. And there he finds the dragon, who weeping, speaks to him, saying—"

"*Marry me,*" Radvyed said in a harsh whisper. When the old woman did not continue, he asked in a low voice, "And what does the young prince do?"

"No one agrees, or has ever agreed. Every time I have heard the story told, the storyteller fails to satisfy, no matter how it ends. Does he run away? If he does, what happens to him and the dragon? Does he kill the dragon, out of disgust, or pity, or cruelty? Does he marry it? If he does, does it transform into a beautiful girl or a beautiful dragon or is he chained forever to hideousness? Does he lie? Is the dragon feigning helplessness and planning to kill him when he comes near? No one knows. It is not a tale that is told often. It unsettles."

The prince stayed silent and still after she finished speaking. Radvyed did not tell her that he had dreamed the story. He stared without seeing at a small green leaf that was hiding a plump berry.

A bird sang out and the old woman stirred. "Give me my basket then, if you're done picking," she said gruffly. Radvyed came to himself with a start, and, pulling himself together, gave her a polite smile and handed her the basket, now filled with berries. She held it on her lap, loosely circled by her arms. The old woman's gaze was uncomfortably keen. Radvyed made a quick bow and turned to go.

"Prince," she called before he had taken two steps.

He stopped and turned towards her. "Yes, I remember, mistress: I will not bring my trouble-making face among you again." To his surprise, she laughed.

"Good! But this is what I wanted to ask you: if you ever learn the true ending to the tale, send me word."

"To what name, mistress?"

"To Starzana of the Kaitiren. The message will find me."

Radvyed bowed again, a little more deeply, and walked away. As he reached the bottom of the gentle slope, he met the path, here a narrow dirt track that cut through high flowering grasses. He followed it around a turn, then glanced over his shoulder. The Wanderers, the blueberry slope, the old woman and her basket, were gone. He faced forward again and found that he was among paths of white shell and beds of lavender, rosemary, savory, and other herbs. A small white marble bench presented itself, and he sat on it. The house, gray river rock with white-framed windows, rose on his left. He broke off a sprig of rosemary, rubbed the leaves between his fingers, and sniffed them absently. Radvyed sat until the stretching evening shadows reminded him it was time to prepare for dining with the Lady of the house.

CHAPTER NINE

T hat evening he had time to notice the dragon and tower motifs carved in the doors before Rue opened them. But he saw no ending to the story.

Over dinner the prince told Hideous about meeting the Wanderers. "You had pricked my curiosity with this tale I had never heard before. I had seen them another time, among apricot trees, I believe, so I asked your obliging garden path to find them, and it led me to blueberry bushes on a sunny hillside." Radvyed smiled. "Your gardens and grounds are most wonderful. Full of surprises and unexpected delights," he added, thinking she must be hearing what she well knew, even if the thorned vine binding her from within never allowed her to wander her estate.

"Tell me," Hideous said.

"About the Wanderers?" he asked.

"Gardens," she said. Radvyed sipped some wine to hide his surprise. Did she not know?

"The grounds of your house are extensive. From the back of the house, facing east, one sometimes looks out on formal gardens, but in the distance one sees the eaves of leafy and cool woods. Other days, masses of flowers crowd up to the house, and beyond them open meadows of sweet grass..."

Throughout dinner Radvyed described for her the lovely places he had found or been led to and told her how gardens changed and vanished, sometimes reappearing, now under heavy skies, now under fair weather. He described the animals, birds, and insects he had encountered, never doubting that he had her complete attention. He could not tell whether she were truly ignorant of her own estate's beauties, or whether she simply desired to hear him recount them. Yet if she did not have the ordering of her domain, who did? Rue? Was Rue truly the Lady Generous, then? How to ask without giving offense?

His talk ceased, and then for a time the only sound was the fire in the grate and the clink of plates as unseen servants cleared the table. A custard with a caramelized sauce was placed in front of him—although Hideous herself never ate sweets—and a carafe of dessert wine, with two glasses. Radvyed poured. As always, she did not drink.

"Tower?" Hideous asked finally.

"Tow—? Oh yes, the Tower. Well, I found the Wanderers—who, by the way, did not make me entirely welcome—"

"Why?" Hideous leaned a little towards him, caught his involuntary recoil, and turned her head away. "Pardon. Do not—"

Radvyed silently cursed himself. "Lady, please do not turn from me." He waited, but she kept her face from him, and he saw that her hands were shaking once more with the tension of trying to control her repulsiveness. He swore at himself again for having wounded her; that it had been an instinctive distaste made the insult harder to bear, he was sure. "Lady, I was not welcome because they thought me too handsome, and so bound to bring discord and strife among them." That surprised her out of her self-pity.

Hideous turned and looked at him. "What?"

"Yes, despite my not looking at nor challenging anyone, the matriarch informed me that neither my behavior nor my intentions mattered a hen's tooth, as we say in my country. She as much as said that murder would soon follow if I did not get my troublesome face away as quickly as possible."

Silence. It was difficult to know what Hideous was thinking. The uneasy conviction that no intelligent, feeling soul lived behind the dim eyes constituted a large part of her repulsiveness. Radvyed forced himself to not look away. *She is a shy woman, unused to strangers, and uncertain of her own charms*, he told himself. *You are the Lady's guest*.

After a moment, the prince filled the silence. The keen-eyed matriarch had reminded him of the fading woman who was never far from his thoughts. "My mother, of course, thinks her son handsome—although not dangerously so, I presume—but that is the way of all mothers, I hear." Again, silence, this time long enough for him to remember that Hideous had not known her mother, and that the mother she did know, Rue, may never have called her beautiful. Or perhaps she did; Rue did not seem to see as others did.

"Tower?" Hideous asked again.

"Did she tell me this favorite story of yours that you would not tell? Well, yes and no. I think I now understand, Lady, why you hesitated to tell it. She told me that no one knows the true ending to the tale and that no teller has ever satisfied an audience with any ending." Radvyed paused, then said lightly, "She did say it begins with a dragon chained in the top of a thorny tower and that a young man—"

"*Prince*."

"Yes, a prince, finds the tower, goes upstairs, and encounters the dragon. But what happens next, it seems no one can say. Do you have an ending that you favor, Lady?"

A log collapsed in the fireplace. The room was very dark, lit only by the low flames. The air smelled of smoke and spice, the thorns' repellent odor faint underneath. They were alone; not even the invisible servants seemed to be about. The dark shadows of the room seemed to cup themselves about the prince and the sorceress, like gentle hands holding a broken-winged bird. The stillness vibrated with a sense of expectancy, or perhaps abandonment to fate. How long they sat in this thrumming silence he did not know.

"Marry me?" Hideous whispered.

Radvyed found that for the first time, he wished he could say yes. He wished he could truly think of her as some well-born young woman, aware of but not yet mistress of the power her wealth, beauty, and position gave her; he wished he could without flinching take her clammy, thorn-pricked, twisted hand, and lead her out to see the marvels of her own house, of her own lands. He wished he knew how to comfort that lonely soul, instead of providing another occasion for her to shrink with self-hatred. He wished he knew the way to say *Yes, I will marry you*, and not feel his gorge rise and his flesh crawl at the very thought. He wished he were more; he wished he were better.

At last, he said, "Lady, I regret. I cannot marry you."

All at once the room became grayer, the fire feebler, even tired.

"Go," grated the horrible voice. And he went.

Chapter Ten

The next day, after a night of confused dreams about the tower tale, in which a sobbing dragon crawled to him, pathetically trying to open its muck-mired wings, shrieking, "Marry me! Marry me!" the prince asked the garden path to take him to the walled garden. It was as high and as thorny as ever, the door just as elusive, hidden, or nonexistent.

Radvyed sat on the gravel path and decided to match the wall in obstinacy. It began to rain, but he did not move, only pulled his woolen cloak more closely about him. He thought of his mother: her kindness, her authority, her love of flowers, her willingness to praise what was lovely or well done and her ability to cool resentment and mend strife. And he remembered more intimate things, too: the note in her voice when she called him, her pride when he had first grown taller than she, how her hand felt on his cheek. How whenever, as a child, he had shown her something he had learned or accomplished, she had said, smiling, "But of course I am not surprised. You are my handsome, clever, wonderful boy." How he had loved to please her and make her proud. Her patience with him, rarely interrupted by exasperation, during the awkward years between child and adult; her high standards for ethics and etiquette; her silly fear of grasshoppers (but not spiders), and the merry laugh, delighted and free, that had first attracted his father. Was she dead even now, as he sat powerless and stupid before this hated wall? His chest constricted, his throat closed, and his eyes burned. Radvyed dropped his head onto his arms, which he had crossed over his bent knees. He wept for the fading of such a queen and woman from the world; and he wept, too, for his own failure to save her.

Because his head was bent, he did not see the thorns softened first by dark, tentative leaves, and then by small, translucent, starlike flowers, opening to the rain and the night. When the prince left to go back to the house, his eyes were blurred by darkness and tears.

That evening, Radvyed could not make himself speak lightly or pleasantly. His hostess's hospitality was a cage; every day he felt himself less a prince, less a son, less a man. As he looked upon Hideous, he could only see an inscrutable, inert, uncanny creature who did nothing to help him to the talisman that would bring healing to his dying mother and wholeness to his land. And yet the sorceress seemed to intend Radvyed no harm, although he was trapped with her in this place where time and thought dragged in sluggish rounds. After dinner he sat, dreading and yet eager for the question he knew must come, for only then could he leave her.

"Prince marries...they live...happy..." Hideous said, the harsh, screeching voice dying away on the final word. Surprised out of his own thoughts, the prince looked at her, at once controlling his inevitable flinch. She held her dull, rheumy, red-lidded gaze on him. Radvyed remembered that he had asked about her preferred ending to the story of the Tower. He did not smile, but nodded.

"If only," he said, "if only it could be told so that ending rang true." Tonight she seemed unusually bold: she kept her eyes on his face. After a pause, Hideous spoke again.

"What is...dancing like?"

"Well, there are many kinds of—"

"No." She stopped to wheeze and grip the table, leaning toward him, her dull eyes fixed on his face. "What is it...*like*?"

She meant, Radvyed realized, what was it like to dance, to move with others with grace, joy, vigor, even intimacy. Had she ever felt any of those singing pleasures in her own movements, in matching them with other dancers? Of course not. How many other pleasures, known to the simplest farmer or villager, were as strange and as wonderful to her as her power, her knowledge, and her house were to him? *She is so lonely. So lonely and not even an exile or a guest. She is an alien among humankind.* And his dark mood was pierced by pity.

"Dancing. Well, there is pleasure in moving freely, yet in a pattern, in matching your movements to music or to the clapping of hands," he began. "There is pleasure in a group dance, when everyone weaves in and out, all of us making something harmonious and alive together. And in the challenge dances, when one shows one's power and stamina, then there is pleasure and pride in one's own strength and agility. Then there are the partnered dances, when one dances with one other, and when you are truly well matched, well, then, I am told, it can be like flying. But even less well matched, it is...well, it is delightful," Radvyed ended awkwardly, not sure how to explain the feeling of whirling about a room with a young woman smiling up at you and knowing that for the moment she had entrusted herself to you.

Hideous kept her gaze on him, even when Radvyed dropped his eyes to his wineglass, unnerved by her intensity.

"Show me," she said.

Radvyed looked up at her. She held out her shaking, thorn-bound hand to him. But she could barely stand. How could he show her—?

"My hand," Hideous whispered.

Radvyed slowly reached out his hand to hers. He held it, feeling its clammy puffiness, the way it lay in his like a dead fish. He felt the hard pressure of the vine that twined about her stiff, swollen fingers, felt even, like pinpricks of acid, the tips of the thorns that pierced her skin. He breathed in the stench, which was ever present under the spiced smoke. Yet she trusted him to show her something of this thing called dancing. He held her hand for a moment. Was that a tremor? He tried to think what his girl cousins giggled about as they told over the triumphs and glories of past balls, what made them sigh at a remembered thrill. Radvyed gave a seated bow, looked Hideous in the eye, and with a smile, asked, "Lady, would you care to dance?"

"Yes," Hideous answered.

Radvyed turned his hand and slid his fingers up under hers until their hands rested palm against palm, the fingers aligned. He slowly pulled his palm back until only their fingertips touched, waited a beat, then brought their palms together again. He turned his hand to the side, their palms still pressed, and laid his fingers over the back of her hand, her thumb caught in the cove between his fingers and thumb. Then he slid his palm around to the back of her hand, and let his fingers drift lightly against her skin as he drew them up from her wrist, until the tallest fingers of both their hands touched only at the tips.

The whole while, Radvyed knew the sweat-stickiness of her skin and the misshapenness of her hand, the wiry pressure of the half-hidden vine and the scrape of the thorns, and yet none of these unpleasant sensations disturbed or distracted him. He was too intent on giving Hideous a glimpse into something that was as unknown to her as the ways of magic were to him. He slowly pressed their palms together again, but this time gently spread the aligned fingers like a fan, and said, "With me, now." And he moved his fingers in between hers and folded them down. She did the same. For a moment their hands remained clasped. Then he withdrew his, gently took her fingers in his grasp, and bowed again where he sat. "Thank you for the pleasure of this dance." Radvyed looked up at her face. She was looking at their hands. Hideous nodded and he opened his fingers.

She laid her hand on the table. Then she looked over into the fire and said, "Go, Prince."

It was not until he was back in his room that he realized that she had not asked him to marry her.

Chapter Eleven

That night the dream had an ending. Again Radvyed approached the thorny tower; again he climbed the spiraling stone stairs to the room at the top, where he saw once more the dragon mired in filth and sorrow. But as he stood there, as he always did in the dream, wondering what came next, the dragon surprised him. Instead of crawling towards him, pleading with him in its usual repulsive and miserable way, the dragon did not seem to notice that the prince had appeared in the doorway. It was looking out a window he had never noticed in his tower dreams before. And while still filthy and unhappy, the dragon was not agitated, but quiet. Radvyed lowered his sword, but not so much that he allowed the tip to touch the muck at his feet. Then the dragon turned its great ugly head towards him, and said, "Here, I give you what you came for." And lifting one of its talons, it slashed open its chest. The prince gasped at the black blood that burst from the wound. The dragon staggered, but held itself up. Its gaze caught his. "I give it to you, but you must take it, take it, and go." The dragon stumbled and Radvyed found himself making his way through the mire toward it. As he came up to it, the dragon swung its head back so that the wound was exposed. In his dream Radvyed watched his hand reach inside the wound and pull out the dragon's heart, which to his surprise was smaller than his fist: it looked more like a child's heart than a dragon's. In the way of dreams, he was then running down the stairs, the heart tucked against his chest, under his clothes. He ran away from the tower with an urgency as vague in purpose as it was powerful in force.

Radvyed jerked awake, gasping and shaking. The sweaty bedclothes tangled about his legs. His hands clutched his chest, but he felt no small child's heart, only the rapid beat of his own. He rolled to his back and rubbed his face. The morning light slipped through the bed-curtains. Radvyed lay there until his pulse slowed and his breath calmed, and the perplexing dream-images faded. When he felt steadier, he pushed aside the curtains and rose from the bed.

Still unsettled by his dream and brooding over the unknown state of his mother, Radvyed asked the path to take him where it would. It led him to the walled garden. His mind dull with grief and the strange torpor of the place, Radvyed did not recognize it at first. The thorn brambles had changed, seeming softer, somehow. Why had they changed now? They never had before, unlike everything else in the Lady's realm. The wall was still high, and now that he came closer, Radvyed could see that the vines that covered it still bore thorns long enough to give one pause. But the thorns were veiled with dark, round leaves, and small white flowers starred the vines, offering a fragrance like pale honey.

Radvyed's heart pounded. With a shaking hand, he gently pushed his arm through the vines, and though the thorns scraped him, they also seemed to shift aside, until his groping fingers found what was unmistakably the latch of a door. Radvyed let his hand rest on it for a moment, hardly daring to breathe. Had the wall taken pity at last? Why? The prince pushed the door. It moved inward a few inches. Carefully, not wanting to offend or upset the guardian briar, he used his other arm to move the vines aside so that he could squeeze his body through thorn, leaf, and flower to the door. The vines fell like a curtain behind him. Radvyed opened the door wider and stepped through into the garden.

It was small, but sunny. A pretty brick walkway surrounded a central square of ground thyme, allowing a visitor to admire the flowers and shrubs growing in beds around the four sides of the garden. A tree—bay, Radvyed thought, but of a variety unknown to him—stood in the middle of the thyme, providing shade for a bench that circled its trunk. He heard the splash of water, but could not see the fountain or stream. The garden that was guarded so heavily was a simple cottage garden. He had expected, without knowing it, something more impressive, more stridently magical.

As Radvyed looked about him, he realized he had no idea which flower was the one that would help his mother. The garden was filled with flowers. He walked along the brick path, examining the blossoms nodding at him. So many, and he knew so little about them: tall stalks with blooms like bright blue buttons; shy, dusky pink flowers hiding behind pale leaves; stems with cascades of golden petals dripping like candlewax; elegant, smooth-petalled flowers of icy white; feathery purple fans that rippled at every shift of air. Radvyed wondered how he would know which flower would heal his mother.

At the third corner, which at that hour was the shadiest part of the garden, the prince found a little spring that welled up and then seeped away. By it was a rosebush. *The inner rose*, had Dris not named it? He crouched down; the colors and textures and sounds of the rest of the garden faded from his awareness. A sphere of silence seemed to enclose Radvyed and the rosebush as he knelt close to it on the brick path. His mind felt clear and certain and calm. He gently shifted a branch of the bush. Among the leaves and thorns there was a single flower. The outer petals were a velvety black, shading to deep crimson petals surrounding the golden crown within. Radvyed touched its stem and felt the quick prick of a thorn. He drew his finger away, paying no heed to the bead of blood on it. With his other hand, he felt for the leather pouch he always kept at his waist, and opened it. Without taking his gaze from the flower, he drew out the pruning hook Dris had given him.

Radvyed lifted the flower's stem up with his pricked fingertip and snicked it with his hook. The flower fell into his palm. Both severed edges of the stem seemed to bleed a drop, but no doubt that was his own blood from the thorn's prick. He stood, staring at the flower in his hand. It gave a perfume like no other rose he knew, yet he could not think how to describe it.

Finally, Radvyed raised his head and said, "Thank you. Thank you." He gave a bow to the garden, cradling the flower against his chest, then turned back to the entrance. He closed the door behind him and pushed past the vines, then broke into a run, for the house was before him, and the path led straight to its door.

The prince burned with urgency. At last the futile weeks, months—he no longer knew how long he had spent here—were over. He had found the flower for his mother. He must return. He could not wait another hour. When Radvyed arrived at his room he saw that his meager baggage was packed. Rue stood in the middle of the room, looking about as if to make sure nothing had been forgotten. He did not stop to look at the furnishings or their carvings or the figures in the rug.

"Mistress," Radvyed said, panting a little from his run. "Mistress, I thank you. I have found what I came for and I must go home." He held out the rose to her, but only so that she might see it; he did not let it go.

Rue looked at it. "Yes, Prince. You have it." Her voice was low and she did not look at his face. Radvyed did not notice her stiff posture or averted eyes. His heart soared. This was the rose he had sought!

"Please tell the Lady of this house of my gratitude for her hospitality and kindness," he said, carefully wrapping the flower in a handkerchief and tucking it against his heart. Rue watched him put away the rose, but said nothing. "And please let her know that I have found the flower and that I thank her most profusely for her generosity in letting me gather it."

Rue looked away again. "She knows you have it."

The prince went on as though he had not heard. "Please tell her I regret that I must leave in haste, but my mother—"

"Yes, she knows," repeated Rue. "May it help your mother, Prince."

"Thank you. And thank you also for your kindness and wisdom, mistress." He had his bags; the flower was secure. Radvyed looked at Rue. "One last favor, mistress. My horse?"

"Yes," she said. She walked to the door and the prince followed. For the last time, she led him through the house, but this time he saw nothing. Radvyed's whole heart and mind were with the homeward journey. When they arrived in the stableyard, a groom led out Belikon, ready for riding.

The prince arranged his saddlebags and turned once more to Rue, but she would not let him speak. "Go," she said. "Take it and go." Radvyed nodded, swung up into the saddle, and pointed Belikon to the stableyard gate, which swung open. He rode out.

If the prince had turned back, he might have seen a cottage in ruins. But he set his horse on the narrow road that opened for him through the dark thornwood and did not look back.

The fall of horse's hooves echoed even in this dim interior chamber. An ember smoldered among ashes in the little gold bowl on the worktable, next to a guttered candle and a bloody knife. A chair lay on its side, as if knocked over. On the floor, a huddled form gasped, torn by tangling thorns.

Chapter Twelve

Belikon ran through the barren, salt-encrusted lands as though he were flying above them. The journey seemed shorter on the return, perhaps because now Radvyed had a shred of hope and direction, or perhaps the flower itself, secured against his heart, worked as a charm might, to protect him from anxiety and despair. Whatever the reason, it seemed to him that he went farther each day and rested fewer nights on the return to his country than he had on his outward adventure. At last, Radvyed crossed into what he barely recognized as his own kingdom, for the salt curse had crept forward and stripped the outer lands of life and movement.

At length he rode past the edge of the salt line. Anxiety and fear hung over the places that were yet untouched. Radvyed used the king's highway now, but stayed at small inns, as he did on journeys in which he did not travel to meet the people. Recognizing by his lack of entourage that the prince was on a private Riding, the townspeople and fellow travelers did not approach him, although they could not help but look and wonder.

No one had certain news about the queen's health, although Radvyed asked whenever he stopped. His need to return to the palace pressed on him harder than the need to gather news, however, so he exchanged no more than a few words late at night or early in the morning with sleepy inn-folk.

At last, one spring evening at twilight, the prince rode into the palace yard. He gave Belikon's neck a grateful pat and handed the reins to the *kunika* who ran out from the stables to meet him. Then he ran up the stairs of the palace and, ignoring the surprise and questions of the people who saw him, made his way to the queen's chamber. Without stopping to knock, he pushed open her door.

His mother lay unmoving on the bed. Radvyed could not tell if she yet breathed. He moved closer, and thought, or maybe only hoped, that he saw the faint movement of her chest. Yet her skin was even more drained of color, right down to her delicate lips and tapered fingertips, than it had been when he had last seen her. Her eyes seemed closed not in rest, but in pain or sorrow, the thin lids tense and twitching. And she was emaciated, the translucent skin shrunken to her bones. Seeing her extreme weakness and fragility, the prince wondered what any flower, no matter how rare and lovely, could do. Swallowing hard, Radvyed turned to his father.

The king sat by the bed, holding the hand of his wife. Was his head grayer; were his shoulders more bowed? At the abrupt entry of the prince, the king's head had lifted, but any reproach he may have been about to utter died on his lips as he saw who stood there: his son, with the mud of the road still on him and his cloak about his shoulders.

"Father," said Radvyed. "Father, I have the flower, the flower from the garden of the Lady Hideous." He knelt by his father's chair and drew out the handkerchief from an inner pocket. He gently unfolded the cloth and offered the flower, as sweet and as fresh as the moment he had first cut it from the bush.

The king stared at the rose for so long, Radvyed feared he was indeed too late. He closed his eyes, crushed by his failure.

"Send for Dris," Arkost said. Radvyed's eyes flew open; the king stretched a trembling hand toward the rose. "Send for Dris now!"

Radvyed gave his father the flower and leapt to his feet. He hastened to the door and spoke to the *strazhen* on guard outside. A *damash*, one of the palace staff, was soon sent hurrying to fetch the gardener. Radvyed returned to his father's side, placing a hand on the bed gently so as not to disturb his mother. He saw that a tear, like a single dewdrop, clung to a black-velvet petal.

Dris was quietly ushered in by the *damash*, who, at a gesture from the king, withdrew. Dris came over to Arkost and saw the rose he held out to her. The gardener took a sharp breath; her hand hovered over the rose before closing on air and returning to her side. Something caught at Radvyed's mind, some connection he should make, but was unable to recognize.

"Dris Rose Gardener," said the king, "here is the flower from the girl Hideous that my son has obtained. Tell us how to help the queen." The king gestured with his free hand first to Dris and then to the queen, his gaze fastened on the gardener's face. His father, Radvyed noticed, still clasped his wife's hand. Dris touched the back of the king's hand holding the rose. The gardener pointed to the queen's eyes and mouth, and then lightly touched her own. She brushed the skin under her nose. Finally, Dris folded her hands over her chest.

The king stood, holding the flower in one hand and his wife's fragile fingers in the other. Gently he touched the papery lids, the bloodless lips. For a moment he held the rose so that its fragrance was breathed in on her next nearly imperceptible breath. Tenderly he parted her gown, exposing the bony chest, and laid the rose over her tenuous heartbeat. He placed her hands on the flower, as though she were holding the gift to her breast. He dropped his hands to his side, then suddenly knelt, gripping the side of the bed, his head bowed. Radvyed knew why. The queen looked as though she were laid out for burial. He put one hand on his father's shoulder and hid his own face, wet with tears, with the other. Dris was solemn and still.

And then, the quality of silence in the room seemed to change. The noiselessness of inexorable decay gave way to the quiet of a spring garden before dawn. Radvyed spread the fingers that still covered his face and peered through them. Arkost raised his head; his hand clutched the bed.

Queen Gladna's breathing deepened and relaxed. The lids of her eyes stopped twitching; the color in her cheeks and lips returned and deepened to their natural hues. The woman who had been skeletal moments before was now merely thin from a long illness. Her hands held the flower and, incredibly, a faint smile curved the rosy lips. Arkost did not dare touch her, but his hand trembled on the coverlet; he fought back tears at seeing his wife reviving before him. Radvyed dropped the hand covering his face. His other gripped his father's shoulder.

With a small sigh, the queen opened her eyes, blinked up at the ceiling, and turned her head. Her eyes met the king's. "My love," she said, "I am rather hungry."

CHAPTER THIRTEEN

Royal heralds carried the glad tidings of the queen's recovery to every corner of the kingdom. Arkost and Radvyed waited anxiously to hear what, if any, effect Gladna's renewed health had on the salt curse. Perhaps only coincidence bound her illness and the bitter tide. Yet as the heralds returned, one by one, they all reported the same news: the salt was retreating. The king and prince and all the people received this news with great relief and wonder. Although the lands within Tamtir that had borne the curse were still damaged, they were salvageable, and already the people who had fled were returning to their *mirenzemi*, farms, and villages. Royal storehouses were instructed to send supplies to the western districts near the mountains and among the foothills that had suffered from the salt, so that farmland could be replanted and the people fed until the new crops were sown and harvested. A week of festival and thanksgiving was proclaimed and the people rejoiced with their king at the return of the queen from the path of the dead.

Radvyed had much to do, resuming duties perforce neglected while he had been away and helping his father sort through business that had been set aside during the anxiety of the queen's illness. Every day that his mother regained strength and health seemed a holiday, glad and sunlit.

One odd circumstance nagged at him. Radvyed came across the gardener, Dris, very often, although he did not go frequently into the rose gardens. Yet it seemed that daily the prince saw her, out of the corner of his eye, or in passing, or standing in a shadow or a doorway, and always she seemed to be watching and waiting, waiting and watching, for him to do or say something. But what? He had found and brought back the flower. She never indicated or explained what she appeared to be expecting.

Radvyed passed Dris again on the stair one afternoon as he mounted to his mother's chamber. He frowned for a moment outside the door, then went in to see the queen. She still had not fully recuperated, but she was well on the mend. Today she sat in a comfortable chair by the window, looking out onto the gardens. A little netted drawstring pouch had been made for the rose; she wore it under her clothes, close to her heart, and her fingers often sought it. The room's air was faintly fragrant with its marvelous scent—as it always was, even with opened windows. When she saw Radvyed come in, his mother smiled and held out her hand. "There's my handsome boy!" she said. He came to stand by her and took her hand in his, grateful all over again for the sparkle in her eyes and the fresh color in her cheeks.

"Sit, sit!" she said, and he sat in the chair next to hers, still holding her hand. "My love," Gladna said, "at last we have a little time together for a talk. Your father tells me that with your help, matters are well in hand...although..." A slight frown disturbed her brow. Before Radvyed could ask the cause of her concern, she shook it off, and smiled again at him. "I feel so well, thanks to this rose!" she said, placing her hand over where it lay. "Well enough to hear from your own lips the story of how you sought and found it, and brought it to me."

And so Radvyed, his hand clasped in his mother's, told her the whole tale: the eerie ride across the salt lands, made possible by Dris's gifts and Belikon's courage; the path cut through the thorny wood, and the cottage found in the clearing; his entry into Hideous's realm, and the changeful nature of the house and grounds; the enigmatic Rue; his encounters with the Wanderers; his dinners with Hideous; the walled garden, which had so long resisted his efforts to breach it, and then, all at once, had opened to give him what he needed.

She listened and asked questions and was silent for a while after he was done.

"My son," she said at last, "You have been charming and handsome ever since you were born, but you have also been honorable and sought to do what is right. Another might have used your looks and your rank to belittle or manipulate others, but that has never been your way." Radvyed waited as she paused.

"But? Mother, I can tell you are troubled. How have I acted wrongly?"

She lifted her eyes to his and said, "My darling, your father and I are very glad that you found the rose that saved me. But something is not fiercely guarded unless it is precious. What did it cost the Lady of that place to give it to you?"

Radvyed sat silent. He had not considered this. He had let himself believe that a sorceress as powerful as Hideous would not miss a single rose, that there could be no cost to her to let him have it. He had not wanted to reflect on his time at her house; he had wanted to resume his life as though his mother had never been ill and his country had not been threatened. Worst of all, he had allowed himself to forget all that he had come to know of Hideous's suffering and loneliness.

"My son. This Lady has given you what I needed so desperately. I know she is repulsive and bears a terrifying curse. But think of the honor she showed you, the kindness with which she treated you, her generosity to those who have come within her domain. Think of how she allowed you to ride away, carrying this precious rose for a woman she had never met, for your sake."

Radvyed remained still and silent. His stomach churned when he remembered his abrupt departure from Hideous's house; his heart burned with shame when he thought of his obtuseness and self-absorption.

After a while he stood and said, "I thank you for your words, Mother," kissed her cheek, and left the room. Gladna looked after him, fingertips to the hidden flower, and sighed.

Radvyed walked, not seeing where he was going. He found himself by the stair to the stargazing tower and climbed it. Standing outside on the high balcony in the cool evening air, he looked up at the bright stars as they began to appear in the darkening sky. For a long time he thought of nothing, only let the stars thicken and the sky deepen. They neither needed nor demanded anything of him, neither judged nor condemned.

But at last Radvyed's thoughts turned to Hideous, whom he had left without a farewell, except through a messenger. He thought of their nights of conversation, her loneliness and self-hatred, her power and her vulnerability. The stars wheeled in the sky as the night hours passed and he thought he began to understand the changefulness of the house and the grounds, the obstinacy and then the yielding of the walled garden. He pondered his mother's words and his conversation with Rue by the stream; he recalled the last evening, when he had shown Hideous a glimpse of the pleasure of dancing. Radvyed remembered her asking, every evening, dogged yet despairing, whether he would marry her. She had not asked him that last night.

The prince saw what he must in all honor do. He knew the goodness of her heart and the strength of her spirit. But to be an exile forever, to be husband to Hideous, whose repulsiveness gave no quarter to familiarity or friendship, who lived under a curse he did not understand...that was a hard road. The night was well advanced when Radvyed left the tower in search of his bed and what rest he might find.

For the first time since he had returned, he dreamed the dream of the Tower. Again he climbed the stone stairs, again he stood in the doorway of the high room. But this time there was no dragon mired in filth. Instead, there was a young woman. She lay in the muck on her side with her back to him. She was dressed in a dirty, shapeless gown, and her hair, what he could see of it that was not covered in mud, was snarled and matted. He moved closer to her—was she asleep? Was she hurt? Where was the dragon?

As he neared, he saw there was some sort of stick—a chill crept over his skin, pricking the hairs of his nape. Radvyed crouched by her and turned her over onto her back. The mud obscured half her face, but before he could look more closely, his attention was caught by the stick that was no stick. Buried in her chest, where her heart would be, was a sword. His sword. She was dead.

Radvyed sat up in a cold sweat. *Fool!* he berated himself as he struggled out of the clinging sheets and blankets. He washed, dressed, and then set about packing his saddlebags, not forgetting Dris's gifts.

Then he went to the king and queen's rooms. It was early, but they were awake. His mother did not seem surprised by the news that he was setting out immediately for Hideous's house. His father looked as though he might object, but when his wife laid her hand on his arm, he said nothing against the plan, although he looked worried. *As well he might*, thought Radvyed. *Who knows when or even if I will return?* But he said his good-byes, went to his rooms to gather his bags, and carried them down to the stableyard. He saw Dris in a corner, but when he turned to speak to her, she was gone.

"Well, my friend," said Radvyed to Belikon, who had been brought to him, ready for riding, by a *kunik.* "At least this time we know the way." He swung himself up into the saddle, took a last look around the palace courtyard, and rode out. He must return to Hideous—pray the Golden Lady and the Dark Master he was not too late. He must marry her, no matter what curses of hideousness and repugnance, uncanny vines and vile thorns, afflicted her. Then they would learn the end of the tale of the Tower, for good or for ill.

Chapter Fourteen

T he prince saw, as he rode, that the kingdom was in good heart, taking strength from the restoration of the queen's health. As he crossed the border, he was surprised that the salt crust had retreated farther than he had expected, beyond the edge of his country. Was the rose's power reaching beyond the confines of Tamtir?

But Radvyed's sole anxiety now was the fate of Hideous, so he did not stop to study the ground or examine the salt line. For the third time he rode through dispirited realms made wastelands by the salt curse. He wondered what could be done to help the lifeless earth, the stricken trees and fields, and the famished people, if indeed any still lived.

Every night, Radvyed dreamed of the Tower, and now it was always the young woman pierced with his sword that he found. Now every night in his dream, after he rolled her over onto her back, he touched the dirty curve of her cheek, and said to her, "I am on my way. I am coming to you." He did not dare touch the sword for fear of hurting her further.

At last the dark wood stood before him. It was shrunken, but harder and thornier: less mysterious, yet more resistant. Radvyed persisted, and with much effort and the help of the pruning hook given him by Dris, he forced a way through the wood. It was evening when the prince and Belikon came to the clearing. He could see the decrepit cottage by the light of the full moon. Not willing to wait until morn- ing, for he was afraid he might be too late, he led his tired horse to the cottage and knocked. It seemed to him even more derelict than he remembered. No one answered. Radvyed pushed open the crooked door, and found himself inside a cramped, low-ceilinged room. Half the roof had fallen in. Was there another room? The moonlight showed him a door letting out, perhaps, into a kitchen garden. He and Belikon picked their way through the rubble and cobwebs to the back door.

They passed through and stumbled into the ruins of the walled garden.

Stones lay tumbled and overgrown with the harsh guardian bramble that had first thrown the prince back. It bore no leaf nor flower. Radvyed looked about. Where was Hideous's house? The ever-changing grounds? His heart froze with the fear that indeed he was too late, that his thoughtlessness had killed the woman who had saved his mother's life. He quickly picketed Belikon near a broken-edged cistern and unsaddled him. Then the prince entered the ruined garden.

There, in the moonlight, was the disgusting body of Hideous. She lay on her side, turned away from him. The silver light did nothing to disguise or diminish her repulsiveness. But Radvyed's mind was not on what his eyes saw, except to know that Hideous was hurt and alone—because of him! He ran to her. Was she breathing? He crouched on her other side, trying to see her face, to understand whether he had irrevocably failed her, but the front of her body was lost in shadow. He could see, to his horror, that a dark, spiny vine, thick as his wrist, wrapped about her torso and limbs. Was he imagining the glints of tiny grains of salt? He lay down on his side on the cold ground facing her, close to her. Were her eyes closed? He groped for her hand and found it; it was clutched against a wound in her chest. There was no sword or other weapon, yet she was injured, injured in addition to the vine's vile curse. He moved closer, pressing against her, entwining his hand with hers, holding both against the wound he could feel was seeping blood. As his hand pressed against the weeping wound, he felt a hard, thorned limb of the vine emerging from her chest. The putrid, noxious smell made him cough and burned his eyes. A forest of thorns pierced her skin; their sharp, acidic spines punctured and burned and tore his own skin and clothes as he clutched her to him. The thorns released their disgusting rotted-meat smell, unchecked by any sweet oil or spicy smoke; the prince gagged but held her fast. He rolled her gently to her back.

The bleeding was slow but constant around the protruding vine, that yes, bore a crackle of salt on its pitted skin. Although Radvyed did not want to let go of her hand, he had to in order to strip off his cloak and use it to staunch the wound. Holding the bunched garment to Hideous's chest, he tried to keep her vine-coiled body close with his other arm, but she was large and the blood made everything slippery even as the salted thorns dragged at skin and cloth.

His voice a hoarse whisper, he said whatever came into his head, trying to will closed the wound he had caused, to will the vine shriveled and gone. "Here I am, Lady. I have come. Here is my hand." He groped for her other hand and clutched it as he half lay on top of her. "Lady, I will marry you. *Yes*, do you hear me? I say *yes*. I am your husband."

Silence.

Radvyed pressed even closer to Hideous, trying to reach her, holding her to him. Their hands were now slick with her blood. The stench made him breathe through his mouth; the thorns seemed to launch themselves from her flesh into his. Was that a curl of vine wrapping around his wrist, his arm? Cold sweat dripped into his eyes, making them burn; his bones ached. Radvyed gripped her hands more firmly.

"Awake, Lady, and I will tell you the end of the tale of the Tower. The ending that you desired."

He could not let this generous, suffering woman die from his stupidity and dishonor. He remembered the dragon ripping open her own chest; he recalled the red-black flower clasped in his mother's fingers. The whole night was waiting for him to say or do something that only he could say or do, but he did not know how to save her. His heart ached as if it had been pierced by one of her thorns. Nothing mattered but that this woman lived. He forgot his hesitations, his parents, his home. Radvyed wrapped an arm around her shoulders and clutched Hideous closer, babbling promises, as if they could undo the wrong he had done her. A prickly tendril wound around his thigh and bit into his flesh.

"I swear I will marry you. I give my heart for yours." Another vine snaked around his chest, tightening, piercing, burning. The stench and his fear choked him, but still he gripped her, spoke to her, refused to accept that he was too late. "I am your husband. You are my wife, my sweetheart, my beloved."

The body he held seemed to jerk as though she had taken a sudden breath, or as if a weak heart had started beating strongly. And then she began to twist and writhe in his arms. Hideous screamed, a hair-raising howl that almost surprised Radvyed into letting her go. The moon hid behind a cloud, delivering both prince and sorceress to darkness. The body he held convulsed and spasmed, contorted and swelled—he could make no sense of what was happening. Hideous made weird, animal-like sounds: snuffles, cries, growls. Thinking only of the wound, Radvyed held on, trying to keep, as best he could, the cloak pressed against her chest. He did not know how well he succeeded in the darkness and confusion, but he gripped her as closely as he could. They were lashed together by thorny vines; they were pulled apart by sucking winds. Was she dying? Was he? All he could think was *stay, stay, stay,* and to his surprise he realized he was saying the words aloud. Then her convulsions and her cries ended all at once, and the dark world stilled. Was she dead? He closed his eyes and drew a deep breath.

The scent of the rose he had given his mother filled his lungs. Radvyed's eyes flew open. The moon revealed itself again and by its light he saw that in his arms was the young woman he had last seen in a tower room with his sword in her chest. He shook off the bloody cloak that had twisted itself around him and held up their laced fi ngers. Her hand was no longer swollen or misshapen or punctured by thorns. He followed the line of her hand, wrist, arm, chest—no ghastly vine thrust from her nor twined around her body. The prince looked at her face. She was no longer hideous.

The young woman, his beloved, his wife, looked up at him, a tenta- tive smile on her lips, her eyes wide and bright. Radvyed's heart seemed to be attempting to come out of his chest and his brain could not make sense of what his eyes were seeing. He was here, with the woman from the tower in his arms, and she was somehow also the Lady of the Rose, who had been Hideous, or perhaps the dragon, but who was now his Beloved, and she was alive, he had not killed her, and so he kissed her instead, and the sweetness and the ardor and the joy of that kiss brought a hundred more roses into bloom about them.

When Radvyed finally was able to bring himself to look around, he saw that the dawn lightening the sky illuminated the walled garden, which now was a riot of flowers within the restored walls, the most lovely and fragrant being the roses. They sat up together.

"You," the prince said, "are a lady of many surprises." Beloved laughed, a new sound. Their clothes were still torn from the thorns' malice, but they saw that their wounds had healed, even the most grievous leaving only painless scars. Holding hands, they stood and wandered the garden. Then Radvyed remembered Belikon and they stepped out of the walls to see how he had fared. He was grazing contentedly nearby, undisturbed by any cataclysms that had taken place in the night. Beloved's house stood before them, warm yellow stone and green shutters, and pleasant gardens surrounded them, not all revealed to the eye at once. The house and the grounds required that one move through them to know them.

The door of the house opened and a woman in brown stood in the doorway.

"Rue," whispered Beloved. Radvyed let Beloved's hand go and she stumbled, her step ungainly as she learned free movement. She walked unsteadily but eagerly to Rue, who had picked up her skirts and was running to her foster daughter. They met and embraced in the sunlight for the first time. Rue's face glowed with joy. She held Beloved close, then leaned back to look at her, then touched Beloved's face, then her hair, and laughing, hugged her again. The cheeks of both women were wet, but their smiles were radiant. It was a while before any of them thought of breakfast.

They did eat, outside in the garden. The people who tended the house and grounds were now visible in Beloved's presence, and very glad her curse was undone. Rue asked that a small table be brought out, for Beloved had spent so many days shut away that she now desired to stay out in the sunlight.

They passed a day recovering from the breaking of Beloved's name curse, but then it was time to think of what came next. Radvyed needed to return to Tamtir, for he had duties to his parents and his kingdom, aside from the bonds of affection. The salt curse still devastated the realms neighboring his own. Yet he was also the husband of the Lady of the Rose. It was Beloved herself who decided their path.

"I wish to see more of the world," said Beloved, "and to meet your parents, your land, your people." Radvyed squeezed her hand as they strolled outside in the sunshine. He had hoped she would return with him, but had not known what he could offer to a woman who had the power and the resources Beloved commanded. "This place gave Rue and me shelter when we needed it. Yet it is also the place of our exile."

"But the gardens, the house—even the air and light—are so, so bound to you—" he began, puzzled and concerned for both her and the *mirenzem*, as he thought of it.

"Yes," Beloved acknowledged. "I claimed it all, cottage, clearing, and wood, long ago. I will release them before we depart." They stood for a moment on a wide slate-flagged terrace, looking out over exuberant beds of dahlias. Their many-petalled red, yellow, orange, white, and pink blooms bobbed in the light breeze. Blue and yellow butterflies flitted above them, dipping now and again to a bright flower; bees hummed as they alit to gather sweetness.

"Claimed? Release?" asked Radvyed, swinging their joined hands gently between them. He turned from the flowers to look at Beloved. "Surely you can still keep this *mirenzem*—this manor holding."

She shook her head, gazing still over the gardens. "No, we mages root ourselves where we live, claiming the land over time, our power saturating our environs..." Her brows drew together in a frown. "Radvyed. It will be difficult for me not to claim land in Tamtir, at least where we live. Are there other mages or sorcerers at the palace already, or perhaps—"

"No," he said swiftly. He wanted no barrier to her coming home with him. "We have no magic in Tamtir; no practitioners of magic live among us. It has always been so, from our founding a thousand years ago."

"No magic?" Beloved turned to look at him fully. "How can that be? When the salt, you say, stayed outside your borders so long?"

"I do not know." A memory rose up, of envoys begging to know what spell or rite they had used to ward their kingdom. He watched a bird hop down a gravel path, feeling the familiar helpless guilt wash over him. "All I know is in Tamtir we have no magic and use no magic."

"Yet the rose healed your mother," Beloved said thoughtfully, looking down at their clasped hands.

"Yes," said Radvyed, glad to leave the topic of Tamtir's inexplicable resistance to the salt. "Yes, so you need not fear crossing the border. You and your magic will thrive there."

She nodded and looked over the flowers again. "On the morning of our departure I will release the Hidden House." So she and Rue had come to call the place of their banishment. Beloved turned so they both looked at the house, all warm stone and green ivy. "We no longer need its protection and will be making a new life elsewhere. And we have tasks to fulfill that can be delayed no longer without harm."

Beloved decided to bequeath the house and grounds to the care of the Wanderers led by Starzana of the Kaitiren, she who had told Radvyed the tale of the Tower.

"I desire that this place remain a refuge for those in need," Beloved told the matriarch. "We may visit, from time to time. But you and your people have the use and the care of it as long as you wish."

The old woman had looked from Radvyed's face to Beloved's and then at their hands, which, as so often, were linked. "And maybe on one of these visits you will be kind enough to tell us the full tale of the Tower," the elder said, "for I see that it has found its ending at last." Beloved laughed and promised.

The people who tended the house and gardens and animals were free to remain at the Hidden House, to go with their lady to the prince's land, or to leave to seek their fortune elsewhere, with a good set of clothes, some tools, and a small bag of coins.

"I who lived so long constrained will bind no one," said Beloved.

Radvyed took her hand and played with her fingers idly. "I am bound to you," he said.

"True," she answered, "but that binding was none of my doing, as glad as I am of it."

He smiled and looked away, following a butterfly's flight with his gaze. Then with a puzzled frown, he wondered, *What tasks does Beloved have?*

Chapter Fifteen

R ue was coming with them. "She must help us find the tower," explained Beloved.

"What tower? Not the one—"

"Yes and no. You will see."

The day before they were to leave, Radvyed was in the walled garden with Beloved and Rue. Beloved cut the roses while Rue held a large basket for the flowers. She took only the flowers, no leaves or stems, using Dris's pruning hook.

When Beloved was done, she cut one branchlet, about the length of her hand from fingertip to wrist, then scored a small wound at the end of the cut stem. She pricked her finger with the tip of the hook and painted the scored end of the stem with her blood.

"Why did you cut yourself?" Radvyed asked.

Beloved glanced up at him. "The rose needs sustenance." As Radvyed pondered her answer, Beloved wrapped the stem in a close-woven, damp cloth. It would go with them to Tamtir.

Rue took the basket of flowers: she would make rosewater, she said. Radvyed and Beloved sat outside on a wide terrace, taking a moment to enjoy the late morning. Butterflies dipped and flittered. Radvyed heard music drifting over the air. Beloved turned her head to hear better.

"It is the Wanderers, I think," said the prince. She nodded. It was a tune with a strongly marked rhythm, though some sort of high pipe was twining about the fiddle's melody. Listening to the music made him think of the Tower dreams and how he had almost killed her with thoughtlessness and unkindness. How to heal the hurts between them, to begin to atone for wrongs? He looked at Beloved, who lifted her face up to the sunshine, seemingly free of resentment against him. Radvyed caught his breath, struck by how the light touched her hair and caressed her skin. Remembering their dance of hands on the evening before he had abandoned her, the prince decided to begin to show her how dear she was to him now.

Radvyed stood. He bowed deeply before his companion. "May I have the pleasure of this dance?" he asked.

Beloved laughed and held out her hand. She was startled when he grasped it and drew her to her feet. "Oh, I thought you meant—"

He guided her hands to the correct positions as they stood face-to-face. He grinned at her. She blinked, flushed, and smiled back at him. Radvyed kept the steps extremely simple, in deference to Beloved's newness to dancing, but she confided herself so naturally to his lead that soon they were whirling down the length of the terrace to where there was a pleasant shade of trees, and his grin had deepened into a smile of delight. As they circled, butterflies flitted about them; he hoped she felt as light and as free as they.

Their dance done, they stood still in the dappled sunlight in a loose embrace, looking into each other's faces. Radvyed said, "I regret it took me so long to understand that you were imprisoned, to see you. I wish that I had said I would marry you that first night."

Beloved's smile became wry. "You were not the first to come searching. You were not the first prince to knock at my door, nor were you the first I asked to marry me. You were not even the first to say you *would* marry me."

Radvyed blinked. "But then how is it that you are here with me and not a princess of some other land?"

"You were the first to mean the words," said Beloved. "When you said you were my husband, you became my husband. Curses cannot be broken by lies. When you named me Beloved, it was because I was beloved by you."

Radvyed entwined their hands, and raising them, looked at them. Then he looked at her, smiled, and said, "You mean, you *are* beloved by me."

Early the next morning, Beloved secluded herself in the walled garden with Rue. Radvyed was not sure what was involved in the releasing spell that Beloved undertook. The two women had arranged a wooden worktable with crucibles and tongs, bone-hilted knives, and variously sized bowls of silver, gold, and stone. Next to the table they had placed bags of dirt, bales of thorn branches, and a copper firepit. Radvyed could make no sense of what they planned to do. Moreover, he could not observe them, for Beloved had told him he was not needed for the spell and he would only distract her as she worked.

After they closed the garden door—Beloved had kissed him, but then shut it in his face—he paced outside the wall, unable to relax. It was hard not to think about the knives. Radvyed tried to distract himself by wondering if he would be able to perceive the moment the spell took hold. Or let go, as it was a spell of release and renouncing? He knew Beloved had spoken with the matriarch Starzana, conferring about what form the Wanderers—those who would remain—preferred for the house and grounds. Once she had renounced her claim, Beloved had explained to Radvyed, the manor and gardens would shift no more. Starzana, who had taken in stride the revelation that Rue was not the only mysterious lady presiding over the Hidden House, had pursed her lips and narrowed her eyes in thought. Was she making sense of the odd seasons, the strange languor that dwelt in the Lady Generous's lands?

He finally sat on a bench facing the walled garden to wait. After a while, Radvyed realized the air had warmed markedly, yet no breeze relieved the still heat. He looked around, and saw he now sat on the border of extensive gardens. Vegetables grew in mixed rows, blackberry brambles romped on the far edge, and in the other direction stood orchards bearing different kinds of fruit, and groves of nut trees; each plant seemed in its proper stage for early summer. He turned the other way and saw the house and stables: large, simple, sturdy buildings of fitted gray stone and slate roofs. A garden enclosed by shrubbery, perhaps for herbs, sheltered near the house. He turned again to look at the walled garden where Beloved worked.

It was still there. The walls were lower, but he could not quite see over them. They were no longer guarded by the white-starred thorns; instead thornless vines, opening trumpet flowers of deepest blue, draped them. Radvyed was surprised at the pang he felt that the thorny flowers were gone. He hesitated by the door, but just as he raised his hand to the latch, it opened from within.

Beloved held out her hand to him and he saw to his relief that she was unhurt and smiling, if a little ash-smudged and disheveled. He took her hand, twining his fingers with hers.

"It is done, Husband."

That same morning, after a late breakfast, Beloved, Radvyed, and Rue rode out, accompanied by those attendants who had decided to follow their Lady to a new home. The thornwood had become a dense greenwood, yet it opened a way before Beloved when she raised her hand and spoke a few words. As they left its protection, they drew their mounts to a halt and surveyed the barren devastation of the salt-cursed land. Beloved's people were silent with horror. They now saw that their Lady's curse had been, for them, a warding spell.

Beloved gazed out on the stricken land, her mouth turned down in pity, her eyes troubled. Then her spine straightened and her jaw firmed. She held out a hand to Rue, who unfastened a wide-mouthed leather flask from her saddle, pulled out the clean rag that stoppered it, and gave it to Beloved. Beloved reached up, broke off a leafy twig from a branch hanging near her, and thrust it into the flask. She rode a little forward of the others before halting once more. After drawing out the twig from the flask, she then swung out her arm, broadcasting the water over the salted land. Beloved rode on, repeating her gesture.

Radvyed and the others watched. *Was it a blessing rite?* he wondered. It would take more than a few sprinkles of water to wash clean and irrigate the land before them. Then Beloved called over her shoulder, "Husband." His heart stumbled; he was not yet used to the name. His wife beckoned.

Radvyed rode forward. Beloved handed him the flask, but kept the green branch. Then she held out her free hand, and he took it in his, a little awkwardly, since they were both still mounted.

"Say my name," she said, looking him in the face. He returned her look and although he was puzzled, he nevertheless obeyed.

"Beloved," he said. She beamed at him. Her smile seemed to call forth a spring of joy from him, so that he laughed a little as he smiled back at her, still holding her hand, for a moment forgetting where they were. Then gasps from the others made him look about and he, too, took a startled breath. Where Beloved had sprinkled the water from her flask, the earth was cleansed of salt and as they watched, fresh green blades of grass and tender sprouts of other plants were poking through the dark earth. The long death-winter was overthrown.

He looked at her. She answered his unasked question. "Rosewater. I am, do not forget, a sorceress—but now no longer poisoned or bound by the curse. We, together, are the breaking and the unmaking of it."

"I should have—" *All this time*, Radvyed thought, *if I had not been so stupid and slow—*

"No, Husband," Beloved said. "Time's ripening, the heart's knowledge, the mind's resolution—these things, if they are true, cannot be forced. You did well."

He looked away, still unconvinced, but willing to let it pass.

"Come. We have much still to do and far to go."

CHAPTER SIXTEEN

After several days of riding northwards, they spied the tower. Its dark silhouette, edged with sparks of orange-and-pink light, stood starkly against the sunset sky. The land here was thickly salted, for the tower, Radvyed now knew, was the source of the curse. He glanced behind him. Here, as wherever they went, a green spring flourished in their wake. The earth was refreshed and renewed, freed from the curse even as Beloved herself was. Birds were returning, insects chirped and droned, and they heard, at night, the cautious sounds of animals creeping forth from their dens and burrows and holes, scenting and exploring. Even people, ragged and gaunt, but still too wary to come close, had been spotted emerging from ruined buildings that the company had thought uninhabited: how the wretches had survived in even such a malnourished state the prince could not begin to guess. Rue, Radvyed, and the others offered food and reassurance to those who dared draw near. Wherever they went, as widely as she could, Beloved continued to bless the land with rosewater from the flask that never seemed to run dry.

The company drew to a halt on the crown of a low hill. Beloved looked for some time in silence at the tower where she had been born. Rue had told him about Beloved's sorcerer father and how he had raped and forcibly married Beloved's mother. Rue also gazed at the tower, and Radvyed remembered that she had once had a life there. Beloved stirred and sighed.

"Tomorrow," she said, and turned away.

When the morning sun struck the crystalline tower, the fractured brilliance of its light almost blinded anyone who looked in the tower's direction. The salt was so thick here that it had created its own landscape of ridges and crags: it was impossible to guess the shape of the earth underneath the bitterness that had spilled from the sorcerer's heart and poisoned and deformed every living thing within sight of the Griefstone. The only sounds were the crunch and creak of the salt as the small party moved about the cheerless camp, and the low moaning of a wind that neither rose to a strength that might cleanse nor dropped to a gentleness that might refresh.

Radvyed was surprised at the size of the tower. He had expected a structure more slender and taller, as it was in his dreams and imaginings. He mentioned his surprise to Beloved and Rue. Beloved said nothing, but Rue said, "It has been many years." He understood then that the tower's own shape had been changed by layer upon layer of salt produced by the font of pride and rage that was his wife's father.

Beloved was silent and somber. As they ate their breakfast, she gazed at the tower, shielding her eyes and squinting against its dazzle. Radvyed looked at the devastated land that lay between their camp and the Griefstone and thought about Beloved's domain in the woods. Her magic had also been constrained, yet she had borne her curse differently. He wanted to know more about her: her past, how her house had not become a second fountain of hatred, why her heart had welled with healing and not spite. He saw her eyes darken and her mouth droop as she gazed at the source of so much malice, her birthplace, where her mother had died and her father—living or dead, no one knew for certain—generated enough ill will to lay waste entire kingdoms. *What an inheritance*, he thought, and was glad when Rue came to stand beside Beloved and put an arm around her shoulders.

Beloved looked at Radvyed. "Only you and I shall undertake this last task." He nodded.

"What will you need?" he asked.

She said, "Rosewater. And your hand."

Rue and the rest of the company did not like letting Beloved and Radvyed approach and enter the tower on their own.

"If there are sorcerous perils, we can deal with them," said Beloved. Radvyed was not as confident as she. "And any beasts or bandits who may linger there," she added.

So while the tower still glittered in the stark morning light, Radvyed gave Beloved his hand, and they walked across the salt toward the source of the curse. The others watched them until prince and sorceress were dark specks against the unforgiving brightness and as the distant figures were swallowed up altogether. Then they turned away from the menacing glitter and prepared to wait as best they could.

Chapter Seventeen

Radvyed and Beloved walked for a while in silence. The terrain became more and more difficult, for the salt crystals grew sharper as they neared the tower. He glanced at Beloved, who was frowning down at her feet. She stopped; he halted, as well. She clutched his arm to steady herself and examined the bottom of her boot.

"Look," she said. Radvyed bent down. There were small holes opening in the sole. Yet the leather was not worn through. It looked as though it had been nibbled, or perhaps burned. He could see glimpses of the skin of her foot. "The salt here is so bitter," she said, "it is eating right through our boot soles."

"Can we use the rosewater to clear a path?" Radvyed asked.

Beloved thought for moment. "No. I think we will need every drop for my...for the sorcerer." She looked at him. "Perhaps we can lengthen our stride a bit and move more quickly?" He agreed. They set off again.

But the salt's bitter bite was swifter than their strides and the tower farther than it had seemed. They had not reached it before their soles were gone, leaving the upper parts of their boots like leather cuffs about their legs and ankles. The salt cut and burned their feet. It hurt to stop and it hurt to walk. They struggled on, even when forced to limp. To break the curse they must get to the tower. Radvyed looked at the woman at his side. Their hands were firmly clasped, for both moral and physical support. During those first days after he had found her in the garden, she had delighted in exploring the freedom of movement she had not known for most—perhaps all—of her life. And now this curse struck her again, in a different way, crimping her light-footed, idiosyncratic gait into a painful hobble. Her feet were bleeding. His were as well, but he did not care about that.

"Beloved—"

"No, Husband," she answered. "You cannot carry me. My blood, our blood—it is part of the counterspell."

"How can you be sure?" he protested, for the first time challenging her knowledge of magic and its logic. "Your poor feet! Let me—"

"No," she repeated, but gently. "Do you think I have not spent years studying curses and how to break them? We must do this."

Time passed; their feet throbbed and burned. They did not look at them as they walked. At last Radvyed said, "You must grant me one allotted day when we are in *my* father's house to shower every comfort and pleasure upon you that I desire."

Beloved was surprised into a laugh. "Gladly. And I will, as a treat, every now and then set you some impossible task—"

"Such as gathering a flower in a walled garden with no gate—"

"—to satisfy your love of chivalry. Carry me over a sea of glass, bring me a necklace strung with stars—"

"Sail the moon's ship seeking the pearl of pearls—"

"Find me a ruby encasing the earth's flaming heart—"

And so they talked, proposing splendid and absurd tasks she might set him, until the pain demanded silence once more.

By evening they had arrived at the tower. The sun was low in the west beyond it: a different dazzlement than the morning's light. At first they could see no door. They crept closer on ragged feet and perceived a passage, once smooth and wide, perhaps—although it was hard to imagine the sorcerer had ever been hospitable or welcoming—but now thickly crusted with the bitter rime.

Through this jagged, narrow passage upward they went, crawling and scrabbling, for the shape of any stairs had long since been overcome by the salt. The tower was high and the way difficult, especially once the light from the entry was obscured. The two of them groped among the sharp shapes, knowing only to keep going up and forward. The salt caught and dragged at their clothes and hair and cut their skin. The only sounds were of ripping cloth, the bumping of their bodies against each other, and their gasped breaths.

At last the passage opened into a wider, half-lit space, where they could stand. Beloved and Radvyed had reached the room at the top of the tower where her father had once laid plans for drawing ever more power to himself. They looked about, wiping with their torn clothing any cuts that trickled blood, and taking a few deep breaths. It must once have been a large room, round or octagonal, with wide windows at each cardinal point of the compass. Now it was a cramped space, with the fading light coming in through an irregular crevice in the center of the salt-covered window facing west.

A fountain of salt in the center of the room commanded their attention. From it their gazes followed how the salt had crept out, over the floor, climbing up the walls and reaching through the windows to slink down and spread its malice onto the earth, impelled by the sorcerer's despair and rage.

Radvyed was silent before the source of so much woe and pain. Kingdoms had been devastated by this one man's malevolence. He could find nothing to say in the face of such will for evil. He looked at Beloved, who limped on shredded feet around what must be the salt-covered form of her father. The fountain raised its thick sharp-edged coils of salt high over their heads before falling in frozen cascades to the encrusted floor.

She was the child of this. Radvyed had known, of course, that she was a woman of great power. But he was at that moment afraid of her as he had not been before, as a child might be when he first realizes that the flames that flicker so comfortingly in the hearth can also, with equal ease and pleasure, devour the house in which he sleeps.

Here we are in a tower again, he thought. *With a dragon of salt malice, impervious to swords and a heart long turned to bitterness. How does one overcome a power that can cause famine and death by merely sitting and hating? How to break a spell that has conquered its maker?*

Beloved stood next to him again, her eyes still on the salt fountain. Then she looked at Radvyed and gave him a slight but encouraging smile.

"Do not fear." At his raised eyebrows, she added, "Yes, it is a very strong spell. But there is no spell that cannot be unmade or undone, just as there is no cloth that cannot be unraveled, no sword that cannot be melted down into steel again. A spell is a made thing."

"Do you know how to unmake it?"

"Rue has told me how it was made: an ill-considered naming by my father and the curse of futility my mother then laid on him, as death and life equally possessed her. You have already undone the ill-naming."

"And the rest?"

"Yes, that is more difficult. This spell seems to be the only thing that my parents ever made together."

"Except for you."

She smiled again. "Except for me. So all the power of my mother's anger against my father, strengthened by her death in childbed, and all the power of my father's rage and frustration went into the making of it."

They were both silent.

Then Beloved stirred, pushing a draggled strand of hair out of her eyes. "They were both beings of great power. But then," she added, "so are we."

Radvyed stared at her in the dim light. "We? I am no sorcerer. What power I have is from my royalty—" She tipped her head, looking at him quizzically. "Or from my looks!" he snapped, his hands clenching and releasing with strain. "Hardly anything this salt spell need fear! I have no lore—"

He stopped speaking as she held out her hand to him. Her palm was cut in many places and dried blood smeared across it in streaks. Beloved's encouraging smile had returned.

She said, "Keep in mind that as the body-child of this mage and this sorceress, even as the spell is the child of their thought and hate, *I* am a force it should fear. You act as a...as a *lens* for me, like a glass that in itself does not produce light, but can allow light to work in more focused ways."

"As when my tutor showed me how to set fire to a dry leaf using a piece of glass."

"Yes. You are the glass. Can you accept this?" She waited as Radvyed considered.

"I am the glass. The spell is the leaf. You are...the sun? My tutor?"

"Sun and tutor both, for I have the power and the knowledge for this." He looked at her, wondering—but then brought his thought back to the task before them. He gingerly put his scraped hand into hers.

"Tell me what to do." Even in the evening dimness he could see the full smile she gave him.

"You let me command you then?" Beloved asked. Radvyed hesitated.

"In this, I am yours to command." She laughed at his qualified assent and he caught the sparkle of her eyes. How could she be so lighthearted with such a work before her, and he with no more idea of what to do than an ox in the field?

She was quiet a moment; he realized she was thinking through how to explain something to him.

"Remember, Husband, that I said a spell is a made thing, like cloth or a sword?"

"Yes."

"When you unmake cloth, you are left with the yarn or thread of its weaving, is this not so?"

"And the unmade sword gives metal for reshaping."

"When any spell is unmade, the power that went into the making of it is set loose. It is no longer controlled by the spell or the caster."

Radvyed thought about that for a moment. "So. When this spell is unmade, this spell that has devoured kingdoms...there will be...*spell-stuff* set loose." Beloved nodded.

"What do you think will happen?" he asked. Beloved said nothing for a while.

"I am not certain."

Radvyed closed his eyes, suddenly more tired than he had ever imagined anyone could be. At that moment, every part of his body that ached, stung, or throbbed delivered its report of distress and fatigue. The rage and misery of the Griefstone seemed to smother the breath in his lungs. He felt himself inadequate to the task before them and wondered whether Beloved would have been better served by another prince as her husband, someone cleverer, wiser, braver...and then he thought of the lands and people still oppressed by the salt curse. Perhaps someone else would have been better, but he was here. A picture flickered through his mind: his mother and father, hands linked, smiling. Radvyed opened his eyes.

"Well. Let us see what remains when you—" He paused when she raised her eyebrows. "When *we* break this damned curse." After a grave look, she held their clasped hands up between them. He was reminded of the evening—it seemed long ago—when they had laid their hands palm to palm, and he had shown her what it could be like to move in harmony and pleasure with another human being. Now their hands were dirty, scratched, and glinting with salt crust and dried blood. But their palms still fit well against each other, the fingers folding into a firm clasp.

"You let me command you, then, Husband?" Beloved asked again, and this time he understood that this was part of their work.

"I am at your service, my Lady, my Beloved," Radvyed answered.

Still holding his hand, she groped at her belt, where she had tucked the flask of rosewater. She pulled it free and held it out to him. "Unstopper it." Obediently he pulled out the rag and kept it in his hand, not knowing what else to do with it.

Then to Radvyed's surprise, Beloved raised the flask and began pouring the rosewater onto his head. He blinked the water from his eyes; a trickle ran into one ear. Amid the splashing he heard her saying, "I give myself to you. I give all of myself to you. I hold nothing of myself back from you. Prince Radvyed, you are my husband and lord, bound to me forever, mine to command and obey." The rosewater poured over him. It streamed off his hair and into his face, down inside the collar of his shirt, and over their clasped hands, for she had stepped close. Radvyed did not mind, for the scent was deeply satisfying to him and the water soothed his hurts wherever it met his skin. Beloved pressed the flask into the hand with which he still clutched the rag. He shook dripping rosewater out of his face and looked at her. She nodded. He raised the flask and, pouring it out over her, spoke in his turn.

"I give myself to you. I give all of myself to you. I hold nothing of myself back from you. Sorceress Beloved, you are my wife and lady, bound to me forever, mine to command and obey." Beloved turned her face up as he poured the rosewater over her and Radvyed watched as it washed away the blood and dirt. It sleeked her hair and made her skin gleam; it trickled and streamed over her clothes. Even in this moment he found himself lost in his delight in her, in the reality of this woman standing there with him, beloved in every feature.

When she knew—and whatever sign she read he missed—that she needed no more rosewater, she gently took back the flask and, still holding his hand, approached the salt fountain. She upended the flask and set it in a crook of the salt coils, so that it could pour out rosewater over the encrusted form of her father. Radvyed was not able to see what effect, if any, this had, for Beloved lightly tugged on his hand and drew him near the western window, from which they could glimpse the last sun streaks of the dying day.

"Dance with me," she said. So Radvyed drew his wife into his arms and on wet, healing feet they slowly circled the room. He guided her through the stately figures of a simple but formal dance; they held eye contact as they stepped and turned. When the dance was complete, Radvyed straightened from his final bow and lifted Beloved from her curtsey. She stepped so close to him that her feet nudged between his. He held her waist lightly.

Beloved placed her hands on Radvyed's shoulders and said, very low, "Kiss me as though I were dying, as though you had no hope of ever seeing me again in life." He swallowed hard, dread shivering through him. Was she being exact, or exaggerating? How could—*she knows what she is doing*, he reprimanded himself. *Your part is to do as she asks.*

Radvyed moved his hands up to Beloved's face and held her gently, feeling the shape of her head beneath his fingers, how soft her skin was on her throat, under her chin, on her cheek. He looked at each feature, so briefly known but so closely cherished, and his eyes met her gaze.

Then he bent his head and kissed her as though the claws of some hell-born fiend were attempting to pry the two of them apart. He gave himself over to her in that kiss, whatever strength he had of mind, body, soul; whatever gifts of pleasure, beauty, charm; whatever longings of will, memory, hope, and desire. If she were dying, she would take him into her so that he would share her death; if there were hope of life, he would pull her to him, out of any abyss, any flame, any flood. He felt her body sag against him, with weariness it seemed, and he remembered the flask of rosewater, essence of her heart, attempting to wash away the bitterness of years, and fear bit him deep. His kiss became even more desperate, fierce, tender, wild, obstinate; he gathered her closer, as if the mere contact with his body could sustain her life. Her hands slipped from his shoulders, too enervated to hold him. Radvyed broke the kiss and pushed his face into her hair. His tears—so useless, so weak—he hid in the softness of her throat, while he pressed her name with silent lips over and over into her skin. So intent was he on his Beloved dying in his arms that it was not until the thunder shook the salt tower and made him stagger that he was aware that the

Griefstone was crumbling about them. Still clutching Beloved to him, Radvyed raised his head and looked about in the gloom.

The world about them ripped apart. The dark sky tore open, and through the rent there thrashed and howled torrents of rain, as if some nightmare water-monster, held back by the fabric of the sky, had fought its way out of a net and now knew no thought but vengeance and rage. The bright flashes of lightning, so close they burned the air Radvyed and Beloved breathed, illuminated a strange landscape, jagged and disintegrating. The thunder cracked above their heads, battering them like invisible fists. The tower listed, an old beast gone toothless and weak, yet still vicious. Whether it was wind or rain or thunder or some other force that caused the tower to sway alarmingly, Radvyed neither knew nor cared. Beloved was now a dead weight in his arms. He wrapped his torn cloak about them both as best he could. Looking out from a window that had lost its rime coat and several stones from its sill, he saw they were too high to leap. He pressed his back to the wall, moving around the perimeter of the room, hoping to find the passage they had used to ascend. Would it still be clear? Would they be trapped within? But Radvyed could think of no other way.

A flash showed him the salt fountain in the center of the room splitting and breaking—was it melting? He noticed no more, for the next moment he almost fell backwards into the passage opening. He turned, still holding Beloved. With one hand he groped for the mouth of the passage, while with the other he gripped Beloved to him. Could they pass through together? Dared he risk it—but what other course was open to him? Another flash cracked through the room. The tower creaked. He must get them out or they would be crushed in the rubble of the falling tower.

They had had to crawl up, so he would try to scramble down now, feet first, with Beloved bundled full-length against him in the tattered cloak. It was awkward, for she was still unconscious, but in a few minutes Radvyed thrust his feet into the scattered, broken stones that had once been a stair and began to move downwards with as much speed and care as he could combine. He had not gotten far—although he had already managed to bump his head and add a new scrape to one hand—before he felt the sharp edges of the salt beneath crumble in a wash of rain. Perhaps some crack in the wall had let in a torrent of wind-driven water. The way suddenly widened and they fell, bumping and slipping. The stones and the water shoved and pushed, until Radvyed realized that he and Beloved had come to a stop. He raised his head, then a hand and arm. Beloved lay beneath him.

A surge of lightning confirmed that they were out of the tower. Now they felt the full force of rain and wind. It seemed the elements would scour off what remained of the skin on their hands and faces. Ceaseless shrieking rent the air, as if a horde of tormented spirits screamed their fury. Coruscating blue fireballs singed Radvyed's sight and exploded with deafening booms. The earth bucked and groaned like a maddened beast beneath them. Would it open, swallowing them whole? Would it spew unknown horrors into the howling, raging, shattering night? Radvyed staggered to his feet, taking Beloved with him, and ran from the precarious tower and its terrifying, unleashed forces. He slipped and fell, turning so that Beloved landed on top of him. He thought dimly that he should get up, get them away, but could make himself do no more than try to shelter her lax, still form with his weary one. And then all was black.

CHAPTER EIGHTEEN

Radvyed was sleeping the deepest, soundest sleep of his life. He wanted to stay in its warm folds, but something chirped annoyingly close by. It seemed like daylight even through his closed eyelids. He really should be rising—had they brought his morning *chelek* late? Now that he thought about it, he was not particularly comfortable. He felt bruised and odd-jointed, like a doll flung to the floor by a bored child. He sighed, then gave in and opened his eyes.

He blinked a few times, trying to make sense of what he saw. Before his nose, grass sprouted, fresh and green as the hope of spring. A little beyond that, Radvyed saw Beloved's face, flushed and relaxed in sleep. He placed a hand on her chest. It rose and fell steadily. His muscles loosened with relief. Now memory came back: the walk across the salt waste, the climb up the tower, the fountain of bitterness, the spell-breaking, and the horrific storm. Yet here they were, alive and together. He smiled. But where was here? Gently Radvyed removed his other hand from under Beloved's head and rolled to his back. The sky was a washed blue with a small cloud here and there: wisps wandering idly in the sunlight. He turned his head and saw Rue sitting not far off.

"Rue," he called, but softly, so as not to awaken his wife.

She responded at once, turning her head, then rising to her feet and coming closer. She sat down nearby.

"How are you?" she asked, looking at him, checking his visible scrapes and bruises. He saw that some of them had been tended with a salve.

"I have been better," Radvyed admitted and she gave a quiet laugh. He made an effort and sat up, then looked out in silence over the changed land. Thick grass waved over low rolling hills. Butterflies and bees hovered over the wildflowers that shone brightly against the new green. Birds fluttered, alit, and were off again, dipping and calling as they flew. Spring, so long an exile, had returned, settling her lovely skirts widely and opening her arms to release bird and blossom.

"Well," he said finally, "it seems she did it."

"*We*, Husband. We did it." Beloved also sat up and gazed about; Rue laughed again. Radvyed felt his wife's hand cover his. He turned his over to clasp hers. His throat felt thick. *She lives.* He gripped her hand a little too hard. Beloved did not complain.

"What happened? Where is the tower? How is it you are here?" Radvyed asked Rue. She smiled at him.

"As to what happened, Prince, surely you know better than I or the others of our company. But I will tell you what we heard and saw after you began your long walk away from us to the Griefstone. After you left, we waited, passing the time by trying to guess how long it would take you to reach the tower, then wondering if you could enter and what you would find there, and puzzling over how you might unmake the spell. Dusk fell, yet we could not rest. We kept silent watch. Then there was a great rush of wind, strong enough that any who were standing staggered with its force. The evening light was dim, but we were able to see a huge black cloud, so high its end could not be seen, crouching over the tower like some fell creature." Rue paused as she remembered the fear of that moment.

"I have heard," she said, "of those storms that are like twists of wind, how they can splinter trees and lift houses. This storm made those tales seem like news of a summer breeze. The cloud settled, covering the tower completely, like a cupped hand. Lightning split the sky and thunder deafened us. We saw the spiral of the storm widen, and we sheltered ourselves and the horses as well as we could, for no one would be able to outrun it. When at length the outer arms of it reached us—such rain! It nearly scraped the skin from our faces. So much water, so fast! It was well we had made camp on a rise; we were exposed but not washed away. We cowered beneath cloaks and blankets, huddled together. The horses ran off. The storm seemed to go on forever. When it was over, it was full night still and we tried to rest as best we could, given the wet and the cold and the fear." She paused again, staring out over the sweet green land. Radvyed had never heard her speak so long. Then Rue smiled and turned to look at them, first at Beloved, and then at Radvyed.

"And then," she said, "we woke. We woke to the sun as it shone on the new grass, the sky as clear and as blue as though the storm had never been. The horses grazed nearby. We looked for the tower, but could not see it. So we packed up and came to find you. And here you were, sleeping like a pair of lost children, and the tower nothing more than some tumbled rocks and a few bones."

"Bones?" asked Beloved, and her hand tightened in Radvyed's. Rue nodded, somber now. They all stood and Rue led them over to what was left of the Griefstone. Large gray stones, their edges chipped and their sides scraped, tumbled on the grass like scattered blocks from some toy tower. In the midst of them Rue stopped. Beloved looked at the bones at her foster mother's feet. It did not seem to be a complete skeleton, any more than the tower's stones were those of the complete structure.

"Stone and bone turned to salt," Beloved said softly, "and this is all that remains after the salt washed away." There was no skull or ribcage. Beloved stood a long moment over the empty relics of malice. Turning, she said, "Let him be buried under what is left of his tower," and walked away. Radvyed and Rue followed.

That evening the camp was full of laughter and lightheartedness; the company reveled in the relief and wonder of the unmade curse. Every now and again someone stopped and stared out over the renewed land or watched birds and small animals investigating freshly cleansed territory. That night they lay in their blankets, gazing at the high pale stars glinting in the crowded sky-fields. The fear and peril of the night before were banished along with the salt, and rest came easily.

The next morning the company broke camp and turned southeast towards the prince's kingdom, Tamtir. At their back they left a low cairn, raised over the few bones of Beloved's father. They called the place Bonemeadow, and so it was always called afterwards in Radvyed's land. In later days, when other people came to settle nearby, the newcomers called it Rosehill, for the wild roses that grew over the old rocks there. They never failed to flower with the spring, no matter how long or bitter the winter.

Chapter Nineteen

Although the company traveled far each day, their journey differed greatly from the rides Radvyed had made to and from the Hidden House. Now they met a land renewed and folk slowly returning to life, like sleepers who had thrown off a long nightmare. The people were gaunt and wary, but they stood among fields and woods bearing the bounty of the warm season, with fresh water easy to find and the sun looking kindly on them. Wherever Beloved went, she lightened hearts and eased minds, as though the faint scent of roses that clung to her were some sort of charm for peace.

As they rode, Beloved wanted to know about Radvyed's earlier journeys, what he had seen, and how he had found her house. He questioned her, too, eager for the details of her past. Beloved told him of living even as a child with the venom-seeping vine beneath her skin and wrapped around her bones. Then, when she had realized that she repelled everyone who stumbled into her wood, she had channeled all her power into trying to make herself lovely, as well as free of her poisonous bindings.

"But beauty was a spell I could not master," Beloved said. Radvyed glanced at her, struck, but did not say anything, as she had not completed her thought. She fidgeted a moment with the reins, gazing between her horse's ears. "It took me a long time," Beloved continued, "to understand that the more power I exerted against my name curse, the more the curse was strengthened. I became more tormented by the vine and more repulsive, not less; I was winding the curse's cruel net more tightly about myself. So I sought to turn my power outwards."

"You mean your house and grounds and the Wanderers and other folk you welcomed," Radvyed said.

She nodded. "Yes. I wanted to make what good I could of our exile. And remember, we mages claim the places we live." Her power had saturated the Hidden House, its grounds, and the wood, even as her father's had overrun his tower and beyond.

Another time, he asked, "How did you come by your store of knowledge, isolated as you were? Surely Rue did not teach you all that you know and understand."

Beloved smiled. "Rue knows perhaps more than you think," she answered. "But you are right. She is not deeply learned in the ways and devices of sorcery." She was silent a moment and then she said, "I drew adepts of lore to me, people who were learned in the understanding of power. They would teach me, for a while, before I let them go."

He looked at her, but she had turned her head away. "Beloved," Radvyed said softly. She held up a hand, as if to hold him off. Then she dropped it, sighing, and turned to him.

"I would lure them to me, and hold them, and make them teach me...then after a time I could no longer abide their captivity, and let them go their way."

"As you did with me," said Radvyed. Beloved nodded. "But you captured me with more than your sorcery," he said. She looked up, surprised. "I came back," he reminded her. She smiled at him then, and he was content.

Often people they met on their journey were drawn to Beloved. They relaxed their guard with her, while ignoring or avoiding her companions. The strangers would drift near, as though she were a hearth fire. They desired to stand by her, hear her speak, look on her as she moved among them. Beloved let them, though sometimes they crowded and jostled her, or clung to her hand or stirrup, or stared, or talked too long, hungry for her attention. When Radvyed saw signs of weariness, he drew her away where she could eat and rest. Beloved would reluctantly acquiesce, recognizing the need to care for herself. Remembering long days of royal duties, he asked her how she could readily accept so many people demanding her presence.

"Husband," she said, "you are asking a woman dying of thirst whether she needs so much water. You have been cherished by an entire kingdom from the moment of your birth. I can see that there have been times when you have found that love heavy to bear, as difficult as that is for me to imagine. But I have had only Rue, my trickle of sweet water in a dry land. I will never be able to think anyone's love for me unimportant or burdensome."

Radvyed fidgeted with a buckle on his boot, abashed and ashamed that he sometimes found his people's love too much. They were sitting after eating, watching the sun set. Beloved looked at him for a while. He kept his face turned away from hers. Since she had a cup of watered wine in one hand and a bit of bread in the other, she nudged Radvyed with a foot.

"Husband."

"Yes?"

"Why did you come back? You had the flower. Your mother was well. I had placed no binding on you, or curse, if you did not return."

He kept his eyes on the pink-streaked sky. How to explain to her? *Dris kept staring at me out of the corner of my eye. My mother asked the price you had paid. I watched the stars move across the sky and their clear, far light showed me the truth of my own actions toward you. Once*

I acknowledged the right thing to do, I could not hide from it anymore. Radvyed was not sure how to explain the weave of duty, honor, and pity that had decided him on the return journey.

"I want to be more than handsome, or charming, although I know these are not qualities without value," he said at last. "I want to be just, to do what is right. I did not know then that I loved you, but I knew I owed you gratitude and even service for your generosity." Radvyed plucked a blade of grass and shredded it, feeling that his words were inadequate.

"Yes," Beloved answered. "You chose to be just, to do what was difficult. You came back, so I knew you to be greathearted as well as pleasing, and that my heart was safe with you." Radvyed ducked his head, but she saw the small smile that he hid, and she grinned before finishing her bread.

Rue bent over a saddlebag and checked the rose cutting from Beloved's garden; it had weathered the journey well so far. She straightened and looked over at Beloved and Radvyed, who sat together, watching the sun sink behind thin, indigo banners of cloud. As the first stars pricked the darkening sky, Rue wondered whether the rose would flourish in its new home. She wondered, too, how Beloved would fare in Tamtir. Rue had never heard of a kingdom devoid of magic, a realm without sorcery. Would her foster child wither or thrive in such a land?

PART II

SCION

Chapter Twenty

Radvyed, Beloved, and their company arrived at the border the next day, entering Tamtir a little before noon. It was not the narrow, less-frequented pass that Radvyed had used on his journeys to Beloved's thornwood. Instead, the company approached from a different direction, having come southeast from the Griefstone. The prince did not seek to travel unnoticed, so they used a broad trade road on which their group of about twenty could ride without being strung in a single file. Radvyed and Beloved wore no finery on the road. The whole company was muddy with travel, yet at the border the guards recognized Radvyed not only by the prince's ring, but by his face. After the usual moment of shock that his handsomeness administered, the guards pulled themselves together. With a gladness that even the best discipline could not crush, they welcomed him and his companions. The company saw a rider leave the guardhouse, mount a horse, and ride down the road before them.

"Who is that? Where is she going?" asked Beloved.

"A messenger to Zolatar," Radvyed said. At her quick look, he added, "The royal city."

As they rode, people came out to meet them, but now it was Radvyed who drew them. The borderlands had been afflicted by the salt curse and the people were grateful to their prince for freeing them from it. Although they had not yet learned of the overthrow of the Griefstone and the unmaking of the curse even outside the kingdom, all had heard the earlier tale: the prince had returned from abroad with a magic flower that had cured his mother and, in saving the queen, had saved Tamtir and its people. So now they threw flowers before the cavalcade and clung to Radvyed's stirrup, and held up children to see the prince, their savior. The company traveled slowly, that the people might see them, and so that the prince could speak to and touch as many as wanted to approach. They stayed at public inns, where people could kiss his hand, offer tributes of song, food, or flowers, or simply stand weeping. Radvyed felt more than usually humbled by the outpouring of love and gratitude. To his mind, it was due to his slowness that these people had been affected by the salt curse at all. But he set aside his own misgivings about his unworthiness, for the people needed someone to whom they could express their relief, their gratitude, and their joy.

Radvyed could not yet announce Beloved as his wife or as the real force that had defeated the curse because she had not yet been made known to the king and the queen; and the people, it seemed to him, were comforted by the idea that it was one of their own who had protected them against the terrible threat. Beloved hung back and held her power close, doing her best to appear an unremarkable member of the company. Yet he wished he could show off his sorceress bride, both for his own pleasure and that she might receive her due.

Beloved had been quiet since the border. When they had crossed, she had suddenly sat up straighter, as if someone had poked her in the back. Radvyed glanced at her and caught a strange expression on her face. She looked at him with wonder and even disbelief. As they rode on, Radvyed worried that something was wrong, but then he thought that she was quiet with the stillness of someone who is learning, assessing, and pondering. When he asked her whether all were well, Beloved smiled and said, *very well, Husband*. Then the needs of his people occupied him, and he dismissed his worry as foolish imagining.

Beloved watched as Radvyed accepted the people's attention and returned it: holding a child on his lap; listening to the tale of an old farmer who had watched his fields succumb to the salt curse; laughing at a girl's trick of making a pebble disappear; and accepting with solemn thanks a little boy's bouquet of flowers. He never showed any sign of weariness and he never faltered in his courtesy, no matter who claimed his attention. Now it was her part to do what she could to aid him, seeing that he had the chance to eat the food set before him and that he had a few hours to rest at night. Beloved knew how to withdraw into herself, and she did so now, unwilling to come between the prince and his people, and also in order to study and to understand better the life that she had chosen. For soon, she realized, she would be recognized as a royal princess. Radvyed had told her that there was no magic in Tamtir. He seemed to believe it. She was beginning to think differently, as she reflected on the unexpected wash of power at the border and the flow of energy between prince and folk. She wondered what his parents and people would make of a sorceress grafted onto the royal family.

At last they reached Zolatar. Some miles from the gates they saw a rider, set to watch for them, turn and urge their steed away.

"It will be difficult to approach by stealth," said Radvyed.

Beloved laughed. "Oh, was that our purpose? You had only to say, Husband, and I would have cast a glamour of invisibility about us. Then we might have been in the king's hall five days or more ago. But I think your people would have been able to pierce it, so strong is their desire to meet you."

He looked at her quizzically. "We do not have workers of magic in Tamtir," he reminded her. "Although who knows what gifts may be granted the servants of the Golden Lady and the Dark Master? Still, I wonder if there are those in or out of the kingdom strong enough to see through any spell you cast."

She shook her head. "You believe that I am the only one with power, or magic, as you call it. But think, Husband: how is it that the salt curse did not cross into your kingdom for so long? It is because there was power—a blessing or ward—that turned it aside."

"I do not know how to explain it," Radvyed said, "other than to repeat that I cannot think who the sorcerer or sorceress could be."

"I have my own ideas," said Beloved. "This ride has given me time to think and has shown me much that I had not known before. But for now, it is enough that the Griefstone is destroyed and the curse broken. I can give all my mind to worrying about meeting your royal parents."

"They will love you," Radvyed said. At her sidelong look, he added, "How can they not? You are Beloved." She wanted to poke him in the side for that, but they were riding and the horse might shy, and she was as yet no more than an adequate horsewoman. So she shook her head instead and was rewarded with the flashing grin that made a dimple grace his cheek.

Their entrance into the city was a culmination of joy. Crowds had waited outside the gates and along the highway, throwing flowers and brightly colored ribbons on the road before the company and showering them with sprigs of herbs: *beda* for victory, *dostan* for plenty, *selia* for joy. The company made their way through the happy crowds at a walk, smiling and waving, glad to be on horseback and so somewhat protected from the crush of well-wishers. It seemed that grief and sorrow held no sway then: there was only the giddy happiness of the people, the pleasure of the sun shining, and the sweet air, filled with cheering and blessings.

At last Radvyed and Beloved and their company passed from the glad clamor of the people to the more sedate, but no less glad, reception at the royal palace. They rode into the courtyard and were met by *kuniki* waiting to take their horses and *damashi* to take their scant baggage. Trumpets called out a welcome; at the top of the short flight of broad steps were the king and queen themselves. Radvyed helped Beloved down from the saddle, steadied her, and took her hand. He led her up until they stood one step below his parents and embraced both his father and his mother. Taking Beloved's hand again, he said, "Mother, Father, I give you Beloved, Rose Lady of the Hidden House. Beloved, I give you my mother and father, Queen Gladna and King Arkost of Tamtir."

Beloved's hand had tightened on Radvyed's with his first words. When she caught his reassuring look, she realized that he had said his words merely as a formula of introduction: he had not felt, as she had, a shiver across the skin, the awareness of a powerful binding.

"Come, my child, let us see you," the king said, and again she felt the power of the words, apparently unnoticed by the wielder. Beloved stepped forward. King Arkost placed his hands on her shoulders. "We owe you a debt we can never repay. Be welcome forever in our house." She accepted his kiss on her forehead.

"Let us see you," said the queen, repeating the king's words, seemingly equally oblivious to their deep ritual power. Beloved turned towards the queen, who looked into her face more acutely than the king had, but still kindly. Gladna took Beloved's face in her hands a moment, then said, "Be welcome forever in our house," before bestowing her own kiss. *I am sealed to them more strongly than they know,* Beloved thought. *How easily they bind us together! Is this what it means to be royal in this country?*

Now they all entered the palace, the king and queen leading, Radvyed and Beloved following, and finally Rue and their companions. At the end of a great hall, lofty doors were flung open before them, and they passed into the throne room. Here all the court was assembled, and its joy, if not expressed as unrestrainedly as the people's along the way, was nevertheless as genuine. A song of victory or praise was being sung by everyone present. The king and queen reached their thrones, turned, and stood facing the hall of people until the song ended. The king raised his hand and the room quieted.

"My people," Arkost said, "we are most happy to share our joy with you at the return of Prince Radvyed, our son and heir." He nodded to Radvyed and Beloved and they turned to face the hall. The king waited as the court cheered, then raised his hand again for silence. "Returning with him is the Lady Beloved, whose flower cured the queen"—another round of loud cheering—"cured the queen, and at the same time freed our kingdom from the dreaded salt curse!" The *mireni* forgot the polish of their court manners and indulged in full-throated shouts, with clapping, and even a few stamps and whistles, particularly from those whose lands lay on the kingdom's western borders. The *dovoreni*, the officials of the palace, managed to preserve more decorum, but not much more. "We welcome the Lady Beloved and name her one of our House for as long as she shall live." More cheers. Beloved's skin shivered again, although it seemed everyone else in the room regarded the words as conferring honor and privilege merely. The king again held up his hand for quiet. "In honor of the deeds of Prince Radvyed, Lady Beloved, and their companions, we will hold a feast and a ball tonight"—the king now dropped some of his solemnity—"and dance as far into the morning as our joy will carry us!" Now there was laughter as well as cheers. "In anticipation, therefore, of this merrymaking, let us go now to rest, to make ourselves beautiful, and to prepare for a night of gaiety and gladness, for the curse is broken, the land is healing, and our son is returned."

Chapter Twenty-One

Radvyed, Beloved, Rue, and the others were led away to baths, fresh clothes, and a few hours of quiet. The *mireni* and the *dovoreni* went their ways more slowly, talking in groups of two or three, discussing the prince, Beloved, and the evening ahead. The whole palace was infused with lightheartedness. Even the *damashi*, Beloved noticed, for whom the feast and the ball meant more work, smiled as they passed by carrying flowers, or baskets of long candles, or cleaning implements. She wanted to ease their work by some small charms—to make burdens lighter, dirt more docile, and water heat more swiftly. But she was new here, and although the king and queen had bound her to themselves and their House, she was reluctant to intrude even with aid. In time, she would understand better the power of the royal family, what forms it took, and how her own might coexist with it. So Beloved did nothing but keep her senses open and alert as she and her company were taken to their rooms.

Radvyed, walking beside her with her hand upon his arm, felt something different about Beloved. She had made herself unnoticed on the road, he knew. Yet here at the palace, she was accepted by his father, the king, and his mother, the queen, so why did he feel that she was making an effort to contain her presence? He frowned and said, "What is wrong, Beloved?"

Surprised, she looked at him. "Nothing, Husband. Indeed, your parents are most gracious, your people pleasant, and the palace splendid."

"You are holding yourself in. I can feel it," Radvyed insisted. "Not quite as before, when you were cursed, but I can feel you doing something—as though you are not wanting to touch or be touched."

Beloved smiled and shook her head. "And you say you have no power. No, no," she replied, laughing, "Do not say again how ordinary you think you are. You are right: I am holding myself in. I cannot explain yet. I must think some more. But do not worry. I am not in pain or distress."

They had to stop speaking then, for they had arrived at the rooms set aside for them, and they were separated. Beloved was borne off by a group of *damashi*, women who were clearly curious about the foreign lady. Radvyed was met by his own *damash*, Pirikon, a middle-aged man who had been with the prince for many years. Rue and the rest of their group were likewise taken to other chambers, attended by yet more *damashi* to prepare their baths and bring them fresh clothes. Beloved had time to glance back at Rue, who was also looking back at her, before a door shut between them. Rue seemed a little—sad? Then Beloved had no time to ponder Rue's expression. For the first time in her life, she was served by people who did not fear to touch her. They helped her take off her clothes and moved her towards the bath. The *damashi* were quiet, perhaps because this lady was unknown as far as temper went—or perhaps they moved gently because they noticed her startlement as they undid her hair and removed her shoes. *A lady unused to being waited on? But then she came from another land—who knew what odd customs they had there.*

Beloved was in the bath before she found her voice and asked to be left alone. Nodding, the *damashi* moved from the smaller bathing and dressing room to the larger sleeping and sitting room. Beloved could hear them setting out clothes and talking quietly among themselves as they finished whatever tasks seemed necessary to them.

She sat in the bath and closed her eyes. Bathing like this, being able to sit in a large tub, was still new to her. Beloved wondered if the first few days or weeks that Radvyed had spent at her house in the woods had been new and strange to him. There, he had said, he woke each day to new furnishings, and the gardens were not laid out in the same way as the day before, and everything seemed to change about him. *Only you and Rue*, he had said, *stayed the same.*

Beloved lifted a dripping foot and spread out her toes, fan-like, then wiggled them. She was still becoming used to having a body that obeyed her whims, a body that could move through the world unobtrusively, if not with perfect grace. She lowered her foot again into the bath. What a wonder it was to move freely, not to be forced to set a tight rein on her body, simply to be able to sit and be. What a marvel, to feel the absence of pain, to know that her body was no longer inhabited and besieged by the thorned vine burrowing through organs and twining around bones, exuding its poison into muscle, blood, and breath. Beloved closed her eyes again.

Her innate power had helped her to heal quickly from the unfamiliar demands of riding. Had Radvyed noticed? It was odd the things he did and did not sense. For one who so adamantly disclaimed all knowledge and awareness of power, he seemed strangely sensitive to it.

The water was almost cold—Beloved had scrupulously refrained from keeping it warm—when a *damasha* came in to prod her out of the tub and into her clothes. Beloved had never worn such garments before, designed for more than modesty or warmth. She turned, feeling the heavy hem swirl, then lifted her arms and watched the fall of her sleeves. Positive pleasure in sensation, in residing in her own body, was also very new to her. Much of her life, beyond the first few years, had been spent loathing the relentless vine binding her bones and perforating her organs, the noxious thorns puncturing her skin from within. She had hated her own self, anguished by her perceived weakness in succumbing to the vine. The freedom from the compulsion to despise herself made her feel like a bird on the wing, rising on some fresh wind into a sunlit sky.

Beloved was led through stone corridors rich with vivid wall hangings to a wide sweep of staircase. She paused for a moment at the top. Down below she saw the prince talking with his parents. Rue stood a little apart from them, yet not with the others from the Hidden House. Beloved had no chance to consider what that might mean, for Radvyed looked up and smiled at her. She placed one hand on the polished stone banister and stepped down.

Radvyed watched Beloved come towards him with her charmingly odd grace, reminding him again, a little, of some newborn animal discovering how to move outside the womb. He took her hand, kissed it, and offered her his arm. Beloved took it as she smiled at Rue, Arkost, and Gladna. She looked beyond them and nodded smiling greetings to the rest of the Hidden House company.

"I have told my mother and father," said Radvyed as the group paced past niches and archways towards the tall doors of the feasting hall, "that we are married." Beloved looked at the king and queen, who were walking sedately before them. She was not able to discern any distress. "Do not worry," said Radvyed, seeing the direction of her gaze, "they accept the marriage. Indeed, I believe my mother knew you were the woman for me before I did." Beloved looked at him, eyes wide with astonishment. "It happens sometimes so, that parents are wise in matters that concern their children," he said, smiling. She looked away, for her own parents had been catastrophically and maliciously foolish.

"Forgive me, Beloved. I did not think," Radvyed said quickly, pressing the hand she rested on his arm. "But do not be sad," he said after a moment. "For has not Rue been your true mother all your life?"

"Indeed," Beloved said.

"And now I bring you two more parents to love you," said Radvyed. After another step or two, he continued, "They wish to share their joy with our people and to make you known as both the Lady whose power healed the queen and as my princess. So they ask that we be married according to the customs of Tamtir in two months' time."

Beloved stopped and turned towards him. "But—"

"They wish you to be known and valued for your own sake and for your gifts to be recognized and honored. We will announce our betrothal in the morning before all the people. And there are more practical matters. It takes time to prepare for a royal wedding. Indeed, two months is practically an elopement."

"I do not understand," said Beloved. "We are married. We are already husband and wife. We are bound strongly—" She broke off. How could she explain to him the nature of the bond between them, so clear to her mind and senses? What he proposed to her seemed not deception, but pointless pretense. She knew he was aware that they were deeply joined. Now she realized that he perceived their union differently than she did; this otherness of understanding frustrated her.

Radvyed watched her for a moment, then took one of her hands in his. "Beloved. You are my wife; I am your husband. No one questions or denies this." He felt her hand relax and he paused.

"But?" she said, her hand tightening again.

"But your husband is a prince who has obligations to his people. My life is not wholly my own. I am…" He remembered her analogy in the Griefstone. "I am, my family is, in part, a lens through which the life of the people is focused. No, that is not quite right…" Now it was his turn to break off in frustration.

Beloved looked at him alertly. "You are saying," she said, "that the people of Tamtir have a right to witness our wedding. It is not something between you and me, or of interest only to your family, or even to the landholders and courtiers."

"Yes." Radvyed, paused, thinking. Then he said, "Remember the story of the Tower? I kept calling the man 'the young man,' but you, and Rue, and even the grandmother of the Wanderers all corrected me—he is the *prince*. He is more than a young man—he is royal, bound to his people and land."

Beloved looked away. "I thought it was his rank, his wealth and strength, perhaps even his prowess and courtesy, that were important. And I do not know that royalty understands itself thus in every land. Yet Tamtir for a long time was untouched by the salt curse."

Radvyed resumed their walk towards the feasting hall. She paced next to him, her hand upon his arm.

"There is much for me to learn," said Beloved at length. "I will bow to the wisdom of your House and your people in this matter."

They had almost arrived at the closed doors. Radvyed took Beloved's hand and kissed it. "Thank you." He smiled. "Wife."

The doors were flung open and the herald cried out, "Their Splendors King Arkost and Queen Gladna! His Radiance Prince Radvyed! Her Grace the Lady Beloved! Her Grace the Lady Rue! The Honorable Company of the Salt-Breakers!"

Radvyed felt Beloved hesitate as they crossed the threshold. The hall was long, high-ceilinged and many-windowed, its stony lineaments softened by tapestries and exuberant arrangements of flowers. The tables sparkled with silver, crystal, and porcelain. Beeswax candles flamed in stands of silver or floated in wide, shallow bowls of water among rose petals. Yet the *mireni* and *dovoreni* and other notable guests outshone the lavish display of the table arrangements and hall decorations. Dresses and robes glittered with threads of gold and silver; necks, wrists, shoes, and hands all threw off the brilliant, fractured light of jewels. The air itself sparkled like golden wine.

It seemed that petty squabbles and more serious grudges were for the moment forgotten, or at least put aside. Radvyed could see the unyielding jaw of that irritable *miren*, the superior smile of that *dovorena*, the impatient eye of a third guest. Yet on the whole, he had never seen so many people of rank together in one place exhibiting so much goodwill. He was about to say something to Beloved, but it appeared that she had already made her own assessment of the mood and the peril of the hall. She took a deep breath, as though she were about to plunge into a lake, stiffened her spine a fraction, and allowed Radvyed to lead her to her place at the king's table.

For Beloved the evening seemed both drawn out and dizzying. There were many new sensations and subtleties to absorb and she was always aware that she was a focus of intense interest. Radvyed attended her at the feast, explaining what sauce went with what dish, demonstrating the proper way to eat a puzzling delicacy, or warning her about a particularly spicy offering. She did not speak much, preferring to watch and notice the interaction of the king, the queen, the prince, and their people. Then the meal was done and the king rose to speak.

His announcement of the betrothal of Prince Radvyed and Lady Beloved was received with the expected exclamations of joy, although Beloved glimpsed more than one damsel who appeared less than happy at the news, and more than one *mirena* or *dovoren* who seemed to have seen a fond scheme brought to nothing. Toasts were announced and drunk, then the king, queen, and their guests made their way to the ballroom. Radvyed and Beloved were among the first to enter, so Beloved was able to turn and watch as the court settled into the room like a flock of gorgeous birds. From the musicians' gallery came a hush, as the last tunings were finished, then a violin sang out the first bars of a melody. The rest of the orchestra fell in, supporting and counterpointing the main line, and Beloved's attention was brought back down into the ballroom by the rustle of a rearranged pattern of people. A space had opened in the center, and Radvyed was leading her into it. She gripped his hand. He turned to face her, released her hand, and bowed—what was she supposed to do? Beloved acknowledged the bow with a slow nod.

Radvyed smiled at her and said, "Will you dance with me?" She could feel the eyes of everyone, benevolent, worried, or assessing: who was this woman who would one day be their queen? The attention made her skin prickle and her muscles tighten. But before her she saw the eyes of the prince who had come back to find her, who had walked into the Griefstone with her, and who had held her cursed hand and danced with her. Her awareness of the room faded a little and her breath eased.

"Yes," Beloved said and gave him her hand.

The steps were not difficult. The tempo of the music was slow and Radvyed murmured directions as they moved. The purpose of the dance was to display them as a couple to the assembly, and in this, Beloved hoped, they succeeded without disgrace. Finally, after they had made a complete circle of the room, some signal, unseen by her, was given, and they were joined by other couples, and the ballroom became a kaleidoscope of richly colored clothes and flashing jewels.

After the first dance, everyone had to be introduced to Beloved; everyone expected to speak with the heir's chosen princess. The names and the faces blurred together: she had never been the center of this many people before, not even on their journey from the Griefstone to the border of Tamtir. In addition, she was not always able to read people's motives and their words seemed to carry, at times, a meaning that she missed.

Beloved became weary. The effort of holding her power close within the bounds of her body, the care taken to perform each action as she believed she ought, the attempt to learn all she could as quickly as she could about her new people and family—the weight of it all seemed too much. But finally the last *miren* was met and spoken to and the last dance had been played. The king and queen closed the ball.

As they walked to their sleeping chambers, Radvyed informed her that in the morning her presence was required. Arkost and Gladna would announce their betrothal to the people from a balcony over the main square. "But after that," he said, "you are free—for the afternoon. What would please you?"

"I would like to meet Dris," said Beloved.

Chapter Twenty-Two

That night, after Beloved had dismissed the *damashi* who had insisted on helping her ready herself for bed, she stood by the hearth in her room, looking down at the fire. The stone walls of the palace made its heat welcome even in summer. She was tired but restless, and she still had to keep her power close within her. It would not do to upset the other denizens of the palace by inadvertently changing the rooms and gardens, for example, which might happen if she let even tiny tendrils of power uncoil. She was not at all convinced that there was no magic, as Radvyed called it, in Tamtir. She had felt the touch of power when they had crossed the border; the royal city felt steeped in it. Yet it seemed only Beloved felt it humming in the cobblestones, floating with the dust motes in the air, and freshening the water with subtle effervescence. She could not simply allow her power to settle into the palace and its grounds. There was another force—entity—presence—in residence.

Her own power was more vibrant, more exuberant, than she had ever experienced, singing through her with ease and clarity and un-strained strength. On the journey from the Griefstone to the border, her sorcery had been free to extend itself. Its depth and range had sur-prised her. She had thought to cleanse the lands between the Hidden House and the Griefstone, but wherever they rode, green renewal had spread from her like a widening gyre. Then she had understood how much of her power had been poured into counteracting the curse's toxins and sealing the constant thorn wounds. Beloved realized that for most of her life not only had her body been bound, poisoned, and tormented, but that her sorcery itself had been trammeled and twisted by the bindings of the name curse. Between the Hidden House and Tamtir she had been able to begin to test the flexibility and strength of both her body and her sorcery.

When Beloved had crossed over Tamtir's border, however, she had furled her power close to her, not wishing to disturb the strong native power of the land and its people. But she could not live permanently like this, with half of herself tied up. She needed to find some way to be freely herself in her new home, to somehow come to terms with Tamtir's power.

Thinking over the evening, Beloved wondered whether being Radvyed's princess would prove challenging in ways she had not anticipated. How often did the royals have such events? Must she attend each one? She had only the vaguest idea of the responsibilities of the ruling House, but she now became uneasy at the thought that she might need to undertake a role for which she had no preparation. In welcoming her, the king and queen had laid new bonds on her. Beloved knotted her hands together. Was her marriage to Radvyed another binding that would imprison and distort her? More pleasant, perhaps, and so more insidious?

Could she claim or make a place for herself in the palace? Would she be able to root her power here? Beloved paced the length of the room, her fingers tangling in her perturbation.

There was a soft knock at the door. Beloved opened it, expecting a *damasha* with some other unnecessary comfort. Rue stood before her.

She stepped back and the older woman came in silently. Beloved shut the door, not taking her eyes off Rue, who stood there, patient and ready, as she always had, as long as Beloved could remember. The older woman's steady brown gaze never faltered; as always, she waited to see what Beloved needed. Rue now stepped closer and raised her hand to touch the cheek of her nursling.

"Troubled, little one?" she asked. She moved her hand over Beloved's hair, in a soothing gesture that had tended many hurts over the years.

Beloved shook her head, then nodded. "Being brought into this House is not so easy. I had not thought about being a princess, only of being free of the curse and being with Radvyed." Beloved stopped, searching for the words to express her uneasiness. "I love Radvyed and I think his father and mother are good people. And I believe I can learn to be a princess and even one day a queen." Her voice rose in pitch, anxiety driving her words. "Yet I am a sorceress before I am Radvyed's wife or princess. I do not know how to join...how to mesh my power with that of Tamtir, a power that, it seems, no one else even knows exists!" Beloved blew out a breath, but could not relax. Rue led her to a divan by the fire and took the younger woman's hand as they sat.

"And now I am bound tightly to them all," Beloved continued, her hand tense under Rue's. "The bond with Radvyed I had foreseen. Only a union as close as the estrangement between my parents was wide could undo the curse of my naming. But he does not come alone! I find myself bound to his parents and his House, and the wedding here will no doubt include words or rites that will bind me further." She turned her hand and clutched Rue's fingers. "Have I entered another prison in order to escape from the first? They use power without even knowing what they do, and only Radvyed guesses my effort to contain myself so that I do not disrupt the kingdom."

Beloved's hand tightened on Rue's. "Will I be overwhelmed, or worse, at odds with the power of Tamtir?"

Rue stared thoughtfully into the fire, still holding Beloved's hand. Beloved, although her situation still seemed untenable, felt relief at having spoken. Her grip on Rue's fingers loosened. She laid her head against the back of the divan and watched the flicker and dance of the flames.

"How odd it is," said Rue, "that when one obtains one's heart's desire, there should be unlooked-for upheaval. How many years did you and I hope and long for the moment that the curse would be broken! How much did we desire that each prince that came would be the one who would undo that name! And now, here you are, uncertain and anxious about your new life...as I am about mine."

Beloved turned her head to look at her. "You? Why are you uncertain and anxious?"

Rue did not answer at once. She stared at Beloved's hand in hers. "Little one, you have a new life opening before you. You have a husband, a kingdom, a wide world to explore. I can no longer be the only one to share your heart and thoughts. You have a new father, a new mother—"

Beloved pulled her hand free so that she could throw her arms around Rue and embrace her. "*You* are my true mother, my only mother," Beloved said fiercely. "The queen, as gracious as she is, is Radvyed's mother. I honor her and I am sure I will learn to love her, but she will never take your place in my heart. You will never be forgotten or ignored by me." She pulled back so she could look the older woman in the face. "I will always need you by my side."

After a pause, Rue said, "I am your mother. But all mothers must let their children go. I must shape a new life, for you will not need me in the same way." She gently disengaged Beloved's arms and again took the younger woman's hand.

"Perhaps not in the same way," conceded Beloved. "You are right. Much has changed. But not my reliance on you, my heart-mother."

Rue smiled at the younger woman. They sat quietly for a while, the snap and hiss of the fire punctuating their silence.

Then Rue said, "Although I am no sorceress, I know your gift and your learning, little one. If you say power abides in this realm, then it is so." Beloved's shoulders relaxed and her hand rested quietly in Rue's. "You are right to worry about how you and Radvyed will marry your powers," continued Rue. "In some ways, this is for all new husbands and wives to learn, but because you and he are royal and full of power, your marriage affects many more people and things. He cannot cease being the Crown Prince of Tamtir any more than you can cease being the Sorceress Beloved." Beloved drooped. "But that does not mean there is no solution," Rue said, some maternal steel entering her voice. "Now, what are you doing tomorrow?"

Beloved told her about the morning announcement before the people and her expressed desire to meet Dris.

"That is a good thought, daughter," said Rue. Beloved looked over quickly at the name, pleased that Rue had used it without seeming to notice. "Of course she must help with the rose. I wonder who this Dris is. Was she not the one who told the king to send the prince to us?"

"Yes, heart-mother," said Beloved. Rue's hand squeezed hers. "And also equipped him for the journey and the thornwood. It was her hook we used to reap the flowers."

Rue straightened a little and pursed her lips. "Dris," she repeated. Then she shook her head. "It was all so long ago...well, we shall see when we meet her." She glanced at the time-candle on the mantel.

"But now it is late, little one, and time for sleep. Some rest and a good breakfast will make all difficulties *seem* manageable, at least."

The women stood and embraced once more, then Rue left the room to seek her own bed. Although the quiet conversation had solved nothing, Beloved felt refreshed and heartened, her restlessness calmed. She gratefully climbed into her bed and slid into sleep.

Chapter Twenty-Three

The next morning, Beloved and Radvyed met the king and queen in the antechamber that opened onto the balcony above the Palace Square. Her husband was looking particularly handsome, Beloved thought, as she watched him exchanging a few words with his parents about the announcement to come.

Radvyed finished speaking with his parents and came to her. "They will make a fairly simple announcement," he said to her, taking her hand and interlacing their fingers. "Then we will come to the front of the balcony and wave and smile and let ourselves be seen. Much easier than last night, for you will not be meeting hordes of new people by name and none of the ones in the square were aspiring to become my parents-in-law." Beloved laughed, and they swung their hands a little between them. She looked at Arkost and Gladna, wondering what signal or moment they awaited.

"Beloved," said Radvyed, his voice serious. She turned to look at him. He was frowning at their clasped hands. "I know there are many expectations and duties belonging to the royal House...I had not considered it before, when we were on the road. All I thought about was bringing you home with me. Yet I saw how even the ball last night made unexpected demands on you. And I do not like how you are somehow holding yourself in, because when you are as—" he searched for the right word—"as *contained* as you have been since we crossed into Tamtir—" Beloved opened her mouth to speak, but he met her eyes and she closed it, waiting for him to finish. "I have been thinking, however slowly, and that *is* when it began—you are closed off or away from me and that feels wrong..." Radvyed shook his head in frustration. "By the Master's Hand, I cannot seem to tell you what I know is happening without a lot of vague—" He stopped speaking, for Beloved had put one hand over his mouth.

"I know," she said. And then, because she suddenly knew it to be true, despite the fears she had wrestled with the night before, she said, "We will find a way."

Radvyed took her hand from his lips, kissed it, and said, "I do not want a prisoner for a wife."

Beloved laughed. "Neither do I wish to be confined or constrained ever again—nor will I be. We will find a way."

At that moment trumpets sounded and they heard the crowd in the square roar. The king and queen walked through the drawn curtains of the balcony door, followed by Radvyed and Beloved. The upturned faces of the crowd made Beloved think of a meadow crammed with wildflowers. Arkost and Gladna stepped to the front railing; Beloved felt the love of the people swell up to meet them, as if it were a radiant, golden wave.

"My people," cried the king, and it was clear that the *my* did not indicate possession but rather union, "we have more joyful news to give you! That the Crown Prince is returned among us you knew." He paused as the crowd cheered. "Today let it be known that he has chosen his princess"—here the crowd's voice swelled again—"has chosen his princess, and she has consented to be his wife and, one day, queen!" The crowd billowed forward in its eagerness to hear more. "My people! I give you the Lady Beloved of the Rose, soon to be your new princess!" Then he and the queen stepped aside, ceremoniously turning and gesturing to invite Radvyed and Beloved forward. The younger couple moved to the balcony railing, her left forearm formally laid along his right. Beloved felt the full power of the crowd's love and approval and she let it sink into her, skin, flesh, and bones, as one might revel in warm sunlight after a long and bitter winter. This was no hardship to endure. She could feel cold and lonely corners of herself that she had scarcely known were there warming and opening in the power of the people's welcome and regard. Radvyed kissed her hand and the radiant wave surged again.

Power, joy, and an urgent benevolence filled Beloved. Scarcely realizing what she did, she brought her right hand to her left shoulder and then flung her arm out, and as it swept wide, from out of the folds of her garment tumbled hundreds and hundreds of roses, falling over the carved balustrade to be scattered by a wayward breeze upon the people below. The crowd's roar foamed up to the balcony in an exuberant wave; people snatched flowers from the air; petals whirled, lifted by the crowd's own motion. Radvyed released her left hand and Beloved opened her arms again and again, and the roses fell until all had managed to gather at least one. Radvyed took her hand again; she was still in a half daze from the people's reception of her. He kissed her, to more happy shouts from the square, and then he and Beloved withdrew to the antechamber. They could hear Gladna speaking a few closing words of blessing on the balcony.

Beloved and Radvyed stood together, his arm about her. They would find a way.

Chapter Twenty-Four

L ater, when they had eaten and changed into clothes more suit-
able for walking in a garden, Radvyed and Beloved, along with
Rue, went to meet Dris. Rue carried the rose cutting from the walled
garden of the Hidden House. The summer day was sunny and clear.
Raked gravel paths wound among the roses. The flowers ranged
from purple-red to pearl-pink to butter-yellow to frost-white. Tiny
many-petalled roses peeked from bushes; heavy velvety roses draped
over trellises; delicate wide-blown roses opened out from tree
branches. Their varied perfumes drifted on the breeze: lush, bright,
intoxicating.

A boy, Dris's youngest apprentice, saw them and ran to fetch his
mistress. While they waited, Beloved looked about at the flowers. She
leaned forward and touched a cool, silky petal with a fingertip. Radvyed's eyes followed the flight of a bird as it dipped and called. Rue
stood still, not fidgeting, holding the cutting in its protective cloth.
After a few minutes, they heard Dris and the boy approaching. The
gardener was a stocky woman, not particularly tall, dressed as one who
tends roses: long sleeves, stout breeches, and a belt on which hung a
pruning hook and a few other tools. A tail of twine dangled from a
large patch pocket; a pair of leather gloves were stuffed in another. Her
straw hat shaded much of her face, but Beloved could see that the dark

gray hair was cut short. Beloved felt an inexplicable, heightened sense of expectation as Dris neared—this woman was more than the Rose Gardener, more than a wise woman. Beloved's heart beat high and fast, and her fingers twisted the folds of her skirts.

Dris stopped before them. The gardener pulled off her hat and stared straight at Beloved. Dris's face was nothing remarkable: the skin sun-wrinkled, as any gardener's might be, brown eyes looking out from under gray brows. The older woman held herself still, her direct gaze unfaltering. Beloved put out a trembling hand and touched the furrowed cheek. Both women caught their breath; then Dris pressed her cheek into the cup of Beloved's palm. The gardener's stance softened, but she did not drop her gaze.

Beloved spoke, her hand cradling Dris's face. "Dris Rose Gardener, I am Beloved who was named Hideous by my father, Besserdech, the master of the tower called the Griefstone, once called Reavinstoft. It was my rose that by your wisdom saved the queen. Will you accept a cutting for the royal garden?"

A tear glimmered on Dris's cheek. Her hand came up to clasp Beloved's wrist, holding the younger woman's hand close. It seemed that knowledge flowed between the women; any words or signs would only be for the others' benefit. After another moment, Dris let Beloved's wrist go, and the younger woman allowed her hand to fall gently to her side. Not looking away from Beloved's face, Dris signed a quick phrase. Beloved smiled, her eyes bright with tears.

The apprentice goggled at his mistress and blurted to Rue and the prince, "She is her aunt!" Rue gasped and Radvyed rocked back on his heels.

I am the elder sister of Lady Beloved's mother, Dris continued. *It is a long tale, but let us graft the cutting first.*

Beloved, tears slipping down her cheeks, moved uncertainly forward, and then, when Dris opened her strong arms, the younger woman fell into the embrace of her only known living kin. Rue smiled as she dabbed her face with a handkerchief; Radvyed brushed his eyes with one hand as he gave a little laugh of amazement.

Then Dris led them to the rose onto which the cutting would be grafted. It was in the central area of the extensive garden, as it had been planted in honor of Radvyed's birth. Dris insisted that they all help in the grafting. She and her apprentice, who introduced himself as Vel, helped the three with their unaccustomed tasks. The prince had rarely himself done such work, and the gardens of the Hidden House had not been tended by Rue's or Beloved's hands. Beloved closely observed every step, absorbed by the process. At last the graft was secured to Dris's satisfaction and the rootstock freshly watered.

The small party then wandered the rose garden with Dris as their guide. Beloved walked next to her, with Vel interpreting as needed. Radvyed and Rue followed, enjoying the garden and the pleasant warmth of the afternoon.

Radvyed looked at Rue, strolling beside him. She seemed relaxed, content to walk with no other purpose than pleasure, and willing to be led among the flowers wherever Dris took them. As she bent to smell a yellow-hearted rose with creamy outer petals, Radvyed thought, *She has brought her child to safe harbor, after many years of hard waiting and sorrow.* He was glad that Beloved's heart-mother had found a measure of peace.

Later that evening, over small cups of sweet wine and a plate of pastries, Radvyed and Beloved spoke of what they had learned from Dris. Rue was not with them; Gladna had particularly requested her company. Alone together, they discussed Dris and her revelations.

"To think that we have had a sorceress's sister in our household for all these years and never known it," mused Radvyed. "It makes one wonder what other unknown connections we have." He bit into a honeycake. "Although our rose garden has been exceptionally fine ever since Dris has tended it," he added, after swallowing.

"That is because you have an exceptionally fine gardener, not because she is a wielder of power," said Beloved. She sat back in her chair, absently running one finger along the rim of her crystal cup. "Dris herself, as she said, has no power as sorcerers speak of it. A curse and a blessing." She caught Radvyed's inquiring gaze. "A curse because the rest of her family was rife with power. She was the ordinary one, alone of all her—*our*—kin. Or that is what I make of the tale of her life before my father attacked them. A blessing because she was not worth the notice of my father, and so she escaped and lived, unlike her parents and brothers who were killed, or her sister, who was taken."

"Yet having no magic she nonetheless knew how to cure my mother's illness."

"One may have knowledge without power," Beloved pointed out. "She comes from a clan of sorcerers, after all." She sipped her wine. "I am glad that she has found a place for herself."

"Beloved, why did you not—" Radvyed stopped, not wanting to reproach her, and yet...

"Yes, Husband?"

"Is Dris's deafness within your power to heal?"

Beloved sighed. "No. I am not even sure that it would be right to do so." She saw that he was startled by this admission. She was quiet a moment, then said, "Dris was born deaf. It is not an injury to be mended. Apparently, no one in our clan was able to help her hear." Beloved continued thoughtfully, "It is possible her deafness is an attribute shared by others of the clan, as height or eye color may be.

I know not." She sipped her wine, eyes pensive. "There may be others of power able to work with the body to reshape its parts and open and close its pathways. I do not have that gift or knowledge." She set down her glass. "I can do nothing for her in this. Yet she seems content and whole, so perhaps I grieve without cause."

Radvyed reached out and took Beloved's hand in his. "I, too, grieve for those whom I cannot aid," he said, thinking of those of his people suffering illness or injury. "And I, too, am not always sure if help is needed or desired."

They sat for a while in the dark, lit only by a few candles and a small fire in the hearth, and gazed out the open window at the stars, remote and orderly and bright.

CHAPTER TWENTY-FIVE

Beloved with great care ladled sun-wine from a large bowl into cups that Radvyed passed to his mother and father. They had gathered in a west-facing room, as the Tamtireni often did, to watch the sun go down. The glass doors were open and the cooling air brought in the green scents of the gardens. When they all had a drink in hand, Gladna raised her cup to the setting sun and thanked the Lady for the gift of the day. Then they all sipped their wine.

"Explain to me why you were surprised," the queen said, taking up the conversation they had broken off as Beloved had concentrated on serving the sun-wine. Arkost sat with his chin propped on his fist, his elbow braced on the arm of the divan. Gladna, seated by him, cocked her head as she gazed at Beloved. The king and queen had not expected that Beloved would not understand the necessity of celebrating a marriage ceremony according to the customs of Tamtir.

"We are already bound," Beloved told them, "and not just Prince Radvyed and I. We two are married because of the broken curses, but you yourselves have also bound me to you and to your House." When Arkost and Gladna looked at her, puzzled, Beloved laughed a little in disbelief. "When you first welcomed me," she added, looking from one to the other. "Do you really not—"

"Beloved," interrupted Radvyed gently. She glanced at him, saw his slight headshake, and although puzzled in her turn, said nothing more. The king and queen looked to their son for an explanation.

"Beloved is convinced that our bloodline, our House, even our people are rife with magic that we wield unawares. I tell her that we are ordinary folk, but..." Radvyed spread his hands. "She is not convinced."

Beloved said nothing, but thought to herself that it was fortunate that the royal family observed all royal etiquette regulating behavior, speech, and protocol. *A House less disciplined could find itself in trouble without even knowing the cause.*

The *seveyati*, priests and priestesses of the Lady and the Master, had chosen the date for the wedding, the fifteenth of the month of Osena. Most of the people who were involved in the planning and preparation felt that a scant two months was ridiculous haste. The appointed day was deemed propitious, however, as it was the date of both the autumn equinox and the new moon.

For balance, a new beginning, explained Dris, writing on her small slate during one of the times that Beloved visited her in the rose garden. She came often to visit her aunt, both for her company and to learn from another immigrant Tamtir's ways and customs. Beloved learned that the ceremony would be outside, in the Forest. Dris pointed towards the thick trees in the distance. *Big clearing, called the Glade. Sacred to the Lady.* Although Beloved did not know much about the goddess yet, she understood the Lady was revered and loved by the people of Tamtir.

"And the Master?" asked Beloved, naming the Lady's consort. "Has He no part?"

Later, Dris said, using one of the signs Beloved had learned, and then waving at the palace. *You go into the Hall and blood the Stone.*

Land and House, thought Beloved. She asked more about the ceremony, but Dris was not yet living in Tamtir when the king and queen had married. She knew only that there was a cup of wine and a loaf of bread shared in the clearing, and a handfasting with the Tree. The Stone in the Hall was very old, older than the palace itself, she thought, and it, too, was sacred.

Food, drink, blood, life, and death, thought Beloved. *I am ever more astonished that they think they do not deal in power.* She turned away from gazing at the Forest, and her eyes met those of Dris. The gardener smiled slightly and Beloved realized that her aunt knew better than she herself did that Tamtir was a place of potent magic. *But it is a wide lake, not a single spring*, Beloved thought.

As the preparations advanced and the day approached, Beloved began to learn about her new role as a princess of the royal House of Tamtir. Since she was literate, she was assigned a tutor, an iron-eyed, long-boned woman in her fifties named Zhelez, who was one of the foremost scholars of history at the College of Learning in the city. She set Beloved to reading the chronicles of Tamtir, beginning with its founding, a thousand years or so ago, as a gift of the Golden Lady, Velaska, and the Dark Master, Predun. She also provided Beloved with books that held the best known and loved stories of the kingdom, including, to her delight, Lionheart. Beloved liked the history tutor, whose manner was a little gruff but very direct. Zhelez did not think Beloved was strange; the scholar merely thought that the princess-to-be was ignorant of her new country. Bards came to teach Beloved music and well-known songs; a dancing master was appointed to teach her the steps of the dances used at court. Her skill and ear for music were no more than average, but she enjoyed those lessons as well. She preferred dancing with Radvyed to her sessions with the dancing master, who was an exacting sort, but intrigued by the challenge, as he put it, of Beloved's idiosyncratic bearing.

Beloved also spent time with the queen, either in her train or seated at her side. She began to understand the duties of the highest lady of the land and how to carry them out, and observed how Gladna spoke and interacted with others. She knew that she was merely scratching the surface of what there was to be learned about being a princess. Yet although Beloved found her new lessons and activities interesting, she did not like having her time so comprehensively scheduled and her studies so wholly directed by others. An afternoon free, to think or to wander or to pursue her own studies—could it really be there was no lore of sorcery in Tamtir?—was very rarely given her. She was also sorry that she was left little time to spend with Rue. She had to carve out a quiet hour taking tea in Rue's room or request time for outings to the gardens with Dris.

Beloved also found herself spending less time than she liked with Radvyed. He had his own duties, and like her, his time was claimed not only for his work but also for fittings for wedding clothes. But now and then, when they were able with clear consciences to leave tutors and tasks behind for a few hours, he would accompany her into the city. Beloved relished this way of coming to know her new people and land. They would go about on foot, hand in hand. While the people recognized them as their crown prince and soon-to-be princess, an etiquette that Beloved did not yet grasp kept Radvyed and Beloved from being mobbed by gawkers wherever they went.

At first Radvyed took her to the market, where Beloved was delighted by all the things on display—fruit, flowers, clothes, jewelry, knives, pots, lace, cakes, spices, musical instruments—what could not be bought or sold here? But then he realized that his bride was fascinated by any skill that required physical dexterity. She was tirelessly appreciative of the craft of smiths, weavers, cobblers, farriers... Anyone performing a skill by hand, from a child weaving a basket under a tree to a man yoking oxen in the livestock market, could catch and hold her attention. At first the people did not know what to make of her as Beloved observed them with deep interest, yet in time they became accepting and proud of her admiration. Between Beloved and the people an understanding was forming, and she felt more at ease with them than with some in the palace.

Radvyed was glad that she enjoyed being among the people, although he did not understand how she could be intrigued with something as ordinary as wool being spun into yarn or a horse being shod. When he asked her about her interest in such mundane things, he was made aware of how very differently she saw the world.

"At my house I rarely ever saw anyone working or making. I read in books and saw in pictures and I heard tales, even looked into others' memories. But I never myself saw someone take a bit of fluff and make thread, or a piece of iron and make a buckle. When Rue was with me she sometimes sewed or did other stitchwork. My eyesight was faulty, then, for the curse interfered, and I could not see well what she did."

"Yet your house was filled with beautiful things!"

"Yes, but I called them into form with my power, sometimes with purpose, sometimes not. No hand made them."

Radvyed expressed his bemusement that a woman who could create by sorcery could be spellbound by watching a baker knead dough or a carpenter making a chair.

"Husband, to me such things are as extraordinary as my 'magic' is to you. Think of it: a little fluff of wool, taken and twisted in just the right way, makes a string. The string can then be meshed with other string to make a cloak. From the back of a sheep, wool can in this way be made into a garment for the queen herself. A lump of metal can be heated and shaped into a form that perfectly suits the hoof of a horse. These transformations of things: wool, plants, rock, metal—go on every day in your kingdom, yet no one seems to find it odd or 'magical.' Yesterday I discovered that the plates we eat from are made from mud. Mud!"

Beloved's enthusiasm made Radvyed laugh, but that evening he looked at the painted porcelain of his plate, and silently agreed with her that its origin in humble clay was indeed amazing.

Chapter Twenty-Six

Finally the wedding day arrived. Radvyed and Beloved, in accordance with Tamtireni custom, had continued occupying separate apartments. They were glad that this prohibition would soon be removed. Beloved felt lonely in her rooms. Although she was interested in all kinds of people, she did not yet feel safe with them: she worried about making a mistake or giving insult where none was intended. She was concerned that she would do something without thought that would appear uncannily "magical," for she was still learning what the Tamtireni considered odd or disturbing. In addition, it seemed to Beloved that some of the people of the palace, both the *damashi* and the *dovoreni*, looked at her with apprehension or discomfort—some because she was a foreigner and others because she was a sorceress. Yet she was to be one day their queen.

Radvyed, for his part, found he did not like to be separated from his lady. He knew his father thought this the natural feeling of a man forced to keep his distance from his own bride, but Radvyed thought it was something more. However, there was no help for it, so he contented himself with seeing her when he could, among the press of duties and preparations, and looked forward to their wedding. Once the marriage rites were completed and they were less busy, he and Beloved could talk about this constraint he still felt she was laboring under, although she did not allude to it or complain. She was not free as she had been after the tower had come down, before they had entered his country. He wanted to learn why.

At last the day arrived. Beloved stood by her window, wrapped in a robe against the cool of the morning. She looked out over the rose gardens and beyond to the Forest. *Balance and newness*, she thought. *They are right: these are good signs for the day.* Then one of the *damashi* recalled her to the duties of bathing and dressing and eating. The festivities did not begin until noon, but the dress was more complicated than her usual garments, and it was plain that her attendants required the whole morning to have her ready.

Radvyed also was looking out his window, which faced the same direction as Beloved's, at about the same hour as she. *Tonight Beloved will be with me*, he thought, pleased. Looking at the Forest, he pictured the Lady's Glade. He had visited the sacred clearing most recently when hunting. All creatures were under the Lady's protection, and every hunter stopped by her Tree, either in thanksgiving for a fortunate hunt, or to petition for success another day. Radvyed had even heard a tale of a hunter, gored by a boar, crawling to her Glade and begging for her aid. He had lost the leg, it was said, but he had lived. *May You and the Master look kindly on this day, our House, and all Tamtir*, thought Radvyed, then turned in answer to his *damash*'s call.

People gathered in the Palace Square all morning. Beloved and Radvyed did not see them, although they could hear the murmur of the crowd. Their rooms were on the garden side of the palace. Because today would be the day prince and lady would ritually come together, the betrothed couple had been kept apart from each other and everyone else. Rue and Dris waited with Beloved in her chambers. The *damashi* dressed the soon-to-be princess, overseen by the royal dressmaker and a *dovorena* who was familiar with the required protocol.

Normally, this office would have been performed by an older female relative of the bride, but neither Rue nor Dris were conversant with the ceremony—or indeed any ceremony of Tamtir. *Dovorena* Namira, a tall, thin, stately woman with dark hair tastefully arranged, projected a calm authority that was very helpful to Beloved: the courtier would not allow her to make a serious error. Beloved had asked for more detail about the ceremony, but Namira advised her not to fret.

"If I tell you details, then you will worry about remembering what you are to do," the *dovorena* explained. "Leave that to me. Trust me, Your Grace. You will be asked to repeat oaths of fealty to His Radiance Prince Radvyed, to the royal House, and to the land and the people of Tamtir. These oaths will be accompanied by ritual gestures—nothing that requires special preparation from you. Allow yourself to be guided, Your Grace."

Beloved usually regarded those of the royal court with some wariness, for she had observed struggles for influence as she had shadowed the queen. Yet she did not sense any double-speaking from Namira. That lady, for her part, had not been perturbed by the sudden insertion of a reputed sorceress into the palace and indeed the royal family. As Namira had no marriageable daughters of her own, she could consider the soon-to-be princess with an impartial eye. She had not found any malice in the young woman, nor had she seen Beloved perform any unpleasantly unnatural feats with her magic.

"It is difficult to move in these clothes," remarked Beloved, looking down at her gown.

"It is also difficult to move in them without dignity," pointed out Namira.

The dressmaker circled Beloved slowly, examining every inch of her creation, now and then reaching out and making an adjustment. She said, "Do not fight the dress, Your Grace. Let it help you. It is stiff to support you through a long day of walking and standing. This is not a day to rush, so the dress will not permit you to hurry. You reflect the splendor of the Golden Lady herself, who shines on us all with kindness. So will you be, moving among the people today. You are unused to its weight and to how it follows your movements. So your gestures will be deliberate and well seen." Beloved looked doubtfully at her reflection in the tall mirror set before her. She did not like having her movements impeded.

"All will be well," Namira said. "Dressmaker, it is a quarter till noon." The dressmaker nodded and turned to pick up a golden sunburst tiara. She set it on Beloved's elaborately styled hair, and made the younger woman turn her head a few times, to check that it was securely settled. Then she relinquished the bride to Namira. The dressmaker and her assistants left the room.

Beloved stood gorgeously arrayed in cloth of gold. Her dress was constructed of several layers, each heavily embroidered. A hint of one rich fabric peeked out through a laced sleeve, another glittered through the fine veil of an overlayer, and two or three more formed the panels of the bodice. Gold lace spilled over her hands. Yellow jewels glinted in her hair and were sewn all over the dress. Gold ribbons and tiny silk flowers added to the sumptuousness, the abundance of splendor. Beloved stretched out one bare foot, which was wholly unadorned.

"It seems odd to be barefoot," remarked Rue.

"It is part of the ritual," said Namira. The palace bells began to ring.

Radvyed also was barefoot and as richly dressed as Beloved. He was clothed in robes of deepest indigo, as elaborately layered as Beloved's costume. His had less embroidery, worked in silver thread, rather than gold. The outer garment was sewn all over with tiny white gems that glittered as he walked. The silver crown on his head bore a large star sapphire. King Arkost and Queen Gladna were to accompany him, as was *Dovoren* Oumyest, the chief protocol officer. Oumyest was a short, bald, man with keen and benevolent eyes. Moving with certainty and precision, he made the people about him feel at ease, perhaps because they felt themselves to be the objects of his benign guidance. Radvyed exited from a lesser door of the north wing of the palace. He walked with his parents, *Dovoren* Oumyest, and several relatives and *dovoreni* towards the Forest.

Meanwhile, accompanied by Rue, Dris, *Dovorena* Namira, and other attendants, including the company of the Hidden House, Beloved used a door from the south wing. They approached the Forest on a wide path on the opposite side of the gardens. The prince and his bride would each enter the Forest at different points, then meet in the Lady's Glade by her Tree. Each party had departed the palace at noon, the time when the bells had begun ringing. Crowds lined both paths into the Forest, waiting and watching for either the bride or groom. When the wedding party had passed, people fell in behind, or walked alongside. Many carried flowers of late summer and early autumn or leafy branches. It was not a boisterous crowd, for it was both a joyful and a solemn moment. Radvyed's robes were heavy and he walked slowly, looking ahead, glad for the support of all the people walking along with him. He could hear them pointing out to each other the bareness of his feet, the richness of his garments, and how his beauty made him as splendid as the Master Himself. *Of Your grace, do not be offended*, he prayed when he heard such comments. *I know I only reflect, Master, Your own magnificence.*

Beloved found that the dressmaker had been correct: if she did not resist the dress, it supported and aided her. She walked slowly, allowing the dress to dictate her posture and pace, with her head pointed forward as directed by Namira.

"You are not seeing those about you yet," Namira had told her. "At this point we are all here to witness what you and the prince are doing and saying. So do not look at anyone or interact with anyone in the crowd." So Beloved kept her attention on the Forest ahead. The path was grassy and cool beneath her feet. She could not help but hear the murmurs of the crowd as they admired her as she walked. She also heard, or sensed, some who were watching her with anxiety, a little fear, and even one or two with suspicion. But as she felt the press and texture of the people's attention on her, she realized that to them she was also a figure of their beneficent Golden Lady, Velaska, moving among them in Her radiant splendor. The uneasiness of some was subsumed under the glad admiration of most, and Beloved felt that not only was the dress supporting her, but also the people.

At last each party came to the eaves of the Forest. When prompted, Beloved and Radvyed each said, at their separate spots, "By Your leave, Lady, I enter Your Forest." Beloved felt as though she passed through a curtain of strings as she entered, filaments of a power akin to that which she had first sensed upon entering the realm of Tamtir. In this place, however, the power seemed more fully present. The invisible tendrils trailed over her curiously, then drifted away, permitting her passage. She looked from the corners of her eyes, but no one else seemed to be experiencing anything similar.

The bride and the groom, with their attendants, entered the Forest and walked the rather narrower, leaf-strewn paths to the sacred clearing. The crowds either followed behind or slipped among the trees, using smaller trails. Birds flitted and swooped among the trees: jays cawed, wrens trilled, flycatchers called, a raven or two croaked. She noticed that even with this number of people, everyone was most careful as they made their way, disturbing the Forest as little as possible.

Radvyed, of course, was familiar with the Glade. However, he had never before seen it prepared for the wedding of the crown prince. The Lady's Tree, which stood in the middle of the clearing, was an ancient elm. There was a table under its spreading branches, and a priest of the Master and a priestess of the Lady stood by it. There seemed to be things set on the table and large jars, chest high, set on the ground, but Radvyed did not study the arrangements because his eye was caught by a flash of gold. He looked at the opposite end of the clearing and saw his Beloved.

Radvyed's breath caught; he could not stop staring at her. She walked slowly forward, her eyes on his. She was magnificent, glowing in gold raiment, the sunlight catching her hair, her tiara; gold sparked with her every movement. She came to a gradual stop, as did he. They were perhaps ten paces from each other. He absorbed her radiance and thought with joy, *Now everyone can see who and what she is. This dress reveals her as no other.*

Beloved found it hard to breathe. She tried not to stumble from the impact of seeing her prince, the most handsome of men, dressed in clothes that accomplished what she had not believed possible: they made him even more dazzling to her senses. His garments did not make him more beautiful, but they gave his beauty a gravity and a depth that made his looks an outward sign of the inner man. *What power is this of the tailor*, she thought with astonishment, *to reveal both the man and the prince? Now all can see the glory as well as the glamour.*

All was silent in the clearing as the prince and the sorceress faced each other, luminous and rapt. The air shimmered with power. Then the moment passed, or perhaps it merely eased.

The king, the queen, and the other attendants of Radvyed and Beloved stepped back. The priest and priestess came forward to greet them. A gold ribbon was bound about one of Beloved's wrists and a dark blue one about one of the prince's. The holy ones tied the other ends of the long ribbons about the huge trunk of the ancient Tree and then the priest directed Radvyed to walk in one direction and the priestess indicated to Beloved to move in the other. The couple circled the Tree slowly while the priest and priestess sang. As the bridal pair circled, they came closer and closer to the trunk, and they passed each other, once, twice, three times. Radvyed stooped under her raised ribbon as they crossed.

They came to a halt facing each other, each one hard by the trunk of the Tree, so close to each other that their garments brushed. They smiled, each having eyes only for the other. Each had a hand and beribboned forearm held up flat against the Tree. At a word from the priest, their other hands came up, the sleeves falling back, and they twined their forearms, laid their palms together, then folded their fingers down, interlocking them. Beloved could see that Radvyed was remembering the first time they had touched in this way, as she was, and now the memory was cleansed of all the shame and despair she had felt that evening—for here they were. The *seveyati*, using fresh gold and indigo ribbons, bound the wrists of Radvyed's and Beloved's clasped hands together. Beloved looked at the complicated knots: they would not come undone easily. She wiggled her hand a little: the bond was not tight, but she and Radvyed were indeed handfast. She glanced at his face; he had an eyebrow raised at her testing of the knots. She raised her own brows; he looked away, stifling a grin.

"Prince Radvyed Kamengorni Mirkamen, Son of Arkost and Crown Prince of Tamtir, Scion of Oak, Rose-Bearer, Curse-Breaker, Scourer of Salt, the Chosen of Predun, do you now of your own free will and desire handfast yourself to the Lady Beloved of the Fire Bird Clan, Daughter of Amarrasal and Sorceress of the Hidden House, Mistress of the Thornwood, Rose-Giver, Destroyer of the Griefstone, Hope of Spring, the Accepted of Velaska?" Beloved listened bemusedly as the *seveyat* unspooled the lists of their titles, which had been produced by *Dovoren* Oumyest in consultation with the chief royal chronicler and master herald.

"Yes," said Radvyed. He knew that Beloved considered them irrevocably bound already. He was beginning to realize that her understanding of what marriage between them meant was a different, more intimate, somehow wilder and more magic-fraught tie than he had thought. Yet he had to admit to himself that it was at this moment that he felt that they became most fully married, here in the presence of *seveyat* and *seveyata*, king and queen, people and Tree. Had he not known from childhood that one day he would be standing beneath the Lady's Tree in her sacred Glade, swearing his life to the woman who would be his consort?

The priestess now took her turn, addressing Beloved. Repeating all their titles, she asked the same question of Beloved.

"Yes," said Beloved. She felt her skin prickle and her bones hum with the power filling the Glade. She could sense the slow seep of sap in the Tree's trunk with one hand and the swift beat of Radvyed's pulse against her other wrist. The silent presence of everyone about them seemed to hold her up; the will of everyone in that clearing was intent on the spell—as she thought of it—being cast.

Seveyata and *seveyat*, one standing behind Beloved and the other behind Radvyed, each placed one hand on the trunk of the Tree, the other on the couple's bound, clasped hands. Together the holy ones spoke:

"Velaska blesses and binds this union in love and in duty, in sorrow and in joy."

Beloved's eyes widened as the words fell upon her and Radvyed. She kept her eyes on his. Did he not feel the weight of the words, as of a mantle thrown over them? But he only smiled at her. She smiled in return, almost giddy with the power swirling through the air like dust motes. She wanted to learn more about this Lady who took such a close interest in the doings of Tamtir.

Then priest and priestess cut the ribbons that tied them to the Tree, leaving a short remnant still tied about their wrists. They dropped their bound hands, and Beloved found that she and Radvyed were holding hands in a natural clasp as they moved to stand side by side. She liked the familiarity of the hold on this day filled with so much that was new to her. The *seveyati* guided the wedding couple to the front of the large table, which Beloved now saw was very simple and made of stone. In front of the table was a circle on the ground, about four paces across, surrounded by a very low wall, also of stone. Beloved wondered about the space, which appeared to contain little except mud. Radvyed tugged at their bound wrists and Beloved looked at him. With a tilt of his head, he signaled that they were to step into the circle and the mud.

Part of the ritual, Namira had said about their bare feet. So Beloved followed Radvyed and stepped over the low wall. Their feet sank a little into the wet mud, which oozed strangely between Beloved's toes. *Now I know why these formal costumes are made to hang above our ankles,* she thought. She and Radvyed were standing facing away from the table and the Tree and towards the people gathered in the Glade.

The priest addressed them. "Do you, Crown Prince Radvyed and Princess Beloved, of your own free will and desire, undertake to bind yourselves forever to the land of Tamtir, entrusted to the House of

Mirkamen by the Golden Lady Velaska, and swear to guard it and cherish it, that it may be a realm of peace and plenty?"

"Yes," answered Radvyed and Beloved. Again, she felt the hum of power, this time apparently emanating from the mud she squelched underfoot.

The priestess bent, dipped her fingers in the mud, and smeared the mud on the backs of each of their hands, on their foreheads, and to Beloved's surprise, over their hearts, heedless of the gorgeous garments.

Then the *seveyata* said, "Velaska blesses and binds this union in love and in duty, in sorrow and in joy." Beloved took a deep breath. But the rite was not yet finished.

The priestess then asked them, "Do you, Crown Prince Radvyed and Princess Beloved, of your own free will and desire, undertake to bind yourselves forever to the people of Tamtir, swearing to govern them, guard them, and cherish them, so that they may thrive and prosper, ruled by justice and clemency?"

Beloved and Radvyed said, "Yes." Beloved was beginning to feel overwhelmed by the ceremony. The power—the *Lady's* power, she realized, in awe—seemed to her senses to fill the Glade and the Forest, as water fills a bowl. The life-binding oaths to husband, land, and folk, sealed by the Lady Herself, twined strong threads of obligation and promise about her very bones. Unease flickered through her. This wedding was so much more than she had expected, even with what she had begun to suspect was going on under the surface of much royal protocol and tradition. She felt lightheaded, and wondered how long they were to stand in the still gently humming mud.

The priest turned to address the witnessing people. "Do you, people of Tamtir, of your own free will and desire, undertake to bind yourselves forever to the Crown Prince Radvyed and Princess Beloved, swearing to serve them, guard them, and cherish them, so that they may rule with justice and clemency, and all may live in peace and prosperity?"

Beloved looked out at the people, allowing herself to see them now. They seemed to her at that moment to be a vast crowd, even greater than the one that had filled the Palace Square when the engagement had been announced to the kingdom. She saw men and women of all ages and ranks, and children, from babes in arms to youths and maidens on the edge of adulthood. Although Beloved had just begun the study of heraldry, she thought she could pick out the colors of every major landholding, or *mirenzem*, of the realm. All, whether noble, artisan, farmer, scholar, herder, or servant of Lady or Master, were dressed in their finest, and most characteristic, clothes. Later she would ask Radvyed about the crowd that seemed to outnumber the trees, like a tide that had swept in, and Radvyed would agree that there were very many, but not as many as she described. Now it seemed to her as though indeed all the people of Tamtir stood before them and solemnly answered, many-throated but one-voiced, "Yes."

The *seveyata* stretched out her arms, her fingers open and spread, one palm towards the people, one towards the handfast couple ankle-deep in mud. "Velaska blesses and binds this union in love and in duty, in sorrow and in joy," she proclaimed. Beloved again felt a surge of intoxicating power rush towards her and Radvyed and she rocked a little under its exuberance. Yet though she was not working to restrict her power, she was not worried that it would show forth in a distressing way. The Lady's power was so pervasive, so strong, Beloved's was contained without her own effort, like a chick under a mother bird's wing.

The *seveyat* spoke now, addressing the people. "Our Crown Prince and his Princess have sworn our oaths and been marked by our earth.

Now they will eat the bread of our fields and drink the wine of our vines, for we are the sap as they are the tree. May they have deep roots and wide branches; may they bear good fruit forevermore." The priestess and priest went to the table. He returned with a loaf of bread and she with a wooden cup. The *seveyat* broke off a piece of bread and handed it to Radvyed, who took it and ate. Then Beloved was given her piece.

As she chewed and swallowed, she thought she had never tasted anything so delicious, so many-layered, so thoroughly itself. It was bread, yes, and if she were a baker dreaming up a recipe for perfect texture and taste she could not have imagined better. But it was more than bread, for as she ate there awoke in her memories of hillsides and valleys, sunlight and soil, and lakes and streams she did not know. Nor did she recognize the hands and faces, the bent laboring bodies, the smell of oxen, the sensations of wielding hoe or scythe, or the sense of muscles tired from holding a plow, binding sheaves, and threshing grain. She closed her eyes and tried to catch the half memories, half sensations, but they slipped away before she could study them. She opened her eyes and saw that the *seveyata* was offering Radvyed the cup of wine. Beloved was a little more prepared now and not surprised that as she drank she was given as well the memories of the places and the days and the people who had made the wine. Again she closed her eyes, hoping to slow the swift play of sense impressions, but they flicked by, elusive as flame.

Beloved opened her eyes. The *seveyati* raised their arms and said together in their strong, clear voices, "Our oaths are heard and witnessed by the Golden Lady. She blesses us with another generation! May She always look kindly on our House, Land, and People!"

The crowd roared their agreement and approval. Beloved felt the goodwill and joy lifting up from the clearing like a huge flock of birds, up above the tallest of the trees, up into the sunlight realms of the Lady, beyond any mountain or cloud. Her own spirit rose with the hopes of the people, and she looked up, opening her free hand and turning the palm upward. Beloved felt as though she stood in a rain of light. Silent words welled up in her: *Yes, Lady, may You ever look kindly upon us all.* She felt a pulse of power, almost like a touch on her head and closed her eyes, overcome. Then she felt Radvyed's hand that clasped hers give a small jerk, as though he were surprised. When she opened her eyes, she caught a flicker of light from the corner of her eye. Turning her head, she saw that on her fingers perched a bird, a small falcon made of flame. She barely felt its weight, although its heat warmed her where it gripped her. Its talons were sun-bright against her hand; its ember-red eye, sharp with intelligence, met her gaze. She scarcely had the time to register the sight or the gasp of the people, for it spread its wings and with three quick beats leapt into flight. It made a low wide sweep of the Glade, just over the crowd's heads, before rising, then seemed to grow larger as it circled higher in the air, leaving bright sparks in its wake. It soared up and out of sight, a glint of gold in the late afternoon sky.

There was a moment of astounded silence and then cries of joy and wonder, buffets of currents of power—of the people, of the Lady, the sacred earth, the royal personages, the *seveyati*, the newly married, the sorceress. Beloved was dizzy and trying to keep her feet, which still slid and squelched in the mud. Radvyed tugged at her wrist, guiding her from the small enclosure. If the crowd before had been solemn, they now were boisterous. As Beloved tried to step over the low stone wall with some semblance of grace, she noticed that people were beginning to sit down and an outdoor meal was underway. She and Radvyed were seated at the stone table along with Arkost and Gladna, Rue and Dris, Oumyest, Namira, and the *seveyati*. As Beloved looked about, she saw that everyone else was seated on the ground and opening wrapped cloths and leather bags, passing baskets of bread and fruit, and drawing cups of wine and water from the large jars near the table. Radvyed offered her some bread topped with a slice of cheese. She took it, but did not eat.

"Is there anything amiss, Beloved?" he asked.

She hesitated, then said, "I am wondering whether this is like the bread we had before." The priestess heard her and turned to look at her.

"Was it not pleasing to you?" asked the *seveyata*; there was suddenly silence at the table.

Beloved bit her lips. Was what she had experienced not common, not expected, not the *point*? She said, "It did please me, as did the wine. How could they not, being gifts of Tamtir and blessings of the Lady? But I did find their...richness...overwhelming."

The *seveyata* looked at her keenly, a small smile tugging at her lips, as though at a private joke. Everyone at the table relaxed. "Overwhelming, yes. Eat, Your Radiance." She laughed a little when Beloved blinked at the title. "Eat and be easy. It is but bread and cheese."

Beloved found that she was quite hungry. She was not alone in her good appetite. The golden dress and the dark blue robes were not as helpful at table as they were in ceremony, she and Radvyed discovered. They had to be careful not to trail a sleeve across a platter of cheeses or dribble the juice of a fruit down their fronts. It was also awkward managing with one hand each, for their wrists were still tied; Beloved gathered that they would remain so for the rest of the day. Their literal handfasting was the occasion for some cheerful teasing, both from those at the table and those seated or strolling nearby. Beloved was unsure how to respond to comments such as "Who has the upper hand?" or "He's a handy man to have about, isn't he?" These lighthearted exchanges were alien to her. But she felt no malice, only goodwill from the jesters, so she smiled at the jokes and tried to follow Radvyed's lead. He seemed to feel no awkwardness nor shyness.

Beloved felt lighter somehow than she had during the ceremony, as if the weight of the rite had left, leaving her nothing more than a happy bride. The Lady's hand had lifted from her head; while that touch had been exhilarating, it had also been difficult to sustain. Beloved turned to Radvyed and noticed with rueful amusement that even mud on his forehead did nothing to dim his attraction. "Tell me about the mud," she said.

Here the *seveyata* leaned forward and touched Beloved's hand. Beloved turned to her. "The mud is made from earth and water from all parts of the kingdom, just as the bread is made with grain from all parts, and the grapes in the wine. It is a sign that Your Radiances are joined not only with each other, but with the land and the people."

Beloved wrinkled her forehead. "A sign? But surely it is more than a sign."

The priestess sat back and looked at Beloved. The priest turned to listen.

"What makes you think that the mud, bread, and wine are more than a sign, Princess?" asked the *seveyata*.

Beloved looked about at the others at the table. Radvyed was half smiling at her, but relaxed, so she was not being upsetting or disruptive, merely odd. Rue continued her meal; it was obvious to her heart-mother, Beloved thought, that powerful binding spells had been cast, but if these people considered them merely signs and rituals, Rue would not argue about it. It had always been enough for Rue to see clearly for herself. As Radvyed's consort, Beloved was in a different position. Her gaze came to the queen.

"Your Splendor," she said, addressing Queen Gladna, "Am I right that you and His Splendor were married in the same way?"

"Yes," said the queen, thoughtfully eyeing Beloved. "Although I must say I did not have a *sozkol* appear in my hand and fly off into the sunfields."

"Indeed, I have never seen such a thing either," put in the *seveyat*, leaning forward with his elbows on the table to see Beloved better. "Was that your magic, Your Radiance, like the roses in the square that first day?"

Beloved hesitated. She wanted to pursue the problem of whether the rite consisted of merely signs or whether the words and things had a more than symbolic purpose. She believed the rite created not just bonds of honor and duty, but also of power and essence, which to Beloved's mind, were rather more difficult to undo or betray. Yet she did not think it would be acceptable to ignore the queen's comment or the *seveyat*'s question. Beloved knew the *sozkol* had not been called by her own power. Yet she wanted time to think about what it meant, that the Lady's falcon had appeared in her hand.

Once again, she was frustrated by how differently she and the people of Tamtir perceived and thought about the world. In her view, the royal family seemed to move lightly and almost naively through a thornwood of strong and even omnipresent power, casually wielding the words, gestures, and materials of what they would call magic, oblivious to the consequences. *Truly the Lady and Master have this people in Their keeping*, thought Beloved. *Or how else can they have prospered with so little knowledge of what they are or do?* Beloved was at a loss as to how to answer the queen or the priest, nor was she sure how to follow her own line of inquiry.

Radvyed shifted next to her, and everyone's eyes were drawn to him. "I do not think it is news to anyone that Beloved comes from a long line of sorcerers on both sides of her family, the Fire Bird Clan on her mother's side"—he gave a small nod in the direction of Dris—"and the Ice Raven Clan on her father's." Rue and Dris had been interviewed by various scholars of heraldry, history, and genealogy since Beloved had come to the palace, so Beloved's story and lineage were not secret. The Rose Gardener's quick dark eyes darted around the table, taking in expression and posture. A tall, freckled herald, Rokena, sat next to Beloved's aunt, interpreting as needed. Dris's face did not give away her thoughts, but she followed the conversation with interest.

Radvyed continued, "We do not have much experience with what one might call powerful magic in Tamtir." Beloved looked at him and opened her mouth to contradict him, and then, catching his eye, shut it, sat back, and waited for him to finish. "Or at least we do not think we do. The princess, who has been steeped in powerful magic since birth, disagrees." Here Beloved noted the sharpened attention of the *seveyati* and disbelieving sounds from Namira and Oumyest. Arkost stared at Beloved, looking like a man who has been handed an unexpected and thorny problem. *Surely he knows that "powerful magic" as Radvyed calls it, exists,* thought Beloved, *none better. His own wife was brought back from the brink of the grave by the fragrance of a flower.* Yet what the king thought of how the queen's return to health was accomplished, aside from his gratitude, Beloved did not know. She looked at the queen. Gladna's fingers brushed the front of her dress, where the rose lay over her skin and beneath her finery. She was listening to her son.

"The princess sees much of the formality of the royal House and the manner whereby royalty and people interact as a series of magic spells or exchanges, the purpose of which are to safeguard the kingdom. Is that not so?" he finished, turning to Beloved.

It was better than she could have said it, but not quite what she perceived.

"Yes," Beloved said finally, unsure how to make the matter clearer. There was a short, slightly uncomfortable silence, broken by Arkost.

"So," he said, "to your mind, Tamtir is a kingdom of unwitting magic users?"

Put like that, thought Beloved, it sounded both silly and as though she considered the entire realm childish at best and idiotic at worst. She felt stupid trying to speak, trying to think with others, trying to make words carry her thoughts from her mind into another's. *Like broken-winged birds*, she thought. Radvyed was quiet at her side. She had to speak for herself. She could only try to speak truly and with respect.

Taking a deep breath and aware that all were now looking at her, Beloved said to the king, "Your Splendor, I do believe that Tamtir is a kingdom steeped in power. To me this makes understandable your successful resistance to the same salt curse that overtook your neighbors. It explains a royal House that has stood for a thousand years. I have long lived with what you call magic and in this kingdom I feel its presence very strongly. Perhaps I will learn that you call what I am sensing by a different name."

"Perhaps the magic you sense is merely you yourself," said Gladna. "You have been under a curse and now you are free. It may be you are moving about in a cloud of your own power and mistaking it for the air of this kingdom. Tamtir is our land and charge, and we have always been a people devoid of the dazzlement of magic." Beloved saw Namira and Oumyest breathe a little more easily and lean back a fraction in their seats. The king's gaze turned thoughtful.

"The roses you gave the people in the square and the *sozkol* to-day—is not their source in you, in your personal magic as a sorceress?"

asked the queen. Before Beloved could respond *No, not entirely, not even for the most part*, Oumyest gave a discreet cough. They looked up and noticed the darkening of the afternoon, the people all about them packing their things, and the *damashi* clearing the table and standing ready to take the chairs.

"It is time, I believe, for the Blooding," said Oumyest, and bowed to the *seveyati*, deferring to their authority in this rite. They acquiesced and all arose. The chairs were whisked away and Beloved and Radvyed were shown a third path, different from either of the ones they had taken into the Forest. The crowd opened before the couple as they walked towards the edge of the Glade where the path entrance lay. Their bound forearms were held up perpendicular to the ground as they paced. Again Beloved's dress came to her aid, supporting her erect posture and making it impossible for her to hurry out of nervousness. The prince, who had been trained since childhood in ceremony, set a slow but not sluggish pace, and matched his stride to that of Beloved. The people had regained their quiet demeanor: the meal had been simply a break from the solemnity of the day, rather than a shedding of it.

Beloved recalled Dris mentioning the Hall and blooding a stone. *More mere signs*, she thought, *that will bind and shape my life. And no one here even sees!* She gasped a little, her heart seeming to climb in her throat, thrumming and choking her. She remembered a bird she had seen in a cage in the market and how it had beat its wings uselessly against the wicker bars, striving for the sky. The ribbons around her wrists seemed like chains and the heavy dress a weight to keep her to the earth. The vows they had sworn coiled about her bones, and she stiffened, remembering the thorny vine's grip. She drew a deep breath, felt the rigid fabric constrict her, and almost sobbed in her panic.

Radvyed's fingers clasped her hand more firmly, as if she had stumbled. The rite again required that they look straight ahead, but he said very low, so that only she could hear, "Beloved? Are you well?"

No, she wanted to say, *I am not well. This is too much, too unexpected, too strong. Because you yourself do not know what we do, I underestimated the meaning and the power of it.* But Beloved saw no point in saying any of it. Radvyed was her husband, and her husband was a prince, the crown prince of Tamtir. A thousand years of royalty now bent her neck to its yoke. She forgot at that moment the radiant joy of midday, the touch of the Lady upon her, and the *sozkol* that had risen from her hand.

"I am as I must be," she answered, unable to lie and say she was well.

Chapter Twenty-Seven

Radvyed remained silent for several paces, still gazing straight ahead with his head erect, as did she. They were in the Forest now and it was almost evening. Beloved wondered what he saw. Shadows were long and dark, and their way was lit by a few *damashi* bearing lanterns: enough to keep them from stumbling, but no more. A raven rasped nearby and was answered by another, far away. Beloved recalled that it would be a moonless night, the first night of the new moon. Yet the darkness did not seem friendly to her. She could feel the shapes of people slipping through the Forest about her, people for whom this Forest was sacred and protective. Beloved did not feel safe. She felt that she was walking towards an unknown doom. The dried mud on her feet, hands, and forehead itched and she longed to wash it off. She thought wistfully of the first days after her name curse was broken, when it had just been she and Radvyed and Rue at the Hidden House, days during which it seemed nothing could weigh on her or constrain her again. Panic rose once more and she fought to control her body, her breath, and especially her power.

"You are my Beloved and I am your Husband," said Radvyed, again in that low voice only for her ears. She closed her eyes briefly and let the words fall on her like cool rain, gentle and refreshing. Then, open-eyed, she kept walking, but listened as her husband spoke to her, his words not like broken-winged birds but like the swift sure flight of a swallow. She let them in; she let them touch her. "I give myself to you. I give all of myself to you. I hold nothing of myself back from you. You are my wife and lady, Sorceress Beloved, bound to me forever, mine to command and obey." He paused, then said, "This was our marriage according to your rites of power, was it not?"

"Yes," she said.

"It was those words and the sign of the water that broke the Griefstone's spell?" *This word,* sign, Beloved thought, *we do not seem to mean the same thing by it.*

"And our kiss," she answered, her breath calming. "In addition to our blood as we approached the tower and our dance...it was a complicated spell." She glimpsed his tiny nod from the corner of one eye.

"I know the rites of this day seem strange to you," Radvyed murmured. "I believe that you perceive—*forces*— at work that we do not seem to acknowledge."

"Yes," said Beloved, relieved that he could see why she might be distressed. Radvyed was silent in thought as they continued their stately way.

"It is difficult for me to understand," he said at length, "how the woman who calmly risked her life in the Griefstone, who without a qualm entered into a bond with me sufficiently intimate and strong to offset her parents' devastating mutual hatred, could be alarmed or dismayed by any rite or ceremony of my House or land."

Beloved was surprised by the laugh that caught in her throat. She bit her lips, trying to maintain an appropriately solemn expression. She concentrated on the leafmeal path under her bare and mud-caked feet for a few more steps before feeling self-possessed enough to answer.

"It seems that we each take as commonplace the power with which we have been familiar since birth," she remarked, "and find perplexing and strange that which we are now encountering."

Although she did not turn her head, she felt his concern for her relax at her answer. "As you learn what it is to be a princess of our House, I hope you will become more accustomed and less troubled by us and our ways."

"Yes," acknowledged Beloved. "Yet—" She did not have a chance to finish her thought regarding *his* need to adjust to being the consort of a sorceress, because they had reached the edge of the Forest, and must speak their formal farewell to its Lady. Namira and Oumyest glided up behind them; each prompted their charge in low tones.

Prince and princess turned together, Radvyed slowly walking a half circle around Beloved, who pivoted on the spot. As one they bowed to the Forest and when again erect, said, "We thank You, Lady, for Your kindness." Then they executed another slow, coordinated turn and stepped out from beneath the trees. Once more Beloved felt the tendrils of power trail over her face and body as they crossed the border of the Forest; once more it seemed to her that she was the only one who perceived them. But the tendrils' touch did not bind, for they slid away as she and Radvyed walked under the open sky, and Beloved remembered the *sozkol* and its free flight.

Before them in the dusk lay the palace as Beloved had not seen it before, large with shadow and mystery. There were only a few dim lights marking a window or a door, for this rite was to begin in darkness. Lanterns bobbed silently about them and she could hear the muffled passage of many people, all accompanying her and the prince to the

Hall. She tilted her head slightly and looked up. A clear night, moonless, the stars thick and bright. The wide milky River of Jewels flowed among the constellations, marking a path to who knew where? *Not I, nor anyone walking the earth*, she thought, and was oddly comforted.

The palace seemed to change as they approached, offering more familiar features when the lanterns came close, withdrawing itself when the lantern light passed. Finally they arrived at a door that Beloved had not used before. She realized that she had thought the Hall they would use for the rite was the chamber in which court gatherings had occurred: hearings, balls, and so on. But this door was low and unremarkable, although in the lantern light she could discern what seemed to be a sign of stars over the lintel. Two of the guard, or *strazha*, stood by the door. As Radvyed and Beloved along with their companions and followers came up to the door, the guards barred their way by crossing their halberds in front of the doorway. *What now?* thought Beloved, and was reassured by the rustle of Namira's garment.

In a loud voice, the *strazhen* on the right demanded, "Who asks to enter the Hall of the Master?"

Radvyed answered, "The Scion of Oak and his Consort, the Mistress of the Thornwood." Beloved remembered *Dovorena* Namira explaining, among the many subtleties of her new life, the titles invoked to approach the Master's Hall. Something about roots and simplicity? Beloved let the thought go, entrusting herself to the rite and the *seveyati*.

"Enter, then, the Hall of the Master. He gives gifts to the worthy," the *strazhen* answered.

The guards lifted their weapons and the wedding couple entered, Radvyed leading Beloved. The door allowed passage to only one person at a time, and they had to turn sideways a little to accommodate their still-bound wrists. The passageway was longer than she had anticipated, for it was even deeper than the thickness of the palace walls, lit but sparingly with torches in sconces. As she set her bare foot on the cool, flagged floor, Beloved was not surprised to discover that here, too, was a threshold marked by power. She did not sense the trailing tendrils of the Lady's Forest, however, but a sudden wash of chill, as though someone had flung at her the contents of a large basin of cold water. She gasped and blinked; a quick shiver ran over her skin. Radvyed looked back at her and she nodded reassuringly at him. She was still cool, but whether that was because of the darkness and lowness of the chamber or because the power that filled the space still rested its awareness upon her, she could not be sure.

They emerged from the passageway and into a large hall. Beloved guessed from its windowlessness and not unpleasant chill that it was underground, or at least partially so. She and Radvyed moved to the center of the Hall to allow room to those still coming through the narrow way and into the larger space. The priest and priestess came to stand near the young couple and they waited as the chamber filled with witnesses from court, city, and countryside. Beloved looked about and saw that the Hall was as dimly lit as the passageway had been. It was a large, high-ceilinged room; marching down the length of it were two lines of tall pillars, one to their right, one to their left. There seemed to be a reddish light down at the far end. The stone of the walls, pillars, and floor was dark, veined with gold and red. She looked up and saw the night sky. At her intake of breath, Radvyed spoke into her ear.

"Beautiful, is it not? The Hall of the Dark Master is roofed with the sky. My astronomy tutor would sometimes bring me here on cloudy nights or during the day, for the stars are faithfully depicted."

Beloved asked, "What season is recorded, then?"

Radvyed's low chuckle right by her ear made her spine tingle. "Why, the autumn equinox as it coincides with a new moon. You see how we are favored." Beloved was not sure that so many portents and signs aligning and converging was entirely favorable. *Too much power, too much meaning, not enough understanding*, she thought. Yet she found the gem-starred ceiling astonishing and lovely. As she gazed, the sight both soothed her and provoked in her a kind of restlessness: *There is more*, she thought without knowing what she meant, *more to know and to be*.

When the Hall filled, the rite continued. *Seveyat* and *seveyata* stepped forward together and walked down the length of the Hall between the high-vaulting columns. At a sign from Namira and Oumyest, Radvyed and Beloved also began to walk; Arkost and Gladna, accompanied by the people, followed.

As they advanced, Beloved realized that the reddish light at the far end of the Hall was a fire in a fireplace. The Hall seemed to be tapering, the ceiling and its supporting pillars lowering. She almost thought there was another narrow passageway to pass through. But as they neared their goal, she saw instead that it was a simple fireplace, of no extravagant size and bare of ornamentation. The large stone set into the floor before the fire seemed proportionally larger than most hearthstones, she thought. The hearthstone and the stones forming the fireplace and the mantel were all of the dark stone used in the rest of the Hall, although here the gold and red veins were obscured, perhaps by use and antiquity.

The *seveyati* turned to face them, each standing on opposite sides of the fireplace. Radvyed and Beloved came near and stopped at the edge of the hearthstone when the priest held up his hand. The *seveyat* waited as everyone in the Hall also came to a stop and the rustles and jingles of clothing had ceased.

Then he said, his voice reaching out into the shadows and distances of the Hall, "Who approaches the Stone upon which the House of Mirkamen rests?"

Dovoren Oumyest stepped to Radvyed's side. "Prince Radvyed Kamengorni Mirkamen, Son of Arkost and Crown Prince of Tamtir, Scion of Oak, Rose-Bearer, Curse-Breaker, Scourer of Salt, the Chosen of Predun the Dark Master," he replied.

"Where is Arkost of Mirkamen and Gladna his Consort? Can they testify that this is their son?" asked the *seveyat*.

Now the king and queen came forward and declared so that all might hear, "We stand before the Master and all Tamtir and swear, this is our son, Radvyed of Mirkamen."

"Who is the woman to whom he stands handfast?" inquired the priest.

It was *Dovorena* Namira's turn to reply; in a carrying voice, she answered, "She is the Lady Beloved of the Fire Bird Clan, Daughter of Amarrasal and Sorceress of the Hidden House, Mistress of the Thornwood, Rose-Giver, Destroyer of the Griefstone, Hope of Spring, the Accepted of Velaska the Golden Lady."

"Is there anyone here of blood or days who can testify that this is she?" asked the *seveyat*.

Rue and Dris came closer to the firelight, Rokena at Dris's elbow.

Rue answered in her steady, clear voice, "I am Rue, foster mother to the Lady Beloved since her birth. Her name has changed, but her heart and her bone are true. I stand before the Master and all Tamtir and swear, this is the Lady Beloved."

Dris then took her turn, signing her answer, which Rokena spoke aloud that the whole crowd might know, her herald's voice penetrating the dim corners. "I am Kaladrisana, known as Dris Rose Gardener, aunt by blood to the Lady Beloved, who is the daughter of my sister.

I stand before the Master and all Tamtir and swear, this is the Lady Beloved."

"You may approach," said the priestess. Radvyed and Beloved walked onto the hearthstone. The flagged floor of the Hall was quite cool, as was the air of the Hall. Yet the hearthstone felt very warm under Beloved's bare feet, almost too warm. It was warmer than could be explained by the fire alone. She felt Radvyed shift his weight a little, then become still.

"You stand on the Stone that guards the heart of the House," said the *seveyat*. "You are called to stand and support the House and guard and rule all Tamtir, both land and people. Do you accept this charge of your own free will and desire?"

"Yes," answered Radvyed and Beloved.

"Kneel," said the *seveyata*. Slowly and awkwardly because of the unfamiliarity of their formal garments and the close-bound ribbons on their arms, Beloved and Radvyed knelt before the fire on the hearthstone. Beloved felt the insistent heat rising from the Stone, not quite comfortable, yet not burning.

"Hold out your arms," said the priestess, gesturing to their bound wrists. They did. Beloved looked at their clasped hands, the glint of the gold ribbon, the deep hue of the indigo, and thought the flames of the fire bent a little towards them.

"Open," was the *seveyata*'s next instruction. She helped them separate and flex back the fingers that had been clasped for hours. The *seveyat* bent over them then; to Beloved's shock, she glimpsed a small dark knife in his hand. Quickly the knife flashed between their hands, once, and again; there was a searing flash of pain. The priestess pressed their cut palms closed and announced, "The Master accepts the Scion and his Consort." Beloved felt a bodiless weight press briefly but firmly on the back of her head—both a gesture of acceptance and of author-ity, she thought, and was not wholly happy.

Then the *seveyata* opened their palms again, allowing the mixed blood to drip onto the Stone. "You offer yourselves and the Master accepts you as living stones of the House of Mirkamen. Seal your oaths with your blood."

Radvyed and Beloved leaned forward and smeared their blood on the hearthstone. The Stone was already stained dark with a thousand years of royal blood oaths. They raised themselves erect on their knees. Beloved felt as though she were kneeling on coals. *No worse than the salt we walked on to the Tower,* she told herself. *The Master wants no faint hearts in His service, I see.* She could feel their blood still trickling from the shallow cuts and was bemused by the mixture of glittering finery and earthy elements: cloth of gold, velvet and gems, mud and blood. *And the night still remains,* she thought, wanting to be alone with Radvyed once more, as they had been before they had crossed into Tamtir and become subject to its proprieties.

The *seveyat* stood before them on the large hearthstone, between them and the fire, so that his silhouette filled Beloved's sight. He raised his arms and in a loud voice announced to all present, "Predun the Dark Master confirms Radvyed and Beloved as blooded guardians of the House of Mirkamen, one day to be its king and queen. May they protect and defend it with their life's blood! May House and Land and People prosper in their time!"

The high ceiling rang with the cries of the people and Beloved felt the brief touch of power again, not bending her neck, but under her chin, lifting her head. The priest had moved and no longer stood in front of them, so she now gazed directly into the flames. The joyful cries had swelled into a song as every man, woman, and child sang the concluding hymn. Then she and Radvyed were raised to their feet and turned to face the people who had witnessed this long day of oaths and joining.

The flames behind them now threw white-blue light; shadows leapt and flickered. Beloved heard the deep chime of a bell, so penetrating that her bones vibrated, and felt the Master's power filling the Hall. Overcome by the awe of the moment—the low tolling, the quiet weight of power, the hymn of exaltation that seemed to suffuse the Hall with glory—Beloved stood, trembling with the force of all the surging love and hopes of the gathered people, all focused on herself and Radvyed. She was too exhausted by the deep-binding oaths and rites of the day to absorb fully or ride smoothly the currents of power, and cried in her mind to the lord of the place, *Master, help me!* A white heat gathered into a point between the palms of their bound hands. Startled, Beloved and Radvyed opened their fingers, so that they bent back like the petals of a flower, and there, between their palms, was a blue-white star. It rose a little into the air, then hovered between them at head height. Those in the front of the crowd fell still; the wave of awareness rippled back to the edges of the chamber, so that there was a heartbeat of stunned silence as all realized what they saw. Then a paean to the Master burst forth from a thousand throats, and the star rose, seemingly carried up by the song of praise. The people sang until the star reached the high ceiling, where it appeared to find a place and set itself among the other gems of night.

Beloved and Radvyed, like everyone else, stared up as the star ascended; Radvyed joined in the singing, and Beloved, although silent, felt her heart lift with the brilliant orb. The song ended and there was silence as everyone absorbed what had just occurred. Beloved looked out over the people, whose faces and figures flickered in the uncertain light of the torches and the fire in the hearth. She was exhilarated but a little weary, as they all were, she thought. The day had given many gifts but had also demanded much of everyone. When would she and Radvyed be left alone together?

Chapter Twenty-Eight

A s it turned out, not immediately, for there was still one more tradition to be observed. Beloved, Radvyed, Arkost, Gladna, Dris, Rokena, Rue, Namira, Oumyest, and the *seveyati* waited patiently at the fireplace end of the Hall while the crowd turned and made its way out into the gardens once more. Gladna was smiling and shaking her head at something Arkost was saying in her ear. The *seveyata* was considering the married couple; the *seveyat* stared at the new star in the ceiling. Rue was her usual calm self, although Beloved sensed that her heart-mother was ready for the day's activities to end. Dris was looking around at the Hall with interest; was it the first time she had been here, or the first time for a ritual?

"There is one more thing," whispered Radvyed in her ear. Beloved turned to look at him.

"What more could there be, Husband? We have taken oaths to land and people, House and realm. We have been bound most firmly together"—she raised their joined hands—"and we have done all this in the sacred precincts of both Sun Lady and Star Master. We have been marked with mud, fire, and blood, and have partaken of bread, wine, and fellowship. I cannot think what has not yet been done to make it clear to all that you and I are married and that I am now most royal."

"Can you not?" came the prince's voice, low, close, and amused. "We have not yet danced, Beloved. And there is still the bedding."

At that she jerked her head around to look at him directly and said with alarm, "Surely not with that whole assembly present!"

At this, everyone in their little group burst out laughing, for she had not whispered but spoken aloud, her tone higher than normal. Only Rue seemed to have shared her misgiving; her face now relaxed into a smile. Even Dris's eyes sparkled with amusement.

"Yes, yes," said the king heartily, "we line them up ten deep around the bed!" The queen gave his arm a playful slap.

"There is nothing to worry about, Beloved," said Gladna. "You will be accompanied to the door by your attendants and some other women. They will help you shed the dirt of the day, then leave you in peace."

"But your man," took up Arkost cheerfully, "will be accompanied to your door by his friends and well-wishers. The men are usually a little rowdier than the women," he added. "But they will not come in, and they do, eventually, leave."

Beloved looked around at the smiling faces, and realized that their laughter had not been unkind. It was only later, when she understood the interactions between people better, that she could see that this moment of mirth had been a release for those closely concerned with the health and protection of the kingdom. They had been watching all day as a strange yet powerful young woman had been bound to their land, line, and folk; they had seen flame fly from her hand like a bird and a jewel rise like a star in their midst. It was reassuring to know that she, like many other brides and grooms before her, could know a little nervousness on her wedding night.

The Master's Hall was empty and they walked back up its length. The flagstones felt cold to her bare feet after the very warm hearthstone. The people no longer watched or observed them, Beloved thought, intrigued. Indeed, they seemed to be hurrying away, most of them, talking quietly together and laughing.

"Where are they going?" asked Beloved.

"There are feasts and dances all over the kingdom tonight, especially in the city. They will be hurrying to their parties and gatherings."

"And we?"

He smiled at her. "A little longer yet, Beloved. There is a ball up-stairs. We must dance one dance, then your ladies will take you away. My gentlemen"—here his father, the king, stifled a laugh—"will drink a few glasses with me and then I will join you."

Beloved wondered if it would be as simple as that, after this day of power-filled signs and solemn oaths, but it was, indeed, that simple. They arrived upstairs in the glittering ballroom, which was ablaze with candles, their flames reflected in mirrors and crystal hangings. The room was filled with the color and scent and chatter of the court, men and women decked out in splendid clothes and sparkling jewels. Musicians in the gallery overhead played carefree melodies that primed the crowd for dancing. Now that all the solemn rites and bindings had been performed, it was appropriate to celebrate the day with lighthearted joy, and this was the mood of the room that Beloved experienced when their little party entered. The froth of people now giving themselves to amusement and frivolity after a day of somber undertakings refreshed her and buoyed her up, so her step also light-ened, and she was able to smile with delight at the scene.

She took in the brightness and color of the room and the green branches entwined with ribbons of gold and dark blue. Flowers adorned the walls and tables, in shades from gold to deep red; they were rich with spicy scent. Then *Dovoren* Oumyest as Master of

Ceremonies announced their presence, and the prince and new princess, barefoot, mud-marked, and with dried blood still on their clasped hands, walked slowly to the center of the room. Their garments were still magnificent, if showing a little the hard wear of the day. That evening many of the doubts and anxieties of the onlookers about this odd, magic-wielding, unknown woman were set aside, if not forgot-ten. She looked at the prince with joy and trust; he looked at her with delight and tenderness—and so they seemed simply a wedding couple, barefoot and handfast like any other. It was true that the prince's beauty shone like a flame and that the princess, royal as she now was, did not carry herself as one would expect from one of the House. But the court had accustomed itself to the force of Radvyed's handsome-ness and Beloved's eccentric grace allowed them not to perceive her real power.

The music started and the newlywed couple danced. The dance was both formal, because with their bound hands their movements were restricted, and intimate, because the dance required them to gaze into each other's eyes. *They are a world within a world*, thought Rue as she watched them, and felt a pang of loss even as she was glad for her heart-daughter. She sensed a hand come to rest kindly on her arm and glanced to the side. It seemed the queen felt the same. After the dance, Gladna and Rue, with Beloved's attendants, came forward to cut the ribbons that bound their hands. Radvyed, supported by his friends, loudly protested that he would not be separated from his new wife. Beloved at first was uncertain, not understanding that this laughing altercation was not a real argument, but then Radvyed caught her eye and smiled, so she did her best to do her part. Only after Beloved's attendants swore that he would find his bride in his bed that night did the prince allow the ribbons to be cut. Then the women swept Beloved off amid jokes, laughter, and humorous advice.

Beloved sat by the fire in the prince's—and now her—bedchamber. She was still barefoot, but she had been undressed and bathed; tonight she had been grateful for the help. Her attendants had brushed her hair and clothed her in a pretty nightgown embroidered with flowers, fruit, and forest animals. After good wishes from the *damashi* and affectionate embraces from Dris, Rue, and Gladna, Beloved was alone at last. She looked about, relishing the quiet. There seemed to be a lot of green branches in the room and more of the spicy-scented flowers. She had just begun to wonder how long it would take for Radvyed to arrive, when she heard loud male laughter and singing that was more hearty than tuneful. Beloved stood, uncertain about what would happen next. "Do not worry; you have no more duties," the queen had reminded her. "Only Radvyed will enter. His friends will accompany him to the door and may well be full of boisterous cheer, but they will soon leave." Beloved had promised to remember. Now, listening to Radvyed's friends jokingly insisting they wanted to come in and make sure those women had kept their word and had returned his bride to him, she was glad of the queen's assurances.

There came a pounding on the door and then Radvyed's voice shouted, "Wife!"

"Yes, Husband?" she answered, and heard the approval of the crowd of friends.

"Open the door!" he demanded.

Beloved, remembering the rote reply she had been taught as she was bathed and changed, responded, "Only to you, Husband! Send your friends away!" More roaring approval.

"And you, Wife? Are you alone? For I want no other in our chamber!" Radvyed shouted his own part to more cheering.

"There is only I to welcome you, Husband," she replied.

"Open the door, then, Wife, that I may come in," he said more quietly; she knew he stood hard by the door. Even the friends subsided a little, waiting.

Suddenly she felt this silly game of shouting through the door was not so silly. This also was part of the marriage rite. She turned the handle and opened the door.

Radvyed was shoved inside the room. He immediately turned and slammed the door closed in the faces of his friends, who pretended to try to follow him in. Beloved was jolted out of her moment of thoughtfulness and into startled laughter. He leaned his back against the door and pulled her to him. They stood there, looking at each other, listening as the friends aired their final witticisms and then moved away, full of plans for more revelry. And then, there they were, Beloved and Radvyed.

He had not just been drinking toasts with friends, she saw, but had also been allowed to bathe and change into more informal, comfortable clothing: matching loose shirt and pants. He looked magnificent still, but somehow more approachable, her own Radvyed, her Husband, from whom she had had to be separate during the time of their official betrothal. But now they were bound together before witnesses divine and mortal and no one could pretend to divide them again.

He was smiling at her, what she thought of as his deep smile, because it was less an expression on his face than a contentment he radiated. She smiled back. The long, lonely years seemed nothing but a painful dream that was fading.

Radvyed said, "May I have this dance?" and when Beloved nodded, he took her more fully into his embrace, and kissed her while turning them in slow dreamy circles until they reached the bed, which was hung with flowers and green branches. Then, still kissing, and though they had this whole night and the sweetness of many others before them, they fell with clumsy urgency onto the bed, and into each other, and made love from joy.

Chapter Twenty-Nine

The next morning Radvyed woke up and rolled over to see whether Beloved was awake. She was sleeping on her side, her face toward him, her hand curled by her cheek. Her marriage bracelet, of silver links and blue stones, was just visible. He glanced down at his own bracelet made of gold and topaz. Rubbing a finger over it, he remembered how they had exchanged them last night, replacing the wedding ribbons with the more durable jewelry. He watched his wife for a while, contentedly listening to her quiet breathing. Beloved's features were relaxed and peaceful. Radvyed's eyes lingered on the curve of her cheek and throat; he smiled. He wanted to touch her skin, to kiss her, but decided not to disturb her. Radvyed rolled the other way and sat on the edge of the bed. It seemed to be early—dawn, perhaps. Cool gray light felt its way through an unshuttered window. Radvyed blinked and looked around. He did not recognize the room. The furnishings were now carved of a lighter wood. *Surely that green stone statue was not here last night.* He became aware that a muffled disturbance troubled the corridor. Radvyed stood and pulled on a robe, still looking about at the unfamiliar furnishings, and walked over to the door.

He opened it and found four *damashi*, three women and one man, in the hall. The man seemed to be counting doors, the youngest woman had a tear-streaked face, and a second woman had an arm around the first and was looking around the corridor with a puzzled but determined air. The oldest woman was looking about her with baffled indignation. It was not difficult to understand the cause of the commotion. It seemed his bedchamber was not alone in having undergone a change in the night. The corridor, formerly tiled with large marble squares of black, white, and russet, was now flagged with glossy stones of pale gold and overlaid with patterned carpets of deep green and violet. The walls that had been hung the night before with a series of tapestries representing scenes of boar hunting, falconry, and archery, were now richly painted with mythical beasts cavorting in a golden-limbed forest. At intervals there climbed up from ceramic pots of indigo and cream a sweet-smelling vine of the tenderest green, with pale blue flowers streaked with pink. It wandered along the tops of the walls, near the ceiling, trailing tendrils. The busts of his ancestors that had lined the hall, each set upon its own stately pedestal, were re-placed with enormous porcelain vases inscribed with swirling designs of cobalt and gold. The whole corridor, thought Radvyed, radiated lighthearted contentment and deep happiness. Unfortunately for the palace staff, they had not spent several weeks in Beloved's Hidden House, and rather than viewing the redecoration of the corridor with amused pleasure, as he himself did, they were instead in a state of disorientation and bewilderment.

"Good rising," Radvyed greeted them. The tearstained young woman stifled a small shriek, while the other three looked at him with relief.

"Good rising, Your Radiance. We are sorry to have disturbed you," answered the eldest woman, Podemina. "Mesha came on this hall to set about her usual work, but when she got here, the hall where she was supposed to be working was not here." The older *damasha* had not completely recuperated from the shock of an entire hallway's appearance having changed overnight, thought Radvyed. The woman looked at him. "Is this your chamber and hall, Your Radiance?"

"It is," Radvyed answered. "I am sorry that you have been upset, Mesha, but there is nothing to fear. If you recall, Princess Beloved is a sorceress. Sometimes things change when she is about."

"The number of doors is the same," said the *damash* helpfully to Podemina, who was slightly mollified by the prince's explanation of the change of décor.

"We beg your pardon for having disturbed you, Your Radiance," said Podemina. She looked around once more, her calm recovered. "Perhaps we should begin work on another floor first." Radvyed nodded. "Come along, Mesha, you can help Tani in the ballroom. Nothing has changed *there*, I believe." And supporting a shaky Mesha with a firm hand under her elbow, Podemina nodded to Radvyed and bustled down the hall, ducking under a particularly exuberant tendril of vine on the way. The *damash* followed more slowly—he seemed to be fascinated by the playful beasts on the wall. The third *damasha* picked up the brush and ashpan abandoned by Mesha and counted her way back from the prince's door to another room. Before slipping inside, she lightly touched one of the pink-streaked blue flowers and smiled.

Radvyed withdrew into the bridal chamber. He looked about the room and sighed. He walked over to the bed and sat on the edge near where Beloved lay sleeping. Leaning over, Radvyed kissed her cheek, then the tender rim of ear peeking through her hair. She stirred, but did not wake. He picked up a hand, kissed it, played with her fingers, and gently but urgently called her name. Her eyes opened and blinked. She smiled at him.

"Beloved, you must wake up."

She yawned and sat up. "Yes, Husband? Is there some marriage-morning rite that we must perform?"

He laughed. "No, my heart. But we seem to have distressed some of the *damashi*."

Now he had her attention. "We have?" Beloved tightened her fingers around his. "What is the matter?"

"The appearance of our chamber and the hall outside have changed. I do not know if other rooms and corridors have also been affected." Startled, Beloved flicked him a glance and then looked about.

As her eyes ran over the room and its furnishings, Radvyed realized that the changes were not immediately obvious to her. He remembered how Rue had required a moment or two to sharpen her sight, or perhaps train it in some other way inexplicable to him, back at the Hidden House.

"Yes, I see," murmured Beloved. "And you say that outside our door as well...?"

"Yes. A young *damasha* was frightened and upset, a *damash* was intrigued, another *damasha* surprised but not overset, and Podemina, one of the senior *damashi*, was annoyed. She felt the new things an affront to the dignity of the *damashi*, I believe."

"A *damasha* was frightened?" Beloved looked around their chamber. "Is there anything frightening in the hall?" She rose and Radvyed stood with her. Beloved pulled on a robe and they moved together towards the door.

"Nothing frightening at all," he said, opening the door, "if one is accustomed to overnight changes of furnishings, paint, and flooring. I think it was the unexpected and startling change that alarmed her, not that she found anything particularly frightening in itself."

Beloved stepped out. She extended a hand and twined a vine tendril about one finger. Then she glanced at him. "And you? What do you think?"

Radvyed smiled at her. "I? I think my wife is content and pleased, and so am I." Then his smile faded a little. "But we are no longer at your Hidden House, and there are more than our feelings to consider."

Chapter Thirty

Queen Gladna waited until late morning to send a message to the newlywed couple, requesting their presence in her sitting room for breakfast in half an hour. Radvyed eyed the *damash* who had brought the summons. It was the same one who had been outside the chamber door that morning.

"And what do you think of the new furnishings, Pelya?" he inquired of the man. "Do they disturb you as they did Mesha?"

The *damash* was a little surprised at being asked, but readily answered. "No, Your Radiance. They do not disturb me." Since the prince continued to look at him encouragingly, he added, "It is only that the new things were so unexpected." Radvyed smiled at him but said nothing more, letting him go.

Beloved was still puzzled that the household staff had been disturbed at all. As they walked to the queen's chambers, Radvyed wondered how early the Hidden House had begun changing its appearance with Beloved's moods, hopes, and fears. She had been tightly bound to the Hidden House. No, how had she called it? She had claimed it. Hence, it had displayed, not so much its mistress's taste or history or wealth, but the treasures and torments of a soul denied almost every normal, more mundane, form of expression. And she seemed convinced that his family line was also magically connected to the earth and people of Tamtir in some way.

As they walked, Beloved and Radvyed evaluated the chambers and corridors through which they passed, but it seemed only their own apartments and the hallway outside had been overtly affected by her happiness. She did not notice, as Radvyed did, the peeping around corners and doors of the *damashi*, or the subtler, but pervasive, assessing glances, tinged with wariness, that the other denizens of the palace cast towards the new princess. The prince saw that his people were beginning to understand what magic might mean, besides throwing roses to a crowd. His mother was right to address the matter without delay. He did not want the people fearing or avoiding Beloved.

At last they approached the door to the queen's sitting room. A *damash* rapped at the door with his fist before flinging it open and calling, "Prince Radvyed and Princess Beloved, Your Splendor!" As they passed into the room Gladna turned away from the window where she had been standing and came towards them, smiling.

"Good rising, daughter," she said, taking Beloved's hands in hers and kissing her on each cheek. Gladna smiled to see the wedding bracelet gleaming on Beloved's arm. "Please, sit down," the queen invited. She gestured toward the prettily set table in the middle of the room. She turned to her son. "Good rising, my handsome boy," she said, and kissed him as well.

He kissed her cheek and answered, "Good rising, Mother."

Once they were seated, Gladna urged them to help themselves from the platters of cheese and fruit and pastries. *No damashi about for this conversation*, thought Radvyed, and glanced at Beloved. She was giving all her attention to pouring herself a cup of *chelek* and trying not to spill it. It was one of the tasks that still challenged her, as it required a dexterity that she did not yet fully possess.

The queen waited until everyone had helped themselves to food and drink, and then said, "There was a surprise this morning on your corridor." Beloved set down the piece of fruit she had just picked up and gave Gladna her full attention.

"Yes," said Radvyed. "A young *damasha* was a bit upset when she saw that the furnishings had been replaced overnight."

"Not replaced," corrected Beloved.

The queen raised her brows, but said, "Not only new furnishings, I think, but also an exuberant flowering vine?"

"Yes, that is new," admitted Beloved. She leaned forward a little. "Were the furnishings frightening or disturbing to the *damasha*? What I saw seemed, to my eye at least, pleasant and pretty."

Gladna set her cup of *chelek* down gently and looked thoughtfully at Beloved. "You do not understand why she found them disturbing?"

Beloved was silent a moment. "The chambers are all accessible, all in the same places as they were yesterday. The stairs and corridors all lead where they have always led, obeying the will of the master and the mistress of the house." *The king and queen*, thought Radvyed. "There are even the same kinds of items in the same places: beds, chests, wall decorations, and so on. I grant that the appearance of these things is changed, and that perhaps the living vine is unusual—although again, it does not seem a plant to inspire fear."

Gladna propped her elbows on the table, clasped her hands, and rested her chin upon them. She regarded Beloved with bemusement. "So it seems no great thing to you that ancient tapestries appear to have vanished, busts of the prince's ancestors are seemingly lost, and the floor originally laid down when the palace was first built has been replaced?"

Beloved looked at Radvyed and then at the queen again. "Your Splendor is saying that the things, the forms themselves, are of great importance to the household? They must stay the same at all times?"

Gladna paused before answering. *She is beginning to realize how differently Beloved has lived*, thought Radvyed. Then the queen said, "Yes."

Beloved frowned in thought. "Yet things change all the time, or else why would you have *damashi* to tend the house? Dirt accumulates, time and use wear things away. Do these changes disturb the household?"

Gladna stared at her daughter-in-law, not so much bemused now, as trying to understand the other woman's thought. "Those are normal, expected changes. Part of the work of the palace staff is to maintain items—unchanged, if you like—by cleaning and repairing."

Beloved sat back. She looked down and picked up her cloth napkin, unfolded it, and held it up. "And when the spinner spins the fiber into thread, and the weaver makes it into cloth, so that it no longer resembles at all either flax or wool, is that change disturbing? Or when the smith melts a horseshoe and reforms it into nails?"

"No," said Gladna slowly. "Those changes disturb no one. They are familiar and one can see and understand each step."

"Can one?" asked Beloved. "To me such work by hands is 'magic.' I can only with concentration pour myself *chelek*, or shape letters with a pen, or comb my own hair." There was a pause as the prince and queen absorbed Beloved's words. Beloved carefully refolded the napkin, thinking. She looked up. "Are your people, Your Splendor, alarmed by seeing a plant grow from a seed, or a tree from a nut? Is every step there known and understood?" asked Beloved.

Gladna's brow furrowed as she sought to understand Beloved's point of view. The queen spoke gently, trying to help Beloved understand in her turn. "No, Beloved, they are not alarmed by seeing plants grow or smiths or spinners at work. But they *are* alarmed by things they know disappearing overnight, replaced by other things that they have never seen before. Plants that appear out of nowhere and overgrow a palace corridor alarm them. These changes are unnatural. That is why they disturb."

Beloved flinched at the word *unnatural*, but then controlled her expression. She seemed to be looking inward again, so Radvyed spoke. "Mother, I think the problem is that for Beloved the changes you mention *are* natural. That is why she is having difficulty understanding why others might find them upsetting. Recall how I described to you the Hidden House."

"Yes, my son," Gladna answered. "I do recall it. And I also recall you saying how you found it strange, disorienting, and difficult to discover a new chamber, a new house, and new grounds every day. I think you would have found it so even if the corridors, rooms, and gardens did not stray about like milling sheep." Gladna was not usually so blunt. She was, it seemed, more rattled than she had wanted to reveal. The queen looked at Beloved, who was still lost in thought. "I would like the corridor, at least, and your apartment, if possible, restored to their former arrangements." Beloved came out of her thoughts and met Gladna's eyes. "Many of the items are heirlooms. I would like the *damashi* not to be upset in this manner in the future. If you would like to change things, you may do it the usual way."

When Beloved opened her mouth to speak, the queen held up her hand. Radvyed blinked in surprise at his mother's severity; Beloved closed her lips firmly. "Radvyed will tell you what the usual way is." She saw that Beloved was not going to protest, and her manner gentled. She picked up Beloved's hand. "You can restore all as it was, can you not?"

Beloved silently nodded, then looked away.

Gladna sighed. "I know you meant no harm, and I am sorry to have to speak to you in this way. The first days of coming into a new family and household are not always easy, I know. We are all learning about each other. Please remember that I am very happy to be able to call you my daughter." Beloved's eyes were rather moist, but no tear fell. She merely nodded once more.

Gladna watched her daughter-in-law's profile a moment in silence, opened her mouth as if to speak, and then closed it. She stood. Radvyed and Beloved rose to their feet.

"Please stay and finish your meal," Gladna said. "I go to reassure the king that all is well: only a minor misunderstanding." She moved to the door, paused, and turned. "The sooner the better, please, Beloved." The queen went out.

Radvyed and Beloved both sat back down. Beloved picked up a fork, laid it down again, inadvertently knocking it against a crystal goblet. Radvyed's hand shot out, catching the cup before anything was spilled or broken. Beloved smiled sadly at him. "To me, such actions are not so simple. But they do not frighten me."

"I do not think of you as unnatural," said Radvyed.

"Was my house so terrible to live in, then? So inhospitable?"

"No." He paused. "It was something new to me, yes, and strange. Is not this palace and its ways strange to you? But I grew to like the ways of your Hidden House. I began to seek out the changes, as clues to what you might be thinking or feeling, as signs to what path or line of action I must pursue."

Beloved looked away from him.

Radvyed moved so that he was back in her line of sight and picked up the hand she had balled in her lap. "I thought your house wondrous, and perplexing, and magical, and beautiful. If I had not been consumed by the fear of my mother's death, I would have enjoyed it more."

She did not smile, but she did not turn away.

He watched her for a moment longer, then said, "You are still puzzled that the form, as you call it, of things is so important to us."

Beloved lifted her head and answered, "Yes."

Radvyed thought about that. "Yet forms are important. Did not the name curse bind you by assuming the form of a poisonous vine?"

"I do not harm or constrain living beings by altering a tapestry. My changes are not permanent or malevolent."

He cocked his head. *She will always see everything differently from the rest of us. Do Rue and Dris also see with her eyes?* The thought flickered in his mind, but at the moment he was trying to help her understand. How could he explain?

"You admire the work of a spinner or a smith," Radvyed said at last. Beloved nodded.

"Consider this then, that these things in the palace—the floors, the tapestries, the statues—everything is made by hand, by the skill of some craftsperson or artisan or laborer. When you change them, people are upset at the magic of it, but they also grieve the loss of those made things, and all the work and knowledge, the history, they represent. They may even think that you value those things as nothing."

Beloved watched him as he spoke, her eyes widening. "I forget. Everything here is made by hand." She bit her lip and looked away. "It is all so strange," she said, almost to herself. She drew her hand from his and passed it over her face. Then she looked back at Radvyed. "I am sorry. I see now...I have been unkind."

He took her hand again. "Not unkind...unknowing." They sat together, each thinking about what was natural and what was strange.

"I am not hungry. Are you?" Beloved said after a while.

"No," said Radvyed.

"Then let us restore all as the queen desires," said Beloved, standing. Radvyed stood as well. She led him a little ways from the table. "Do you recall how everything was before?"

"Yes."

"Good." She kept his hand in hers. "Let us begin at the far end of the corridor and proceed towards our bedroom at the other end. Close your eyes and imagine we are walking down it, with everything as it was."

A short while later they were treading the corridor leading to their apartments. Radvyed had been charged with examining everything and informing Beloved if something was not as it should be. If he noticed something unfamiliar, he stopped and told her. She would hold one of his hands and place her other hand on the irregular object. He would hold the image of what the object should look like in his mind, thinking about its meaning and history. When he looked at the thing again, it would be as he had remembered it, down to the last detail and sign of wear. He found it odd, but it was plain that to Beloved this was a slightly tedious but not particularly complicated task.

"Can you do this with anyone's aid?" Radvyed asked after they had made sure their bedchamber was returned to the state of the day before. He adjusted his wedding bracelet. The weight felt strange and warm on his wrist. "Or is it only because of our bond?"

She looked away from him, as if remembering something she was not particularly proud of. "It depends on how determined I am to see into another's mind, and how capable their resistance is," she said.

"Also, many people have vague thoughts and memories, whereas you hold all these things firmly and clearly in your mind…but you are right, our bond helps."

She sat down in a chair by the fire, now once more upholstered in a rusty brocade shot with gold thread. She was subdued, no longer the joyful young woman who had illuminated the Glade with her radiance just the day before.

Radvyed sat on the arm of her chair. "Is it truly that necessary to you, to change the appearance of things where you live?"

She laid her head back against the seat and looked up at him. "Necessary? No. Only one more thing to remember, to be careful about."

He stroked her hair back from her face. "Are there so many?"

She closed her eyes, smiling at the question. "Remember that in the Hidden House was the hidden Hideous. No *dovoreni* or *damashi*, no adoring people, no charming but royal in-laws, no rules but those that Rue and I devised."

"No handsome prince," he teased. At last he won a genuine laugh from her. She opened her eyes and smiled at him more freely. The hazy worry that had begun to form in his mind faded away.

"True! And being with him is well worth an accommodation or two to the life of a princess."

"I think," said Radvyed, drawing her up and into his arms, "that we newlyweds have had a very strenuous morning."

"Oh?" said Beloved. "Is the prince tired from walking to his mother's sitting room, breakfasting there, and strolling back?" Radvyed was pleased that she was learning to tease him back in this way.

He began to turn her slowly in a couple's dance around the room, enjoying the sparkle in her eyes and relishing the way she entrusted herself to him as they moved. "Awoken by disturbed *damashi*, summoned to the queen's presence, lectured on the nature of being and change, and used as an assistant in the magical restoration of various objects and rooms."

Beloved laughed and he swirled her once more.

"I feel faint merely thinking about it," Radvyed added.

"Perhaps you should lie down, then."

"Perhaps I should," he said, and with a last vigorous twirl, he swung her onto the bed, then fell down beside her. And as he had hoped, no sadness lingered in her face. "Perhaps I should," he repeated, and rolled towards her, and kissed her.

Chapter Thirty-One

For a week there were no further changes to the palace or the younger royal couple's apartments. The *damashi* recovered their equilibrium and Beloved's days were full of various resumed lessons and studies, helping her to understand better how the kingdom was run. She liked to learn and she knew how to observe and listen. As before the wedding, one day her lessons might involve following the queen about for the morning; another day she might tour the city with Zhelez, her history tutor. Radvyed picked up duties that had been too long neglected or temporarily assigned to another. The chamberlain, *Dovorena* Pravlyana, was asked to present a plan for the prince and his new princess to tour the kingdom, so that Beloved might be introduced more widely to the people.

A month after the wedding, the king and queen held what they called an informal ball. The purpose was to give the prince and new princess another opportunity to mingle with *mireni* and *dovoreni*, as well as merchants, artisans, and scholars resident in Zolatar. Beloved and Radvyed were expected to speak a few words to each of the hundreds of guests. Beloved was to learn as many faces, names, and histories as possible, with Radvyed as her guide. The guests, for their part, were still taking their measure of the new princess. Some rumors about a redecorated hallway had spread, in the sensational and inaccurate manner of rumors, and people were wondering what kind of person Beloved was: Was she truly magical? How foreign was she? Was her father really an evil sorcerer? Was the new princess amiable, kind, shrewd?

It did not take many conversations for Beloved to realize a few things: an informal ball had its own etiquette; Radvyed was a skilled politician and diplomat, all while seeming merely a charming and handsome prince; and, most disconcerting of all to her, most of the people she spoke with had very little idea of what the salt curse was, how the queen had been healed, or what magic was. Beloved's life had been based on the fact that power (or magic, as Radvyed and his parents called it) was an elemental force: she was taken aback by the tacit assumptions that the dangers and depredations of the salt curse were exaggerated (this from those whose lands were far from the western borders) and that the queen had been cured by some foreign concoction that Tamtireni apothecaries were now replicating in their stillrooms. Beloved's casting of thousands of roses upon the crowds that first day was seen as a charming trick, rather than the powerful expression of her response to the people's joy that she knew it to be. The latest episode of redecorating portions of the palace was seen as an immature prank by some and as a high-spirited joke by others. Whether by the queen's will or the discretion of the *damashi*, or both, most thought that Beloved (and possibly Radvyed as well) had physically moved one set of furnishings out and another in.

On the whole, Radvyed thought, Beloved was taking his people's ignorance of the ways of magic fairly well. She did not seem to feel the need to correct anyone, although she was so surprised by their not taking sorcery seriously that she hesitated to respond to their remarks. Beloved did cast him a few incredulous looks when some imperious dame or pompous youth explained to her how no curse could possibly be as strong as the salt was said to be (*Mere exaggeration by simple minds, my dear!*) or that the queen must not have been as ill as the king had feared (*For she recovered, which speaks for itself! How could she have been deathly ill?*). Radvyed handled these obtuse and tactless interlocutors so adroitly that they never realized that they had been dismissed, but instead retained a memory of the prince listening cour-teously to them. *The princess, though—she seemed a little less gracious. Well, she is a foreigner, poor thing, and still somewhat awkward.*

The ill-informed and oblivious were easier for Beloved to understand, however, than those who believed a light tone of malice gave their manner a sophisticated edge. While no one was stupid or malev-olent enough to insult the princess to her face, there were those who could not resist testing her with pointed wit, trying to see how sharp Beloved was, how alert to shades of meaning. Would she respond in kind, with thin mockery? Would she crumple at a hint of unkindness? Or would she even have the intelligence to realize that she was being pricked? Radvyed himself did not know the answer, although he knew that if Beloved did not understand that she was being tested, it would not be from lack of wit on her part, but only lack of experience at court, and in interactions with other people generally. Subtlety had not seemed to be a hallmark of her dealings with people thus far in her life.

There had already been one or two conversations that had caused Beloved's eyebrows to draw together. Radvyed observed that she marked those speakers, following them with her gaze, as he guided her to other guests. *Yes*, he thought. *She noticed. And she is now thinking over their remarks.*

It was a few moments later that Beloved found a chance to say to him, "Husband, that woman in the dark blue—*Dovorena* Galetza, I believe—and the man in red—*Dovoren* Panovri—"

"Yes, Beloved?"

"It seemed to me that their words were not straight, were…" She broke off, frustrated at not being able to articulate her discomfort with the conversation. "Their words did not match what they were saying," she said.

"Yes. Sometimes people, especially at court, have, as you say, words that do not match their meaning."

"Why?"

Radvyed gave a laugh, not sure how to begin answering. "Words can be used as weapons or tools, as you know." She nodded. "You have experienced them at the best and worst extremes, but sometimes people like to play games with them, sometimes friendly, sometimes less so."

One of the king's ministers then came up to them, desiring to present to them a woman who turned out to be an important merchant. After they had finished their talk with her, Beloved returned to their earlier topic.

"How is it that some of your people would play unfriendly word games with you, the prince?"

"*Dovorena* Galetza and *Dovoren* Panovri were not playing games with me, or at least not directly. They were trying to find out about you, to learn what kind of person you are."

"But why in that way?"

"They are close in rank to the royal house. Their ancestors have married into our House before, and their children might marry my cousins or other relatives. So this edge to their talk reminds me that I am not so far above them, and so, since all your rank derives from your marriage to me, neither are you."

They broke off to greet some more people. Radvyed spoke to a passing *damash*, and they were brought fresh glasses of wine and a small plate of finger food.

When they were alone again, Beloved said flatly, "They are not equal to you in rank. They have some small power, but it is obvious to anyone who can see that your House is royal and theirs are not."

Radvyed blinked at her, not sure what to say.

"And," she continued, "if they think my rank, or command of power, derives solely from my marriage to you, they are stupid."

The prince was surprised into a laugh in mid-drink. Beloved reflected that he even choked on his wine gracefully, and felt herself still more awkward in comparison, as she tried to stand, drink, eat, and converse without mishap.

"Beloved, I do not think they perceive rank as you do. Let us agree that if they are stupid, they deserve your mercy more than your anger."

She gave him a straight look. "I do not like it when people say one thing and mean another."

The prince sobered. "Sometimes being indirect can avert hostilities when a frank declaration would only inflame them." He saw that Beloved was still not convinced. She said nothing, but looked away. "Beloved," Radvyed said, and she looked at him. "Here I know how power is wielded. Trust me. No one here means you real harm. They test only your quickness, your temper, and your courage."

She held his gaze and the line of her mouth was stern. Radvyed caught a movement out of the corner of one eye: someone else to be presented.

"Beloved," he said again, willing her to listen to him. Her eyes still on his, she gave a short nod, then took another sip of wine before the next introduction.

Radvyed thought that after their exchange, Beloved seemed more wary when people were presented to her, and he was sorry for it. She had begun, he thought, to relax as she had in the outerlands, immediately after the curse was broken, when ragged people crept out of nowhere to receive the warmth of a word from her or the ease of her touch. Once they had crossed the border, she had pulled herself in; then, when the king had introduced her to the people out on the square, she had radiated joy. The past few weeks, Radvyed now understood, Beloved had been trying to find the right level of openness. Now she was more guarded, but he hoped as she became more accustomed to the ways of their people, she would be able to adjust to them more comfortably and naturally.

Yet he thought that on the whole all was going well, until they turned and found *Mirena* Lioda and *Miren* Rezh before them, with their respective spouses. Lioda and Rezh held lands close to the royal city, the former on the northern edge of Zolatar and the latter to the southeast, and they enjoyed the small intrigues and petty rivalries of the court. Their lands were well-run, but they were both known more for tight justice than for open mercy. Radvyed smiled and presented them and their spouses to Beloved, who had stiffened slightly as soon as their eyes met hers, but she also smiled, if not with great warmth.

A few idle remarks on the weather were exchanged, and Radvyed began to think they would be rid of the smirking pair with no trouble when Lioda, idly turning a jeweled bangle on her arm, said, "Lady of Light, what a hideous dress that girl has on." She looked at a girl, no more than fifteen, who was indeed wearing an unflattering gown. Beloved had gone still at the word *hideous*.

Radvyed ignored Lioda's comment. He was about to ask her husband, Krotok, about his falcon, when Rezh said, "Yes, she seems to be cursed with parents with no eye for fashion. Her father is a spice merchant, salt and seasonings, you know, and her mother seems to be from a family of gardeners."

Radvyed kept his face easy and neutrally pleasant. The relationship between Beloved and the master of the Griefstone was not a secret, but the royal family had not emphasized it. The fact that Dris was her aunt was made public, of course, during the rite in the Master's Hall. The two were prodding Beloved, to see how she would react to having her family and her past alluded to: would she understand their references? Would she be abashed or apologetic?

Radvyed pretended not to understand their remarks and so hoped to deprive them of the satisfaction of having scored a hit. Krotok was looking at his wife with a confused but resigned expression. *Mirena* Trula, Rezh's wife, did not understand the point of her husband's comments, but she knew that he was saying something a little unkind, and she looked anxiously first at the prince and then at the princess. Beloved's face was stony and she said nothing. She seemed to be staring at a point over Lioda's right shoulder.

Lioda laughed and turned her bracelet again. "I wonder if her mother chose her dress? Truly, such parents are nothing but a grief to their children."

Rezh smiled thinly at his friend's response, but his eyes stayed on Beloved's face.

Radvyed glanced at her. Beloved looked calmly resolute. She brought her gaze to Lioda, first to the glittering eyes, then to the slight, malicious smile. Her eyes dropped to the jeweled bangle, and finally to the *mirena*'s dress, which was embroidered with twining flowers about the bodice and overskirt.

"Indeed, a lovely dress is a beautiful thing," said Beloved, and her hand reached toward the *mirena*'s bodice. The arm with the bracelet dropped, and Lioda stepped away from the unexpected gesture, but

Beloved's finger touched one of the flowers on Lioda's dress, high on the shoulder. "Beautiful and fragile," said Beloved, and the flowers writhed into life like enchanted snakes, up and down Lioda's dress. The woman shrieked and tried to pluck off the twisting flowers with both hands. Then the flowers burst into flames before quickly dying down. Lioda stared in horror at the black-and-ash-gray lines of burnt embroidery.

Beloved was not done, however. "One does not choose one's parents," she said softly, and lightly touched the elaborate twist of green silk at Rezh's throat before the shocked *miren* could back out of reach. The silk turned to a dark, muddy slime.

There was an uproar. Trula fainted into her beslimed husband's arms; Krotok pulled his wife aside, to keep her from saying something to the princess that the *mirena* would later regret. People nearby had stepped back aghast; people farther away pressed forward to see what the commotion was about. Radvyed saw his father, who was on the other side of the ballroom, dispatch someone to investigate the situation and report. The queen already had a *dovorena* speaking in her ear; Gladna's face was expressionless.

Radvyed turned to see what had become of Beloved in the confusion and saw her standing alone. Everyone had clearly decided that to be within reach of the princess in this mood was not wise. His wife's face was unreadable. In one hand she held a goblet of wine; the other was a fist at her side. She was a single, silent, still figure, alone amid the swirl and bustle, the gasps and exclamations of the crowd.

The prince watched her for a moment, but Beloved did not look at him. He pressed his lips together and turned away.

CHAPTER THIRTY-TWO

The ball limped to an end. *Damashi* were summoned to escort Lioda and Rezh to private chambers where the indignant *mireni* could tend to their lacerated feelings and spoiled garments. The queen announced a sudden headache and needed the care of her loving daughter-in-law forthwith; both royal ladies withdrew. The king and the prince remained to do what they could, each with their own charm, to soothe the rattled and dismayed guests and to calm the speculations and gossip of others who had instead found the events deliciously shocking.

When Radvyed returned to the bedchamber he shared with Beloved, he found her talking with Rue on the divan before the fire. He stood for a moment in the doorway, watching them. They fell silent and looked at him; Rue stood. She gave her heart-daughter a quick kiss and pressed Beloved's hand. Giving the prince a look full of meaning, which he decided he was too tired and irritated to decipher, she left.

Radvyed looked at Beloved, who was still sitting on the divan. She said nothing, but from the defiant expression on her face, he surmised that she was not planning to apologize. Radvyed did not want to discuss the affair now. He knew that there would be more than enough discussion the next day—with Beloved, with the king and queen, with the Council, and who knew who else. He was weary, angry that Beloved had not trusted him to handle the pettiness of the two courtiers, and frustrated with himself that he had not been able to avert the incident.

All he said was, "I am tired."

She nodded and rose from the divan. She did not approach him, but made herself ready for bed. That night they did not hold each other.

In the morning, Radvyed looked at his wife sitting across the little table where their breakfast was set. She was eating, but while she usually relished her food, today she seemed to be forcing herself to eat. She was quiet and did not meet his eyes. Beloved did not defend or try to explain her behavior of the night before. Radvyed was not sure she understood why it was objectionable, and not just because she was untaught in court life. What normal social life of any kind had she had? None at all—the tiny circle of herself and Rue, and the occasional detained mage or faltering prince. It was remarkable that her behavior at times like last night merely seemed ignorant and callous, rather than malicious and feral. Yet all the more reason to lean on the guidance he had given her to navigate the situation.

Or perhaps she simply does not know that people apologize and explain—that there can be amends, he thought.

He said, "Beloved." She looked at him and swallowed. He tried to read the mixture of emotions on her face. Defiance? Regret? Confusion? All that, perhaps, and also sadness. He held his hand out across the table. After a moment she laid her own in his. Their wedding bracelets clinked as they touched.

"Beloved, I understand that you were angry at their unpleasant game. But I asked you to trust me to deal with such situations, and you did not, and I was hurt and angry. Now we must calm people who wonder whether you can control your temper, and what *Mirena*

Lioda and *Miren* Rezh could have said to merit such retaliation. You cannot go about harming people with magic."

Radvyed saw her jaw set. Perhaps because she was refraining from pointing out that the *mireni* had not actually been harmed. "But one may go about harming people with words?" she said instead.

He sighed and reminded himself she was not being deliberately obtuse. *All is new to her. I must explain without accusing.* "Of course one should not go about hurting people with words or anything else, unless..." Here Radvyed stopped, realizing that his sentence was leading him in an unfortunate direction. Beloved might be new to Tamtir and to all kinds of interactions with other people, but she was not slow of understanding.

"Unless they deserve it?" She began to draw her hand away; he gripped it more tightly. She stopped.

"Listen, Beloved. When I asked you to trust me, I meant that you should trust me to deal with any unkindness. There are ways, expected ways, that one rebukes or corrects those who have given offense. And you do not have the authority—" He broke off when she gave an exasperated huff, her hand twitching under his.

"We are married. I am the princess. I am now, as I have been often told, of the royal House of Mirkamen. Do I not have the right, even the duty, to address offenses?" Beloved's unwavering gaze held challenge.

Radvyed swallowed an oath. "Yes. Yes, you do. But you do not yet know how. And until you do—"

"I see now," said Beloved, pulling her hand away. He let it go. "It is you who do not trust me. What if I had burned that woman to death where she stood? What if I had not merely covered the man in slime but in some foul poison? You do not trust my judgment in these matters, but more, you do not trust my knowledge and mastery of my power."

Radvyed said nothing. She was right. Not he, not his parents, no one in Tamtir, except Rue and Dris, really trusted Beloved with her sorcery. How could they? She was a stranger, she was possessed of powers none of them truly understood, and in addition, she was a young woman with the social education of a hermit. He sat back in his chair, his fingers gripping the armrests.

Beloved knotted her hands in her lap.

Radvyed took a deep breath and forced himself to relax. *If I can reason with the ambassador of Beshimia, I can reason with my wife.* He said, "You are right. We do not trust you. We cannot trust you until you know us better and we know you, and your magic, better. But can you believe me when I say that burning her dress and turning his cravat to mud was not the best way to handle their insinuations?"

Beloved looked at him, then away, and nodded.

"Magic is frightening because we do not know what it can do or what you will do with it. But everyone knows what damage words and blows can do, and people have learned how to anticipate, avoid, or defend against those kinds of harm."

Beloved nodded again. Radvyed looked at her averted face unhappily, not liking that there was a barrier still between them. *How I wish my words could do more good, but I am neither bard nor teacher.*

"Will you refrain from using magic in ways that frighten or disturb others?" asked Radvyed, and watched as Beloved bent her head and put a hand to her eyes. "Is it so much to ask?" he asked, his voice low.

She was silent, then said, "What uses of my power do not frighten or disturb?"

Radvyed drew breath to answer, but Beloved took her hand from her face, shook her head, and said quietly, "I will try to do as you ask."

He picked up her hand and pressed it to his lips. She looked at him, a look that was somehow both sad and—angry? He would have spoken again, but she drew her hand away and asked him to pass her the jam pot. Radvyed hesitated, seeing Beloved's lip tremble, but then decided he had made enough demands. After winning his point, he should now allow her to direct the conversation into less fraught paths. So he smiled and passed her the jam pot. In a few moments they were speaking of their plans for the day and he told himself to leave off worrying. He would do as she asked and trust her.

There was no avoiding a meeting with his parents about the incident of the night before. When they came into the queen's sitting room, the king was also present. Arkost was not sitting, but stood leaning with one arm on the mantelpiece, staring into the fire with his brows lowered. Gladna sat in her chair by the fire, calmly writing a letter at a delicate little table. Both looked up when Radvyed and Beloved were announced. It was noticeable that the *damasha* opening the door kept her distance from the princess. Beloved's posture stiffened, so that her spine was almost rigid, and she kept her hands close to her sides. Radvyed had a flash of her as Hideous, back in the Hidden House, trembling with the fruitless effort of controlling her ugliness—but then his mother spoke and he lost the quicksilver image.

"Beloved," said the queen, and her voice was both gentle and firm. "Please explain to me why you did what you did last night."

The king stopped leaning against the mantelpiece and crossed his arms over his chest. He did not appear to think that any reasonable explanation could be forthcoming.

Radvyed began, "Mother—" but fell silent when Gladna raised her hand.

"Radvyed, I heard your account last night. I would like to understand Beloved's views."

Radvyed tried again. "Beloved and I have spoken this morning, and she says—" He stopped once more, obedient to his mother's gesture.

"My son," said Gladna, "I understand that you care for your wife, and so you should. But Beloved and I must be able to speak to each other without you in the middle. Indeed, the princess must form direct connections with many, in the palace and out. You cannot stand between her and everyone else, no matter how good your intentions are."

Radvyed knew this was true, but he felt Beloved's inexperience and vulnerability keenly. He looked at her. She nodded. He gave both wife and mother a slight bow and went to stand by a window. His father caught his eye and Radvyed was a little cheered to see Arkost's slight smile. Then the king glanced at Beloved, the smile faded, and Radvyed's heart sank.

"Your Splendor," said Beloved, her voice clear and steady. "*Mirena* Lioda and *Miren* Rezh were using their words to hurt me. No more than little stings, it is true, but unexpected and painful. They were also harming with their words a girl whose only fault that I could see was to have a dress and perhaps parents they did not like. The prince told me that sometimes people use words this way to find out what other people are made of: are they strong or are they weak? So I thought, if they are trying to see what I am made of, why not give them what they seek and show them?"

Radvyed heard his father snort and glanced at him. He was surprised to see that the king had not reacted in anger, but was trying to stifle his amusement. Arkost turned back to the fire, composing his face into solemn lines. Radvyed had seen that very expression more than once after one of his own youthful escapades had ended unexpectedly. He looked at his mother, who kept her courteous gaze on Beloved.

His wife continued her account. "I taught them that I am not stupid, for I understood the stings that were hidden under their words, that I do not like being stung, and that I, too, can sting without warning. And now their curiosity is satisfied."

There was a moment of silence as the three Tamtireni contemplated the straightforward approach of the royal House's newest daughter.

At last Gladna said, "Beloved, I can see that you had your reasons for how you behaved, and that you did not act as you did because you simply took a dislike to *Mirena* Lioda and *Miren* Rezh, as some might think who did not hear the conversation."

Beloved frowned. "I *did* take a dislike to them. They are small-hearted and unkind."

"Yes, but not an unprovoked dislike. However, one cannot go about making one's dislike so open and—spectacular."

Beloved was puzzled. "They made their unkindness plain. That seemed to distress no one."

"That is not true, Beloved," Radvyed intervened. "Their spouses were uncomfortable and embarrassed. I also was not pleased."

"But you said and did nothing, nor did their husband and wife. How is it that they may be unkind, but I may not answer?"

The queen replied, "You may indeed answer, Beloved. It is the manner of your answer that is causing—let us say, more trouble than those two are worth. If you had answered with barbed words of your own, no one would be disturbed. Setting a person's clothes on fire is seen as an overly forceful response, as if you had swatted a fly with a hammer."

"It is not just a question of deeming words less damaging or forceful than action, Beloved," Radvyed added, as he watched her think about what his mother had said. "The use of magic is strange and frightening—I know, I know"—he broke off as Beloved turned to him, already drawing her breath to interrupt—"I know you consider that we are steeped in magic, and cannot believe we would be disturbed by a little thing like a cravat changing into slime after the rites of our wedding day. Please understand that we do not believe we have magic in Tamtir, and that even if we do, it is not used or manifested in the way that you use it."

"So," said Beloved. "Everyone here wields words as sword or shield, and they have learned how since childhood. But I have not, and when I answer differently, I disturb and frighten everyone."

"Because no one knows what you *can* or *will* do," said the deep, gruff voice of the king. "You throw off calculations when you act unpredictably. That upsets people."

Beloved pressed her lips together, staring over Radvyed's shoulder and out the window, seeing the Lady's Forest dark on the edge of the gardens. She thought of her life as Hideous, and to her surprise, discovered that there had been benefits to being a disgusting monster. People were too horrified, intimidated, or repelled to tell her what to do. No one was surprised that she had power and used it. Because the curse had poisoned and strangled her body, limiting her free movement and her interaction with other people, she had been nearly immobile and almost wholly isolated.

In her now liberated body, however, she looked like other people. She appeared normal. The court saw a young, foreign woman who was a little unpolished and somewhat ignorant. The healing of the queen was not generally attributed to her rose, for everyone "knew" that that was impossible. Yet even the king, queen, and prince—her own Husband!—had difficulty remembering that Beloved was not merely a young woman. Her peculiar history as well as her heritage of sorcery made her very different from any of them, no matter how many rites were performed to graft this unlikely branch to their tree.

I am still a monster, she thought, and the Forest blurred before her eyes. She blinked, straightened, and turned to the room. Arkost, Gladna, and Radvyed were looking at her with concern.

"Your people must not be disturbed," said Beloved.

"Beloved, it could have been answered differently," said Radvyed. "Please trust me to deal with these things, as I trusted you in your affairs."

Beloved looked at him. "Did you?"

"You will learn," said the king. "It takes time, but you will learn."

"Indeed, you have learned much already," added the queen.

"Is there any time I may use my—magic?" asked Beloved. There was a pause.

"What do you want to do?" Gladna asked.

Beloved looked at her, knowing that saying simply, "Breathe," would not make sense to them, even though that was the word that rose to her lips. She looked to Radvyed. His perfect brow was wrinkled, and he was looking at her, but not seeing her with his eyes. He looked like a man who was hearing a piece of far-off music and was trying to catch the melody.

He knows something is not right, she thought. *Help me, Husband.* But she could not think what to say and so said nothing.

"When you think of something you want to do, Beloved, let Radvyed know, and then we will see," said Arkost. He came away from the fireplace, clapping his hands in a way that made it clear the discussion was finished. "Good, I am glad we were able to have this little talk. And although it was not an appropriate way of answering and you should not do it again," he continued with a bit of a smile hidden in his beard, "I think you have discouraged at least two from thoughtlessly unkind speech."

After exchanging a few more words, the king and queen left to go about their business for the day.

Radvyed and Beloved returned in silence to their rooms, each lost in thought.

"Beloved, all is not well with you. I can feel it," said Radvyed as soon as the door shut. "Tell me."

Beloved turned and looked at him. *You are so perfect, so loved,* she thought. *You have been cherished and have known your place in the world since you first knew there was a world. Everything is easy; everything makes sense to you. Except me. Your face and your heart, your inner and outer selves are reflections of each other. Mine did not match when I was Hideous, or at least I strove to prove they did not, and yet they do not seem to match now. So I am still hidden.*

But what she said was, "I am strange and monstrous. The opposite of you."

Radvyed's jaw dropped and he looked at her, stunned and appalled. "*What?*"

"I am. My power is frightening, unnatural, disturbing."

"Your *power* may be, but *you* are not!"

"Radvyed, my power is part of me! It is like saying my blood is terrifying but I am not!" She took a breath and then, hearing his answer once more in her mind, looked at him with shocked eyes. "Do *you* think my power is unnatural and disturbing?"

His hands—hands that had loved her so sweetly, had touched her hair, her skin, had made her feel like she was precious and lovely—hung by his sides as he tried to find words.

"It is a part of you I am still learning," Radvyed said at last. "The breaking of the Tower—the outlands healed—the days in the Hidden House—the rose from your inner garden that still refreshes my mother—all these are proofs of the depth and range of your magic, and yet none seem to have yet exhausted you. It is all new to me, that such magic exists and can perform such works. But unnatural and disturbing, no, Beloved."

Now he came to her and put his hand to her cheek, cradling it. "You are what you are and are nothing like anyone I have known. You are like a beautiful plant or bird brought from a faraway land. You are not unnatural. You are rare and fascinating. And I am lucky to be your husband," he finished, bending towards her to murmur his last words into her hair.

Beloved closed her eyes. She felt his kiss on her ear, and sighed, and let herself be persuaded that all would be well.

Neither Radvyed nor Beloved thought about the imported plants or birds that sometimes sickened or died in the land to which they had been brought as specimens or pets: stunted, forlorn marvels in hothouses and cages.

Chapter Thirty-Three

From then on Radvyed noticed a difference in how Beloved carried herself. *She is holding herself in again,* he thought, *even more tightly than before.* Earlier, when she had crossed into Tamtir and then she had arrived at the palace, she had held herself close because she was a guest. She was assessing the new place, the new life, even the newly freed body she found herself in. Now she contained herself because she had been warned against doing anything startling or unusual.

He did not think that was the result his mother had aimed for. The queen, no doubt, had thought that asking Beloved to refrain from redecorating the royal heir's apartments while sleeping and to forbear expressing her annoyance by setting embroidery on fire was the equivalent of asking children to leave porcelain ornaments alone. But Radvyed realized that there was something more at work.

For one thing, Beloved was still learning what was considered "usual." As she had told Gladna, activities that everyone else saw as ordinary she found remarkable, even fascinating. For another, curious, active children were pointed to appropriate times and places to exercise their inquisitiveness and restlessness: *Do not touch the porcelain here, but you may explore the woods there.*

Beloved said nothing to Radvyed to suggest she suffered discomfiture or uneasiness. Troubled by a vague but persistent disquiet, he inquired whether she were well. Did she lack anything, or require some amenity or service? Beloved smiled and assured him she was hale and in need of nothing. When he asked directly about the undefined constraint he felt sure she bore, she kissed him and said she was simply settling into life at the palace. In the end, he allowed himself to believe that what he sensed must be only the awkwardness of a stranger adjusting to new circumstances.

But Beloved had discovered that she could take nothing for granted. She had assumed that her official marriage to the prince had made her a full part of the House, but now she saw this was not so. The House must shape her, form her, train her into proper princesshood. She wondered why it felt so much like being pruned, even caged. The clamp she set on her power hindered it from rooting into the palace, into Tamtir, leaving her untethered and insecure. Yet Beloved could see that the more tightly she controlled herself and watched her every gesture, the more people seemed to relax around her—although a few, Beloved thought, would never feel at ease.

It was a little more than two weeks after the incident at the ball that Beloved woke very early, when the pale gray of false dawn was just revealing the world outside. Yet the window did not let in much of that faint light. Something seemed to be obstructing it. Something that was not a shutter—although the nights were cold, they had left the shutters open last night and had closed only the frames paned with thick glass. She slid out of bed, careful not to disturb Radvyed. She looked back at him, savoring the sight of him asleep, sprawled on his stomach, the pillow bunched under his head in that way he had, his face sweetly at rest. She stood and paused; she felt strange this morning, leaden and stiff. Puzzling over her odd achiness, she went to the window.

As she drew nearer to it, her heart seemed to freeze for a moment, then to beat once more with horrible, painful, slow thumps. Her stomach gave a sickening dip, then knotted. She could not open the window more than a thumb-length. Peering through the crack between the frames, she saw that a thorny vine had grown over the window, with dark branches as thick as her wrist, and long barbed spines, and no flower or leaf. She tried to look out and around, but could see very little between the limbs of the monstrous plant. And then a sword of anguish pierced her right under her heart. Her vision blurred, then darkened.

On the twisted branches glinted tiny grains of salt.

Chapter Thirty-Four

R advyed sat up in bed. A chill draft brought the sound of a few chirping birds; he could hear the *damashi* outside the room about their tasks. The chamber seemed darker than it should be at this hour of the morning. Beloved was not beside him.

He glanced at the window, then stared at it. Why were there bars over the window? He rose and went to it, then stopped short when he saw the thorny vine and the specks of salt that glittered on its twists and knots. Radvyed stood by the barely open window, unable to move, scarcely able to think. At last he turned away and went to pick up his dressing gown.

Where was Beloved? Should he consult his parents? Rue? His eye fell on the little table between the two armchairs by the fireplace. A sheet of paper was held down by a carved paperweight. He snatched the paper up. The carefully formed letters said, *I am sorry.*

Rue found him an hour later. Radvyed was sitting in one of the armchairs. His personal *damash*, Pirikon, had come to bring in breakfast and draw a bath, but had been alarmed at how the prince had not responded when spoken to. Beloved's *damasha* had also come to Rue, unsure of what to do. Both had been shaken by the prince's unresponsiveness, the growth over the window, and the absence of the princess.

Radvyed sat with his head in his hands. At first Rue thought he was hunched in despair, but then she realized he seemed instead to be listening. To what? For what? She moved to the other chair and sat. After a few minutes Radvyed raised his head and looked at her. His handsome features were strained with anxiety and grief; the easy sparkle of his usual manner was absent.

"She has left," Radvyed said. "She was miserable here and she left."

"I do not think she was miserable," said Rue.

His laugh was bitter. "Look at that window. Thorns and *salt*."

Like her name curse. Like the salt curse. He did not say it, but Rue heard the unspoken words. She watched him for a moment, noting his tense shoulders and his hands dangling uselessly between his knees as he propped his elbows on his thighs.

"She chose to live with you here," she said.

Radvyed shook his head and looked away, but made no answer. He fidgeted with his wedding bracelet, frowning as he stared at it. The door opened and the king and queen entered. Radvyed looked up and then away, ashamed. His wife had found life with him so intolerable that her own magic had forced her to flee.

"What is this?" asked the king, shutting the door. "Pirikon came to me with some tale that you were still and silent and the window barred..." He stopped speaking when he saw the twisted arms of the thorny vine writhing over the window. The queen also saw; she gasped. Arkost looked a long moment, then turned his attention back to his son. Rue had stood up when the royal couple had entered and Gladna now sank into the vacated chair and took her son's hand. He did not meet her eyes.

"Radvyed," said the king, "my son, what has happened here?"

The prince said nothing for a moment, then said, "Beloved has left me."

Arkost took a deep breath; Gladna gripped her son's hand more tightly.

Rue said, "No, Prince, she has *not* left you. She has left the palace."

All three royals turned to stare at her.

"Prince, we have all seen the close bond you share," began Rue.

"A bond that is clearly a chain," said Radvyed.

"No. Did she ever say as much to you? When she spoke to me, she was only worried about taking up a new life as a princess, and how her power might join with yours."

"But the bond has made her a princess," said Radvyed, ignoring the implication that he had any magic.

"Yes, but the marriage bond is not what traps her. It is the *palace*." Rue saw that she was making no sense to these people for whom the palace was home.

"Your Splendors. Your Radiance. At first I did not understand the need for a royal palace. No, let me explain," she said, raising her hand and so cutting off whatever the king and the prince had been about to say. The queen merely looked puzzled. "Why, I thought, do they not live among their people more simply? And then I came to understand two reasons—no doubt there are others—the people need a palace, but so does the royal family."

Rue saw that she had their full attention now, although they were not sure what this had to do with Beloved's unhappiness. "The people need the palace, because they need a large and visible place to be the seat of their royalty. Here they can come for arbitrations and petitions. Here they can gather to mourn and to rejoice. Here they can express the flower of their beauty and wealth; here they can treasure and protect the royal bloodlines that are bound to them and their land. Here they know they can find *you*." The king and queen had not quite followed the part about the bloodlines being bound, but Rue did not stop to explain.

"At the same time," she continued, "the royal family needs the palace as a place of repose and possible privacy. When you are out, you are the king, the queen, and the prince, and you are obliged to be available to your people. I saw this, Prince, as we traveled from the border to your city. I saw also that you were relieved to come to the shelter of the palace, where you can also be Radvyed, and not merely the prince." They were all listening closely—this part they understood, although perhaps they had never expressed it in such terms before. The palace was indeed where people and royalty could meet while respecting and fulfilling the needs of both.

Rue took a deep breath before continuing. "But Beloved is *not* royal." The king opened his mouth to protest, but shut it when his wife put her hand on his arm. Rue explained, "Beloved is not royal in herself, although she is royal by marriage. She has been grafted to your stock. She has consented to learn to become a princess. But for her, the palace is not where she can be Beloved. The palace is where she is a princess, and she does not have the same rest or relief here."

Rue decided not to broach the issue of a mage claiming the land where they lived. She could see no way to convince them that Tamtir was saturated with power. It would only distract them from what they could understand and grapple with.

Arkost made a wordless, huffing noise and turned away. Rue understood he was hurt. And indeed, they had done everything they could to make Beloved welcome. They did not understand that her power was of a different kind, because they, the royals, did not believe they possessed what they called magic.

The queen was gazing at her hands, folded in her lap. She looked up at Rue. "Explain a little more, please, how it is that we have hurt your heart-daughter, when we tried only to provide joy and comfort."

Rue came to Gladna and knelt before her, covering the tightly gripped hands. "You have done nothing wrong, Your Splendor. This... this is the rocky period of adjustment that, I believe, happens after many a marriage." Rue remembered talk among those who had ended up at the Hidden House; she reached further back, into the time when she had been a daughter and a servant. "Some find they cannot tolerate their sisters-in-law. Others realize that their husband is absent-minded about money. The prince and Beloved... It seems it is not easy to join lives, even when people love each other, even when they are bound together in rite, power, and royalty. Misunderstandings happen. Surely you and the king know this?"

The queen nodded then looked at the window. "But for it to be manifested so spectacularly..." She looked back at Rue, who, incredibly, had a wry half smile tugging at her lips.

"Well, Your Splendor, our children are rather spectacular. And Beloved, you know, was never taught—never learned—never required—to express herself in a tasteful or tactful way."

Arkost strode back to where the women were. "But what is upsetting her?" he asked. "What about being a princess is so confining? She lives at the palace. She has every useful or beautiful thing at her disposal. She has a husband who adores her and in-laws well-disposed toward her—indeed, eternally in her debt. The *damashi* like and respect her, even if they sometimes find her a little unnerving, but they are adjusting. She can ride, she can enjoy the city, and—"

"She is required, every minute of every day, even while sleeping, not to trouble or frighten others with her 'magic,'" said Rue in a low voice, intensely enough that the king let himself be interrupted. "She is asked, for the sake of others, not to use or manifest a power that is as natural and as essential to her as your sight, or your right hand, or your royal authority. And not because someone else has chained her power. No, she is to trammel herself. How long, Your Splendor, would you be able to endure, day after day, reminding yourself that you may not open your eyes, or stretch out your hand, or give the least order, render the most inconsequential judgment? Because others would find that too disturbing?"

The king stared at her, taken aback. Rue kept speaking. Indeed, Radvyed had never heard her say so much. "Her power is not a party trick, or something she dabbles in, or even an occasional burst of wonder. Her power is a part of her and she has been required to wrap it in chains. The rules, the etiquette of being a princess, the manner, all this she can learn and assume when needed. She may even, growing into her bond with the prince, become fully royal, but she cannot stop being a sorceress because—now that she has healed the queen—there are those discomfited by having an unknown woman of great power living at the palace."

"Enough," said Arkost. "Enough. It is clear that a grave misunderstanding of Beloved's nature has led to this difficulty, although we had no notion that we were confining her so."

"Why did she not say something," asked Gladna. "Why did *you* not say something, Rue?" Rue looked at the king and queen but found nothing more to say.

"I think that neither Rue nor Beloved knew how to explain the situation to us," said Radvyed. The others turned to him in surprise, almost as though they had forgotten he was there. "And perhaps Beloved believed she would be able to find a way...yet her magic needed to claim... I had hoped...but I should have insisted. I should have been able to persuade her to tell me..." He got up and walked to the window.

"I knew she was troubled." He turned away from the thorn and the salt. Rue could almost see him putting his grief, fear, and, yes, anger, into a mental strongbox and locking it. "The question now is what to do," said Radvyed.

"I wonder," said the queen, "whether Dris might provide some good counsel."

Dris was sent for. As they waited, they said nothing. Gladna continued to gaze at her folded hands. Arkost paced up and down the room, every now and again shaking his head or tugging at his beard. Rue stood by the small fire, staring down into the flames. Radvyed sat next to his mother in the other chair, intent on his own thoughts, wondering what to do next. Go after Beloved? Wait until she returned of her own will, if ever?

There was a knock on the door. Dris, upon being bidden to enter, walked in with her usual unhurried gait. The gardener stopped to bow before them all. The king gestured toward the window. Dris took one look and strode over to examine the vine more closely. She was careful not to touch it. After a few minutes, she turned towards the others, eyebrows raised expectantly. Arkost picked up a slate from the table by Radvyed. He wrote quickly, explaining the situation and Rue's thoughts. Dris nodded. She did not seem surprised or amazed, but then she did not wear her thoughts on her face. She took up the slate.

Not uncommon with sorcerers to have troubles in marriage even if bond is true, not a mere alliance of powers.

You do not believe Beloved has left Radvyed for good, then? wrote Arkost.

No, Dris replied. *Bond is true. Maybe not everyone knew, as bond rooted, a time of settling?*

Gladna sighed and then laughed a little. "A time of settling. Yes, of course, as Rue pointed out, one does expect such a time after every marriage—or indeed any other change within a family. But somehow I thought that because Beloved and Radvyed are joined by magic as well as love, there would be no misunderstandings, no uncertainties, no...settling. Very foolish, now that I think of it."

"Yes, yes," said the king, "But now this girl has run off thinking she cannot be Radvyed's wife, and we do not know where she is, or when or whether she plans to return, and then we must explain that thing"—he waved towards the vine at the window—"and Beloved's disappearance without causing panic or fear." No one commented on the king calling Beloved a girl, as though she were some flighty damsel bent on frivolous rebellion against long-suffering parents. Arkost resumed pacing, crossing and uncrossing his arms: he was worried for her.

"Your Splendor," said Rue. "Please remember that this has been an eventful year for Beloved. First she bore the anxious days when the prince first visited us. She almost died when he left to bring the queen her flower. She almost died again in breaking the salt curse. The name curse was broken, and she has had to learn how to use her newly healed body and how to be among people, who although they do not pity her nor fly from her because she is hideous, are frightened of her power. She has left the only home she has ever known to come to live among people who know nothing of the sorcery that has shaped her whole life. She has discovered a kinswoman and been made part of a new family. She has become a princess and a wife. She has been struggling to repress her power. It is no wonder to me that she became overwhelmed."

Arkost stopped pacing and threw up his arms. "But why did she think that she had to bear her burdens alone? Here is her husband, here are we in this room—"

"She has not yet learned that others may help her," said Radvyed. "She thinks she is the one who helps everyone else. She is the Lady Generous, she is the curse-breaker, she is the one with strength and knowledge. Forgive me, Rue," said Radvyed, bowing to that lady, "for I know that your love and care were the only good things in her life for most of her days, but I think Beloved does not know that people, even powerful people unhindered by any curse, still need others."

Dris stirred and bent over the slate. *Prince must cut down bitter-wood.* Radvyed stared at Dris, who gave a sharp nod.

"Son, go with Dris and do as she advises," said Gladna, "for she knows much, it seems, of magic and growing things." Gladna smiled at Dris, and the gardener bowed. "Lady Rue, will you be good enough to come with the king and me to discuss how the palace may be made more of a home and less of a cage for our Beloved? For it seems we have invited a *sozkol* to live among us and then been dismayed at seeing sparks. Yet she is a princess as well. Let us think what we may do."

"I would be happy to, Your Splendor."

The three of them left. Radvyed could hear his father proposing two or three advisers who might also be invited to the discussion.

The prince remained alone with Dris in the room he had shared with Beloved. He glanced again at the window, then gave a small smile to Dris, despite his heavy heart. "It seems you always have gardening tasks that only I can do." He pointed at her, then himself, then mimed wiping his brow of toilsome sweat. "Let us see if I am able to perform this one to your satisfaction." Again he pointed at Dris, this time widening his eyes and placing a hand on heart to indicate the hope of pleasing her. He was gratified when one corner of the gardener's lips quirked up.

Chapter Thirty-Five

After Radvyed had dressed, he and Dris went outside. By now it was almost midmorning and the late autumn air was clear and chill. They came around the corner of the palace wall and had, for the first time, a full view of the bitterwood vine. It twisted like a many-headed, spike-skinned snake up the wall to the window. It had not grown much past the window, and as yet it had not spread farther up or over, but it did not take much to imagine the horrible plant growing until it gripped the whole palace, from foundation to towers, in its monstrous tentacles. Now it lay against the wall, brooding, glittering with bitterness.

They gazed on it for a moment, then Dris rang one of the deep-toned bells stationed throughout the gardens. Soon an under-gardener appeared, brushing dirt from her clothes flusteredly when she caught sight of the prince. She halted, wide-eyed, upon seeing the vine. After a brief exchange with Dris, she ran off. A few moments later, she returned with another undergardener, the two of them bringing kindling, a small load of wood, tools, and a ladder. Radvyed kept looking at the vine while Dris gave directions.

When she had finished, the prince turned, and she handed him a small axe, then nodded at the vine. He looked carefully at the axe, hefted it to judge its weight and the best hold. It seemed to be a plain axe with nothing magical about it. Radvyed put the edge to the foot of the vine, preparing to hack it off at the base.

"Prince, no!" exclaimed the first undergardener, who had introduced herself as Tseva; the other one, Leshin, also cried out. Radvyed straightened and looked at them. Dris held her hand up, palm out towards him, clearly signing *stop*.

Tseva answered his silent question. "Your Radiance, you may not cut it down like that. Where will it fall?" Radvyed flushed. He had only been thinking of cutting the bitterwood down as quickly as possible.

"How, then?" he asked.

"Your Radiance must use the ladder," said Tseva, and Radvyed saw that Leshin was propping one up against the wall alongside the bitterwood vine. "Then you must cut each branch and throw it down to us. We will burn it." Radvyed looked around and saw there was a small fire laid ready in a wide iron bowl, serving as a portable firepit, and that Dris was pulling on thick leather gauntlets.

"I, too, will need some gloves, then," said Radvyed, gesturing towards Dris's hands. Dris again held up a hand, guessing his order. She met the prince's gaze and shook her head. He stared at her, then looked pointedly at the thorny vine, then back at her. She again shook her head.

Radvyed bit back a sigh and looked up the full height of the vine. *Best get started.*

Leshin held the ladder as Radvyed climbed; the prince had the axe tucked into his belt so he could use two hands. He stopped a few rungs from the top of the ladder and looked to see where he was in relation to the vine. Its farthest-reaching fingers were above the level of his head, but Radvyed thought he had gone high enough. He looked down at the others, who were rather farther below him than he had expected. Their faces were turned up towards him, ready. Leshin seemed solidly braced. Radvyed spared a moment to wonder what the undergardeners thought of the monstrous vine that had grown overnight below the prince and princess's bedroom window. Then he shook off all distracting thoughts and pulled the axe from his belt. He was only a little more skilled with the hand axe than he had been with the pruning hook. *Really,* he thought, *I had believed my education to be quite thorough, but some gardening lessons would not have been amiss.*

Then, trusting the undergardener to hold the ladder steady, Radvyed leaned into the palace wall with his hips to brace himself. He gingerly grasped a branch and began, rather awkwardly, to hack at the base of it, where it joined a larger limb. The wood did not give way easily, unlike the brambles that had guarded Hideous's cottage, and the thorns bit and burned into his hands with their salted spines. Radvyed hacked the branch free and called out before dropping it down. Dris picked it up and threw it onto the fire, which leapt up with a deep yellow flame before falling back into sullen blue flickers. The fire gave off an unpleasant dark smoke that dissipated reluctantly. Again and again Radvyed hacked, called, and dropped; the branch burned and the fire flared. The morning wore away as the prince doggedly attacked the vine. His hands were bloody and slippery, so he worked slowly, wishing neither to injure himself more than he could help, nor to harm his helpers below.

Every now and then Radvyed would pause and wipe the sweat from his face with the back of his hand or the shoulder of his tunic. He felt dully that he had been working at destroying the bitterwood for days on end. The sun struck him with unfriendly heat, the vine did not seem to become smaller, and he was hot and filthy. His hands were torn up as badly as his and Beloved's feet had been on their walk to the Tower.

As Radvyed hacked and his hands throbbed and stung and the sweat dripped into his eyes and made his clothes sticky, he thought of Beloved, who had fled from him, very likely at the sight of this vine. He was angry with her for leaving—not even waking him up!—angry that she did not trust him, or think that he might help her cope with what she feared. He was angry that he was bound to this woman who could make him feel inadequate, useless, and insubstantial.

And yet, Radvyed thought, tossing down another branch, and pausing to wipe his slippery hands on his ruined tunic, *what am I to her but a good-looking man, needful for spell-breaking, pleasant to pass the time with, of high blood and perhaps some charm, but otherwise burdening her with another cage, another name that binds her?* And he felt, to his horror, tears of frustration, anger, shame, grief, longing—too much all at once, too much to understand or feel—pressing out of his eyes and mixing with the sweat on his face. Then he was glad to hack at the vine, for it was a simple task that let him hit back at his oppressive feelings; he could lose himself in it and empty his mind of worry, self-doubt, and uncertainty about what would happen now. The next branch was all he needed to think about. He ignored his tears as he made himself ignore his bloody, salt-burned hands, the heat of the sun, and the smell of the fire.

The day passed on, but no one suggested stopping for food or rest. The prince remained fiercely focused on one thing only: cutting down the vine. From time to time he heard, as from a distance, voices that came and went away, and he noticed, on the edges of his awareness, that the light had changed and the shadows had shifted, but he did not stop, until he moved his foot down to the next rung and struck the ground with a jolt. He stumbled, grabbed the ladder to steady himself, and hissed at the pain. He raised his head and looked around.

Leshin still held the ladder. *How long has he held it? His hands must be cramping,* thought Radvyed. The undergardener did not smile at his prince's clumsiness, but watched to make sure Radvyed had found his feet. Dris turned to throw the latest branch onto the fire. Tseva stepped back as the smoke billowed and faded. Radvyed looked at what remained of the vine. A branchless trunk, maybe two feet in height.

Now that he had woken from his concentration, Radvyed saw that it was dusk. As the heat of exertion faded, he shivered. The autumn air chilled the sweat on his skin. He felt afresh the pain, the aches, and the heart heaviness. Yet he was not finished. Radvyed took a deep breath and squared his shoulders. Leshin had moved the ladder. The prince knelt and finished cutting down the vine. He sat back on his heels and sighed with relief. *Done.* He laid the axe down, only to find that a square-bladed spade had been set down next to him. He raised his eyes and looked at Dris in the dim light. The small bonfire gave some illumination, and Leshin had lit a lantern that had been brought at some point during the day's work.

Dris returned his gaze. Tseva, her voice low, said, "I am very sorry, Your Radiance, but the root must be dug up and destroyed."

Radvyed with great effort did not say what he felt at that moment about Dris and her proclivity for setting him impossible tasks with imperturbable authority. He squatted for a moment longer, wiped his face with his sleeve, did not examine his bleeding and blistered hands, and stood.

"Very well," he said. He picked up the spade.

Tseva showed him how best to wield it. Radvyed dug up, by lantern and firelight, the dark, gnarled root, glittering with salt. After he had loosened the soil about it, he handed the spade to Leshin, and knelt once more. As the others watched, he worked his hands underneath the root and, grunting from pain and exertion, lifted it free. He was surprised that the root was not larger, and said so.

"You have done good work this day, Your Radiance," said Tseva.

Dris rested a hand for a moment on his shoulder and gave him a brisk nod.

The prince bore the root over to the fire and threw it on. He stepped back quickly, for a large flame of deep bright yellow leapt high, dark smoke hissing from its tip. They all watched as the root settled to burn with the bitterwood's low blue flame. When it was all but done, Radvyed looked up from the fire. To his surprise, his mother and father had joined them. His father nodded and his mother brushed her eyes with her hand, but they said nothing. Dris watched the embers and last flickers of flame. The two undergardeners stood solemnly—*as if they are witnesses,* thought Radvyed—staring at the remains of the fire.

Radvyed looked up. The stars had long since revealed themselves and now were engaged in their stately nocturnal dance, giving no notice to the small smoky fire far below. Gazing at their bright, cold cleanness, Radvyed felt himself filthy, and aching, and very, very tired. He looked down again. The fire had finished burning. To his dull surprise, there was nothing left but a few dark ashes that were already being scattered by the brisk night breeze. He looked at Dris. She bowed to him and to his parents. Then she and her helpers gathered the ladder, tools, lanterns, and firepit and walked away into the dark gardens.

Radvyed stood with his parents, too weary to think. After a moment, his father came to him and put a hand on his shoulder. "You have done well, son," Arkost said, "but now you must rest."

His mother also came up to him, took one of his bloody hands in hers, looked at it, then held it gently to her cheek. "Yes, my handsome son, you have done well. Now come inside, and bathe, and rest."

Radvyed said nothing, but willingly walked between them as they led him back to his chamber. There he let himself be bathed and cared for before he tumbled into bed and slept. He dreamed of Beloved dancing with him that first day of her freedom as the butterflies wove bright paths in the air above the terrace.

Chapter Thirty-Six

The next morning after getting dressed and eating breakfast, Radvyed found his father alone in the king's study. King Arkost was seated behind his desk, staring at but not seeing a paper he held in his hands. Radvyed wondered if it were another report about an unseasonal hailstorm. This autumn there had been three or four, pecking at the edges of the kingdom, and damaging harvests. Arkost looked up when his son walked in.

"Good rising, son," Arkost said and waved Radvyed to a chair. He watched as his son sat. "So. Are you well? Your mother did not want your sleep disturbed after yesterday's work. How are your hands?"

Radvyed held up his hands, which were wrapped in light bandages that left his fingers somewhat free. "Better, Father. Rue gave me a salve last night, or at least I think it was Rue. But I hope that Dris has no tasks for me today."

His father smiled. "No, no, she has not turned up this morning."

They sat for a moment in silence.

"Well," said the king. "And what are your thoughts about the situation with Beloved?"

Radvyed looked for a moment out the window and then back at his father. "I think I should find her," he said.

Arkost watched him. "You do not think that she will come back in her own good time? If she felt confined here, will she see you as a jailer bringing her back to prison?"

Radvyed took a moment before replying. "That is a risk," he said. "Yet she also seemed to believe we valued her little once she had healed Mother and broken the salt curse. If I do not follow her, will she not then think we are relieved that she left?" The king frowned. "I will find her and speak with her. If she desires to stay away..." Radvyed stopped speaking. He would not, of course, force her into a life that ill fit her. *First find her,* he told himself.

His father nodded. "You may be right. That was your mother's thought and Lady Rue's as well. Make sure she knows that we welcome her home and we are devising ways to accommodate her—what did Rue liken her magic to?—her extra limb, or sense, or what will you. To accommodate *her.*" He tapped his fingers thoughtfully on the desk. "And this claiming or rooting or...well, that rite or spell that Rue and Dris explained, and which I do not yet fully understand." The king held up a forefinger. "But she must also learn to live—no," he added, seeing his son preparing to protest, "not in any painful or diminishing way. I mean she must learn to accommodate herself the way a strong man does not clap a fellow on the back with his full strength, or the way neither you nor I make our authority felt by oppression."

Radvyed picked up a silver-specked paperweight, then set it down again.

The king said, "As I understand it, while she was under the curse and living in her cottage or palace there in the middle of a thorn forest, she let her magic go as she willed, and that worked well for her household. But being a princess, as she has realized, is a different thing. How did Dris put it? She has been transplanted here, but no plant grows the same way in two different gardens."

Radvyed was silent. His father, or Dris, was right. He and Beloved had married each other; it was not an alliance of convenience with clear terms, or an annexation of one by the other. He nodded. They must find the right soil for Beloved. She must consent to grow in it.

Chapter Thirty-Seven

Radvyed stood in his bedchamber, staring out the now un-obstructed window. It was early afternoon of the day after Beloved's disappearance. He considered which direction Beloved might take. Neither Rue nor Dris had had any helpful advice. Beloved seemed to have left on foot, in the early morning. No one had noticed her departure, but perhaps she could alter her appearance. In any case, even an unobtrusive cloak and a ducked head would have let her out of the palace unobserved. The *strazha* were more interested in those coming in the gates than in those going out.

Where would she go? His saddlebags and gear were placed by the door. A cloak was draped over a chair. He wore his riding boots. One hand held his gloves—larger and thicker than his usual ones, as his hands were bandaged—while the other raked through his hair. He was ready to ride out, but did not know in which direction to search.

Radvyed left his room and made for the high tower where he liked to stargaze. From the balcony at the top he could see the country all about him. He absently shook the wrist that bore his wedding bracelet: it was prickling his skin. Radvyed paced slowly, hoping for some sign, some internal flicker, some memory or thread of logic that would point him in the correct direction. Rubbing his skin under the bracelet, he scanned the horizon as he circled the tower. His eyes met the smudged blue line of the Sinevy Hills to the east of the city. He remembered telling Beloved about them one morning when he had brought her up here. The hills were rocky and thin-soiled and sparsely populated, but their stubborn rough grass was the favorite pasturage of sheep that gave wool remarkable for its fineness and strength. The people of that district were tough but hospitable, and their wool, combined with the crimson dye they obtained from berries that grew high among the rockier crags, were goods that traders sought eagerly. She had been more intrigued by the description of the high, scrubby hills than that of other, gentler, landscapes.

As he thought of the villages and slopes of the Sinevy Hills, his bracelet hummed and prickled more strongly. He looked down at it, surprised, then back at the eastern hills. Curious, he walked to the western side of the tower. The bracelet's hum quieted; the prickling gentled and faded. As he approached the east once again, the hum strengthened, the links pinched, and the gold of the bracelet glowed more warmly. He looked from it to the blue smudge of hills that seemed to call to the bracelet Beloved had clasped on his wrist. He felt an almost physical tug when he relaxed his arm. He lifted his wrist and stared at the glowing, humming bracelet. More of Beloved's magic? He could think of no other cause for the bracelet's odd behavior. Well, then. He would try the Sinevy Hills.

His decision made, Radvyed returned to his chamber. After he directed a *damash* to carry his things below, he went to bid farewell to the king and queen. Radvyed told his parents that he would begin by searching in the direction of the eastern hills and that he would send messages as he may. They kissed him and he left, clattering down the front sweep of stairs that led to the courtyard where a *kunika* held his saddled horse. After a quick word of thanks, Radvyed swung himself up onto Belikon. Nodding at the *strazha* at the gate, he passed through and into the city.

Radvyed did not expect to make much headway that day. By the time he had gathered what he needed, decided which direction to follow, and spoken with Rue, Dris, and the king and queen, it was well after noon. Then he needed to make his way out of the city, and although Radvyed was not dressed to attract attention, there was little he could do to disguise his face short of wearing a mask. Even though the citizens of Zolatar could see that their prince was about on private business, he made slower progress than he liked, for many lingered to watch him ride by, and always there were those who were struck still or otherwise overcome by his beauty. Between the gawkers and the bedazzled, the sun was well advanced in its westward path behind him when Radvyed arrived at the eastern gates. Although it was later than he had hoped, he judged that he had yet a few hours before true darkness fell.

As he left the royal city behind him, the travelers became fewer and Radvyed could urge Belikon to a swifter pace. He kept alert for any signs that Beloved may have passed this way, not sure what he expected to find, but confident that some trace of her presence would make itself known. The bracelet had settled into a steady soft hum. He had no real idea how many miles she might be able to travel in a day on foot. Her mobility was still new to her and her limits untried. Radvyed had been impressed at how well and quickly she had learned to use muscles that must have been exercised very little for most of her life. He had asked her about it, and she had looked at him, surprised. "But then," she had said, "butterflies fly as soon as they are free of the cocoon." Beloved was remarkable, but Radvyed did not think her swifter on foot than he on horseback.

On the other hand, Radvyed thought, as he slowed Belikon to a walk, there was no reason for Beloved to keep to the road. She had, as far as he knew, no destination, aside from, possibly, the Sinevy Hills. But once free of the palace and the city, she need not rush. Radvyed had thought he might encounter her at an inn along the main road, but now he saw he had been led astray by conventions of travel. Would Beloved believe that she could take her rest in an inn full of people who might be frightened if a flowering vine or fruit tree grew in the night, to say nothing of changed furnishings or rooms? He did not think so. Had she spent last night in a field or under a hedge? Had he passed where she may have left the road, and wandered across country?

Radvyed drew Belikon to the side of the road and stopped. He looked back and pondered possibilities. As he had ridden from the city, the villages had become more widely spaced along the highway. The last village had been some miles back, but the farmhouses visible from the road were still rather frequent. He doubted she had left the road at a point behind him, then. How he would know whether she had diverged from it at some point ahead, he was not sure. The hum and prickle of the bracelet comforted him now, although he hesitated to place full credence in a buzzing bit of jewelry. Radvyed kneed Belikon forward. Nothing to do but go on until dark, keeping his eyes open for what he might see.

Dusk had softened the sky and the first stars glinted high and clear when he saw a farmhouse set back a bit from the road. As he rode closer he could see through a window a woman lighting a lamp and setting it on a table. Her head turned as she heard hoofbeats and she seemed to speak to someone else. Radvyed rode up to the door, the hood of his cloak well up. Three dogs came forward, not menacing, but investigating the strange horse and rider; one gave a short bark.

Before Radvyed had finished dismounting, a barrel-chested man had appeared at the door, his arms crossed.

Radvyed took a step nearer. The man said nothing, but watched him.

"Good setting, master," said Radvyed. The man grunted and waited.

"Might you have food and shelter for the night for my horse and me?" asked Radvyed. The man looked at Radvyed's horse, noting the animal's noble lines and proud head. He looked again at Radvyed, at the fineness of the stranger's cloak and boots. The cowl of Radvyed's cloak was pulled forward against the evening chill, leaving his face in shadow. Radvyed stood quietly, letting the man look and make up his mind. The woman came behind the man and peered over his shoulder.

"Who is it, Van? What does he want?" The look she gave was a little friendlier than the man's but not less sharp.

"A *miren* or *dovoren*," rumbled the man, "who needs a night's shelter."

"Does he indeed?" said the woman. "Then let him in, Van, and you take that poor horse to stable. There's room and there's fodder."

Van eyed Radvyed once more, then he stepped forward, grasped Belikon's bridle, and began to lead him away.

"Thank you," said Radvyed. Van merely grunted again and led the horse around to the back of the house.

"Come in, master, come in," said the woman. "We were about to sit ourselves down to supper. Come in and take off your traveling things." Radvyed followed her into the house, taking off his riding gloves and thrusting them into the wide leather belt he wore at his waist. His hands were still sore despite the bandages. The woman moved off and began laying a third place at the table. "My name's Alya, and that was my husband, Van. He's not a great talker, but he's a good man. Now let me take—*oh*."

Alya had turned back to Radvyed to take his traveling cloak from him. While she had been talking and setting the table, he had removed his hooded cloak. He held it now over one arm. She stopped in mid-sentence when she turned and saw his face. Although it was dark outside now and the kitchen was lit only by the fire in the hearth and the lamp on the table, the light was enough for her to see his face and be struck by it. In Radvyed's mind flashed a memory: dinner with Hideous, with one candelabrum and a small fire in the hearth, and Hideous attempting to keep out of the light. Alya was silent, staring and clutching at the back of a nearby chair.

"I thank you, Alya, for your hospitality," said Radvyed. He was not sure if she realized he was the prince, or whether she thought he was merely a handsome man.

Her eyes swept down to the badger and oak of the heir's ring, which he wore on a chain around his neck. Frowning a little, she looked at his ungloved, bandaged hands and gasped. Her own hand on the chair back whitened, but she took a deep breath and looked at his face again. She bobbed a bow, her right hand over her heart.

"It is our honor, Your Radiance," she said, "to offer you the welcome of our house." Her eye caught the cloak still over his arm. "May I—?" she added, holding out her hands.

"I thank you," said Radvyed, and gave her the cloak. She hesitated, uncertain what to do with it. Finally, she hung it up on a peg by the door next to other pegs holding outer garments. Van came in.

"Van," said his wife, putting her hand on his sleeve, "Van—"

Her husband looked at her and then at Radvyed. He blinked and flicked a glance at Radvyed's right hand. He blinked again to see it injured, then his gaze rose to the ring on its chain. He met Radvyed's eyes with his own, then gave his own awkward bow, and said to his wife, "Well, Alya? His Radiance is hungry, no doubt."

Alya stared at her husband a moment, then gave a quick, brisk shake of her head and said, "Yes, yes, of course. Please sit down, Your Radiance." She followed her husband's lead in treating their unusual guest as unexpected but not impossible. The men sat and Alya served three portions of a firm grain pudding with toasted cheese and a thick stew. Then she poured some ale for them all and sat down. The three said thanksgiving to the Lady and Master for the meal. There was a moment of awkwardness during which Radvyed waited for his hosts to start eating and they waited for their prince. Then Alya, beginning to recover from receiving royalty on her doorstep, dipped her spoon into her bowl and ate. There was silence as all three gave their attention to their food. Van and Alya darted discreet glances at Radvyed, no doubt wondering why the prince was here, alone, and not on an official outing. Radvyed contemplated what, if anything, he should say about his errand as he relished the good cooking and excellent brew. He hoped Belikon had done as well with the stable fare.

Finally, they were done with their meal. Alya got up and began to clear the table. Radvyed stood when she did.

"No, no, Your Radiance," she said, apparently thinking he was about to offer to help clean up, "you and Van go sit outside for a bit while I get things in order." The prince was surprised—he was not accustomed to being shooed out of the way—but followed Van outside into the cold night. There was a bench against the wall by the door and they sat, wrapped in their cloaks. Van got out a pipe and started to fill it from a pouch at his belt.

Radvyed looked up at the stars. Here, away from the city and the palace, they seemed closer and more numerous than ever. He thought that if he stretched out his hand, he might be able to pick up a fistful, as he might some sand on the shore. Not for the first time did he marvel at the splendor of the Master's work.

"Seems odd," Van said after a few minutes of quiet smoking. "Your Radiance traveling alone. Did you not get married some weeks back? To that rose-girl, the one who broke the salt—Lady Beloved?"

Radvyed smiled in the darkness. *Rose-girl.* Van did not seem disturbed in the slightest by Beloved's magic. Of course, he had not encountered it directly. Radvyed leaned his head back against the wall and stretched his legs out in front of him. Still gazing at the stars, he said, "Yes, she is Princess Beloved now." He paused and Van blew a ring that melted into a veil against the stars and then faded away. Radvyed asked, "How long have you and Alya been married?"

"Well-nigh on forty years."

"How did you meet?"

Van said nothing, so Radvyed turned his head, still leaning against the wall, and looked at him. The man was grinning at some old memory.

"I sense a story there," said Radvyed. He was not sure, but it sounded like Van snorted.

"Oh, aye," he said. Radvyed turned back to the stars and waited. "Alya lived over in Perikrost, east of here right before the hills," said Van. Radvyed nodded; he knew it, of course. "I took my family's grain to market there and sometimes livestock. Or I'd be sent if we needed something from town." Van paused and blew a few smoke rings. "And one day at the fountain in the middle of the square, I saw the prettiest girl in the world filling a bucket of water. I knew right then I wanted her to wife. But I also saw that she had many a town lad about her with the same idea. Well, I took my mule up to water at the fountain, thinking maybe I'd say a word or two, if I could think what to say. That's when some town boy gave me a shove, not liking me getting between him and Alya. But he shoved a little too hard, and as I went back, poor Alya got a dunking. So now he and I are fighting, each glad of a reason to break the other's nose and defend our lady's honor." Van paused and smoked some more.

Radvyed waited, but Van seemed disposed to smoke and stare at the stars all night. "And then what happened?" he prodded.

Van chuckled. "Alya got herself out of the fountain and took that nice oaken bucket of hers and whacked us each right smart on the head. Then she got herself some more water and trotted back home, leaving us laid out and bleeding. Now the other fellow, when he pulled himself together, was pretty annoyed with her and left her alone after that. And the other town lads seemed to think that a wife that not only *could* but *would* knock your head off was a wife they didn't need, no matter how pretty."

"And you?" said Radvyed.

Van laughed. "Well, Your Radiance, I said to myself, now that's my girl. I knew she wouldn't be one of those who smiled at you when she was mad then got back at you when you weren't looking for it. My brother married a girl like that—a beauty that could turn your head in her young days, but you never know what she's thinking." He puffed a bit. "He don't seem to mind, though," he added. "Likes a bit of not knowing, I guess, to keep things interesting. And she's still a fine-looking woman."

"And besides impressing her with your brawling skills," Radvyed said, smiling when Van snorted again, "how else did you win her?" He wanted to hear how this farmer had won his wife after knocking her into a water trough. He was curious how someone else's courtship had followed an unusual course.

"Well, I just hung about. Whenever I could go into town I'd be there and I'd help her with whatever her work was if I could, and I'd bring her the odd gift, and her brothers and sisters kept an eye on me, and her father and mother asked around and found out about my family and our farm and so on. She didn't talk to me much but she didn't tell me to go either. Then one fine day we're back at that fountain getting water and she turns to me and says, do I have anything to say to her or don't I. And I say yes, I'd like her to be my wife. And she says, are you moving to town? And I say, no, I'm a farmer. And she says, well, I guess I'd better marry you before your crops die of neglect." He paused. "Now that girl knew I was putting in my share of work at the farm, but she also knew my heart wasn't in it, 'cause I was worrying about whether one of those town boys would come to his senses and snap her up. I fidgeted her, she said. So the next week we got married and she left town and here we are."

Van and Radvyed sat some more in easy silence, feeling the night cold, listening to an owl call, and watching the stars. Radvyed wondered, as he gazed up at the dark, glittering sky, where Beloved was and what she was doing. He was not worried about her physical safety, for he felt sure she could use her magic to protect and provide for herself. He was troubled that she was lonely and felt out of place where he had hoped she could feel at home. *I am not enough, after all*, he thought. *I am only pretty looks, an easy manner, and a princely bloodline. And honor*, he added, thinking of their conversation before they had crossed into Tamtir. *But even that is not enough.* He looked away from the stars and down at his bandaged hands, folded across his stomach. *What can I offer her, if the palace does not suffice? If her magic cannot settle and root there? And yet, I am as tied to the palace as this man is to his farm.*

He must have sighed, or shifted, because Van said, "Why is Your Radiance here, heading into the east hill country, and not with your new wife? That's no way to treat a bride, if you don't mind my saying."

Radvyed turned his head and looked at the older man. In the faint light from the window he saw Van's face, weather-roughened, a little hard, but also with a steady-eyed, open look. He sat patiently, ready to serve his prince with talk, with silence, with the simple companionship of another man who did not always understand his wife.

"My lady does not like the palace," Radvyed said at last. "She finds it strange and lonely there, although we love her, and have tried to make her welcome. I go in search of her, to assure her of my love and the king and queen's, and to see what would ease her life there."

Van nodded. "A new life is like a new shoe," he said. "It pinches and chafes for a bit at first, but then it takes the shape of the foot, and fits nice and snug. My Alya, now. Took her some months to get used to life on the farm and living with my family and all. Or my brother what married his pretty Ellana, bad temper and all. Her people are sailors, and he moved to a sea town to please her. He said it took a good while before he stopped being bothered by the fish and tar smell, and the screams of the gulls." Van knocked his pipe against the bench. "You'll find your lady, Your Radiance. Because if it's a love match, which from what news we get here, it is"—he shot a glance at Radvyed, who was grateful to the shadows hiding his heightened color—"then she's wanting to be found."

Radvyed could think of nothing to say in answer. Then Alya came to the door, asking Van whether he planned to keep His Radiance up until daybreak, and the men went inside.

Radvyed lay in the bed that the kind couple had, over his protests, given up to him. They were sleeping in the loft. He wondered whether Van was right in saying that Beloved wanted to be found. Had he missed her diverging path? Would she go across country? Was he wrong in thinking she would head for the hills? Had she acquired a mount at some point? How long did she think to be away? He was tired but anxious, and frustrated at not knowing how to find her. Then he remembered what Beloved had told him about the Tower dreams, when he had asked her why and how he had had them. "Perhaps I had no other way to speak to you," she had said. He thought also of his wedding bracelet humming when he had stood on the tower facing east.

But I have no magic, he thought, and an image of Beloved's incredulous face came before his closed eyes. He smiled despite himself. *Very well,* he thought, *and no harm, at least, can come of it.* He settled himself on the edge of slumber. Resting his braceleted wrist on his chest, Radvyed imagined how he must look on horseback as he had been that day. He thought of himself calling, *Beloved, where are you?* as he rode. Holding that picture in his mind as his bracelet faintly thrummed, he sank into the tide of sleep.

Chapter Thirty-Eight

The next morning, with a belly full of Alya's good food and more provisions tucked away in a saddlebag, Radvyed bade the couple farewell and rode away. Back on the road, he held Belikon to a brisk walk. It was early and he was riding under a pale pearl sky toward the east, where the vault overhead was already streaked with pink and gold. When the sun lifted herself over the ridge of the hills, Radvyed pulled his hood forward to shield his eyes. Otherwise it was pleasant riding; the few fellow travelers on the road seemed too sleepy or too intent on their own business to take much notice of a lone rider on a fine horse. In an hour or so he sighted Perikrost. Although he knew a strong desire to see the fountain by which the courtship of Van and Alya had begun, he decided to avoid the town. He was eager to find Beloved and knew that if he entered the place, he would move slowly, for word would spread that the prince was there. The bracelet was indifferent to the town, as far as Radvyed could tell. So, he took Belikon off the highway and onto a narrow road that skirted Perikrost and met a wider track, which wound down from the hills, to the northeast. This wide track crossed the highway farther down in the valley; Perikrost sat where the two ways met.

No one was using the byway around the town and Radvyed reached the hill road without incident. He had not been a mile on it, when it branched again, the main track running northeast to follow a shallower slope of the hill, and a bridle path rising more steeply eastward. The land became rocky here, and the bends sharper. Obeying the pull of his bracelet, Radvyed dismounted and led Belikon. They came around another turn where the ground rose sharply and something caught the corner of Radvyed's eye. He turned to look and stopped. Belikon bumped the back of Radvyed's head and blew down his neck. Radvyed stared at the small green vine that grew by the side of the rocky path. Its green was a darker, glossier color than that of the grass around it; it was a young relative of a climbing plant he had seen before. There was a glimpse of white. He bent, lifted a few round leaves, and saw small starry white flowers, guarded by long hooked spines.

Radvyed carefully withdrew his fingers and straightened, gazing at the plant with a small smile. He stood for a moment, one foot braced on the higher ground of the path ahead, one gloved fist on his hip, the reins in his other hand. Of course he had seen that plant before. It had guarded his lady's walled garden. Now, improbably, a shoot of that distant vine grew on this hillside, right next to the path. He did not doubt that it was a sign of Beloved.

Radvyed looked around him. Was this a token to say she had passed this way or was it a marker of the road she had taken? He looked beyond Beloved's vine and thought he could distinguish a yet smaller footpath that branched off the track he had been following. The grass was so tough and low, and the soil, where it showed through, so rocky, that discerning the way was not easy. He held out his arm: the thrumming bracelet tugged at him. Radvyed determined to follow the indistinct trail. Before pressing on, however, he bent and broke off a small, leafy twig from the young vine, and tucked it into his belt. Squinting into the sun, he led Belikon onto the faint path.

After about an hour of winding upward around boulders and tussocks, Radvyed began to see sheep grazing, with a few goats and the occasional cow, and from time to time he would spot a child in the distance, sitting under a scrubby tree, and watching the livestock. Encouraged by these signs, he walked on, still leading Belikon, and keeping a sharp eye on the vegetation on either side of the path, in case Beloved had left other tokens. Presently the ground leveled and there was a sort of natural terrace in the side of the hill. The track widened and smoothed. He had arrived at a village. A wall of fitted stones without mortar ran along his left side, while an orchard grew on his right, continuing a little ways down the shoulder of the hill. The trees were small but well established. As Radvyed approached the village gate, he heard the sounds of a smithy. His bracelet buzzed.

The smith's yard was just on the other side of the wooden gate set in the stone wall. The track widened into a flat area that allowed space for a village square and some buildings on both sides of the main street. Radvyed passed with Belikon through the gate and stood just inside, taking in the village. On the left were a tiny inn and a few houses made of the local gray stone and roofed with slate. Up the slope of the hill beyond that first row, other houses nestled. On his right opened the smith's yard. And there, seated on a stone bench against the village's outer wall, sat Beloved, watching the smith at his work.

Radvyed stood silently looking at her. The relief of having found her, apparently unharmed and untroubled, almost made his knees buckle, before swiftly transmuting into hurt and anger. How could she sit there, relaxed and at ease, her hair glinting in the sun, not a scratch on her, not a care in the world, while his heart had been gnawed by anxiety and fragmented by doubt? While the whole palace was cast into an uproar? Once more he felt humiliated and abandoned: his wife trusted and valued him so little, and resented her new life so much, that she had left him. The frustration and the shame of it overwhelmed him again. Seeing her safe and well while he stood unnoticed and miserable made him feel like a stranger, cut off and separate from her.

Perhaps I should go, he thought. *Here she is, seemingly well able to take care of herself, happy and free of the unbearable burden of being my wife and princess*—he knew that he was descending into self-pity, but persisted—*let her wander, then. She has done enough for me and my House. And if she never returns and I have no heirs—well, that is what cousins are for. I will not be her jailer.*

At that moment, Beloved turned and looked at him. Perhaps she had heard the jingle of harness or a shadow had caught the corner of her eye, or perhaps she had sensed the strength of the emotion within Radvyed. Her gaze met his; her face became solemn and wary. All at once Radvyed was tired. What had he done to make her look at him like that? He led Belikon into the smith's yard and hitched him to an iron ring set in a post. He walked over to the bench where Beloved sat. She moved, whether to make room for him or to put distance between them, he did not know. He sat down, setting his elbows on his knees and looking straight ahead. The smith, after a pause in his hammering, resumed his work.

They sat in silence for a while. Radvyed was glad that she did not know what to say or do either. The smith kept at his work and they watched as he turned the piece—it looked like it might be the strap for a door—occasionally pulling the bellows string to get the needed heat. The smith was a tall man, not bulky but wiry, and Radvyed knew that although the man kept to his work, he was also aware of the silent couple sitting on his bench. But the smith was not, it seemed, a chatty or curious man, for he said no word.

"I like to watch him work," said Beloved, and Radvyed inclined his head towards her to hear her better over the clanging of the smith's hammer. Radvyed still did not look her in the face, but he felt her glance at him. He heard her swallow, then she said, "See how he tames fire to his purpose and even makes iron take the shape he desires? By his strength and skill he harnesses flame and bends metal."

Radvyed felt a tightness grip his chest, but he answered, over the quickened beating of his heart. "And he does not mind the sparks or the heat."

"No," she agreed. Her hands twisted in her lap, then stilled.

Radvyed was not sure he understood. Was she saying she was like the smith or was she like the fire? He turned his head and saw that she was biting her lip and that her eyes were wide and she was blinking fast. His anger and his shame slipped away. Beloved had not meant to hurt or humiliate him. She did not always know she could call on him for help and comfort, or how to come to him when she felt burdened or overwhelmed. At the Griefstone she had claimed his aid with authority, for in working magic and breaking curses she knew what had to be done and how. But in the everyday round of living with other people, of loving a circle of people, even of being with him, she was unsure.

Rue she had always loved and been loved by and had always lived with; their histories as well as their lives were entwined. With Radvyed, however, Beloved found herself intimately bound to a man she deemed honorable, yes, and even brave; he was courteous, kind, and affectionate. Yet the knowledge of him that only time could bring was lacking. She was off-balance and nervous, not realizing that the close bond she had with Rue, born of their severe isolation, was not commonplace. Now, as at those long-ago dinners with the prince at the Hidden House, she was anxious and uncertain. She still half-expected to repel him, still thought that, without the magic of their joining, he would never have married her. *Indeed*, Radvyed thought with surprise, *perhaps she believes that in breaking the curse of her hideous vine-bound captivity, I became blinded by magic, and now am compelled to see her as lovely. Whereas the curse was broken because my heart knew her loveliness before my eyes did.*

Radvyed reached over and picked up one of her hands and held it between both of his gloved ones. Beloved looked up at him. He lifted her hand to his lips, kissed it, and, meeting her eyes with his smiling ones, said, "Beloved. Will you come home with me?"

She began to smile and tried to say something, but could not, and instead pushed her face against his shoulder. He put his arms around her and she flung hers around his waist, clutching at him, her face still pressed into his shoulder. He turned to lay his cheek against the top of her head and saw that the smith had stopped working and was watching them. After a moment, the smith gave a nod and took up his work once more.

Once they had composed themselves, they drew apart. Deciding that since they were not there in their official role as royals, no one would be shocked if the prince sat his wife on his knee—and if they were, he did not care—Radvyed lifted Beloved and sat her on his lap. She put her arms around his neck and looked at him. Then she asked about his journey, whether the king and queen were angry, and about the state of the bitterwood vine.

He told her that his parents were not irate, but sorry that the daughter-in-law they had tried to welcome had instead been made so uneasy. "And the bitterwood vine—I am surprised you do not know." Radvyed could feel she was smiling although her face remained solemn. "You *do* know!" he said, narrowing his eyes a little and jostling his knee. Beloved grabbed his shoulders to steady herself and laughed.

"I know that something happened. And I know what happened to me. But I do not know exactly what did happen."

"As you might imagine, since Dris was called in to advise us—the king, the queen, Lady Rue, and myself—her plan involved presenting me with an impossible task to be done with an inadequate tool." Radvyed grinned to hear Beloved laugh again.

"We were standing there outside looking at the wretched thing and she hands me an axe, and has a man hold a ladder, then tells me that I—and only I!—must cut the thing down, thorn, branch, and root."

Beloved sobered. "Poor Husband," she said. "I am sorry." He held her closely to him, then loosened his arms and sat back. He kept his riding gloves on; he did not want to show her his bandaged hands.

"It took all day. As I cut and threw down branches, Dris and the others burned them. That is all."

Beloved cocked her head. "Nothing else?" she asked.

"No, why, did we forget to do something? Is it growing back?" Radvyed asked, alarmed.

"No, no," she replied. "Only…what day was this?"

"The day you left."

Beloved looked off, her gaze not seeing the village before her. She seemed to be counting back the hours. Radvyed waited, watching her. Then she looked back at him.

"That day, what time did you begin cutting?"

"About midmorning."

"From the time you began cutting, I could feel it."

His chest tightened and he gripped her a little harder. "Did I hurt you?"

"No. No! I could feel it, like—like weights were being removed from my arms and legs, my neck and shoulders. When I left the palace, I could barely walk, but as the day went on, the pain and the heaviness slipped away, until by nightfall I was moving freely. But…" Beloved became thoughtful once more.

"Yes?" he prodded.

"But there was something more. Not only a relief from the heaviness and the pain, but a new feeling. I am not sure how to describe it. Somehow, I did not worry anymore. I slept so well that night."

"Oh? Where?"

"Outside. I rolled myself up in my cloak and slept outside." Radvyed turned his gaze away. "Did you worry?" she asked. "But who or what could harm me?"

His face dimmed and he still did not look at her. "It seems the only one who can and does harm you is your husband."

Beloved straightened and gave a little shove to his shoulder. "Enough," she said. "You can hurt me because I love you. Do you wish me to cease loving you?"

"No. Nor do I wish to continue hurting you." They sat in silence, Beloved considering his profile as he stared straight ahead.

Then she said, "You know that when we first set out from the Hidden House I had never ridden before?"

He turned his head to look at her. "Yes. You did not complain, however."

Beloved gave a small shrug. "What would complaining have accomplished? We were already riding slowly because of the need to heal the land and meet the people who came to us. Nevertheless, those first days of riding were not at all comfortable." Radvyed nodded. He had helped her up and down from the saddle; he had seen how she and the others from the Hidden House had had to become inured to long days of riding. "My muscles ached," continued Beloved. "I was sore. Everything seemed awkward and strange. I was sitting on top of a small moving hill with a mind of its own. And all around me, everyone else seemed to have been born to the saddle."

"I was," said Radvyed. "I believe I first sat a pony at the same age that I was learning to walk."

Beloved nodded. "I was sure that I would never manage. And yet the horse and I were working together with good will. By the time we arrived at the royal city, riding was beginning to seem not the completely unnatural and odd thing it had been at first."

"So, we are learning a new skill and it is only reasonable to expect discomfort and awkwardness," Radvyed said.

"Not only are we studying a new skill, we are learning together. Like two animals who must pull a cart. I saw a team of oxen the other day as I walked. They were having trouble settling to their task."

Radvyed laughed. "So, we are two beasts yoked! And both of us used to pulling alone. Very well, then, Beloved: no more grumbling. You are here with me; the sun is shining; and you will come home. Of what do I have to complain?"

"Nothing, Husband," she agreed. "But perhaps your horse has a grievance." Radvyed turned, and saw Belikon had stretched his neck to drink from a trough in the smith's yard, which was near the post the reins had been tied to.

"Indeed," Radvyed said. After tightening his arms briefly about her, he set her aside. He walked to Belikon and laid a hand on the horse's flank in silent apology. While Belikon finished drinking, Radvyed neared the forge where the smith worked. Beloved wandered over to stand by her husband. After a few moments the smith rested from his work, looked at the prince, and bowed with his hand over his heart.

"Good day, Your Radiance."

"Good day, Master Smith. I thank you for letting my lady and myself make free of your yard—and my horse of your trough."

"She's a sweet girl, Your Radiance." The smith smiled at Beloved, who smiled back. "It is our honor and our pleasure that you choose to sit with us."

"Your wife is here then? May I thank her also?"

As the smith went to the little house behind the smithy and called through the open door, Beloved said, "Yes, a very kind woman, a spinster. She let me watch her spinning wool into yarn."

Radvyed looked down into her face and smiled. "I know you love to see such work done," he said.

"She even let me try to spin, a little! Not with her wheel, but with a...a drop spindle." She gestured to suggest the shape of the tool. "But I only produced a bit of thick, lumpy yarn."

The smith's wife came out to meet them, making the customary obeisance. "Our thanks, good mistress, for your hospitality," said the prince, taking her hand. Beloved smiled at the woman, who was as thin as her husband. The deep grooves between the spinster's brows and beside her stern mouth suggested she did not always welcome strangers into their yard.

Yet under Beloved's smile the village woman's face softened and she said, "It was an honor and a pleasure, Your Radiance, to serve Princess Beloved."

"Husband, you would not believe the fineness of her spinning!" said Beloved. "And she showed me some of her work in lace—like cobwebs, and dyed red with the *somredin* berry." Beloved looked to the other woman to make sure she had the correct word; the spinster nodded. "Sometime we must come to the shearing, which I would very much like to see."

Radvyed said, "Perhaps we may make a Riding to see it." The smith and his wife smiled at this, pleased. While Radvyed asked the smith about stabling for Belikon and about the inn for board and bed, Beloved walked over to the stone wall, where a few low shrubs straggled.

"What plant is this?" she asked the spinster, who had followed a few steps behind.

"It is an herb whose oil is good for healing burns, Your Radiance. When I married Smith, my family gave me some, for they grow well on my people's hillside. But here, no matter where I plant them or how I tend them, they do not flourish. Yet even these poor leaves give some good oil."

Beloved fingered a few leaves, a small smile on her lips. "I am not so handy as you," she said, "but what my hand can do, I give you in return for your kindness to me." And she touched a branch or leaf of each shrub, then turned to look at the woman, who stood, uncertain of her princess's meaning.

"Thank you, Your Radiance," said the spinster politely.

Beloved laughed and walked back with the still-perplexed woman to where their men were speaking. "Do not worry, mistress! You will know what you thank me for before long. But it is my thanks to you."

Radvyed and Beloved then left the smith and his wife. Radvyed untied and led Belikon. They went up to the village's small inn, which was a tavern with an extra room or three for guests and a stable with a few extra stalls for guests' horses. The people they met acknowledged them by laying their right hands over their hearts and giving a slight bow, but did not approach them.

Beloved was surprised. After they had seen Belikon safely into the hands of the tavern's *kunik* and had closed the door of their room, she said, "On our journey from the border everyone gathered to greet you, but here, you are treated more as someone else's *miren* rather than as their own prince. Yet I have been learning that the royal blood belongs to the people even more than it belongs to your House."

Radvyed took her into his arms and replied, "Before it was more like a Visiting. This is a Riding. And there is also the Tithing to explain. But my lady, I most humbly request," and here he bent to brush her temple with his lips, "that all explanations be delayed, until more urgent matters have been attended to." He kissed her neck just beneath her ear, then pressed more kisses along her throat.

Beloved agreed.

Chapter Thirty-Nine

That evening, although the tavern was perhaps a little more crowded than was usual, Radvyed and Beloved dined undisturbed. After they had finished their meal, the prince pushed his chair around so that it faced the room, and said, "I believe you all know that I have recently married," for all the world as though he were a neighbor returned after a long trade journey. "This is Princess Beloved, also known as the Lady of the Rose." Beloved, straightening in her seat as she was introduced, felt at the prince's words the surge of love and—*power* was the only way she knew to name it—sweep towards them. She accepted it into herself; with some surprise, she noticed that so did her husband. As he asked for local news and the villagers responded, she could feel the power eddying about the room. The people gave to the prince and to her; they, especially the prince, returned it to the people. Each exchange enriched and strengthened the power, until she felt almost giddy with it.

At length there was a lull and Beloved asked her own question. "Tell me, what is the tale of the orchard outside your wall? For nowhere else on these hills have I seen as many trees, and nowhere fruit trees at all. How came they here?"

"That I can answer best, Your Radiance," said the tavern host, "seeing as it's my great-grandfather as planted them." He waited until the other voices who had undertaken to tell the tale quieted. "Now, my great-granda, he was a traveler," the man continued. "He went often down to the low flatlands beyond the hills. On one of those travels, he met a girl, and married her, and brought her back home. But the girl had never lived in our hills before, and she found them strange and bare. She grew sick, her heart still in the flatlands, where her people had orchards and the wind, she said, blew sweeter, and life was not so hard to get from the earth. So the next time he traveled, he brought back with him plum saplings, and she chose where she thought they might grow best. To teach her that there was softness in the hills, he gave her two lamblings, and he traveled no more, because he had trees and a flock to care for."

"And she?" asked Beloved. "Was her heartsickness cured?"

"Who knows the secret heart?" said the tavern host unexpectedly. "But the lambs and the orchard gave her something to care for that needed her strength, and they had nine children, and she stayed."

The next morning, when they left the village, Beloved paused by the trees outside the walls. She stood considering them, then turned her face about, seeking something. Radvyed thought that she might be sensing the direction of the wind. She moved until the wind was blowing at her back and she was facing the orchard. Then she loosely held her hands palms out and chest high before her, drew in a deep breath, and gently but steadily blew. It looked almost as if she were piping, but there was no pipe or reed. She played, as it seemed to Radvyed, a soundless tune, her breath mingling with the breeze, and then weaving with it among the branches of the trees. When she was done, she lowered her hands, closed her eyes, and was quiet a moment. Then, apparently satisfied with her work, she opened her eyes and walked back to where Radvyed and Belikon were standing, awaiting her. Radvyed raised an eyebrow inquiringly, but she merely smiled and said, "So you said we might return for the shearing, and you called it a Riding?"

As they made their way down the steep trail, Radvyed told her about the ways by which those of the royal House went among the people. Beloved had thought that the royal family had only freedom to move within Zolatar, the royal city. She had believed every excursion from the city would result in the kind of travel they had known from the border upon their return from the Griefstone, but that had been an unusual case. Then the prince had returned victorious from a great feat, a benevolent sorceress in his train. Add in the people's relief at the breaking of the salt curse, and it was no wonder his way homeward had been unusually slow.

Radvyed explained that every ten years, the royal family made a thorough, formal tour of the kingdom called a Tithing. The last time, about five years ago, he had been old enough to help in fulfilling this duty apart from his parents: he had toured the south and west, while they had taken the northern and eastern districts. The purpose of these journeys was for the members of the royal House to come into contact with as many people and as much territory as possible. As Beloved listened, it was obvious to her that these tours served to strengthen the sacred and powerful bond between the royal House and the rest of the country: they were not merely an essential element of an ancient and wise tradition of governing, as the prince considered them. Radvyed and his parents viewed the Tithings as crucial to the unity of the kingdom: since anyone could present petitions to the king, queen, or heir during these journeys, the tours were important means of both upholding justice in the realm and understanding the needs of their people. But there were also more pointed excursions, called Visits. The king, queen, or heir could Visit a particular *mirenzem*, town, or hall and stay as long as the royal deemed it necessary.

Visits were made for a variety of reasons, not all of them welcome to the hosts in question: to shore up local authority, to investigate *mireni* or officials accused of wrongdoing, or to participate in a district festival, for example. Finally, there were Ridings, informal travel by the royals. During these trips, while the people might acknowledge the royal person present among them, they did not approach, unless, as at the inn the night before, the royal gave a sign that he or she was available. Since they were on a Riding now, he and Beloved would be able to move freely, Radvyed said.

They made their way walking, leading Belikon down the hill path, the morning sun behind them. He told her about the thrumming of his wedding bracelet. She nodded and said that hers had become cool as she had distanced herself from the palace, only warming again the afternoon of the day before.

"I hoped that meant you were near," said Beloved.

Radvyed stopped and showed her the sprig of her vine where the smaller way joined the larger. Beloved bent down, touching a leaf lightly. When she straightened, she said, "I had a dream the night before that you were searching for me. So when I decided to follow this other path, I left a sign." He looked at her, bemused. She looked back at him, her head cocked, uncertain why he was staring at her.

"You left a living flower not native to this place as a sign?" Radvyed asked.

"Yes," Beloved answered, still puzzled. "I felt sure you would recognize it."

"So I did," he said, smiling at her. "I only wondered how."

"Oh. A bit of grass, twisted together, wetted with saliva, and planted," she said, her gestures describing the twisting, moistening, and setting into the earth of the plucked grass.

"And magic," Radvyed said. "A spell," he added, when she did not agree right away.

"A spell, I suppose you would say. Or an intention. Or perhaps persuasion. How would you have left a sign?"

"I might have made a pile of small stones or an arrangement of sticks—whatever material was to hand."

"That is what I did. What would you call the power you used to move one stone upon another? Magic? A spell?"

He shook his head and laughed. "No. Perhaps I would call it an *intention*. But not *persuasion*." Radvyed looked down at the little plant, a little rueful, still smiling. Beloved kept her eyes on him, her gaze quizzical. Then they continued down until they were but a mile or two from Perikrost. He told her the story of Alya and Van's courtship.

"I would like to find this famous fountain," Radvyed said. "Although I think it must be by the far gate. In any case, we should get you a horse. And food."

"Will you not be recognized?" Beloved asked. "I know this is a... a Riding," she said, still unfamiliar with the terms of royal movement within the kingdom. "But do you wish to have it known we are here?"

"Now that you are with me and we are returning home, I do not mind being known," he said. "Before, when I traveled to your thornwood, the task was too urgent for me to give any thought to anything or anyone else. I could not allow myself to be distracted. When I came to find you this time, I was anxious, and—" Radvyed broke off and was silent a moment. "I did not hide myself from Van and Alya," he said, and she knew there was something she had missed, that she was not perceiving here. "Do you wish to be unknown, Beloved?"

She thought for a bit, as they stood by the road, Belikon cropping the grass on the wayside while the two humans spoke together. "It is still a little strange, although not unwelcome, this being known and—" Beloved frowned, searching for the word she wanted.

"Being known and beloved?" Radvyed said.

She half laughed. "Yes, being known and beloved as Princess and Lady of the Rose, one of the Company of the Salt-Breakers, Consort of Prince Radvyed…" She could not recall any of her other names and titles from their wedding day. She looked at the walls of Perikrost and the roofs visible above them. "Let us find a horse for me and food for us both. Perhaps we will catch sight of the fountain, too," she said. Now that they were off the hill track they could ride, either one or both on Belikon's back, but they chose to walk beside him as the town was not far and they wished to talk.

As they approached the town gate, Radvyed felt Beloved begin to do what he thought of as drawing herself in. He put a hand on her arm and she slowed, turning towards him.

"Do not," he said. Her brows came together but she did not ask him what he meant: she knew.

"But I do not wish to disturb—"

"Do not trammel yourself," he said. "Let us see how this…this grafting of your magic to our royalty plays out." Radvyed saw that she hesitated. "Please," he added.

"As you wish," Beloved said. "I will not trammel myself, as you put it. Yet I will not be heedless. I shall be…as royalty on a Riding."

He smiled. "Let us see then what may come."

CHAPTER FORTY

Perikrost was a bustling town, full of its business, and while people were surprised and pleased to see the prince and his bride, they greeted the couple with the customary slight bow and hand on heart, but otherwise did not approach. The Tithings and the Visits also had another purpose, thought Beloved. By guaranteeing the attention and the presence of royalty at certain known times, the people were kept connected to their ruling House. They were not hungry for contact with them. Once a man wept over the prince's hand and another time a woman was unable to resist touching Beloved's garment, but it was plain from their disapproving glances that the other townspeople saw these actions as indecorous, even boorish.

Yet there was something different, thought Radvyed, from other Ridings. Beloved made a difference. In part this was because she herself was still new to the people: her history, her role in breaking the salt curse, and the simple fact of her physical presence were new to the fabric of their lives. Although the townspeople were discreet, they were curious. More found business to do in the streets where they passed, and reason to come out of doors just as the royal couple came by, than on other, similar occasions. Yet their interest could not be explained only by the desire to catch a glimpse of the new princess or even of a mysterious sorceress. They would have been curious about any recent royal or magic-wielder, but they lingered because they were fascinated by Beloved herself. This did not surprise Radvyed, as he himself found her intriguing. After a short while of being in Perikrost with her, however, he began to realize that his people were charmed by his wife because she was so clearly charmed by them.

As in Zolatar and the hill village, she admired any display of skill or craft, no matter how commonplace, from the work of the butcher to that of the cobbler, from the child making wreaths of dried flowers to the weaver displaying cloth made from the wool of the hill flocks. She noticed with pleasure the calls of the vendors, the haggling at store counters, the way the laundry was beaten to cleanliness in the washhouse of a square. The people felt the genuineness of her interest, the simple respect that she had for the skill of their hands and for the ways they shaped and moved through their lives, and they responded with warmth and even courteous familiarity.

For her part, Beloved felt like a flower opening in sunlight. During their ride into the royal city from the border she had held herself in; during the heady time of the first days at the palace, she had felt almost drunk on the waves of power that washed over her from her acceptance and welcome from the king and queen and the people of Tamtir. Now, while she still felt the energy of the people flowing towards her and the prince, she did not feel overwhelmed. Since she was not concentrating on holding herself in or coping with surges of strong power, she could let herself move out towards the people. As Beloved felt the townspeople's warm reception and how their initial formality softened as their princess watched them work or asked them questions, she sensed them respond to her, not only as Radvyed's bride, but as herself. Beloved allowed herself to relax a little more and to enjoy the time in Perikrost.

Radvyed noticed as the day wore on that after they passed, the autumn flowers in pots by doorways seemed fuller and brighter and the trees planted in squares and by houses more vigorous. They ate at an inn: Radvyed, now on the alert for signs, saw when they left that the buds on a late-blooming trumpet vine against the front wall had burst into flower, releasing its intoxicating fragrance. When they bought a horse, a small potted lavender shrub by the stable door seemed to grow a little, stretching itself in the afternoon light. He was pleased at these small, unobtrusive indications that Beloved felt at ease.

Radvyed and Beloved looked for the place where Alya and Van had met, but Perikrost, at the foot of the hills, was well supplied with water, and most squares had a public fountain. In late afternoon they considered how much farther to go that day. Beloved wished to meet Alya and Van, so they decided to travel at least as far as their farm.

Accordingly, they made for the western gate, called the Cloth Gate, for it was by that way that the local woolen goods went out to the rest of the kingdom. In the square before the gate there was a fountain, which they decided was the one of the fateful brawl. It was a popular meeting place, and there was, along with the fetching of water and the press of animals, a fair amount of flirting and jostling among the young men and women. Beloved and Radvyed did not linger to watch, however, as they wanted to be sure to reach Van and Alya's farm before dark.

As they rode away from the town, Radvyed brought his horse near hers and asked Beloved what she thought of her first foray out "untrammeled."

"I liked it very much. I am becoming used to how much power they give us. And of course now it is not in the huge waves that it was a few weeks ago." She saw that Radvyed was staring at her, puzzled.

"What have I said?" she asked.

"Who gives us power? What power?"

She focused a moment on her mare, Tisha, who had spied a patch of interesting flowers by the roadside and needed to be recalled to her business. Then looking at Radvyed, Beloved said, "The power you get from your people. You yourself said you were a lens for them."

"Do you mean magic? I know you love to watch people work, do, make…but there is no magic here, no sorcery. My people, we of Tamtir, our blood has no magic."

Beloved glanced at him before looking ahead at the road that passed steadily under their horses' hooves, like a rough ribbon unspooling before them. "I am always surprised by how sincere you are when you say such things. It is very clear to me that the magic, as you might call it, of this realm, of this people, is in many ways more complicated than the power that lives in me. My bloodline has sorcery dense within us, bone, breath, and blood. Yet the power in this land is like a web binding everyone to the land, to the royal House, to each other. The longer I am here the less I wonder that the salt curse was baffled at the border."

Radvyed did not answer. He loved his country and his people, of course, but he hardly thought of them as magical, as Beloved insisted. Magic, to him, meant something exotic, strange, a little frightening but also thrilling: a shimmer of glamour over tales of kingdoms far away and long ago, in which mysterious maidens suffered cruel spells cast by evil warlocks and unlikely heroes, helped by a peculiar crone or two, brandished bright swords at the moment of seemingly inevitable defeat. It was with deep surprise that he realized that his own life of the past months fit that description well. *But of course*, he thought, *I should have known the moment I understood the story of the Tower.*

They rode on in silence. Radvyed was trying to absorb the idea of Tamtir as a magical kingdom and himself and Beloved as figures in a tale. Beloved saw that he was thinking through what she had said and so did not speak. She was content to look about her, to glance over her shoulder at the Sinevy Hills, which distance was beginning to soften to a smoky blue, to feel the animal moving steadily beneath her, and to share silence with the man riding at her side. She thought she would never stop noticing these simple pleasures of a body moving freely through the world.

The sun had begun her evening show, gathering her skirts of orange flame and blue cloud before sinking out of sight, when they saw the buildings of Van and Alya's farm a bit above and back from the road on the right. They turned into the cart track that led up to the farmhouse. Beloved looked about her, but the light was quickly fading, and she saw no more than the darkening shapes of buildings behind the house, and could only distinguish what might be the stables. Overlaying the farm smells of animals and earth drifted the lighter smell of some plant grown for beauty and not usefulness. She saw a white cat slip around a corner. Three dogs, large and curious, came around to the front. The horses shifted, but after the lead dog gave a series of short barks, the canine trio settled near the door and merely kept a watchful eye on the newcomers. Radvyed turned to her with a smile.

He nodded towards the dogs and said, "Van and Alya's doorbell. We wait here until the master or the mistress of the house comes." They did not wait long. The shadow of a man broke away from what Beloved had decided was the barn and strode towards them. As he neared, the light from the house window caught him.

He looked up at his mounted visitors and said, "How may I—" Then he stopped short, looking quickly from Radvyed to Beloved and back. Radvyed grinned at him. Van laughed, a little breathlessly, for how often does one play host to the crown prince in a lifetime, never mind a week? Clasping Radvyed's stirrup with one hand while he briefly put his other over his heart, he said, "Well, Your Radiance, I see that she indeed let herself be found and glad I am to know it. How may my wife and I serve you and your lady?"

"If it is not too much trouble, we seek shelter for the night."

"Of course, of course! And have you yet eaten?"

"No, not yet."

"Then you shall sup with us." Van turned toward the house. "Alya! Alya!" he called. When his wife answered with an inquiring shout, Van smiled at Beloved, and replied, "Visitors, wife! They stay for supper and sleep!" Alya came to the door, wiping her hands on her apron.

"Visitors?" She saw first that the newcomers were mounted on good horses and wore well-made clothes, then she looked at Beloved, who looked back at her. Alya's gaze moved to Radvyed, and she gasped, automatically bowing with her hand on her heart, then looked back at Beloved, at Radvyed, and finally at her laughing husband. "Visitors! Honored guests, you mean, you wretched man! And here I am in my apron—"

Radvyed said, "I hope we are no trouble?"

"Trouble! Of course not! Just—just a surprise! Please be welcome to our house, Your Radiance—and Your Ladyship—or is it Radiance—"

"I am so new to my change in state," said Beloved, "that I am not entirely sure myself how you should address me." Radvyed had dismounted, handing the reins to Van. He went to Beloved's horse to help his wife down. Van gathered the reins for her horse as well, then led both animals away towards the barn.

"You may be called Princess or Your Radiance," said Radvyed.

Alya had meanwhile managed to get over her first startlement at the unexpected and exalted visitors. "Come in, come in, Your Radiances!" She threw open the door and the warm light from the lamp on the table spilled out into the dusk-dark dooryard. The dogs drowsily shifted into a more comfortable pile and shut their eyes. Radvyed took Beloved's hand and they stepped into the embrace of the house.

Chapter Forty-One

Dinner was simple but satisfying. Beloved, as Radvyed was noticing was her way, drank in the details of the place. She flustered Alya a little by her close attention to the room around her, to the objects in it, and to how the mistress of it all moved about her house, ordering and working. A friendly quiet prevailed and Beloved wondered a little at the lack of conversation, until she remembered that in the hill village there had also been reticence until the prince had signaled his openness to talk.

Settling back in his seat when the meal was finished, Radvyed smiled at Van and Alya and said, "So, what news since I was here last?"

Van laughed and Alya smiled; she stood and began to clear the table. Beloved glanced at Radvyed, who gave a nearly imperceptible shake of his head, so she sat back a little in her chair.

Van replied, "I'm afraid nothing as interesting as a royal visitor. And nothing to interest a royal guest." Van was speaking to Radvyed, but his eyes rested on Beloved's face; she, in turn, was quietly watching Alya. It was clear that the princess was not sure how to behave. *She is not haughty*, Van decided, *or frightened. She feels herself a stranger here and she does not wish to give offense. And perhaps she is a little embarrassed at her flight from the palace.*

Alya returned to the table; she had determined her task now was to serve her guests with conversation. She turned to Beloved. "The prince said you were traveling, Your Radiance. Did you stop at Perikrost?"

"No, I went around and beyond, up into the hills, to a village with an orchard outside the wall and a smithy just inside the gate," Beloved readily answered. "The village is called Nagorna." Van and Alya nodded in recognition. "But on our return," Beloved continued, "we did come through Perikrost. The prince and I were trying to identify the fountain you threw your husband into."

Van half choked on a laugh, while Alya repeated slowly, "The fountain I threw my husband into."

"Yes," said Beloved. "Or was the prince telling me a false tale?" She glanced at Radvyed. "Did you not say that when they first met, she threw him into a fountain?"

Alya was now eyeing her husband. "I don't remember throwing him, exactly," she said, while Van grinned at her, "though I'm not saying he wouldn't have deserved it if I did. I do remember him jostling with another one with more brawn than brain, and in their need to get their own animals watered first, they ended up pushing *me* into the fountain." Beloved looked at Van, who was now shaking his head mournfully, then back at Alya, who was maintaining her air of stern disdain.

"They pushed you into the fountain?" said Beloved. "What did you do then?"

Alya turned to the princess. "Well, what should I do? I got myself out, with no help from either of those great oafs, I might add, and picked up my good oaken bucket, and—" Alya broke off, plainly wondering whether announcing that she had joined the brawl was really in keeping with her pose of offended dignity.

But Van had no doubts. "And cracked us both in the head with it and went off home, leaving two poor men bleeding in the street!" Beloved was not sure what her reaction should be. She was startled by the violence of the story and confused that Van, the prince, and even Alya, who allowed herself a small, satisfied, reminiscent smile, appeared amused.

"Not before filling my trusty bucket, I didn't," said that good woman. "And as for bleeding, *pff!* A little cut on your forehead. It didn't seem to do much harm to you and it didn't put you off, either, because there you were again the next day."

"The other man wasn't!" Van said, and laughed. "But I was careful about jostling Alya after that, let me tell you."

"As you should be," said Alya. "It was good for you to know right off that I won't be pushed around."

"But, Prince," said Van reproachfully, turning more fully to face Radvyed. "I never told you that Alya here threw me into the fountain! Conked me with that iron-hard bucket, yes, but not dunking me in water!"

Radvyed laughed, watching Beloved out of the corner of his eye. "Yes, I regret that I misrepresented you and your good lady to the princess." He turned to Beloved with a solemn face, but she thought he was still laughing. "Beloved, I have wronged this good man and his wife. It was *he* threw *her* into the fountain, while *she* struck *him* with a bucket. Pray remember the true tale should anyone inquire."

Beloved smiled hesitantly back, still uncertain how to understand their relaxed talk or how to respond appropriately. She knew she should say something and so said what she was wondering. "But then, after such a beginning, how did you come to marry?"

The other three laughed as though she had said something very funny, but Radvyed could see that she had asked the question seriously. After a moment, Alya realized it, too.

Still smiling, the farmwoman answered, "Well, it wasn't all a bad way to begin, was it? Van here learned that I'm not meek nor timid and I learned, when he showed up the next day, that he wasn't put off by a woman who would not put up with such nonsense. And then over the next weeks, he kept showing up, and we'd talk while he helped me with my work. You can find out a fair bit about a person working side by side. And since he came to me, my family grew to know him, too. So by the time I asked him how long he was planning on hanging around me and shirking his work at home"—here she was interrupted by an indignant *oi!* from Van, and her smile widened—"by that time, as I say, we knew each other about as well as you can before getting married. So I decided he would do. It helped that he hadn't knocked me into water or anything else since that first day."

Beloved turned to Van. "And you? What made you come back and *court* a woman who hit you with a bucket?"

Van laughed and reached across the table to take his wife's capable, work-roughened fingers in his own calloused hand. Beloved watched as they twined and folded their fingers together, her eyes lingering on their wedding bracelets of dyed leather. "Well, I'll admit that it can put someone out to be dunked in water unexpected-like. And that water coming off the hills is cold! But I noticed, once I could sit up and shake some thought back into my head, that she used that bucket no more than was just. One hit on the head to each of us and she was off. Not a word of scolding, no, not even the next day when I saw her again. I had done wrong, she had given swift justice, and no more was said about it in blame or reproach until this very day. Well, a woman like that is worth something, and I don't grudge the cut it took to learn it about her." He stopped and considered. "And then," he added, "you can see my Alya's a lovely woman. As a girl she was the beauty of Perikrost, and beauty casts its own spell, maybe making a man not think the way he might otherwise."

Radvyed glanced at Beloved. She, of all people, knew how potent a spell beauty or ugliness could be. Van and Alya did not know or did not remember that Beloved had been under a curse of hideousness for most of her life. Radvyed was uncertain how she would react to Van's half-joking assertion that Alya's beauty had drawn him with spell-like power.

But Beloved was calm, looking at Alya and Van thoughtfully, her gaze flicking down to their joined hands, then back up to their kind eyes. Their faces bore the story of their years passed together, not without trouble or sorrow or even anger, but also not alone.

Beloved said slowly, "Indeed, beauty has its own power to draw and even to give hope. When the prince first came to my house, I was bound by a curse as strong as the salt."

Van and Alya were quiet now, listening. Radvyed watched his wife as she spoke, noticing how the firelight caught at her hair and flickered across her cheek, and how her eyes, although resting again on the entwined fingers of the older couple, seemed to look inward, as though she were gradually seeing some truth in her mind as it emerged, word by word, from her lips.

"When the prince came, I had spent my life hidden away, shamed and trammeled by my repulsiveness and agony." Alya stifled a distressed sound. "And when I first saw him, so handsome..." Beloved was silent, remembering, then resumed her thought. "His handsomeness was a gift to me, a candle in darkness. That such beauty existed, that I could be allowed to behold it, that the curse could take from me so much, but not this, the pleasure and the wonder of looking on his face...and then he stayed, and spoke to me—always kind, always courteous, although that could not have been easy—it was as if a ray of sun, a breath of wind, had come into my life. He was water in a salt land." She was quiet again, then said, "It was long before I let him go." She stopped speaking and lifted her cup to her lips; the other three were silent.

The fire popped. Beloved looked up, belatedly worried that she had said too much, that she had made them uncomfortable, that she had said something to offend the prince's dignity. But Van's lined face held sadness and compassion as he looked at her; Alya had tears in her eyes and her lips were tightly pressed together. Radvyed took Beloved's hand and laced his fingers between hers, in that gesture that always recalled to her the night when she finally was able to release him. He looked at her, then away, and Beloved realized that she had never said this to him, what it had meant to her, having him there at her table, night after night. What she had said was true: she had received his presence as a gift unlooked-for, amazed that she should be, after so much misery and loneliness, allowed this man's company for even a brief while. She was still astonished that he had returned to her, that he had found the way to free her, that he had come once again in search of her, that he was even now sitting by her and holding her hand.

But now it occurred to her that the silence was perhaps oppressively serious. "I am sorry," Beloved said in a low voice that was almost a whisper. "I am sorry. I did not intend to make everyone sad. Please forgi—"

She broke off as Radvyed squeezed her hand and she looked at him. He was shaking his head, but there was a smile, small but real.

"Not sad, Your Radiance," said Alya, after dabbing her face with her sleeve. "Not sad, but sorry to think you had been so unhappy. We had heard you had been under a curse, of course, but we heard more of the end of the story, you see. Our prince went and found the flower that saved Her Splendor, the queen, and then returned and broke the salt curse and won the Rose Lady for his bride...it all seemed a grand and splendid story. But now I see that for you, inside the story at the long and painful end, as it were, for you it was not so grand and splendid."

Now Beloved's face shone with remembered happiness. "Oh, but, Alya," she said, leaning forward and putting her hand on the woman's arm. "Alya, it *was* grand and splendid to open my eyes and to know that I was free. To have the prince there beside me and to know that he had come back, that he had found the way. That joy no bard, no storyteller could tell, and have it in full." Radvyed thought of the Tower tale and wondered whether even now its ending satisfied.

Then he looked around and saw the others did not know what to say next; it was up to him to help them to firm ground again. "But, Alya," he said with a grin, "you, too, are a heroine. How was it, at the time, to be in the Tale of the Fight at the Fountain? Sad or splendid?" They all laughed and regained their equilibrium.

"Well, Your Radiance," said Alya as they rose from the table and prepared to retire for the night, "I can't say it was either sad or splendid. *Soaked*, is what I'd say."

"Ah, lass," whispered Van in his wife's ear as they sought their hastily made-up bed in the loft after an evening neither would forget for the rest of their lives, "you were splendid then and you are still."

Chapter Forty-Two

The next morning, Radvyed and Beloved said their good-byes to Alya and Van while an early mist rose from the ground and a pale sun peeked over the hills. Beloved looked back when their horses joined the road and saw the couple still standing and watching them, Alya in her apron and Van with his leather jerkin, ready to return to their tasks as soon as their honored visitors were out of sight. She felt their love and their kindness reach towards her and she raised a hand in farewell, realizing a moment later that she had released more than her good wishes. She watched as a dormant vine that clung to a trellis by the front door woke and stretched out new leaves. A trumpet-shaped flower of deep blue opened right over Alya's head. Beloved bit her lip, decided that the vine's freshness was not too implausible, and turned Tisha to follow Radvyed as Belikon trotted ahead.

It was during this day of riding that Beloved realized that beauty could be an actual inconvenience. When she had ridden with the prince and their company from the border of Tamtir to the royal city, he had of course not sought to travel unnoticed. His face had been bared, his ring worn openly, and his horse, clothes, and manner had proclaimed his lineage. But now, when he would like to travel with less notice, it was difficult. His horse was a fine one and would always draw attention. He could, and did, wear clothes that while marking him as wealthy, did not necessarily proclaim his royalty. He did not seek to draw attention to himself by his manner: no showy horsemanship, no loud talk or laughter, no exaggerated gestures. But as contained as he kept himself, the arresting beauty of his face and form caused every person he met to stare, miss a step, even stop whatever they were doing: speaking, walking, working. They soon enough realized who he was and since it was obvious he was not on a public journey, they refrained from approaching him, merely giving the little bow with a hand over the heart. It helped that he rode and did not stop or slow. But it was clear to Beloved that everyone needed to shake off the effect of his handsomeness almost as though they were trying to resist a charm or spell. Some seemed more affected than others, but everyone felt the effect of looking on the prince as he passed by.

Beloved thought about how he could further restrain the power of his looks. His deeply cowled hood, for example, if pulled up, might hide quite a bit of his face. Of course, it would also eliminate much of his peripheral vision and in warm weather be uncomfortably hot. He could wear a veil. There were fabrics so fine that one could see through them even as one's face was obscured. This, too, might be uncomfortable, and why should the prince not be allowed the fresh air and sunlight, or even rain, should he desire it, on his skin? A veil would not help him travel unnoticed anyway. Without one he was recognized by his beauty; with one he would be recognized by his hiddenness. And why should his people not have the blessing of beholding him, if he went among them? No one seemed hurt or offended by his presence. Rather, she thought, people seem to look as though they had been given a gift, like discovering a flower among high rocks or opening a door to a warm, firelit room on a cold, wet night.

Radvyed and Beloved did not say much on the way back to the city. Beloved was not yet a good enough rider to converse easily on horseback and the prince was not inclined to speak while on a well-used public road. They traveled slowly, both in deference to Beloved's rudimentary riding skills and to accommodate the needs of themselves and their horses. Dusk had purpled the air when their horses' hooves rang on the cobblestones outside the palace gate. The *strazha* saluted and let them pass. Beloved drooped in the saddle. Radvyed looked at her with sympathy: for someone still as new as she to riding, a day on horseback was no easy thing. As they came into the stableyard, *kuniki* ran up to take their horses. The prince dismounted, handed the reins over to a *kunika* with a word of thanks for both the stablewoman and Belikon, and went to Beloved's side. A *kunik* had helped her down from her mount, and she now held tightly to the man's arm, as her legs were unsteady beneath her. A second *kunika* had taken charge of Tisha. Radvyed thanked and dismissed the man helping Beloved, then took her arm himself.

"Come, Beloved. Let us reassure my father and mother and Lady Rue and Dris. They have all been anxious for you."

Radvyed led her from the stableyard through a less impressive entrance to the palace, much to Beloved's relief. She did not want to climb the grand sweep of stairs on her tired legs. As they moved through rooms and halls, she noticed that the *damashi*, the *mireni* in residence at the palace, and the *dovoreni* acknowledged and saluted them. Yet aside from a startled blink or a quick breath, the prince's handsomeness did not affect them as strongly as it did the people outside the palace and city. *They have learned to live with his beauty*, thought Beloved. *Can they not become accustomed to me?*

Chapter Forty-Three

Arkost and Gladna were in one of the royal family's private apartments, a room made not for entertaining, but for a few people to relax informally. The chamber was still larger than Alya and Van's house, but it was arranged not for display or mingling, but for quiet conversations, letter writing, or a game of cards or of foxes and hounds. Beloved was unsure what to expect, although Radvyed had told her during their journey home that his parents were not angry.

"They were hurt and confused, as was I, to learn that you had fled the palace in distress and without a word to anyone. When I left, however, they were making plans for how to make our house a shelter and not a cage for you."

"You speak of me as of a wild animal," she said, her step slowing and her brow furrowing.

He was silent and then said, "Not an animal, no. But you are wild in that you are not tame. Or, better, you have needs that are different from those of many people. The things that bring others comfort may make you uneasy and what makes you easy may bring others discomfort."

They were approaching the door to the private apartments. Beloved said, her voice low and troubled, "I will never truly belong here, in the palace. No bread eaten or blood shed can change that."

Radvyed halted and turned to her. He held one of her hands in one of his, then nudged her face to him, urging her to meet his gaze. His eyes held hers as he said firmly, "You do belong here, and no shadow of fear or clutch of doubt will change that. You *and* your magic. You are the sorceress Beloved and I am your husband."

She gave him a subdued smile, but he did not return it until she admitted, "I am Beloved, you are my husband, and so I belong here in your house."

"*Our* house."

"Our house," she agreed. The smile he gave her dazzled her into a happy laugh.

The *damash* opened the door and they turned to face the room. Arkost and Gladna stood there in the candlelight, for full dark had fallen. Radvyed could see in their slight stiffness and the careful smoothness of their faces the remnants of their anxiety. He drew Beloved into the room and the door was shut behind them.

Before either of his parents could speak, Beloved let go of Radvyed's hand and stepped forward to stand alone before them. "I am sorry to have caused you anxiety and trouble," she began, but was interrupted as Arkost came to her, his arms open in a gesture of appeal.

"That the one who saved my queen's life and this kingdom felt so wretched in my house that she was driven to flee it will never cease to shame me," the king said, his voice more gruff than usual.

There followed a brief time of confusion. After embraces, confessions, and apologies had been exchanged, Gladna rang for tea, and stronger drink as well, to be brought. She also requested that Rue and Dris both be notified of Beloved's safe return and invited to join them.

"We will not discuss today, Beloved, the ideas that the king and some of the Council have put forth for your thriving," said the queen as they settled into comfortable chairs and recovered from the relief and high emotion of their greeting. "Time enough for that tomorrow. We merely desire to assure you that we are very happy that you have returned, sorry that you felt the need to go, and eager to discover how we may together encourage you and your magic to settle and thrive in the palace."

After that, serious matters were set aside and the royal family enjoyed a quiet hour together of talk that was not problem-solving or rule instructing. Rue, then Dris, soon joined them, and satisfied themselves that Beloved was well and in good spirits. Beloved appeared at the Court dinner that evening and if she was quiet, she was also smiling. It was seen that the prince and his parents were also untroubled and at ease, and so whatever rumors of ill will or distress had been circulating died down.

No one noticed, in the relief of that day, the clot of ravens circling the palace, before settling to roost on the roof above the princess and prince's chamber.

Chapter Forty-Four

Beloved sat up in bed, in the cold bleak light that paled the world before dawn. She looked to her side: there slept her husband, undisturbed by whatever had pricked her awake. She marveled once more at how there seemed to be no angle, no pose, no mood that made him less than breath-hitchingly handsome; then she felt again the unwelcome chill in her bones that had first roused her. She looked about the room: there was no danger that she could see in the shadows or sense in the air. Beloved slid her legs to the side of the bed and slipped out, unwilling to disturb her sleeping husband until she had a better idea of what was troubling her. She walked across the thick carpet to the window. After opening the glazed panes, Beloved slid the bolt and softly opened the shutters. To her relief, no bitterwood vine, thorny and salted, met her gaze. She peered down and looked about: there had been no new growth in the night. So this was not something that was arising from within her. Beloved turned and picked up the wool robe laid across a nearby chest and put it on. Again she returned to the window, considering, breathing in the morning chill. As she looked out, she thought about the prickle of unease that was strong enough to wake her from a deep sleep. A warning of danger? Or even—

There, there it was again—every hair on her body stood up, and she felt as though a cold hand had brushed the skin of her face, blindly seeking. Beloved closed her eyes and focused on the cold, clammy touch, distinct from the morning air. Deliberately she scraped her palms against the rough-cut stone of the outer sill, and felt the sting of shed blood. She spun out her power, using her shadow-self to follow the trail of the touch back: out of the palace, out of the city. She had not cast forth her shadow-self for some years, but now she followed the cold touch as she might trace with her finger a gleaming thread in a tapestry, over field and homestead, *mirenzem* and temple, forest and water, until the border of Tamtir itself was left behind. And still her shadow-self pursued, the tether of power stretched but holding, her body taut by the open window, her hands gripping the stone sill, her eyes closed and blind.

Outside the kingdom's borders, the trail itself was stronger, but her own power thinned and strained, anchored only by her blood, unable to draw on a deeper claiming. She could no longer discern the lineaments of the lands she passed through, but pursued the filament of strange power through a dense gray fog, until it ended in the clenched hand of a tall, bony woman with ash-white hair and dark, stony eyes. To Beloved's confused gaze, it seemed as though the woman's dark garment was decorated with feathers of some kind, but then Beloved realized that the shapes were hands. Others in the room, mages and sorcerers, fed their power through their splayed fingers into the bony woman. Beloved was not able to sense more than a rough estimate of how many—perhaps fifteen. Together they were strong, strong enough to break hills, reverse rivers, shape weather. But they wielded more than brute force, for they were skilled enough to weave their disparate filaments of power into a single seamless ribbon and searching, found and touched her as she slept.

Beloved clamped close her horror and fear. She must not snap her tether to her body. She must not give herself away.

For they did not know she was aware of them. At least Beloved did not discern any sign of consciousness of her presence. Her shadow-self, attenuated at the edge of her range, was perhaps too faint and unlooked-for. If they meant to attack her, if this were a trap, surely they would have harmed her at once. Beloved recognized neither the focal woman nor the place. They seemed to be in a high room—only a few stars and the quarter moon could be seen through the window. She kept her shadow-self still and quiet.

The bony woman's face tightened in concentration; her body trembled with tension. "We have her at last—I have found her. How long did she plan it with that pretty princeling, to hold the salt in place until all kingdoms but his own were broken? And now he is called Savior—and she, she is the Lady who made it all possible." The bony woman snarled as she spoke, almost as if to herself. Beloved did not dare do anything to let any of them suspect she was aware of them; she was not sure she could do anything, her shadow-self was so distant from her body. The bony woman, aided by the others, no doubt, had, it seemed, cast a seeking spell to find Beloved: the touch of it had woken her. Apparently, they had not thought she would—or could—notice the trail of power, much less follow it back to them. The bony woman stood, her right fist still held out in front of her, almost panting in her anger, a little spittle at the corner of her mouth. A few of the others present seemed to shift restlessly. Then the focal mage splayed her fingers wide, her palm facing Beloved's watching, bodiless shadow-self. The bony woman's eyes narrowed and her snarling voice dropped to a hoarse whisper.

"We are not dead. We do not forget. You erred, you filth of your bitch mother. We will crush you as you have crushed us. You, your handsome fool, and his lying parents. *You and all you love will be cut down. We are not powerless.*" And with her last hissed words, the woman thrust her palm forward, as though she were trying to break someone's nose.

Beloved had only enough time to think *beacon spell*, before her shadow-self's head snapped back as if at a blow and she felt herself flying back along the path of power she had traced, but this time she recoiled violently, her tether spooling too fast, lashing her with pain. Her awareness slammed back into her body, her eyes flew open, and if she had not been clinging to the stone sill she would have fallen backwards to the floor. As it was, she struggled to stay upright and gasped for breath. Beloved's head reeled and she thought she might be sick. Every muscle ached as if she had been pummeled. An unpleasant trickle made her nose itch; when she put her hand up to it, it came away wet with fresh blood. Beloved fought down another surge of nausea.

Radvyed stirred in the bed, then sat up, looking around for her. When he saw Beloved, he rose from the bed and hurried to her.

"What is wrong, Beloved?" he asked. He saw her face and hands and muffled an exclamation. After hunting up a handkerchief, he handed it to her. When the bleeding from her nose had stopped, he took her hands and examined them. As her breathing steadied, he let her hands go and put an arm around her. "Tell me what is wrong," he demanded.

She held out a hand, eyes closed, and took several deep, measured breaths. He waited. Once she had composed herself, she looked into his concerned face.

"We must speak with the king and queen. Now. Tamtir has enemies and they are planning to strike."

PART III

Flame

Chapter Forty-Five

Radvyed persuaded Beloved that the meeting with his parents could happen over breakfast. He wanted her to recover herself fully after what had obviously been an ordeal, but he saw that she would not rest until she had told them whatever she had learned or experienced by the window before dawn. She had said something about being wakened by a seeking spell, which she had traced with her shadow-self, and then there were malicious mages and recoils and some other spell. He asked her to explain further, but she shook her head.

"Better one time, with the king and queen," she said.

They entered the queen's sitting room shortly thereafter. A sideboard had been set up with platters of breakfast meats, breads, cheeses, and fruit, and a small table set for four. By the sideboard a *damash* hovered, ready to assist. Arkost and Gladna were already seated, their breakfasts in front of them, cups of hot, sweet *chelek* steaming by their plates. Beloved and Radvyed sat and were served. Gladna smiled at the *damash* and dismissed him, requesting that the royal party be undisturbed.

Arkost asked how they had slept and recommended a *tervi* pastry. Once the door had closed behind the *damash*, however, he dropped all small talk and looked straight at Beloved. He wiped his mouth with his napkin, cleared his throat, and said in an entirely different voice—what Radvyed had always thought of as his father's no-nonsense voice—"We are listening."

Beloved put the roll she had been buttering back down on her plate. She pushed her plate away, clasped her hands on the table, and said, "What I have to tell you may seem strange. I ask only that you let me tell all of it before you ask questions, Your Splendors, Husband." She met the eyes of each of them in turn and after each had nodded assent, began her tale.

In plain speech, without attempting to make a story of it, she reported what she had experienced in the early hours of the morning: the sudden awakening, her opening the window and looking about, the filament of power that Beloved traced with her shadow-self, the faraway room with the bony, angry woman and her company of mages. Beloved repeated the words the unknown woman had spoken and then told her listeners how she had been thrown back into her body. "Then I said to the prince we must speak with you at once," she finished.

There was a moment of silence around the table. Gladna lifted her cup to her lips and sipped her hot drink. Arkost frowned down at his eggs and half-eaten pastry. Radvyed reflected that his wife had done nothing to soften the fact that this unknown mage thought him pretty but foolish, nor had she emphasized that the people of the lands between the Griefstone and Tamtir thought of him as a hero. She also had not concealed the insult to the king and queen. He set aside thoughts of her disconcerting straightforwardness, however. He was deeply unsettled by the ease with which this company of mages had intruded into their bedroom and into Beloved's very sleep, not to mention the physical repercussions she had suffered from both her overextended shadow-self and the foreign spell.

"How did the bony woman dismiss your...your shadow-self, when the mages did not seem to know you were conscious of their doings?" Radvyed asked.

"My shadow-self recoiled with the force of the casting of the beacon spell," Beloved explained. Radvyed frowned. Beloved anticipated his next question and added, "A spell that marks me, so that I may be found again at will." Radvyed opened his mouth to pursue the matter, but his father spoke first.

"What I do not understand," said the king, "is why you are not dead or otherwise gravely harmed." He looked up from his plate and at Beloved. "Why, given that this person and her associates can muster quite a bit of magic—power—and consider you filth, and so on, did they not simply injure you when they had found you?"

"I believe they desire, or certainly the focal mage desires, a more thorough revenge, Your Splendor," answered Beloved.

Arkost frowned, his fist rapping the table restlessly. "Yes, but...I can understand their resentment and hatred: our kingdom was untouched by the salt curse for many years and we were unable to provide reasons for this protection. Then suddenly, the child of the sorcerer whose power is known to be the cause of the curse appears, throws some water about, breaks the spell, and marries our son. They may even know that one of our household, who provided our son with guidance, turns out to be her aunt. It looks suspicious; it seems incredible. This is no accident, they reason; this is no coincidence. So yes, the hatred I understand, and the desire for vengeance. What I do not understand is the strategy. Why not kill you immediately and then attack and destroy us after?"

Gladna said, "Perhaps they are able to cast—what did you call them?—seeking and beacon spells, but a killing curse is more difficult over this unknown distance." She looked at Beloved. "You say there may have been as many as fifteen mages in all." Beloved nodded. The queen continued, "And perhaps they, or at least the bony woman, are not thinking as clearly as they might. They are caught in the grip of grief and rage. They want revenge, the more destruction the better: *We will crush you.*" Gladna cocked her head, looking at Beloved. "I wonder if they meant to inflict a nightmare on you and they woke you instead. Perhaps they want us to feel fear, because it is not merely our destruction but our suffering they desire."

Radvyed listened to his mother speak calmly of their enemies' malevolence and wondered at her fortitude. *But then*, he thought, *she has so recently been close to death. Perhaps feeling death's shadow pass over you makes you stronger.* A thought flickered and caught at something in his father's earlier words and reminded him of a history tutor's teaching—*accident, coincidence, conspiracy.*

"Perhaps they have already struck once," said Radvyed. The other three turned to him. Beloved nodded; she followed his thought. "Perhaps they have already struck," he repeated, "although unsuccessfully. Mother, what caused your sickness? Why is it that only magic could heal it?"

Arkost shoved to his feet and began to pace. "*We are not powerless,* they say. Yet perhaps they are careless or arrogant. Beloved, you say the other mages were feeding the bony woman power?" he asked.

"Yes, Your Splendor. I could not see clearly, but I sensed they were joining their power to hers or lending her power."

Arkost crossed his arms, one hand pulling at his beard, and scowled at the wall opposite as he thought. Finally he gave his attention once more to his companions. "The Council must meet, as soon as may be. Beloved, thank you for your swift tidings, as troubling as they are." He strode towards the door, his restless energy filling the room. The others rose from the table, their meal forgotten.

"Your Splendor," said Beloved, addressing the king, "I, too, must be at this Council meeting."

"Radvyed will sit for both of you at the Council. You are not yet ready for understanding or dealing with the complexities of the court," responded the king gruffly as he yanked the bell pull to summon a *damash*. "Although," he added, "you may be asked to give a direct report to the Council. We shall see."

"Your Splendor. It seems plain that there will be sorcery—magic—involved in this attack or attacks. I know about magic, more than anyone in this kingdom, as far as I know."

Arkost turned towards Beloved more fully. Gladna and Radvyed were standing at their places, the prince with his napkin still in one hand, the queen looking at Beloved thoughtfully.

"The question is, how far do you know? What can you do?" the king retorted. "You have spent your life, as far as I can determine, captive to a curse and unable to break it yourself. My completely unmagical son had to do it." Beloved flinched. Radvyed took a step forward, but was halted by the hand his father held out.

Radvyed could see from her stiffened posture and drawn brows that Beloved had not expected this challenge. In her mind, the Tamtireni were all swimming blindly in a sea of power; only their careful observation of the rites and traditions given by the Lady and the Master and guarded by the *seveyati* kept them from disaster. She had not expected her own knowledge and experience of magic to be dismissed as unreliable.

Beloved stared at Arkost, for the moment speechless as she grappled with his skepticism.

At last, her voice touched with disbelief, she said, "Your Splendor thinks I played no part in the downfall of the Griefstone or the healing of your queen?"

Gladna's hand moved to touch the flower she still wore at her neck under her dress. She said nothing, however, merely watched as sorceress and king faced each other. Radvyed also was quiet but alert.

"How much was knowledge and skill, and how much was the wisdom and feats of others, and even luck?" answered the king. "I do not know. Without the knowledge of Dris, without the heart of Radvyed, without the wisdom of Rue, where would you be? Still imprisoned in your curse?"

Beloved took a deliberate breath. Radvyed felt that drawing in of herself that meant she was placing all her power under tight control. "Without the rose ripped from my heart, your queen would be dead. Without my understanding of the curse, the Griefstone would still be standing and salt would be choking every hill and valley from your western border to the Rasovel Sea—"

"You have great power, yes, but you are not mistress of it—or why would you have fled last week, and why would that monstrous vine have grown outside your window?" Arkost demanded, turning as Radvyed opened his mouth to speak. "A vine only you, my unmagical son, could destroy." The king shook his head and gestured at Beloved in exasperation. "Now is not the time for blundering or for holding the hand of a girl as she learns what it means to be responsible for a kingdom and a people!"

Gladna moved next to her husband and rested her hand on his arm. He glanced at her, flushed, and took a deep breath. "And this morning," he said more calmly, "foreign mages were able to attack you as you slept, and place a spell on you to mark you for death or disaster. You are not invulnerable, far from it."

Beloved's head came up, acknowledging his point. She kept her gaze steady on the king's face. "You do not trust me, neither my knowledge nor my skill," said Beloved, her hands clenching and unclenching at her sides. "But I have sworn solemn oaths to protect this people, land, and House with my life. I must be allowed to do what I may to defend and protect Tamtir, or bring more curses upon us all." Radvyed stood next to Beloved and placed a hand on her shoulder. She looked up and saw that he was looking at his father, unsmiling.

Arkost set his jaw. "What do you wish to do?" he asked at last, his voice quieter.

"I thought to speak with Dris and Rue. I need to consult my books and discover more about beacon spells and how they work. It may be that I can remove or obscure it. You have scholars also, learned in history, geography, and other lore. We do not know where these mages are, which kingdoms or lands they speak for, or what they may or can do. The temples also may offer some wisdom or insight."

The king looked at her for a long moment, then said, "I do not know whether to be relieved or distressed. I had feared you planned to cast some powerful protective spell beyond your skill or ability. Now I hear you simply wish to consult loremasters and archives. I do not know what to think. Is this how you fulfill your oaths?"

Beloved's back was very straight and her gaze direct. "I, the sorceress whose power cured your wife's death-sickness and whose knowledge and deeds broke the deadly salt curse, will consult Dris Rose Gardener, my aunt by blood, by whose knowledge the queen was saved, and the Lady Rue, the only surviving member of my sorcerer father's household and the woman who raised a cursed sorceress from infancy, although she herself possesses no power. I will further consult anyone learned in any field of knowledge or lore or holiness that will help us to name, find, and discover the actions of the company of mages threatening the health and welfare of this kingdom and this House. Yes, Your Splendor. That is how I begin to fulfill my oaths."

The king turned away from Beloved; the jerk of his shoulder said he had little hope in results from her plans. "You may consult with Dris Rose Gardener and the Lady Rue and whomever else you wish. Who knows what useful piece of knowledge you may uncover? But you will not take any action nor pursue any policy."

Beloved said quietly, "I will gather wisdom, nothing more, for you are right: I know nothing of policy. I wish only to be allowed to protect, as fully as my powers permit, this House and land."

Arkost looked at her and it was clear he was not sure what she might be able to accomplish, but he gave a regal nod, and said formally, "The prince will be your liaison with the Council and ourselves." Then he turned to the *damash* who had entered the room and began giving him orders. Gladna paused on her way to the door, laid her hand on Beloved's arm, and gave her a small but warm smile.

"Who knows what might be our best hope? I would not have thought a flower from a hidden garden could persuade death's hand to pass over me. Yet the king must use his powers as he can, as well."

Beloved nodded. Now that the moment was past, she was wondering whether it was correct etiquette or wise strategy to inform the king of her course of action. Her conviction that sorcery would play an important part—perhaps the major, even the only part—in the coming assault had carried her through her confrontation with the king, but now it occurred to her that others, whether his wife, his son, or his *dovoreni*, did not speak to him as she had done.

After Arkost and Gladna had left the room, Beloved looked at Radvyed. He smiled ruefully. "He does not really believe that you have designs on his authority. But not many people aside from my mother speak as though they believe themselves equal to the king—not as you do, without malice or envy or contempt. He is unused to it. We all are." He cocked his head and added, "And the news you brought us has disturbed him deeply."

Beloved came to him and held out her hand. Radvyed took it. "What do *you* think, Husband, of my desire to consult with Dris and Rue, and whomever else might know anything about mages and power?"

Radvyed looked at their joined hands. "I think it is an excellent idea." After a pause, he said, "I met you under the curse, I lived in the Hidden House, I held you as the name curse was broken, and I was with you when the salt curse was undone. But my father—all that is a wondrous tale to him, not something real. Even my mother's sickness—well, people fall ill every day, and sometimes they live, and sometimes they do not—even the healers do not always know why or how."

Beloved nodded.

Radvyed considered the events of the past few days. "And the bitterwood vine—that was real enough, but it seemed to happen, as the other things did, without your control. Add in the events of this morning... To him, I think, counting on magic to protect the kingdom makes as much sense as counting on the clouds—for sometimes they are thunderheads and sometimes they are wisps, and never do they heed the wishes or will of us who walk under the sun and stars."

Chapter Forty-Six

Later that morning, Beloved sent messages to the temples of Velaska, the Golden Lady, and Predun, the Dark Master, asking for a few *seveyati* of learning to come to her that afternoon to consult on an urgent matter.

"I had best write the letters," said Radvyed, after glancing at the time-candle burning on the mantelpiece. He sat down at a table and bent to his work.

Rue, Dris, and the historian Zhelez had already received Beloved's requests. Zhelez had added to her reply that if Beloved were interested in lore about magical feats, Her Radiance may wish to consult a well-versed bard: should Zhelez bring along one she knew, a certain Pevetos?

Yes, sent back Beloved in her painstaking hand. *Please do.*

The prince finished the messages for the temples and gave them to a *damasha* outside the door with instructions to see them delivered. Then he gave Beloved a swift kiss and left for the Council meeting.

She stood for a moment, looking at the door after he had gone. The king's words from that morning came back to her. *Now is not the time for blundering or for holding the hand of a girl as she learns what it means to be responsible for a kingdom and a people.* She bit her lip. *He is right*, she thought. *What do I know of such things? I ruled only my house and even then, I did not always know what I did.*

"Nonsense," said Rue half an hour later after she had listened to Beloved accusing herself of ignorance and inexperience. "You have not ruled a kingdom, it is true, and there is much yet to learn, and we shall hope you have the chance to learn it. Yet think what you have done and what you have learned. You know some curses may not be directly resisted: they must be undone. You know spells often have in their very making the key to their unmaking. You were able to create a haven of peace and plenty amid disaster and deprivation. You earned the title of Lady Generous. You gave new life to ruined lands. You laid down your very life for another."

Beloved frowned at the floor. "I did only what seemed right at the time and what I knew to do to help."

"Yes," said Rue. "And you will continue to do what is right and to help as best you know and can."

Beloved contemplated the fingers she was twisting together in her lap, looked up at Rue, and gave a small smile. "As always, I will be guided by you, heart-mother."

Rue smiled and said, "So now you say." Then, sobering, she said, "Tell me again of the encounter with these angry mages." They spent what was left of the morning talking over the event. Rue was troubled by the combined strength of the mages as well as their malice. The matter of rooting Beloved's power in Tamtir, whether on the palace grounds or elsewhere, had now gained new urgency. Beloved needed to discover how to graft or join her power to that of the kingdom. But she had never heard of a sorcerer performing any such feat.

Setting aside that formidable problem for the moment, the two women gathered books from a trunk brought from the Hidden House and researched beacon spells. Beloved pulled out a map she had been using when studying Tamtir's history and they looked at the countries that abutted the kingdom's borders. Neither of them, however, had much knowledge of the history of the region, so they turned their minds to lists of known clans and lines of mages, their guardian spirits, and their different disciplines and inclinations.

Later that afternoon, Beloved looked around at the people who had come in answer to her summons. One of the rooms in the apartments that she and the prince shared was a room just for this—for "privy counciling," as Radvyed had joked. There was a large oval table. Her chair was slightly more elaborate and larger than the others and was placed at one narrow end. She had little idea of how to arrange the seating, so had asked Rue to sit opposite her at the other end and invited the others to take a seat, in the hope that no offense could then be taken.

Dris was to Beloved's right. Kashan, a scribe specially trained in rapid notetaking for hard-of-hearing councilors, was seated between the two women. He was a small, neat man with quiet eyes and quick fingers. Dris had a slate larger than the one she usually used on the table before her. She could easily look at Kashan's notes, and he would read aloud her contributions to the privy council's deliberations.

On the other side of Dris was Loucha, the *seveyata* sent by the Lady's solar, or temple, in answer to Beloved's missive. She was a sturdily built woman of perhaps sixty or so; Beloved was uncertain, as she was still unpracticed at reading age in faces. Her short, curly red hair was graying, and her pale blue eyes had fine lines at the corners. Loucha had brought with her a junior in lore, a younger woman with black hair and brown eyes named Baleka. Baleka was offered as a secretary for the council; Beloved gratefully accepted.

Beyond Baleka sat Rue, at her end of the oval table. To Rue's right was Mesaz, a priest from the Master's forge, as Predun's temples were called. He was a large man, rawboned and sunken-eyed, with big-knuckled hands and shaggy dark gray hair and beard. Next to him was Zhelez, Beloved's history tutor. Both Mesaz and Zhelez had brought their own writing materials for notes. At Beloved's left hand sat Pevetos, the bard whom Zhelez had recommended. His dark hair was braided back from his narrow face. His long-fingered hands were folded before him on the table, and he used this opportunity to study the new princess with bright hazel eyes.

Beloved had never presided over a similar gathering before, although she had some idea, from her shadowing the queen at that lady's work, what to do. Nevertheless, as she looked around at the polite faces turned her way, Beloved was aware that watching a woman who had been leading councils of established advisors for thirty years was very different from presiding over her own little hastily summoned group. She tried a smile: Gladna always seemed to begin this way.

"Thank you all for coming at my request. I am grateful for your time and I believe you will find the purpose as urgent as I." She glanced down the table at Rue, who gave a slight nod. Beloved continued, "I was awakened this morning by an inadvertent warning of what I believe will be an attack on Tamtir." Now she felt the sudden sharpening of attention of everyone at the table, except Rue, who already knew the topic to be broached. Spines straightened, faces expressed more than polite interest, and some people leaned forward. "The king and queen have already been notified and are even now meeting with the full Council." Mesaz, Loucha, Baleka, and Pevetos all nodded; Sonza and Zevedan, the *seveyati* who had led the rites during Beloved and

Radvyed's wedding, sat on the Council, as did a representative from the Bardic Hall.

Beloved continued, "I believe that the attack will be sorcerous—magical—in nature. Their Splendors have agreed that I may gather some advisors, learned in history and lore, to consider what form a magical attack may take, and how it may be countered. And so I have asked you here today."

Beloved stopped, uncertain how to proceed. Baleka's quill scratched as she wrote. The others looked at Beloved expectantly.

"Perhaps, Your Radiance," prompted Zhelez, "you might tell us more about this warning."

Beloved flushed with embarrassment. "Yes, of course." She related to them what she had earlier told the king and queen. Beloved also mentioned the king's questions about why these enemies did not harm Beloved immediately and the queen's theory that the angry mages desired Tamtir's fear and suffering as well as the kingdom's destruction.

Dris's face was hard to read; she seemed to be thinking over what Beloved had said. Baleka stared at Beloved and had to be nudged into taking notes again by Loucha, whose eyebrows were raised but who otherwise betrayed little reaction. Rue sat quietly; she had heard the story earlier. Mesaz drew his brows down over his deep-set eyes and glared at his hands, folded before him. Zhelez steepled her fingers and rested her elbows on the table, her gaze contemplating Beloved with surprised interest. The bard, Pevetos, eyed her with an odd smile that Beloved was unable to interpret.

Beloved said, "Does anyone have any thoughts?"

"You followed a filament of power, you said," observed Pevetos. "While your body remained in your chamber?"

"Yes, I followed with my shadow-self," said Beloved, not understanding the point of the question.

Loucha and Baleka exchanged glances; Mesaz lifted his eyes and pursed his lips, as if reassessing Beloved.

"Do you have any thoughts," Beloved repeated, "on the threat that faces Tamtir?"

"You are certain," asked Zhelez, "that this was not simply a dream that you experienced? The early hour, the excitement of the past days—it is not difficult to see how these things might lead to troubling dreams, Your Radiance. To imagining you visited vague enemies as a *shadow-self*."

Beloved sat back in her seat. "Am I to understand," she said, "that there is a question as to whether the event I have related actually occurred?" There was an uncomfortable but stubborn silence. Rue drew in her breath and folded her hands and looked at them as she laid them on the table. *She thinks there is no point in continuing,* thought Beloved. *But I do not have that choice. I need whatever scraps of knowledge these people may have. I have sworn oaths.*

"Are there others wondering, as Scholar Zhelez is, whether I was dreaming?" she asked. People exchanged glances. Dris looked about with impatience, but did not make any comment.

"Your Radiance," said Mesaz, his deep voice matching his dark eyes. He spoke softly, however, and did not appear to be intending insult. "As Scholar Zhelez has noted, this has been a time of intense emotions and significant events. Your arrival in a strange land, your marriage to the prince, the many demands of your new life, as a wife and a princess—it is easy to understand how one so young and inexperienced could feel overwhelmed."

"You think I cannot distinguish dream from reality." Beloved's tone was neutral. She did not bring up the pain, the nausea, the bloody nose. The physical repercussions of the spells would only serve to reinforce in their minds her fragility in her new life.

"Say, rather, that when reality is lived so intensely, as in your case, it can come to seem dreamlike," answered Mesaz.

"I am young and inexperienced. The life of the palace has overwhelmed a girl whose whole existence has been chained to one small place with almost no one else for instruction or companionship." Beloved's voice remained flat as she stated what was being implied by the councilors.

Loucha shifted in her seat. "It is understandable, Your Radiance. No one thinks the less of you for it."

Beloved felt her power aching to expand outside of her skin. She took a moment to pull herself in, to hold herself tightly. Then she asked, "Besides my youth and inexperience, is there another reason why you question my account?"

"It is unheard of," said Loucha. "No one, not even the most holy or learned of the *seveyati* can do this—this bodiless travel and hearing and seeing people many leagues distant. What you call the *shadow-self*—it is true that the *seveyati* can walk the sunfields and starplains while waking, but their souls do not travel to other earthbound people."

"But I am a sorceress, not a priestess, holy or otherwise," said Beloved.

"Yes," Loucha answered, then stopped.

"Yet the Lady herself gave a sign to me," said Beloved, referring to the *sozkol* that had flown from her hand on the day of her wedding.

At this Loucha shifted again.

"Or do you not believe it was the Lady?" asked Beloved.

"She has never given such a mark of favor before."

"And the Master's token?" Beloved turned to Mesaz. What would he say about the brilliance that had risen from her palm and the prince's?

"It is unprecedented," he admitted. She stared at him a moment, looked again at Loucha, who did not look away, and then moved her gaze around the table. Beloved took the time to order her thoughts as well as to try to read her councilors' faces: she had not expected such fundamental objections.

"Let me understand you all. A stranger comes among you and saves the dying queen that none of the *holiest* or most *experienced* were able to aid. During the magic rites"—here heads snapped erect and eyes narrowed—"the magic rites," Beloved repeated, "of her royal marriage, she receives unprecedented signs of divine acceptance. Then the magic-wise stranger who has sworn to protect you warns you of an attack on your kingdom, and you think she is an overwrought girl who has suffered a bad dream?"

There followed another uncomfortable silence. Rue continued looking at her hands; Dris surveyed the others seated around the table with a look of exasperation.

Beloved realized she was angry. Very angry. It was not only that she needed to hold in her power; she needed to hold in her fury. She had spent a long time, after her early years of futility, learning to redirect her frustrated rage, to use her energies to plan and study and do what she could to make her own life a worthy one. It surprised her to find that her capacity for deep anger had outlived her name curse. *Inexperienced? Confused? Unable to tell dream from waking? And these are the ones I have called together, hoping for wisdom!*

Yet they may still have something to offer. Besides, to whom else could she go? Beloved closed her eyes and remembered a *kunika* at Perikrost she had noticed settling a restive horse. Crooned, she had, and gentled it with her touch. Beloved imagined doing that with her anger and the crackling power that was eager to serve it. *Be at ease. All will be well. Be at ease.*

She opened her eyes and looked about. Her councilors seemed a little apprehensive; Pevetos had lost his smile. *They are wondering whether this overwrought girl might singe their garments, perhaps,* she thought grimly. *No, I shall astonish you all with my composure.*

Beloved took a deep breath and tried to think of another way to set the task before them. She recalled Queen Gladna discussing with Beloved a tricky meeting she had sat in on. *Sometimes, you need to find a new way to let someone see a problem. Then they can let go of whatever was distracting them from the point.* Beloved looked around the table once more.

When she spoke, she used careful formality to maintain self-control. "Very well. I am uncertain what proofs I could offer to satisfy you. The only likely ones will be offered as time passes, yet the advent of these very proofs is what I hope to avert. I remind you only that I have told my tale to the king and queen and they have accepted it as true. For now, I ask you, if you would, to consider the problem as—as a thought problem. Let us, for the purpose of our discussion, assume that there is a threat such as I have described. Where would you go for guidance; what tales or annals or records would be of use?"

Everyone sat back and settled to thinking. *How strange,* thought Beloved. *They prefer to think about a problem they believe to be imaginary, rather than the same problem when presented as real. Why waste time and thought on what one believes does not exist? Yet I suppose they must indulge me, as I am nevertheless Her Radiance, Princess Beloved.*

As she waited, Beloved looked down the table and caught Rue's eye. Her heart-mother gave her a tiny, ironic smile and Beloved knew that they were both remembering a time when Beloved had compelled others to put their learning at her service. Yet as frustrated as Beloved was by the lack of urgency felt by the councilors around this table, she did not desire to coerce anyone anymore.

She was ashamed that she had ever used force against others whose only fault had been in having knowledge and experience that she herself had lacked. On the other hand, how else could she have learned the ways of sorcery, and without the learning she now possessed, would she have known how to break the Griefstone? Books holding this kind of knowledge were almost as rare as such people and usually better guarded. Would it have been possible to obtain what she needed without duress? Beloved did not know. She only knew that it had become more and more difficult for her to hold another person captive, until finally only wayfarers seeking shelter from the curse and princes pursuing worthy deeds stopped at the Hidden House. Except for Radvyed, she had let them leave when they would.

"Your Radiance," said Mesaz, breaking into her thoughts. "I would like to know more about this group of bitter mages." Beloved nodded for him to continue. The *seveyat* seemed to be taking seriously her suggestion that the gathering consider her account as though it were factual. "You say that many mages were feeding the focal woman power. How was this done?"

"They all had their hands on her." Beloved held up her right hand, spreading the fingers. "At first, I thought they were a feather design of some kind on her robe, but then I realized they were many hands. I do not know of another reason for them to touch her so. To reach across so much territory with power—I would be very surprised if a single person were able to do that. Why would she not have acted sooner, if she could have acted alone?" Beloved thought then of Radvyed's idea that perhaps the angry company had already acted, by striking at the queen. She would think more on it, however, before bringing that idea before her council.

Mesaz nodded. "Then one might ask, would it be possible to separate the group physically?"

"They are far beyond our physical reach, I think," said Loucha. "You are right that one aim must be to disrupt their ability to combine power. But without knowing who they are or where they are, it is hard to see how this could be accomplished." Beloved silently agreed. She noticed that to her left Pevetos had his eyes closed. A finger of his left hand tapped softly against the edge of the table. Dris at her right was writing on her slate.

"Your Radiance," said Zhelez. Beloved looked at the historian. "You say you were standing at the window of your bedchamber when you felt this—pull—of power. Did the pull give you a sense of direction—and would this direction correspond to the same direction experienced bodily, that is, not as a shadow-self?"

"Yes, Scholar. I was looking straight out the window of my chamber, which faces east. The pull of power came from my left, that is, north. And yes, it would correspond with what one might call ordinary or material geography. The draw of the Griefstone was so strong, for example, that we would not have needed a map to find it, even if Rue had not been with us. And Prince Radvyed's connection to Tamtir is so powerful that we had no need of the map to find the road after the Griefstone was broken."

Kashan turned to Beloved and she nodded. He read from Dris's slate. *Can you describe the woman who spoke? I might know of her or her clan.*

Beloved closed her eyes for a moment, calling up the memory. Still with her eyes closed, she answered, "She is a tall woman, thin and bony. Her hair is very pale, very short. Dark eyes. Her robe is also dark, but with a gleam—probably silver thread in the weave—the better to absorb the power the others feed her." She paused, holding the memory in her mind's eye.

"Is there anything else in the room, Your Radiance?" This was Zhelez again, speaking softly so as not to jar Beloved's concentration.

After a moment, Beloved replied, her eyes still closed, her hands braced flat on the table before her. "I sensed, rather than saw, the other mages, aside from their hands." She paused, willing herself to notice more. "There is a small window, high up, over her left shoulder," she said, speaking slowly but with certainty. "I can see the third-quarter moon, a bright star riding above." She was quiet again. "The window is stone. Above the arch is carved a raven, wings outspread, beak open."

Two or three people gasped. Beloved stilled, the hair at her nape prickling, her fingers suddenly cold on the table. She had not noticed this detail before. She opened her eyes and looked at Rue. Rue knew that raven, just as Beloved did, and the knowledge was not welcome. Dris's eyes met Beloved's. *Yes, of course,* thought Beloved, *Dris would know.* Mesaz's and Loucha's gazes were keen; Pevetos's brows were lowered over his clear eyes; Baleka was looking at Beloved uncertainly.

"Your Radiance, this raven—is it a simple decoration or is it a sigil?" asked Loucha, leaning forward.

Beloved blew out her breath on a shaky half laugh. She looked at her hands, still flat on the table. Then she looked up and said, "It is a sigil. I know it, but not as well as some here at this table." She nodded at Rue and Dris. "It is the Ice Raven, the sign and guardian of my father's clan."

Everyone except Rue and Dris sat back. All kept their eyes on Beloved. She had dropped her gaze back to her hands, still flat on the table, fingers spread.

Now Mesaz spoke. "Many clans and houses have birds as signs, and ravens are honored by more than one. Are you certain this is the mark of your father's clan?"

Beloved looked at him, then drew her hands back closer to herself. She thought for a moment, then flung her left arm out to her side, snapped her fingers, and pointed. There was a burst of flame accompanied by a whooshing sound. The flames died down and the startled councilors shifted—Pevetos cautiously, for he had had to duck Beloved's arm as she gestured—to look at the wall to Beloved's left. Still smoking, a sigil had been burned into the stone of the wall. It was a raven, wings spread, beak open. They looked at it in silence. Whether they contemplated its significance or the fact of it being burned into rock, Beloved did not know.

Mesaz spoke. "Thank you, Your Radiance. That is indeed the sign of the Ice Raven Clan." Beloved nodded and looked around the table.

"Thank you, Scholar Zhelez, for your suggestion that I examine my memory of the incident more closely. I think we all need time to think about what we have discussed today. I request your attendance here, tomorrow morning, at the fourth hour."

She rose, thereby signaling that the others could also rise. Beloved stood at her end of the table, looking at her small group, but not settling her gaze on any one person. *Remember*, Gladna had told her, *as a royal your gaze has weight. Where and at whom you look and for how long has meaning. Cultivate a middle-distance gaze that sees but does not single out.*

Beloved was still learning to read people. For most of her life the only person she had spent any time with was Rue: she could read her heart-mother's expressions, gestures, and silences well. But the refugees and strays at the Hidden House had been invisible in her presence; the teachers, while usually visible, were few, and almost all of them frightened or angry. The Wanderers she had observed only from a distance. So as Beloved watched this gathering disperse, she was not sure what to make of the councilors' glances, postures, or silence.

Dris was one of the last to leave. Before she went, she put a hand on Beloved's shoulder and squeezed. Beloved saw that her aunt had a small smile playing on her lips. Dris glanced over Beloved's left shoulder and Beloved turned and looked—and closed her eyes when she saw the Ice Raven sigil, still smoldering. She opened her eyes, sighed, and turned back to Dris, who gave a bark of laughter before turning away.

After they had left, Beloved and Rue stood at each end of the oval table, looking at each other. As so often, Rue waited.

"I had not expected to be challenged on the truth of the seeing," said Beloved.

"They do not know you. Remember, they have heard your story, but what they know of you, the princess standing before them, is that you are a young woman who has appeared from somewhere far away and who knows little of what any Tamtirena your age knows." Beloved blew out her breath in exasperation and turned her face away, staring at the unblemished wall to her right. "Daughter," continued Rue, and although Beloved did not turn, the younger woman listened, "trust takes time."

Beloved looked at her. "How much time do they need? What more must I do? We may not have time."

"I do not know."

Beloved pushed her chair in so she could move around the table. The sigil of the Raven caught the corner of her eye. As she moved towards the door, she nodded at it, and said, "What do you make of it? The Ice Raven?"

Rue folded her lips and shook her head, wordlessly telling Beloved that she was not sure. She waited for her heart-daughter to precede her through the door into the sitting room of Radvyed and Beloved's chambers.

Beloved glanced at the time-candle set in a sconce by the fireplace. Halfway through the twelfth hour—someone would bring *chelek* soon and something to eat. At the palace the court dined at the sixteenth hour, later than Van and Alya. She had a moment of longing for a quiet evening with the kind couple; all worry and care seemed somehow smaller and more manageable in their steady presence. *Was it because the house was smaller?* Beloved wondered, aware of the absurdity of the notion even as she thought it. And yet it seemed that everything was larger in the palace: rooms, meals, people, problems. *And joys*, she added to herself, as Radvyed opened the door and came in.

Chapter Forty-Seven

B eloved was almost becoming used to the catch of her breath when she first saw him and was amused that Rue thought she had controlled her own reaction by presenting an expressionless face. Beloved did not hide her pleasure at seeing her husband, especially when he looked about, saw her, and smiled. Not a full grin, but a quiet, glad smile that told her he was happy to be with her again. *I am learning his face*, she thought. *Now I have only a few score more people to learn how to read.* Radvyed nodded a greeting to Rue, then came to Beloved and kissed her cheek before moving towards the chairs placed near a small table where the *chelek* would be set when it arrived. He waited until the women joined him before sitting down.

"How did your council fare, Beloved?" he asked.

Rue gave a small snort and Beloved sighed. Radvyed looked from one to the other, raising his eyebrows. "Trouble?" he asked.

"They thought I was recounting a dream," answered Beloved.

Radvyed's eyebrows rose higher and he looked at Rue, who nodded in confirmation, before he turned back to Beloved. "A dream?"

"It was early morning, I was half asleep, I am young, the past few weeks have been demanding and eventful, and besides, what I recounted is impossible," explained Beloved.

Radvyed's eyebrows snapped together. "They believe you called them together to listen to a *dream*?"

Beloved gave a short laugh in response. "They believe that *I* believe I had a true seeing. But they do not consider that I am able to distinguish dream from reality," she answered.

"Dris does," put in Rue.

"Yes, Dris does," agreed Beloved.

"With all respect for your aunt, Beloved, that will not sway them. Her judgment may be suspect. She is not a scholar or a *seveyata;* she is a foreigner, and she is of your blood." He pondered a moment. "And there would have been little point bringing up your physical reaction. They would only seem causes, rather than results, of your seeing."

"That was my thought," said Beloved.

A *damasha* opened the door and a second began to bring in trays from the cart standing in the hall. The three watched in silence as the women set down the tray with the *chelek* pot and cups, then brought in and arranged the plates with bread rolls, cheeses, and fruit. Finally they brought in some honeycakes and linen napkins. One asked whether anything else was needed. Upon being told no, and thanked for their service, they left. The three in the room could hear the two *damashi* murmuring as they rolled the cart away.

Rue helped herself while Beloved concentrated on pouring them all cups of *chelek* without spilling any. Radvyed frowned at the plate of rolls for a moment before taking one, breaking it open, and reaching for the cheese plate.

"This is not an auspicious beginning," he said. "Did you spend the entire meeting explaining that it was not a dream?"

"No, I decided that was a fruitless task," Beloved replied. "Instead, I asked them to pretend I was telling them of a true event: what would they suggest then?" Radvyed turned amused eyes to hers.

"And did that work?" he wondered.

"Yes! Husband, it was so odd. I tell them of a seeing in which an unknown group of mages is plotting against Tamtir, and they barely regard it, because they are considering whether a sorceress *could* travel by means of a shadow-self. Then I ask them to *pretend* that I could do so and that the seeing was real, and they immediately give their attention to a threat they do not believe exists." Radvyed laughed and Rue smiled into her cup.

"Clever, Beloved," he said. "Now you can gather their ideas without arguing about whether they are needed. So what came of it?"

While Radvyed peeled a yellow *grushla* fruit, Beloved told him. Radvyed's eyes did not leave her face as he swallowed, wiped his lips, then his hands, with his napkin, and leaned closer to her, crossing his arms and resting them on the table. His face was very serious.

"The Ice Raven? Is that not the sigil of Besserdech's clan?" Beloved noticed Radvyed did not say, *your father's clan*. She was not sure whether he was trying to spare her feelings or whether he did not like to think that the master of the Griefstone was his wife's father. Perhaps both.

"Yes," she answered. Rue put down her cup and reached for a honeycake, her smiling mouth close to laughter. Radvyed looked at her, then at Beloved, as he refilled his cup.

"I would not have thought this detail to be quite so amusing," he observed and blinked in surprise when Rue let a laugh escape. He turned to Beloved, who was blushing. "Beloved?" he asked.

Beloved looked at her fingers as she fiddled with the handle of her cup, her color still high. "I was asked whether I was sure that the sign was indeed the Ice Raven."

Radvyed frowned in disbelief that someone had questioned whether Beloved recognized the sigil of her own father's clan, but said nothing, awaiting her conclusion.

"So I showed it to them," Beloved said. Rue snorted, but Beloved's eyes remained on the cup handle.

"Come, Prince," said Rue, rising. She laid her napkin on the table then moved towards the council room door. Radvyed, after a glance at Beloved, stood and followed Rue into the other room. She gestured towards the far end of the wall to the right. He came farther into the room, moving around the table to the left so he could see better what was depicted. There, burned into the stone, was unmistakably the sigil of the Ice Raven Clan. He gazed at it for a moment, then turned to Rue.

"How...?"

"After she was asked whether she was sure that the raven was indeed a raven, was indeed a sigil, and was indeed that of her father's clan, she pointed at the wall and, after the flames had died, that is what remained."

Radvyed looked again at the wall and shook his head, half smiling. He walked back into the sitting room. Beloved was still fidgeting with her cup, her eyes away from him. Radvyed squatted by her chair, reached out a hand, and covered her restless fingers. They stilled, but she did not look at him.

"Beloved. I take it they accepted it was the Ice Raven, then?" He heard Rue's amused huff, but he kept his attention on his wife.

"Yes," she muttered.

"Is it dangerous for that sigil to be burned into our wall?" he asked. Rue was silent. Beloved turned to him; her fingers came away from the cup and clasped his.

"No, Husband," she answered. "My father was evil; the Ice Raven is not. I do not say that the Ice Raven is good, either. But my father's will was his own. Yet if it disturbs you, I will remove it."

Radvyed thought for a moment.

"Let it be, then," he answered, then rose, took his seat, and chose a honeycake. "We must now consider what can it mean that there is an Ice Raven carving in the room the enemy mages chose for their gathering." He bit into the cake and, after he had swallowed, said, "Did anything else go forward?"

"No," replied Beloved, and she, too, picked up a honeycake. Rue poured herself another cup of *chelek*; at a nod from Beloved, she filled her heart-daughter's cup. "We come together again tomorrow. I thought it good to give a little time for thought and study." Radvyed nodded. They were all quiet for a few moments. Beloved looked up from the embroidered flower on the tablecloth that she had been tracing with a finger.

"And you? How did the Council go?" she asked. Radvyed sighed and sat back, resting his arms on the arms of his chair.

"Since the king and queen take this threat seriously, there were no suggestions that you may have been dreaming or imagining the seeing. There is, of course, a great deal of uneasiness. We are not used to magical attacks." Beloved and Rue looked at him.

"Not used to magical attacks? What was the salt curse? What was the queen's illness?" Beloved asked. Radvyed held up a hand.

"Say, rather, we are not used to thinking of ourselves as dealing with magical attacks. The queen's illness is not understood by all to have been caused by magic. There are those who are skeptical that it was *cured* by magic: they think your flower was simply the proper exotic herb."

Beloved's eyes widened and her jaw dropped a little.

Radvyed saw her expression and continued, "The salt curse, well, yes, it is hard to deny that *that* was caused by magic. But it was not a targeted attack at Tamtir, and we held it off for a long while—if without understanding why or how, also without much trouble. There remains a sense that even if a magical attack is imminent, we cannot be harmed." Beloved's posture grew rigid as he spoke and she clenched the wooden arms of her chair.

"And the king and queen?" she asked.

Radvyed looked at her and sighed once more, but no longer about the Council.

"Beloved," he said, leaning towards her and again putting a hand over one of her tense ones. "My parents heard you and are acting. Never would they have brought this matter before the Council if they did not consider your account true." Beloved's body softened as she listened. "They and I know you can tell dream from waking. But, Beloved, many on the Council are struggling to understand something that is strange to them. An army on the march; bandits; pirates: these kinds of threats are understandable. But a woman who menaces Tamtir from a land far away, who, it seems, can cast a hex of some sort on the Lady who broke the salt curse? That is frightening and unsettling." Beloved nodded to show she heard him. Radvyed left his hand over hers, but eased back in his chair a little, giving her time to think.

"I know too little," Beloved said. "Not only about this enemy, but about how the power that sustains this kingdom and its people is invoked. Is it held? Does it flow? Can I join my own to it? I do not know. But until I understand better the forces that sustain and guard Tamtir, it is difficult to know how to prepare a defense—much less a counterattack."

Radvyed raised his brows. "You wish to counterattack?" he asked in surprise. "Of course we must defend ourselves against harm. But there is no need to seek out conflict, surely." He looked at her a moment longer, his gaze perturbed. "We are a peaceful people."

Beloved laughed, half in frustration, half in sadness, and gazed down at their joined hands. Looking up at Radvyed, she met his eyes. "Yes. They have threatened us. Why should we wait for them to act if we can strike first? Although if I believed about some kingdom what they believe of Tamtir, I, too, would attack with as much terror and destruction as I could muster."

Radvyed pulled back, his hand sliding from hers.

Beloved looked at him with unhappy eyes, her lips pressed together. She said, "Now you learn, Husband, that I am indeed the child of my parents. Rage, the need for retribution, the desire to lash out—I understand all these." He opened his mouth to speak, but she raised a hand and he was silent. "But I have sworn oaths," Beloved continued. "These mages cannot be allowed to take their vengeance. I will not permit my father to claim any more victims, at least not among those I am sworn to protect."

Radvyed swallowed, but could not loosen the sudden grip of disquiet on his heart. Recapturing Beloved's hand, Radvyed leaned closer to her.

So low that Rue, sitting at the same table, could barely make out the words, he asked, "And is it only because of the oaths you swore and the anger you bear your father that you will guard land, people, and House? Is it only because of your fear of what curse may recoil upon you if you fail of your oaths?" His gaze, usually so clear and steady, was troubled and uncertain.

Neither of them noticed as Rue quietly rose and removed herself to the far end of the room, where she could not hear what they said.

Beloved and Radvyed stared at each other in charged silence. Beloved was shocked by Radvyed's sudden intensity. She was taken aback that he needed to hear what was so evident to her—what she thought was obvious to the world.

"You are my life," she said, speaking each word distinctly, wanting there to be no doubt. After a pause, because her husband did not ease at her words, she continued in a voice matching his in fierceness, "You won my heart. I gave it to you freely, never expecting to see you again, though it cost me my life. Do you not see? What can separate us, when I have given you my heart and you have proven you will not relinquish it?" She meant that he had come after her when she had fled in her panic at seeing the thorn over the window of their bedchamber. His posture softened, but he was still staring searchingly at her. She moved closer and reached for his other hand.

Beloved tightened her hands on his and said, "I put a thornwood around me and you cut through it. I hid myself in a shape-changing house, and you stayed. I guarded my heart with a wall with no door and you entered. I was repulsive and you held me. I told you a story that never could be and you made it true. I ran in fear, lost, and you followed, found me, and brought me home."

The tension of his face softened as he listened. She realized his own worries and doubts had been plaguing him, although they did not manifest themselves in thorny vines.

"Radvyed," she said, using his name as she rarely did, "Husband, I love you. I will not leave you. And loving you, I take into my care that which you love and value. One day I hope to love as you love. But until then, out of love for you, and to honor the oaths I have sworn, I will protect and guard Tamtir to my last drop of blood and my last flicker of power."

Radvyed closed his eyes and leaned his forehead against Beloved's.

"I am a fool," he said lightly. Beloved was surprised into a laugh and disentangled one hand so she could bring it up to his cheek. After a moment they both sat up, blinking. Radvyed regarded the remains of their small meal on the table.

"I could do with some wine," he said. Rue rose from her seat at the other end of the room to summon a *damasha* to clear the dishes and bring a pitcher of sun-wine. Radvyed fought down a blush. Rue made no sign, however, that she had witnessed a scene between husband and wife, so he tried to set aside his embarrassment.

Another point occurred to him. "What have you learned about beacon spells? Will you be able to remove it?"

Beloved shook her head. "No. We spent the morning among my books, and all authorities agree. The spell is set by—" she hesitated, trying to think how to explain to someone who did not study magic. "It is set by binding a marker to my blood itself. It cannot be removed except by total exsanguination of the subject."

He stood and paced a step or two. "That is not good news."

"No. Nor have I yet found a way to obscure or weaken it." She sighed.

Radvyed took a turn around the room, his brows drawn, his mouth serious. After a moment he looked at Beloved, who was staring into the middle distance, lost in thought. "We are to dine with my parents tonight," he informed her. "Not a large gathering. Tomorrow morning the Council is scheduled to meet again at the third hour. It may well take much of the day. I am certain your presence will be required, both to present your testimony, and to advise on how best to prepare and defend Tamtir."

Beloved gave a helpless little laugh, shaking her head.

"By that time you will have spoken with your privy council," Radvyed reminded her. "It may well be that they also will be summoned. After some thought the king sees your reasoning."

Beloved nodded; she was glad the king was no longer angry. The *damasha* came in and began clearing the table. Radvyed smiled at the woman as she went about her business and she ducked her head, flushing. A *damash* appeared with three goblets and a pitcher of sun-wine.

After the *damashi* had shut the door behind themselves, Beloved accepted the goblet of wine Radvyed offered her, and said again, "I know too little. For example, I understand that part of our wedding day was the binding of the two of us to each other. But there were also rites to connect us to the land and to the House. Yet this can hardly have been the first oath you have taken to protect and defend Tamtir."

"No, of course not. Like everyone, I was dedicated to land and hearth when I was very young," answered Radvyed. He took a sip of his wine. After he had lowered his goblet, he noticed both Rue and Beloved staring at him. He looked from one to the other, his brows raised in question.

"Like everyone?" asked Beloved. Rue shook her head. Radvyed took a deep breath and set down his goblet.

"Like everyone in Tamtir," he amended. Observing that the two women had resumed gazing at him in silence, he added, "Everyone in Tamtir is dedicated to the land they live on and the hearth of the house they live in when they are quite young—just beginning to walk and talk, at about two years."

Beloved and Rue looked at each other. Beloved seemed to find this information significant. Radvyed was not sure why.

"Husband, are you saying every child takes part in a rite that binds them to Tamtir?" Beloved asked.

"Yes," Radvyed replied. "When a child is about two years old, weaned and walking, they are dedicated to land and hearth," he repeated. "Of course, a parent or other elder takes the oaths for young children. When ten years old, children take the oath themselves."

"Describe this rite to me," demanded Beloved.

He blinked at her insistence, but complied. "I am sure you noticed every house, even in the city, has a small *zelohn*—a green space with shrubs, or flowers, or a tree—attached to it. That is the gift of the Lady to the household, just as the *kamin*, the hearthstone, is the gift of the Master."

Radvyed stopped. Beloved and Rue were listening, leaning forward, their eyes fixed on him as though he were imparting information of the utmost importance, instead of explaining the most common and basic custom of his people.

"The rite is similar to the one we participated in: the child stands within the *zelohn* and swears to love and reverence Tamtir and help tend the corner of it in the household's care," he continued. "And the same with the *kamin*. A small cut is made in the child's palm, and the blood is shared with the *kamin* as a sign that the child will help tend and protect the house."

Radvyed then explained to Beloved and Rue that adults, when they married or changed households, also swore oaths to their new land and house. The two women sat in silence when he had finished, thinking about what Radvyed had told them.

"Who are the Master and the Lady?" asked Beloved. Radvyed turned to her, blank-faced. She explained her question. "I understand the Lady is mistress of the day and the Master's realm is night, but why does she care for the land and why does he guard the house?" It seemed some things had been so evident to the Tamtireni that it had been considered unnecessary to explain them during her scheduled studies.

Radvyed frowned at the obviousness of the answer. "Because she is the Gardener, who cherishes all life and makes everything grow and thrive. The Master is the Smith, who builds and crafts and defends."

Beloved's eyes widened and she sat back in her seat. "So the Lady's fane is the Forest and her—her sign of presence, the Tree. And the Master's sanctum is the foundation of the royal House and his sign is the Stone."

Radvyed nodded. "But why, Beloved, is this important? Surely you already knew the people are loyal and that the Lady and Master are honored for their gifts to Tamtir?"

Now it was Beloved's and Rue's turn to stare at Radvyed with puzzlement.

"Because this gives greater insight into how power *works* here!" Beloved replied with exasperation. When Radvyed raised his hands in a gesture of frustration, Beloved's voice sharpened. "We do not have time to argue whether you have power—magic—here or not. If what you say is true, then Tamtir—land, houses, people—*all* of Tamtir is steeped in magic—in *sorcery*, in the gifts of the Lady and the Master, whatever you call it here. I had never imagined such a thing. In the clans of my father and mother, the power runs as in a river, through each member, branching here, drying up there, but in *us*—we can live anywhere; we can choose to look to any god or goddess or guardian. We claim the land we live in, yes, but there is no sworn oath or duty to it. And so it is with any mage or sorcerer I have ever heard about. But here, it seems the land is drenched in power, houses are built by it, and people and royalty share in it—I am no longer surprised Tamtir has stood for a thousand years! Thank the Lady and Master that I have kept my power close. It is no wonder that mages from outside are bitter and vengeful when what they perceive as sorcery has been used to defend Tamtir, but other lands were left to the curse."

"Why did they not repel the curse themselves? Why is it the task of Tamtir to defend or tend other lands?" demanded Radvyed, rising and pacing once more.

He thrust his hands through his hair but could not dislodge the memory of the wastelands created by the salt generated by the Griefstone—by the father of the woman here in this room: the ragged, gaunt people, wraiths in their own land; the rimed earth; the black and dry trees. So much suffering, and so many years of not knowing how to relieve it. The only thing he had been able to do to help was to find this woman, who now was both the heart of his heart and a cause of unease—had she not said the magic and the hostility of her bloodlines flowed in her? Her parents' sorcery had stolen her childhood, devastated kingdoms, and destroyed the master of the Griefstone himself. That seemingly bottomless power filled her. Was she fully mistress of it? Of herself?

Radvyed dropped his hands and turned to look at her—his princess, his wife, his Beloved. She stood, too, facing him. She sensed something was wrong. He almost laughed to himself. Her privy council and some on the great Council questioned whether magic could exist powerful enough to enable a seeing across distances measured in kingdoms. *He* knew such powerful magic existed and existed in her.

They stood staring at each other, Beloved's face passing from anxious puzzlement to wariness. *Yes, my Beloved*, Radvyed thought, *you seem so young and untried. It is difficult even for me to remember that in hard-won knowledge and suffering you are senior to many of us. And you do not* look *like someone whose veins run with a magic that can crush fortresses and overthrow spells that older, more desperate mages could do nothing against.* He made himself see her as she was—more than wife, princess, young woman in a strange land—forced himself to recognize what she had been trying to tell him: she was a sorceress of ability and knowledge, who nevertheless knew herself to be young and untested in her power. Beloved was a river that had been dammed and was now free, swelling the riverbed that was its right. Yet it was so strong and wild, it also found other paths in its course to the sea.

As Radvyed looked at her, he realized she was still, too still, as she stared at him. He saw Rue out of the corner of his eye, seated at the edge of her chair, arms on the wooden armrests, hands curled around the ends, her nails biting into the wood. One of Beloved's hands trembled; she controlled the movement. He remembered her hand on the table, back at the Hidden House, when she was Hideous, shaking as she tried to hold herself in, tried to repel him as little as possible.

"Beloved," Radvyed said, taking a step toward her, holding a hand out. Her eyes were wide and staring.

"You think I am a monster still," she whispered. He froze, his hand still hanging in the air between them.

"No," he said.

"Yes," she insisted. "You do not like it when I say I can understand the bitter mages. It is not only because they have declared themselves the enemies of your House and of Tamtir."

Very well, he thought, *let us hear this. Better this than another vine, another flight.* "Why else, do you think?" he asked, and he kept his eyes on her, his voice steady.

Beloved swallowed and said, "You asked why they did not repel the curse themselves. You know the answer—because they *could* not. And now you look at me and you see the sorceress who *did* have the power to destroy it. You begin to see the power I have. You begin to think where it comes from. You begin to wonder about having such a creature in your kingdom, your house, your—your bed." Tears were leaking down her cheeks. She did not notice them and they dripped off her face. Radvyed remembered standing in the Griefstone, pouring the rosewater, brewed from the attar of her own heart, over her head, moments before the salt gave way. But he said nothing yet, for she was still speaking.

"In the story, the dragon turns into a girl," she said. "But the girl, I think, keeps her dragon heart, no matter what her form. She is a dragon. A monster." Now he did step toward her and took one cold hand in his. With his other hand, he touched her cheek.

"You are no monster." He was able to say this firmly, honestly, and without hesitation. He had blundered. Because of his moment of fear, his Beloved had been hurt to the quick. How had he allowed himself to forget every choice she had made since the moment he had walked into the thornwood? She looked away, but he stroked her damp cheek, silently asking her to look at him. She did.

"You are no monster," he repeated. "Even in your despair and rage and loneliness, you could not make yourself compel your teachers to stay. You opened your house to wanderers and exiles. You let me bear away your inmost rose for my mother's sake. You destroyed your parents' two-fold curse by rejecting their choices. You seek to understand your ignorant husband's land and ways."

Beloved shifted her feet and opened her mouth to interrupt. "Yes, *ignorant*," Radvyed continued. "Ignorant of much of the reality you inhabit, yet expecting you to live as though you do not inhabit it."

"The vine," she said. "I—"

"The vine was a way of you speaking to me when I did not or could not otherwise hear you, as were the tower dreams," said Radvyed. She blinked and her spine lost some of its stiffness. "Did the people of Nagorna think you a monster?" he persisted. "Did Alya and Van? Do any of the artisans and shopkeepers and so on in the city think you a monster?"

"They do not know!" she said. "What of the *damasha* who was frightened by the changes I made to the tapestries and statues?"

"What of the many witnesses who saw a *sozkol* appear in your hand and who saw a gem rise from your palm? Beloved, do you think my House, my line, has never had those who chose evil over good? Their own gain over the welfare of Tamtir?"

Her jaw dropped. "But the oaths—the Lady—the Master—" she stammered.

"Why do you think these oaths are sworn? We must get Zhelez to give you more history to read. But the point is this. You are right that I was struck anew just now by the realization of the power you wield. You are also right that I do not like that you can understand the resentment that drives our enemies. But every choice I have seen you make has been born of great-heartedness and the desire to serve those in need."

She bit her lip and shook her head. "My flight. And *Mirena* Lioda and—" Radvyed took her other hand and noticed that the iciness of her skin had faded to coolness.

"You are allowed to be afraid, to be sad, even to be angry, without being a monster," he said, moving closer to her, speaking low. "All of us mortals who walk under sun and stars have moments we regret. We are not monsters because of them." Beloved leaned forward into Radvyed, pressing her forehead into his shoulder.

"Well," said Rue, standing up and brushing her skirts with brisk hands, although Radvyed thought her eyes looked rather bright and liquid. "No one ever said the first year of marriage was an easy one and now I know why. I need a little calm and quiet before the next council. Daughter, I go to my own chambers. Prince, I leave you both to ponder the bitter ones' next move."

Beloved broke from Radvyed to cross to Rue and embrace her. Rue smoothed back Beloved's hair, gave her heart-daughter one of her faint smiles, and left.

Beloved turned back to Radvyed. She wiped her cheeks with her fingers before remembering some of her lessons in deportment, then hunted in her sleeve for a handkerchief. He came up to her, took the square of linen from her hand, and blotted her face. He gave her back the handkerchief and led her to the cushioned easy chairs near the fireplace. They each sat in what were becoming "their" chairs.

"So tell me," said Radvyed. "Why were these bitter mages not able to break the salt curse themselves? Am I right in thinking they are strong in power, if they are able to cast spells from far away?"

Beloved was feeling rather worn after the intense emotions of the past hour or so; she was glad to turn her mind to a problem that demanded some calm thinking. "They were not able to repel or unmake the salt curse because they are not I—or more precisely, they are not *we*." She looked at Radvyed, expecting him to say something, but he frowned and waited for her to continue. "Only I and my bound husband could undo the intertwined curses of my mother and my father, in part because I share my parents' blood and so their magic, in part because a bond of unity was needed to counter their distorted bond, and in part because I myself was the focus or the point of convergence of both curses— my father's curse on me and my mother's curse on my father." Radvyed nodded.

"These mages, of course, could not act as I did," Beloved went on. "But they also are weaker than the intertwined curses of my mother and father. My father was an extremely powerful sorcerer and the reason, Rue and Dris tell me, he chose my mother to be his bound wife was that she was also very powerful. He hoped, Rue says, to beget a child. Then, training from birth the offspring of two powerful clans, he planned to amass the power and wealth he desired." She paused. Radvyed looked at her, tilting his head.

"You were born," he said. "Were you not healthy? Did you not have magic? Surely he could have made you into the tool he desired—or at least, he must have thought so."

Beloved shook her head. "Rue says he never had anything to do with babies, for he considered them disruptive, weak, and contemptible. I am his only child. He laid the name curse on me as soon as he saw me, so deep was his disgust at seeing my newborn self. My mother died in childbed, cursing him with her last breath. He kept me and Rue under his eye, but he saw nothing remarkable about me. After a week he cast us out."

Radvyed tried to imagine being cast out from house and land as an infant. It was no easier to imagine Rue's plight: charged with a week-old baby who needed constant care and feeding, and driven to a remote cottage to raise the child as best she could, alone and un-supported. No wonder, he thought, they were sometimes abrupt and awkward, these women whose lives had been so restricted in some ways, although strangely free in others.

"Who do you believe the leader of the enemy mages to be?" asked Radvyed. "I am troubled that they gather under the sigil of your father's clan."

Beloved shook her head, frowning. "I do not know," she answered. "I know little of my father's clan. He was not one to value friendship or affection. Although great ambition such as his would seem to require allies, I think he was too arrogant and grasping to seek partners in his plans: he took my mother by force and he had hoped to create his own subordinate confederate in his child. But I know little about him, except for what Rue tells me, and she was young when she left his service to care for me. There are some tales told of him, from before the salt curse, but not many were eager to tell them to me." Radvyed could well believe that few would be anxious to feed the daughter of such a man stories of his malice and destruction.

"Just such knowledge is what I hope will be brought to the privy council tomorrow morning," she continued. "Do the scholars, the bards, the *seveyati*—do they know anything of the Ice Raven Clan, or of any magical attacks? Can they say what the Lady or the Master may or will do to protect Tamtir? What can the people do? What wards are set on the land and dwellings? What role do the members of the House play in the defense of Tamtir?"

Radvyed pulled back his head a bit in surprise. "What role do we take? We lead the *strazha*." At Beloved's inquiring glance, he said, "The *strazha*, the guard. You have seen them here at the palace and in the city. They keep the order of law and lead and assist when there are disasters, such as fires or floods. They are also trained to fight."

"But where will you lead them?"

"Wherever the attack is," he replied, not seeing her point.

"Husband, a magical attack is hard to predict. If a fighting force attacks, then you know it must approach and cross a border. Even if it comes by sea, it must approach the coast. Watches can be set, and—and people sent out—"

"Scouts and spies," he said.

"Yes, scouts and spies. But if your thought is true, that the first strike at Tamtir was the illness of the queen..."

Radvyed sat back in his chair, his brows low. "They are not constrained in the same way as a conventional fighting force is by geography," he said. "Nor is there any reason at all that there would be a point of attack we could deduce or discover before the attack itself." He rubbed his face with his hands. "Another piece of bad news."

He dropped his hands and looked at Beloved, who looked solemnly back at him. Then he picked up one of her hands and interlaced their fingers. They sat for a long time, staring into the flames licking at the logs in the fireplace, saying nothing, and thinking of how to counter an attack from an enemy who did not need to consider great distance nor the requirements of an army.

CHAPTER FORTY-EIGHT

The next morning, Beloved was again at the head of the oval table in the privy council room. She sensed the change in the mood of the room more than she read any subtle clues of posture or expression. Several had brought their own writing materials for taking unofficial notes for their personal use. Today they were here to work, not to humor a new and high-strung foreign princess.

Several factors had brought about the change Beloved perceived. First, King Arkost and Queen Gladna were taking Beloved's warning seriously. The advisors of Beloved's privy council had returned to their temples and halls and discovered that their colleagues who had been summoned to the great Council had no doubt the threat was real.

Arkost and Gladna were not rulers who allowed themselves to be drawn into speculation or exaggeration. Ever since the queen's long illness and her recovery, they no longer dismissed works of magic or curses out of hand, as some in the Court still did, or think them foreign machinations and intrigues that "did not happen here." Even when Arkost had challenged Beloved's control of her power, he had not denied the flower had healed his wife by magic. Furthermore, the royal couple were beginning to consider, albeit with skepticism, Beloved's insistence that Tamtir and all its people, including the royal House, were steeped in magic.

In addition to the king and queen, the *seveyati* of Tamtir's main solar and forge, both located in Zolatar, were also anxious to discover an effective counter to a magical threat. While they may question the holiness, judgment, and mystical ability of the princess, the servants of Velaska and Predun did not doubt the possibility of forces operating on an invisible plane. The *seveyati* did not endorse those who hoped that, should such an attack indeed occur, the Lady and the Master would immediately and directly protect Tamtir and its people.

"At no time in our history has the Master intervened in this way," said Zevedan, the head smith at the main forge in Zolatar to Mesaz. The senior *seveyati* were eating a meal together before the temple's evening benediction. "He gives gifts, yes; he teaches, yes. But the use of those gifts, the doing, he requires of us. For if we will not act to guard as we have all sworn blood oaths to do, why should he?"

Mesaz nodded and sipped his wine, then told Zevedan of the privy council and the sign of the Ice Raven. The older priest chuckled when he heard of the sigil burned into the wall, but then he sobered. "That young woman is powerful," he said. "The sooner we all accept that, the better it will be for Tamtir."

Sonza, the *seveyata* who led the royal city's main solar and tended the Lady's Trees both there and in the Glade, listened attentively to Loucha and Baleka's report of the privy council. None of the priestesses of Velaska expected the Lady to descend in a chariot of flame, arrows of fire at the ready to defend Tamtir.

"I told the Councilors, yes, the Lady loves us all, and cherishes all living things," Sonza said. She and the other two women sat discussing the day's meetings in the sunset chamber of the solar late that afternoon. "But the land of Tamtir, both tilled and wild, is a gift she gives us. We have all sworn, with our feet in its earth, to tend and serve the *zelohn* in our care. Why should she save a people that abandons its charge?"

The women paused, sharing a moment of silent agreement. Then, as the red rays of the setting sun reached through the wide window, they turned toward the west, lifting their faces and offering their palms as the Lady bid them her daily farewell.

Similar exchanges had taken place in the guildhall of the bards and the hall of the scholars. Time spent in research and consultation with colleagues had turned up scraps of information and suggested avenues to pursue. The scholars, bards, and *seveyati* valued the skills needed to perceive and understand the unexpected or unknown, each in their own fields of knowledge, art, and mystery. Once they had time to shake off the shock, they made an effort to give this new experience of magic in seemingly unenchanted Tamtir room to show itself and be known.

Therefore, the group gathered around the oval table in the small council room no longer regarded the threat to Tamtir as hypothetical. Beloved looked about, noticing that everyone kept to the same seat as previously. Her gaze met briefly the eyes of each person around the table. Body language was difficult for her to read. Yet it seemed to her they were ready to listen with more than the politeness of the day before. She took a steadying breath and, after flicking a glance each at Rue and Dris, began.

"As you know, we are meeting again to take up the subject of our discussion yesterday," Beloved said. She kept her body still, contained, her power furled: *I am not a temperamental monster.* "If any have questions about the threat I relayed to this council yesterday, please ask them. If not, I would be glad to hear what wisdom a night of thought has brought forth." She eased back a little from the table after having said her opening piece, which she had rehearsed with both Radvyed and Rue.

Zhelez, after a quick look around the table, faced Beloved.

"Your Radiance," she said, "we do not have any records of magical attacks on the kingdom of Tamtir." Seeing Beloved's shoulders droop, the scholar added, "But that does not mean there have been no such attacks." Sensing the surprised reaction of the others, Zhelez turned to address everyone at the table. "Scholar Panemi, who is a member of the Council, informs me the king and queen have suggested that it is possible Tamtir would not have recognized magic at work. For example, an unusual storm or a widespread illness may be caused by magical means rather than natural ones. The Famine in the tenth year of Queen Kudaya," she said, naming an event from two hundred years before, "is an example." The bard and the *seveyati* nodded; they, too, had heard this idea from their colleagues on the Council.

Baleka looked up from her notetaking. "Is it possible the recent hailstorms in the Rechnayeg and Bogatravy *mirenzemi* are such attacks?"

Everyone looked in surprise at the younger of the two priestesses. Baleka flushed.

"My family is from Rechnayeg," she said. "I know that the *zernuka* crop was lost, and they had to quickly sow winter *pasheno* instead."

Zhelez nodded slowly. "Yes," she said, "and these storms are indeed unusual. His Splendor asked the last time hail had fallen in the Koleben Plain, and it was a hundred and twenty-three years ago."

There followed a short silence as the council thought back over the events of the past few months in light of possible hostile action.

Mesaz cleared his throat, and everyone turned to the Master's *seveyat*. "If you will permit me to raise another topic, Your Radiance?" he asked. At Beloved's nod, he continued, "I am concerned about this beacon spell that you say the bony woman put on you, Your Radiance," he said. "Are you able to nullify or strip it?"

Beloved nodded again in acknowledgment of the question. "Unfortunately, no, I am not, from what Lady Rue, Dris Rose Gardener, and I have been able to remember and to glean from texts of magic lore." Clothes rustled and chairs squeaked as people shifted, taking in the unwelcome news. "Beacon spells are set by binding a marker or tag to the subject's blood itself. The only ways to undo the spell are by the subject's death or by completely draining the subject of blood." A silence followed, as everyone absorbed the realization that the "subject" was Beloved herself.

"Unfortunate, indeed," said Mesaz. "A grave disadvantage."

"And yet," said Zhelez thoughtfully, "Her Radiance is, as I understand it, a wielder of powerful magic." At Beloved's surprised glance, the historian said, "I spent last evening reading closely the reports from where the salt reached into Tamtir, as well as the accounts of your companions."

Loucha leaned forward, her bright gaze on Beloved. "Your Radiance, Sonza tells me that at the wedding feast in the Lady's Glade, you advanced the thought that we in Tamtir practice magic continually. That far from being without magic, we are swimming in it from our birth."

Pevetos widened his eyes and gave a huff of surprised laughter; Zhelez cocked her head, considering the idea. Mesaz turned his dark gaze to Beloved; Zevedan had also passed on this intriguing idea to his fellow priest. Rue took in the group with her steady gaze, watching for ridicule or fear. Dris, always reacting a little later than everyone else as she had to wait for Kashan's notes, sat back with an expression that said this time she would wait while everyone else caught up to *her*.

Beloved moistened her lips and chose her words to be as clear yet as inoffensive as possible. "I do not believe the people of Tamtir are practicing magic continually. But I do believe the rites observed—for example, during the dedication of children and at wedding ceremonies—could be considered spells that create bonds of magic. They are not only oaths of honor or duty."

Zhelez frowned as she examined the idea. "Then in your view, Your Radiance, the kingdom of Tamtir, from the humblest holding to the royal palace itself, is bound together by magic spells, and not law or tradition, or the care of the Master and the Lady?"

"No," Beloved said. She saw Zhelez raise her eyebrows. "No," she repeated. "I believe the rites of power are *added to* the forces of law, tradition, duty, and love. They create bonds of a different kind."

"As a bond of blood is different from a bond of duty," said Rue. All turned to her, for she did not speak often. "Both forces may be at work, distinct, but reinforcing each other."

"But then, would it not be possible for both forces to be at work, pulling *against* each other?" asked Pevetos. "Many songs and stories are about this. One's heart decrees one course of action, one's duty another, for example."

Beloved went very still, feeling goose bumps unpleasantly prickling her skin. She answered, "Yes. That is possible, as my own history makes clear." Pevetos dropped the hand that had been stroking his beard and looked at her. She kept her eyes on the middle of the table as she controlled her voice. "In my case, a father's curse laid on his child and a wife's curse against her husband." *And a child's self-hatred, her power turned against herself,* she thought. She continued, "And a daughter's rejection of her parents. Magic, as you call it, was only one of the forces at work, although perhaps the most spectacular."

Pevetos pressed his lips together and flushed with embarrassment at having been so tactless. "I am sorry to have caused you distress, Your Radiance," he said. He wondered whether he were alone in forgetting that what seemed an intriguing tale to others was a painful, personal past to the strange young woman sitting with them.

Beloved recovered enough of her composure to look at him and nod, accepting the apology. There was a pause. While they all knew the dedication of a child, the union of a couple, or the swearing of fealty were powerful oaths and promises, Beloved knew they had thought of them as natural and ordinary. A sunset is an amazing yet everyday event.

"Your Radiance," said Loucha, "perhaps here is an unlooked-for defense or protection." The *seveyata* had everyone's attention. "Mages seem to think in terms of individuals, not of peoples or kingdoms. Perhaps because they carry so much power within themselves—if I understand correctly how they gather and use magic—they do not see people who are not sorcerers as threats or worthy targets. But look at the attacks we know of or guess at. Your father—excuse me for touching on your family history, but it is instructive—desired a daughter of a powerful clan as his wife. He did not need to conquer a kingdom or even an estate to obtain her."

"Yet the Famine in the time of Queen Kudaya and—possibly—the recent hailstorms suggest that mages are not unaware of how to weaken a populace," pointed out Mesaz.

Loucha frowned. "It is not certain that either Famine or storms were caused by magic. But the queen's illness was, for it resisted non-magical cures. It targeted a single, eminent person. And from what Her Radiance recounted, these mages do not seem to be acting on behalf of any one kingdom or realm."

Dris's gaze sharpened with interest; she nodded.

Zhelez agreed, "It is true that the mage clans do not swear allegiance to a kingdom or royal House, but keep their own small territories. They do not care for arable land or mines or similar resources. They hold small keeps, with a little land, and make themselves hard to find. We do not know much about them, in fact, for they are fond of secrecy."

Dris raised her eyebrows and crossed her arms, but did not dispute Zhelez's words.

"But do you see?" persisted Loucha. "These mages disregard the people. Their own bloodlines are like deep rivers of magic, sorcery concentrated and gathered over generations. Why should they worry about overcoming the defenses of magicless people, no matter their numbers, if mages never have to cross a border or face an army? But if what you say is true, Your Radiance, and Tamtir is held together—people and land—by bonds of magic, then while the mages may have rivers of magic to work with, we have an *ocean*."

Beloved nodded. "But how to harness this power? How to direct it?"

"As to that, Your Radiance, I was hoping you might have an answer," replied Loucha.

Beloved gathered her thoughts. "Alas, I am one of those whose magic runs in the blood, channeled by many generations. And I have spent much of my life apart from others, isolated. I am not of Tamtir."

Mesaz leaned forward and placed one large hand flat on the table. "Not so, Your Radiance, not so. You are now one of us," he said. His dark eyes seemed to bore into Beloved. "Yes, one of us. Your feet know the wet earth of the Lady's *zelohn* and your blood marks the Master's *kamin*. You have eaten the grain of Tamtir and drunk our wine and our water. You are bound—hand, heart, and body—to the Crown Prince himself. The Lady has accepted you; the Master has received you into his service. You are now of us."

Beloved looked around the table. The others nodded in agreement. Rue met her eyes and Beloved saw her heart-mother's faint smile, reassuring and steadfast.

She swallowed, then said, "I am grateful for this acknowledgment, but—"

"It is more than acknowledgment," broke in Loucha, ignoring Mesaz's quick frown at her interruption of the princess's reply. "You are of us—the ocean of power that is Tamtir must be available for you to use."

Beloved stared into the *seveyata*'s face, which was lit by hope, and she felt her ribcage constrict, her heart stop and then beat once, twice, out of rhythm. *She cannot know what she is saying*, Beloved thought, *or she would not radiate such relief.* Could Beloved link her power to that of Tamtir? And if she could, if somehow the Lady, the Master, the land itself did not reject her presumption, could she channel and wield that vast sea of power? She thought of the night the Griefstone fell and felt her hands press hard into the table beneath her palms. The eager light faded from Loucha's face and Beloved realized she had been staring at the priestess in unresponsive silence.

She took a deep breath. Her voice sounded strange to her own ears when she answered. "Yes, that is true. I may be able to draw on the power of land and people, for, as you say"—here she turned her face to address Mesaz as well—"I am of you, bound in power." Beloved did not look at Rue, whose smile had faded; she did not look at Dris, who had sat up and now held herself in stillness.

Pevetos noticed the quiet watchfulness of the two women whom he thought of as the princess's protectors. His bard's mind saw them as a lioness pacing at her side and an unhooded falcon on her wrist. Beloved herself still eluded the nets of image and sound he used to understand the world.

"Your Radiance," Pevetos said, before anyone could inquire into the details of how Beloved could draw upon the magical resources of Tamtir, "am I right in thinking that as yet we do not know what form a strike might take?"

"Yes," said Beloved. She lost a little of her stiffness as she addressed this shift in topic. "I was hoping there might be records or memories of past assaults, so that we may plan our defenses. Perhaps we may find out more about the Famine, or the recent hailstorms, or discover other possible forms of hostile magic."

Pevetos nodded. "Indeed, there are many tales of curses and evil spells that have taken hold in other realms. Last night several of my colleagues and I recalled them."

He stared over Dris's head and listed the magic-caused disasters the bards had brought to mind: "Plagues of darkness, locusts, rats. Sleeping sickness, forgetting sickness, limb-binding. Unquenchable wildfire, earthquakes, ice storms, floods, sandstorms. Transformation into beasts of various kinds, as well as attacks by packs of feral animals." He lowered his gaze and continued, "Then there are curses that strike at individuals or families, not whole kingdoms: the gold touch, ungovernable fear of fire or water, loss of memory, despair, and foreknowledge of the death of loved ones."

He did not mention, Beloved noticed, name curses, mysterious life-sapping illnesses, or salt curses. Was that because the songs had not yet been made, or because such things had come to pass in these living days?

A heavy silence held the group as they considered the daunting list of catastrophes.

Zhelez stirred and said, "And do the bards also tell of the measures taken to counter or to end these troubles?"

"Often what is required is that the mage be identified and killed or that some beneficent magic sufficiently powerful to overcome the malicious spell is performed," replied Pevetos.

"As in the case of Her Radiance," said Rue. There were small, startled movements as the Tamtireni in the room again realized that occurrences that for them were the stuff of tales were events in the personal histories of three of those present.

Loucha spoke. "Is there some way to narrow down the possibilities? Do the spells, for example, fit the perceived insult or otherwise have a discernible connection to the people struck by the curse? Or can all mages of a certain level of power perform whatever spell they wish? The *seveyati* may provide a parallel. We of the Lady may walk the sunfields with our spirits. Yet even our most senior and most holy may not venture onto the starplains that open themselves to the *seveyati* of the Master." She glanced for confirmation at Mesaz, who was across the table from her.

"This is true," he answered, his rumbling voice thoughtful. "What are the strengths, then, of the Ice Raven Clan? I confess I know little about the mage clans, aside from knowing they exist and learning their sigils and names as a novice. None live near our borders, and we have—we *have* had—little to do with magic—that *kind* of magic here."

"The Ice Raven is the lord of the sky."

All turned, surprised to hear Kashan's light tenor after the deep baritone of the *seveyat*. He continued reading Dris's reply. *He claims the realm between the ground and the sky leas as his domain, or so said the clan. The Ice Raven is sly, clever, and unreliable.* Dris's face was impassive. *He brings death.*

The room was silent as all absorbed Dris's grave words.

Pevetos pursed his lips and said, "A trickster, whose claimed realm is boundless, and who brings death." He rubbed his forehead with one hand. "A formidable adversary."

"For whom is he unreliable?" asked Rue. "For it is not necessarily the Ice Raven himself, but only a mage or clan that looks to him that threatens Tamtir."

Loucha nodded. "Indeed," said the *seveyata*, "he may be indifferent in this dispute. Yet surely mages that place themselves under his sign have certain preferences in spells, even if they are not constrained."

"The sky," mused Mesaz. "That could point to any number of weather disasters—flooding rains, lightning, gales and twist-winds...hail..." He did not look at Loucha as he added the last hazard.

"Not rain, perhaps," said Pevetos. "He is the Ice Raven after all. Perhaps the colder weather ills only, which may leave out lightning as well. And if we agree his realm is the sky, then may we decide we need not prepare for earthquakes or similar land disasters?"

"The curse on my father manifested as salt, not a weather spell," said Beloved, pleased that she could speak of her father without a tremor. All paused as this point was given thought.

"Your Radiance, was this a deliberate spell he cast?" asked Zhelez. "If I recall, when the Royal Historian interviewed His Radiance about the Griefstone, the prince said Besserdech was still within the tower. He himself was encased within the salt, his body corroded by it."

Beloved remembered standing among the ruins of the tower in the sunlight and staring down at what bones were left of her father's skeleton. She took a moment to be sure her voice would be strong and answered, "Yes, that is so. The salt curse was not, I believe, a deliberately cast spell. It was born of my mother's curse and my father's bitterness. The salt was like a fountain, coming out of him, poisoning everything."

Zhelez's gaze sharpened and she said, "This would agree with your theory, then, Your Radiance, that mages hold magic in themselves like a river of power. Here, no doubt because of the curse laid on him by your mother, the power turned to fruitless malice, expressed as salt—but it did not stop flowing. Your father no longer had command of it, but the river was still there."

Beloved thought of her years attempting to break her name curse on her own, efforts that merely served to make her more and more hideous, noxious, trammeled, and trapped. *Like a dam stymying a rapid, but giving no outlet. The river of my power churned in on itself.*

"Yes," Beloved acknowledged. "That is so."

"To whom do you look, Your Radiance?" All heads turned towards Baleka, and the *seveyata* looked down, embarrassed at the sudden attention and at her own effrontery. Nevertheless, she continued. "That is, you do not seem to follow your father's clan and look to the Ice Raven. Do you have a guide or protector whom you call on?"

Although all the Tamtireni felt the abrupt change of topic was gauche, once the subject had been raised, they, too, were interested in the answer. What were the princess's allegiances? What aid might they hope for?

Beloved met Baleka's eyes, then the gazes of each person at the table. Rue, she knew, shared her thought: *I look to no one, for no one has helped me.* Sudden images flashed before her mind's eye then: roses spilling from her arms to the crowd below, a *sozkol* soaring upward, a star trembling between her fingers and those of the prince.

As her eyes came to Dris, she saw an uncharacteristic weariness in the face of her mother's sister. *She is of the Fire Bird Clan,* Beloved realized, *even though her blood carries no power. How was it that the*

Fire Bird failed my mother's clan? How is it I never made the connection before, that my mother's sister may have looked to a guardian as a member of a mage clan?

The expectant silence brought her thoughts back to how to reply. "I do not believe the Ice Raven to be evil or malicious, despite my father and our recently revealed enemies," Beloved began. "No more than the Lady or the Master are to be blamed if a farmer beats her mule or a shopkeeper cheats a buyer." She looked at the *seveyati* and they nodded, conceding the point. "Yet I do not feel an affinity with the Ice Raven." She paused for thought, but did not miss the general quiet exhalation of relief. "The Lady and the Master have accepted me as someone entrusted with *zelohn* and *kamin*, as new blood in the royal line, and as a sorceress." Again, she looked at Mesaz and Loucha.

Mesaz nodded in agreement.

"But I do not think," said Loucha, "that the Master and the Lady—*interest*—themselves in mages the way the Ice Raven, or the Fire Bird, or the Snow Deer, or the Lightning Snake, or any other guardian of a mage clan does."

"Because the Lady and the Master cultivate and guard Tamtir as a whole," said Zhelez.

"Yes," said Beloved. "So they accept me and perhaps are glad to add whatever strengths I have to Tamtir, but their eye is on the well-being of the whole kingdom, and not on me or my line."

"Although your line may be of more interest now that it is joined to the royal House," commented Pevetos.

"Indeed," agreed Beloved. "And yet..."

"And yet, Loucha is correct that the Lady and the Master will likely hold aloof, at least more than a clan guardian might," said Mesaz.

There was a pause as everyone tried to recall any time in history or tales when the Lady or the Master had directly intervened to avert disaster.

"Is there some rite that binds guardian and clan together?" asked Mesaz. "Some promise, oath, or form of fealty?"

Beloved looked to Dris.

Her aunt nodded and wrote. *Yes, an oath, disciple to master. Guardians guard the knowledge the disciple seeks. They do not guard the disciple.*

Dris watched as this information was absorbed by the others, then, seeing already the questions they were poised to ask, erased her earlier words and jotted a new comment. *Disciple and master. Over time, clan lines looked to the same guardian. But the oaths are between an individual mage and the guardian.*

Mesaz, Loucha, and Baleka frowned as they considered this. Pevetos tilted his head, bemused.

Zhelez wanted more clarification. "At what age does a mage take this oath? And what is the oath?" she asked.

There are tests of skill before a mage can petition to be a guardian's follower. The mage must be at least thirteen years of age. Few are ready until sixteen or so.

"Petition?" asked Zhelez.

Dris nodded. *Petition. One must ask the guardian to accept one. The oath is sworn. The disciple promises to serve and obey the guardian for a certain period of time. The guardian promises to teach the disciple during that time.*

Zhelez sat back. "It is an apprenticeship," she said.

Dris's brows drew together, considering the historian's assessment. *Yes, but the terms are many years—fifteen, twenty. When the term is ended, the relationship may continue, but now without strict obligations.*

"A contract no longer binds them?" suggested Zhelez. She seemed intrigued by the idea, whereas the *seveyati* appeared shocked. Dris nodded sharply.

Yes, no more contract. Dris added, *Guardians do not like permanent commitments.*

Beloved thought about this new information. Did Dris have any relationship with the Fire Bird? Or had her aunt grown up watching the others of her clan be accepted as worthy, while she could never hope to be, due to her inability to channel and manipulate power?

"Therefore," said Loucha, "it may well be the Ice Raven holds no particular malice towards us, although some of his followers—or even former followers—may use what he has taught to harm us."

"Yet let us not forget," said Pevetos, "that the Ice Raven delights in tricks and illusions...and that indeed all the guardians are, as far as we know, more capricious than our Lady and Master."

Mesaz turned his dark eyes to Beloved. "Your Radiance, have you taken or do you plan to take an oath to study under a guardian? You say you have no affinity for the Ice Raven. I am glad to hear it, whether he bears us malice or no. But is there another to whom you would look?"

Beloved gazed down at her folded hands on the table before her. She still spent time simply looking at her freed body, admiring its capable form, its responsiveness to her will. Now she looked at how her interlaced fingers stacked, making a small room: the tops of her palms meeting to form the angle of two walls and the polished wood of the table the floor. She remembered another room, deep in this very palace, the Hall where she had felt the hand of the Master touching the back of her head and then raising her chin; she felt once more the fleeting touch of the Lady in her Glade, a lick of flame and a bird flying into the sun. Beloved became aware that the silence was becoming heavy—of course, she had not yet answered. She looked up.

"I am not the sworn follower of any guardian," Beloved began, then stopped, and wondered whether what she would say next would anger the *seveyati*. "I believe the Lady and the Master have taken me under their protection as—not a follower—but as more than a new bride of the royal House." She looked at both Mesaz and Loucha. His gaze was assessing; hers was—satisfied? Beloved could not decipher anything more; she sighed inwardly and continued. "Yet, it may be that I require in addition a guardian to guide my studies of magic." She thought of the loremasters she had coerced; she could not blame them for concealing this path to more knowledge and power. "I know little of this practice, for those who knew did not desire to teach me," she concluded and flushed, embarrassed at what she did not know and why.

Dris commented, *The Fire Bird knows of the living flame—including the sap that fires all growing things. You are drawn to this.*

As are you, Aunt, thought Beloved, and wondered again whether Dris had entered into any contract with the guardian of her clan.

"Fire is the Lady's element and She is the Gardener," said Loucha. The *seveyata* turned toward the gardener, her voice sharp and her eyes flashing. "Is there anything of sun or sap the Lady does not know?"

Everyone's eyes turned to Dris, who remained unruffled. *No one denies the Lady's knowledge or greatness,* replied Dris. *She is kind to all who tend their* zelohni *and generous to Her* seveyati *who walk the sunfields. But I have not heard She teaches mages or desires to. Am I mistaken?*

How Kashan managed, with his measured voice, to convey Dris's respect for Loucha as well as her tartness and bluntness, Beloved did not know. There was a humming silence while everyone waited to see whether Loucha would take offense. Then the priestess laughed, and the tension of the room eased.

"In truth, the Lady is no teacher of sorcerers. Although I believe Her Radiance is wise to recognize that the Lady takes a special interest in the princess and her use of magic." Loucha's bright gaze touched on Beloved before moving to Mesaz. "Does the Master likewise have His eye on Her Radiance?"

"The Master, like the Lady, teaches us, but He does not enter into contracts with individuals," said Mesaz; his tone made it clear such an agreement would be, in his estimation, beneath the Master's dignity. "Yet I believe He does watch over Her Radiance in a particular way." He saw Beloved swallow and caught a sudden small movement from Rue to his left. He turned to Rue. "How could it not be so? Her Radiance, if our theories of magic are correct, may be a disruptive force in Tamtir."

Beloved felt the blood drain from her face. Was Mesaz suggesting she herself was a danger to Tamtir, an alien monster, after insisting she was of Tamtir?

Rue saw Beloved's stricken face and the older woman's heart went out to her foster daughter. "Indeed," Rue said coldly, "she disrupted the illness that was killing the queen."

Mesaz was surprised, for Rue usually said little and he had not thought her hostile. But then he met her angry eyes and he glanced up the table towards the princess, who was sitting stiffly. Pevetos, sitting on her left, glared at him. The *seveyat* realized he had not made himself clear; he was not usually so clumsy.

"Your pardon, Your Radiance, and Lady Rue," Mesaz said, bowing to each woman from his seat. "Your Radiance, you are a new and potent element in the—let us call it—the *economy* of magic of Tamtir," he explained. "It is no wonder you have drawn the attention of both the Lady and the Master."

Rue settled back; Beloved relaxed her posture and gave a small nod, acknowledging his words.

Then Beloved glanced at the time-candle set into the wall on her right, farther down the room. "There is a repast in our chambers prepared for your refreshment," she said, taking refuge in formality. She felt bruised from the morning's discussion. "Let us eat, then gather once more at the tenth hour. Our task remains: how to identify and counter a magical strike?"

Beloved stood and all the others rose to their feet. She gestured to Rue, who led everyone from the room. Beloved took a moment to make sure she was composed enough to produce the light talk appropriate for such times. She did not look at the burnt outline of the Ice Raven as she left the room.

CHAPTER FORTY-NINE

Beloved, in her role as hostess for this little party, was able to hang back until everyone else had helped themselves and sat down. Late fall's cool sunshine spilled through the tall windows, filling the chamber, and providing a welcome contrast to the privy council room, which was lit by small, high, half-moon windows. Beloved set a casement ajar to invite some fresh air within.

She thought Queen Gladna, were she there, would have noted who was sitting and talking with whom, in addition to making charming small talk, but Beloved felt that was beyond her resources. She contented herself with noting that the energy of the room was quiet but not unhappy and moved toward the sideboard. Rue appeared at her side. Beloved glanced sideways at her heart-mother. Rue said nothing, but gestured for Beloved to hold out her plate so Rue could serve her some of the grilled *melzahn* Beloved liked so much. Beloved smiled as Rue added a few other things to the plate, including a floury roll and some soft baked cheese. Rue touched Beloved's arm.

"Go, sit, eat," the older woman urged. And Beloved obeyed, Rue's love for her settling like a gossamer shawl about her shoulders—light, warm, and comforting. She restored herself with her meal at a table a little apart from the rest. From time to time, Beloved remembered to make a general comment and to invite the others to enjoy another helping of food or drink. Although she did not know it, both Rue and Dris were keeping a watchful eye on Beloved, letting the others in the room know Her Radiance was not to be accosted.

Pevetos eyed the princess as she smiled up at the *damash* who was pouring wine into her goblet. The young man was at ease with this foreign sorceress. He made a comment to her and she laughed. The *damash* had to move away to attend to someone else, but he seemed reluctant to leave her side. *She has charisma,* thought Pevetos. Was it because she was the vessel of magical bloodlines? Was it because her history, or at any rate what had yet been told of it, was like something out of an old tale, edged with mist and touched with stardust? She had, also, an air of having just been born—everything seemed new to her, yet although she was young, she was a woman grown. He wondered how he could ask, without giving offense or pain, about her life before her arrival in Tamtir.

A little ways off from where Pevetos sat musing over his spinach tart and ham, Loucha sat with Mesaz. She had let Baleka go sit with Dris and Kashan. As far as Loucha could tell, Dris remained aloof from the conversation—*too busy being a watchdog,* thought Loucha—but Kashan amiably chatted with Baleka as he neatly ate a *linti* tart. A good break for the younger woman, Loucha thought. *These sessions have been more intense than Baleka had anticipated.* Loucha finished buttering a roll and sipped her wine.

"What do you make of Her Radiance?" she asked her fellow *seveyat.*

Mesaz glanced at the princess, who was, with some awkwardness, peeling a piece of fruit with a small knife. He chose a morsel of cheese from his plate and placed it in his mouth. After swallowing, Mesaz said, "The Master has accepted her."

Loucha nodded. *Yes.* She herself thought the young woman was earnest, well-intentioned, and promising. But the reason Loucha was willing to work with her and believe in her was because the Lady had approved her.

Dris and Zhelez, after conferring together during the break, presented to the privy council their belief that the focus mage was one Khaladona, Besserdech's elder sister. Beloved was astonished to discover that she had yet another aunt, this one on her father's side. Dris thought Khaladona was a decade or more older than Beloved's father and that she had a maternal rather than a sororal relationship towards him.

From what Dris—and Rue, upon consultation—recollected, Khaladona believed Amarrasal, Beloved's mother, had lured Khaladona's younger brother into marriage. According to Rue, Khaladona had appeared after Amarrasal's death and proclaimed that the whole train of events was a convoluted plot by the Fire Bird Clan to destroy her brother. That her brother's wife was dead, Khaladona dismissed as a calculated risk. That Besserdech had virtually exterminated his wife's clan when he had raped Amarrasal, she brushed aside as a second fatal miscalculation on the part of the Fire Bird Clan. Beloved had blinked at the line of twisted logic, but none of the others at the table seemed surprised.

Noticing Beloved did not know what to make of such illogical reasoning, Pevetos said, "Your Radiance, history and song are filled with the distortions of reason brought on by rage, jealousy, and thwarted love. Lady Rue tells us Besserdech himself did not agree with his sister. He seemed to dislike her as much as he disliked everyone else. Yet she preferred to think that he had been duped than to admit he had no love for her. These things are sad in any family, but they are disastrous when others are brought into the reach of harm, as may happen when the family wields power—whether of wealth, arms, or blood."

Dris and Rue further proposed that Khaladona had gathered the other mages from lands stricken by the salt curse, many of whom had lost a great deal of influence and wealth as the realms about them diminished. In addition to spreading her story of the treachery of the Fire Bird Clan, Khaladona may have promised revenge to those who desired it and provided a target of envy for those who cared little for anyone but themselves.

Mesaz and Loucha committed their temples to walking the starplains and sunfields, seeking the wisdom of the Master and the Lady among the sky leas; the temples would also try to glean what they might of the Ice Raven and his followers.

"For all birds," said Loucha, "seek light."

"Who knows," added Mesaz, "what devices the Ice Raven may have contrived?"

Beloved was not sure what the *seveyati* meant when they spoke thus, but she saw from the others' nods that this was considered useful action, so she said nothing against it. She resolved to ask Radvyed about it later.

The privy council concluded that the Bitter Ones—for so the group had fallen into naming them—would strike at what the foreign sorcerers perceived to be the heart of the kingdom. In part Beloved's advisors based this reasoning on the theory that the queen's illness had, indeed, been the first attempt to harm Tamtir.

"But they disregard the people, as we have said, and aim at individuals," said Zhelez, summing up the thoughts of the gathering. "I believe they may discount the royal family and perhaps even the *seveyati*. Now that they have found you, Your Radiance, you must appear to them to be the sole worthy adversary. It was you, after all, who healed the queen and destroyed the Griefstone."

Beloved shook her head and held up a hand. "Not I alone, Scholar. The prince took the cure home to the queen and together we brought the Griefstone low."

"But this, too, they do not seem to comprehend," said Baleka. "If I understand Dris Rose Gardener and Lady Rue, many of the rites and observances that are universal in Tamtir are not observed in other lands. So they may underestimate our strengths."

"They have spies," said Mesaz. He had sat awhile with his eyes closed, searching for the weaknesses that the enemy would find and exploit. "They must. And what better spies than birds? They do not send white ravens, no—but if the Ice Raven claims the sky, how many birds can they call to do their bidding?"

This was a chilling thought. Zhelez turned to Beloved and said, "Your Radiance, they will strike at what they believe to be the heart of Tamtir. What do you think that will be?"

In Beloved's mind flashed a picture of the sacred Tree on the day of her wedding, a silent, other-than-human witness; she thought of the ancient, bloodstained Stone laid among the supports of the royal palace.

Beloved said, "Knowing what I know, if I wished to destroy Tamtir, I would strike at the Lady's Tree and the Master's Stone. I would poison or otherwise kill the Tree; I would crack or crush the Stone."

The Tamtireni flinched at the blasphemy. Rue and Dris nodded.

Loucha said, "Yet it is still unclear what they know or what they make of whatever news their spies"—she glanced at Mesaz—"may bring them."

"It is always so," said Zhelez.

Beloved was thinking that there was not much more to be accomplished this day, when there was a knock on the door.

"Enter," said Beloved. She, together with everyone else, gave an involuntary gasp of pleasure when the prince opened the door. Radvyed's face was solemn.

"The king and queen," he said, "request the presence of the Lesser Council in the Great Hall. They desire that all councilors shall be present and advise Their Splendors. The Lesser Council shall present the results of its deliberations before the Great Council and be informed of those of that body. Please rise and follow."

Chapter Fifty

T he Great Council was usually held in its own chamber. It was composed of the king and queen, the prince, administrative officials or *dovoreni* appointed for their skill and ability, senior *seveyati* from the temples of the Lady and the Master, representatives of the major guilds and halls, and leading *mireni* from all over the kingdom. Today, to accommodate the princess and the Lesser (or privy) Council, all were assembled in the Great Hall. This decision had been made not only to find room for more people, but so that the princess could be seen and heard by all. Three long tables formed a U. At the table that formed the shorter crosspiece of the U were seated the king and queen, with Beloved to the king's right and Radvyed to the queen's left. Down the two long lines of the other tables sat the rest of the Council. The members of Beloved's Lesser Council were seated at the end of the table nearest to her, with Rue to her right.

Beloved looked out over the full Council, which, numerous as it was, still seemed a little lost in the open space of the Hall. Their faces were turned towards King Arkost, who was standing and explaining that the princess had been meeting with a Lesser Council to discuss what form a magical attack was likely to take, when it might come, and from where. The faces of the councilors were grave. After the king had finished and sat down, they gave their attention to those who formed the Lesser Council. Eyes lingered on the princess, Rue, and Dris.

Radvyed, watching the councilors, saw that while most of those present accepted the right of Rue and Dris to be there, as the only ones with firsthand knowledge of mages outside of Tamtir, the Tamtireni were still uncertain as to the reliability of the foreign women's knowledge. As for Beloved, those who had known her longest—the *dovoreni* whose work kept them in the palace and those used to seeing her about the royal city—by and large accepted her as they did the other members of the royal family. They had no complaints: the princess had undertaken the oaths and observed the rites; she was learning the business of ruling; she was kind and respected the people.

The *mireni*, who spent less time among the day-to-day doings of palace or city, were less certain of Beloved's temperament and judgment. They were the ones who were most likely to suspect still that the princess had merely had a powerful dream and no real seeing of the Bitter Ones. The *mireni* had been at the wedding and all the rites of that day; they had seen the *sozkol* and the gem; they had heard the story of the rose and the salt. And yet.

The new princess had been appallingly ignorant of the most rudimentary truths about the Lady and the Master. She seemed unable to converse with people in a normal manner. Either she spoke with disconcerting candor, or her whole face and body closed up like a shuttered window. Yes, she had knowledge of magic, but look at her judgment: the fracas with *Mirena* Lioda and *Miren* Rezh; the redecorating of an entire floor of the palace on a whim; the odd tale of a poisonous thorny vine and her flight into the country, only a few days before. And this farouche girl was what they had to rely on to save them from possible ruin?

None of this was said, although the prince and his parents understood the undercurrent of doubt. Yet they hoped that seeing the respect that the Lesser Council accorded Beloved would help skeptics to listen to her without prejudice.

Beloved understood only that she was being put to the test. She had wanted one of the others to be the spokesperson for the findings of her privy council, but Radvyed had said she must be the one to speak. Baleka had been writing a summary of the day's work when the prince called them; this document now lay under Beloved's hand. Arkost allowed a sufficient pause for everyone to study the Lesser Council and prepare to listen to the princess. He turned to Beloved and nodded for her to rise and address the assembly. Beloved drew a breath and stood.

It was one thing, she discovered, to stand on a balcony and have exultant, joyful crowds below you, or even to have a group of seven or eight gathered around a table. It was altogether another thing to stand in the Great Hall before the king and queen and the fifty or so members of the full Great Council, whose polite but unreadable faces waited for you to explain what little you knew. Beloved took another breath and the paper in her hand rattled a little. She glanced down at it, then out over the Council, and began.

She forgot, of course, the proper opening formulas as she began her report. Radvyed watched as a few of those listening bristled at the abruptness of the start of her speech. But her listeners' concerns with protocol faded as they heard what she had to say.

Beloved told them that the privy council believed it had identified the leader of the mages as her own paternal aunt, one Khaladona of the Ice Raven Clan. She explained the theory that the other sorcerers were ones Khaladona had gathered from those who had been directly or indirectly harmed by the salt curse. The three most likely targets for an attack were suggested: the Lady's Tree, the Master's Stone, and

Beloved herself, upon whom the beacon spell had been placed. She pointed out that someone who had learned the ways of magic from the Ice Raven may well have at their disposal birds as spies. There followed a list of the kinds of attacks an Ice Raven mage might deploy: blizzards, ice storms, illusions, perhaps some form of death strikes. Finally, Beloved explained that because she was now strongly bound to Tamtir, she should be able to call on Tamtir's common reservoir of power—a comparative ocean—to counter a targeted attack.

After Beloved finished speaking, she sat. Every eye was fixed on her and a horrified silence held the Hall captive. Even those on her privy council were startled at how dire the situation appeared when spelled out so starkly. Radvyed heard repeatedly in his head Beloved saying she believed herself to be a specific target. King Arkost rose to his feet.

"Thank you, Princess Beloved, for that report of the dangers you and your advisors believe we are facing," he said. Beloved nodded. The king addressed the Council. "Who would speak? We are eager to hear your thoughts."

A stout older woman stood. Beloved thought, from the emblem pinned on the woman's garment, that she might be one of the *mireni* of the western borders, and so one who had had experience of the salt curse.

"I am concerned," the *mirena* said, "that our enemy is the aunt by blood of the princess. Has she some hold or power over Her Radiance? Should Her Radiance remain near the palace or even in Tamtir, if she is a target, marked, as she says, by this beacon spell? Does her presence endanger innocents?"

Beloved became so motionless as to seem a statue of herself, her gaze fixed above the heads of the Council. Rue made a sudden irate motion and Dris glared at the *mirena*, who stood stolidly awaiting an answer.

"Princess Beloved," said Arkost, "will not be exiled from the palace or from Tamtir. She is of Tamtir and of our House. In addition, we do not believe expulsion would be a wise use of her knowledge or skills, or an effective countermeasure against the enemy. If the princess were to be exiled and then captured by these malevolent mages, for example, would that not render Tamtir more vulnerable, not less? They would still resent our prosperity and desire to destroy us. As to her connection to her aunt, she herself will respond." He turned to Beloved and she rose to stand next to him.

"I had no knowledge of this sister of my father before today," Beloved replied. She was holding herself in so tightly, she was vibrating with the tension of it. After taking a breath to steady herself, she continued. "If the *mirena* is asking whether I feel any allegiance to the woman whose brother raped my mother and forced her into marriage, and who cursed me and abandoned me, no. I do not. I remind the *mirena* that my father's tower and the salt curse were broken by Prince Radvyed and myself." Beloved sat down as soon as she finished speaking. The *mirena*, a little flushed, nodded and sat down.

A man stood, on the early side of middle age. His hands and his plain dress suggested he was an artisan of some kind. "I keep hearing about this idea that we have magic here in Tamtir," he began. "Well, I've never heard of it until Her Radiance came among us, not from the *seveyati*, not from the scholars, not from the *mireni*, not from anyone. Now we're asked to believe that some mage and her friends are going to bring ice and death upon us and destroy Tree and Stone, and Her Radiance says, she'll just use all this magic I've never heard of that's lying about Tamtir to fend them off. I'll tell you now, this sounds like a tale to amuse my little ones. It makes no sense to me."

"And yet you have seen proofs of magic at work in our kingdom, Master Strolit," answered Arkost. "Few were there to witness with their own eyes the recovery of the queen from her illness, but many saw the *sozkol* fly from the princess's hand, the star arise from her fingers, and the roses that she bestowed in the Square that first day."

Master Strolit shook his head, unconvinced. "A bird, a jewel, a few flowers. Is this the power that will shield us from an evil death, even if the threat be real?"

The king answered, "If your concern is that Her Radiance has little power, may I mention once more the queen's health and the overthrow of the Griefstone?"

Radvyed glanced at his father. They had expected contention and the need to air all doubts and fears. His parents remained calm: these debates, the questions and answers, were part of the purpose of the Council. But looking beyond his father, he saw Beloved was not tranquil. She was controlled, her face closed, but he could see the quick rise and fall of her chest. Rue and Dris, too, unused to Council sessions, were grim-faced. Master Strolit did not sit; he was still unsatisfied.

Another person rose to join him, a *miren*. He was an older man, tall and elegant; his lands lay near enough to Zolatar that he would be aware of palace gossip, yet far enough that he would not see the royal family frequently. "And what of the incident with *Mirena* Lioda and *Miren* Rezh? The impulsive changes to the palace overnight, causing heirlooms to vanish? The salt-covered thorn on the very grounds of the palace and the princess's flight, abandoning the palace to the vine? If Her Radiance has power, then it seems that either her control of it is uncertain, or her commitment to Tamtir and the royal House is weak."

Rue glared at the *miren*, her eyes narrowed in anger; the bard, Pevetos, spoke quietly in her ear. Dris's face hardened and her eyes were stony. Beloved surged to her feet. Her chair crashed down behind her.

"Weak?" she repeated, and her voice, although low, was so intense, it was audible to everyone in the Hall. She reached up and grasped the neckline of her bodice with both hands. Radvyed knew in that moment what she was about to do and could only watch, helpless. Beloved yanked open her bodice, sending buttons flying. Everyone about her was rigid with surprise. She grabbed the neckline of her chemise and ripped it, pulling the torn garment aside to expose her sternum. To the left of it, an ugly red scar marred her smooth skin.

"This," Beloved hissed into the shocked silence, "is the mark left on me when the prince took the flower from my garden and brought it here, to Tamtir, to save your queen from certain death, a woman I had never met nor seen. Since then I have sworn oaths to Lady, land, House, people, and Master. From other flowers of that same stem came the renewal of the outerlands and the downfall of the Griefstone. Do you think that was a small spell, requiring little power or skill?"

No one answered or even moved. This went beyond debate and hearsay and wild tales. The scar seemed to twitch on Beloved's skin as everyone in the Great Hall stared at it, both fascinated and repelled.

The *miren* and Master Strolit sat down. But a woman arose, a crown of white braids about her head, with high cheekbones and a thin mouth. She was Selya, the head of the healers, and Radvyed knew that she felt it keenly that they had been unable to help his mother.

"I still see no evidence of power," Selya said, "whether used well or ill. The queen's health—the illness came upon her mysteriously and it passed the same way. The bird and the star—they are the work of the Lady and the Master, who can do as they will. That scar on your chest—badly tended, badly healed—is from a sword or a knife. Even this seeing, or warning, or whatever you choose to call it—how reliable is it? I require evidence, not stories or fables."

Radvyed rose, but before he could reiterate his testimony regarding his mother's cure and the end of the Griefstone, he saw the gathered councilors recoil as one, eyes wide with—shock? Terror? He looked to his right, beyond his mother and his father, and saw that Beloved faced the healer. His wife was enveloped in flame.

Chapter Fifty-One

Beloved began to shake. Something was building inside her, giving her such a surge of power that she felt at that moment she could do anything: level the palace, cover the kingdom in thorns overnight, burn stone. It took her a moment to realize this power was not coming from anyone in the Hall, or from her spell-bonds with any of them, or through the magic rites—*still unacknowledged! still denied!*—that tied her to House and land. The surge of power came from deep within herself, from a source that would never run dry nor falter. Then Beloved was at last able to name it: rage.

Through her anger, which only the discipline learned in years spent in misery and loneliness allowed her to control, she saw she was indeed her parents' daughter. Here was this people, endowed with land, shelter, benevolent interest from Lady and Master, handed down, guarded, and cherished for a thousand years. And here was she, her inheritance—what? Power, yes, power of fire and blood and green sap, but also a rage that blasted through her veins like molten iron: hot, destructive, and unstoppable. *This* was the force that broke a dozen kingdoms with its salt bitterness; *this* was the grim ferocity that had paralyzed the potency of a hated spouse and laid a curse on a newborn child, still bloody from birth.

Beloved found this rush of rage both exhilarating and terrifying. These oafs—who did not even know, much less understand!—the power through which they moved and acted, these closed-hearted, soft-headed people spoke to her, she who had given her heart, her heart, her own bleeding heart, for their sake, they spoke to her as though she were a child, as though she were stupid, as though she were weak or scatterbrained, while the problem—did they still not see it?—was that she was old, older than they by far in grief and darkness, and resilient enough that she could make a haven from exile, and strong enough that at this moment she could crumble the stone and wood of this very palace to sand and splinters, should she wish to speak the word.

Yet at the very same time, Beloved felt she held the reins of a runaway stallion, who had gotten the bit between his teeth and had just sighted a challenger over the hill, and this magnificent, unbroken animal cared nothing at all for whether she stayed on his back or no, and he gloried in his speed, his fire, and his aggression. *Let the palace fall, then*, the stallion might have called, had he cared, *let the palace fall, if it is too weak to stand!*

Radvyed, Arkost, and Gladna were all on their feet. They were looking at her as though a dragon from the old tales had been dropped into their midst, all smoke-hardened wings, flaming breath, and glittering scales. Beloved herself felt taller, as though she were expanding, but through gritted will alone she drew her power into herself; she shaped it, in her mind's eye, into a whirling sphere of wind-whipped flame, and she set it where her heart should be. The others stood still, wary and silent.

Beloved spoke and they flinched at the way her words seemed to gleam in the air before fading into smoke.

"Open your eyes," she said, her voice low but carrying. "Open your eyes and see. I am no child. I am not ignorant. I am no tamed creature or exotic pet. Any bindings on me are ones I have permitted, to soothe *your* fears, to calm *your* anxiety, to preserve *your* peace."

Radvyed vaulted over the table and came to stand in front of her, drawing Beloved's gaze from the healer, stiff with shock, to himself. Beloved looked at him. There was her husband, the child of every good thing: power, bloodline, beauty, love, adoration, nobility of character. She felt a wave of longing and her rage billowed higher; in its distorting grip she hated herself for this weakness of love and desire. She compressed the rage back into its burning ball.

"You labor yet under bindings you did not choose," said Radvyed.

"Name them, whatever you think they may be," she replied, her power still held by her, but no longer hidden or dampened: everyone could see the ball of flame.

"Marriage. Royalty. Loyalty to the land of Tamtir."

She laughed; the king drew in a careful breath and the queen lifted a hand and let it fall. Radvyed stood, his hands open at his side, motionless, his eyes never moving from that face of frightening radiance.

"Because I have been harnessed does not mean I must remain bound," said his wife. "Do you think you could keep me, handsome prince, if I wished to go? Do you think this building could stand, if I willed it to fall? Or this land thrive, if I willed it to fail?" She spoke, wanting them to see, to know her for what she was: only half civilized, if that, as they understood it, her blood and breath glittering with a power they hardly allowed themselves to recognize. "I am still a monster, if no longer Hideous. Until you see me for what I am, our bonds are but frayed ropes."

There was a moment of throbbing silence, as Beloved and Radvyed stared into each other's eyes.

"Say your will, then," Radvyed challenged her, unsmiling, soft-spoken. "Will you bring down destruction on this land and this House? Does your angry heart demand this payment for our smallness and ignorance, for our attempts at taming you, for the loneliness of your power?"

Beloved held his gaze and snarled her answer. "No, I will not. My anger may demand what it will. I am yet mistress of it."

She sensed that the stance of the king and queen eased a very little. But there was still plenty of tension in the room. *Yes,* she thought at the gathered Council, *I am to be feared. I am the nightmare from a story that has ripped the roof off your house. You cannot drive me off and you cannot keep me close. What then will you do?*

"Then do you forsake us? Cut us off from you as unworthy? For you know what you call our power, you say, better than we do ourselves."

Beloved said nothing, but the whirling fire at her heart threw off unruly sparks. She kept her eyes on his and heard her own breath quicken. There was not enough air in the room.

Radvyed kept silence and his gaze did not move from hers.

Beloved trembled with the force of containing her power and of mastering her hurt and rage.

Radvyed searched for a word that might reach her, help her remember the trust they had built between them, the bond of love as well as duty. *What is it you want of me? What is it you think I can do that a Lady who wields so much power cannot do for herself?* The prince remembered that day by the stream with Rue. *But I have married her,* he thought, *and freed her from her curse. What more does she need from me now? Perhaps only to stand before her in her rage, and not look away, not renounce her.* So he stood, presenting no threat, waiting, listening. He would remain until she told him to go.

Beloved stared at Radvyed and she saw, at last, the form of his power. He was earth, standing before her, a mountain with bones of stone, crowned with oak. Earth, which would absorb any lightning flung on its chest; earth, which remained after the retreat of every flood; earth, which even when swept by fire or gale, allowed only its surface to be disturbed or rearranged. Earth, accepting bone and seed, death and life. Steady, enduring, patient, fruitful.

At last Beloved spoke, her eyes never leaving her husband's. The queen was not sure whether the note of wonder in her alarming daughter-in-law's low, quiet voice was only imagined.

"I do not cut you off, Radvyed of Tamtir, neither you nor your people. You are worthy, and more than worthy. I break no oath nor bond."

Beloved felt her power settle back, calm, into a deep-currented river. The runaway stallion shook out his mane, slowed to a trot, then a walk, and then bent his head to graze. She released the ball of fire and the flames faded into her blood and bone. She stood now, a young woman like any other, if somewhat disheveled, before the statue-still Council.

Radvyed took a step toward her, still looking into her eyes, and held out his hand. "Neither do I cut you off, Beloved, Rose Lady of Tamtir. I see you, and you are worthy, more than worthy. I break no oath nor bond."

Beloved leaned toward him and placed her hand in his. The table separated them, so she could go no farther. He raised her hand to his lips, then let it drop. He placed one hand on the table and leapt over it to join her. They looked together over the assembled members of the Council, who were silent with stupefaction.

Beloved laced her fingers with Radvyed's. She knew she had behaved badly. She did not know how to make amends. To the tense faces before her, she said, "I ask only to be allowed to serve Tamtir as I have sworn to do, using all my power and skill."

King Arkost spoke then. "Let the Council be adjourned. We will meet again tomorrow in the Council chamber at the fourth hour." Then he and Gladna turned and left by a side door, followed by Radvyed and Beloved. As the door closed behind the younger couple, they heard the rising babble of voices as everyone in the Great Hall began to exclaim, to argue, and to speculate, as if the royals' departure had unfrozen every tongue and limb.

Chapter Fifty-Two

The king, queen, prince, and princess withdrew to the queen's sitting room. *Damashi* brought in food and drink. Arkost stood by the fireplace, resting his elbow on the mantel, frowning at one booted toe as it nudged a pattern on the flagstone. Gladna had settled herself in her favorite chair, her full skirts comfortably spread, and her arms laid on the armrests. Beloved stood a little ways inside the door, uncertain. Her fingers were still laced with Radvyed's and she was grateful for his solid presence at her side. The younger couple waited for either Arkost or Gladna to speak.

After the door shut behind the last *damasha*, the queen looked at her son and his wife, then drew her brows together a little. "Beloved, my dear, would you like to change your dress?"

Beloved looked down and realized that her torn gown and chemise still fluttered about her chest, exposing the scar. "Yes, of course," she said. Letting go of Radvyed's hand, she held the two edges of the chemise together and ran her finger up the tear. Turning to Radvyed, she asked him to hold the ripped bodice of her gown together, and once more ran her finger along the ragged edges. He took his hands away and he and his parents saw that Beloved's clothes had been mended without stitch or sign of darning. Or buttons. *Did this bodice not have buttons?* Radvyed shook away the inconsequential thought.

Gladna stared for a moment, laughed, and shook her head a little.

Beloved looked about at them. "Oh. Should I not have—"

"No, no," said the queen. "It is well. One is so used, however, to thinking of magic as something displayed in great or terrible deeds, that one does not think of its everyday uses." She waved towards the table that had been set. "Come, children. Sit and eat." Radvyed and Beloved moved toward the table. Beloved glanced at Arkost, who was still by the fire.

"I am sorry," she said.

"Yes?" said Gladna. "For what?"

"I should not have spoken so to the Council." Beloved hesitated by a chair; she did not sit. Radvyed also remained standing. He wanted to know what his parents thought. He knew they were not angry, but beyond that, he was not sure.

"It was not polished or tactful, perhaps," conceded the queen. "And yet, I am not sure we have the time for much more tact. Your allegiance and your power were being challenged and you had to answer convincingly, which you did."

Arkost snorted a laugh and moved away from the mantelpiece and toward the table. "Yes," said the king, "I believe we are all now persuaded of the seriousness of your commitment to the defense of Tamtir and the fact that your magic is more than the sleight of hand of a traveling conjuror." He took a seat at the queen's side. "Sit, sit," he said, waving a hand at the younger couple. "The day's work is not yet done." After another moment's hesitation, Beloved sat down. Radvyed sat on his mother's other side.

The queen poured *chelek* for all of them. "Yet I am distressed, Beloved," she began, then paused to reach across the table to touch Beloved's arm, for the princess had frozen with her cup halfway to her lips. "I am distressed to learn about your scar. Does it pain you? Do you need—"

Beloved set her cup down, *chelek* untasted. "No, no, I am not in pain, Your Splendor," she said. "Keep your flower," she added, for Gladna's hand had gone to her breast, her fingers hovering over the place where the rose was still tucked away, close to her skin. "The scar is..." Beloved's gaze slid to Radvyed.

She had once called the scar ugly; he had put his fingers over it and said that the ugliness was all his, for he was the one who had ripped the rose from her garden and left without looking back. There had followed a half-playful, half-serious argument. In the end they had agreed that the scar was a sign of courage on her part and faith on his.

"For you returned," Beloved had said, "so it is a scar, not a death-wound."

Radvyed had kissed it and said, "It is both glory and shame to me, then."

Now, seated around a table with his parents and drinking *chelek*, Beloved said, "The scar is a reminder that though there is suffering and fear, both can be overcome." Radvyed smiled at her and reached for a jam tart.

"Battles leave scars," agreed Arkost. "Is that *sladky* cheese?"

Gladna looked between the two younger ones, then said, "Very well."

"What concerns me," said the king, spreading some soft cheese on a slice of toasted bread, "is when this attack may come and what form it might take. Ice storms, say: what does one do against those? Or illusions? Illusions of what? How large? How widespread? And this knowledge that the Ice Raven brings death seems only to add formless dread to our planning. Brings death how? Plague? Poison? Invasion by man or beast?" He took a bite of bread and cheese.

"I would like to know more about how you would be able to draw and focus power from the land and the people," said Radvyed, helping himself to some greens dressed with a honey sauce. He picked up his fork but did not gather a bite, instead turning his gaze on his wife, who was avoiding his eye. "Beloved?"

She said nothing, but moved a few morsels around on her plate with her fork. The king and queen finished swallowing their food and set down their utensils, looking between Beloved and Radvyed in the silence that was becoming more strained by the moment. Finally Beloved gave a small sigh and looked Radvyed in the eye.

"The way I did before," she said. Radvyed set down his fork, the greens untouched, and leaned towards her.

"The way you did before," he repeated. She nodded. "The way you did before, in the tower, when you used the power of our bond to unmake the salt curse." Again Beloved nodded. Radvyed was not done. "The way you did before, in making yourself—or was it us—the focus, or lens, as you explained it to me, of all the power used in both the making and the unmaking of the spell."

"Yes!" Beloved burst out, frustrated. "Only this time I alone will be the focus." She knew the cost. She also was afraid, not so much for herself, but of failure. An ocean of power to tap, to channel, then to wield—how? Against what threat or force?

Arkost said, "Surely that is to the good, that Beloved knows what she is doing?" His son swung around to face his father.

"She almost died! I carried her half dead from a tower that was falling as we fled!" Radvyed shouted. His father said nothing, only looked at his son. Gladna laid a hand on Radvyed's arm as he fought to get himself under control. Before she could speak, Radvyed turned back to Beloved.

"How many times will I have to hold you as you die?" he asked.

"As many as needed," Beloved said without stopping to think. His eyes narrowed and she realized the question had not been awaiting an answer.

The queen, who had rarely seen her even-tempered son so out of his usual ease, spoke up. "Then we are fortunate that our House is signed with oak and badger, two creatures who know what it is to hold fast," she said. Her words had the desired effect of breaking the glare between Beloved and Radvyed. Beloved turned to the queen with widened eyes.

"Of course," said Beloved, "I had forgotten. Foolish of me. You have your own guardians and guides in addition to the Lady and the Master who watch all Tamtir." Seemingly reassured, she began to eat. The prince was not placated.

"I am glad that you are comforted by the sigil on my ring," Radvyed said, not sounding glad at all. "As the wearer of the ring, I feel less than tranquil."

"You have not let go of her yet," said Arkost. "I see no reason to worry that you will slacken now. No, the strength of the pair of you is not in doubt. The when and against what are."

Radvyed looked in exasperation at his wife, then at his parents. *But really*, he thought, *what more was there to say?* Beloved would act as she must, and that being so, it was his part to keep her alive, whether by his love, by their marriage bond, by the guidance of spirits, or by his sheer unwillingness to yield his wife to the maw of death. No one liked it; no one had to like it. It was what must be done. Radvyed huffed out a breath and picked up his own fork.

They spent the next hour talking over and over and round and round the possibilities of when and what. Then a message came from the Lady's solar. *Lady's Glory*, it said. *Too far away? When is the birthday of Her Radiance?*

The queen held the note in her hand after reading it aloud. "It seems they are considering significant dates," she mused. She looked up at Beloved. "Days such as the solstice and equinox are sacred to the Lady and the Master," she explained to Beloved. "Lady's Glory is the summer solstice, the fifteenth of Letena." Beloved had already learned that Tamtir had been established during the summer solstice centuries ago. "But do such things have any meaning in the workings of magic?"

Beloved nodded. "Yes," she replied, "the movement of sun, moon, and stars are often taken into account, especially in the casting of large or difficult spells. Liminal events, such as births, deaths, and marriages, evoke the energies of two states of being—" She saw from the slightly lost looks on the others' faces that she was veering into more specialized theories than she had time or need to explain. She brought herself back to the question at hand. "Yes," Beloved repeated. "Events of the wheel of seasons as well as dates attached to particular individuals can have special significance, and therefore power, in spells."

Gladna looked back at the letter. Arkost, standing at her shoulder, said, "Glory too far away—yes, perhaps so. It is another six months, almost. Of course we do not know what they are planning." Again his frustration at working in ignorance was plain.

"When is your birthday, Beloved?" asked Radvyed.

"Near the winter solstice," she said. "The day of my birth is also the day my father laid the name curse on me. I do not know for certain whether I was born on the eve of the solstice or on the day itself." She and Rue had not celebrated either birthdays or solstices. "Rue would know the hour."

The *damash* sent to call Rue to the queen's sitting room found Beloved's foster mother in the palace gardens, sitting on a bench. Nearby Dris walked among the winter-dormant rose plants, her rough gardener's fingers brushing them as gently as a butterfly's wings. The late afternoon sun was pale, but the air was clear, and both women were relieved to be out of council chambers, whether privy or great.

The man delivered his message and departed. Rue had just risen to obey the summons when she said to Vel, who was straightening the edging stones of the path nearby, "Does one often see so many ravens over the Forest?"

Vel looked, following her gaze. "No, mistress," he said. He hastened among the roses after Dris to point out this anomaly to her, while Rue with more than usual briskness entered the palace. She would be sure to mention the ravens to Beloved and the other royals.

The birds circled a few times, then dropped like a dark net onto the expanse of upraised bare branches below.

Chapter Fifty-Three

"Your birthday was the day of the winter solstice, in the dark before dawn. Your mother died before the sun rose. Another week and we had left the tower," Rue said as she stood by Beloved in front of the cheerful fire.

How different this room is from the chamber of Beloved's birth, Rue thought. Here in winter's gloom the firelight painted tongues of warm light on everything: the comfortable furniture, the rich colors, the kind faces. She remembered that long-ago night, almost twenty-five years ago, now. Only a girl herself, really, although she had thought herself old enough then. Rue remembered the dark, cold room, the dying fire, the dead woman, and the terrifying, sorcerous master brooding and scowling over the silent, swollen body of his wife. A log falling in the fire brought Rue back to the present moment in the queen's sitting room. Rue touched Beloved's hair—*you have always been beloved by me*—then dropped her hand to her side.

"Do you mean to say that man sent you out into the dead of winter alone with a week-old infant?" demanded Arkost. Rue looked at him.

"He was angry, and not a kind or thoughtful master," Rue replied. The king snorted at her calm answer, but the queen was not distracted from the main point.

"Beloved was born the day of the winter solstice? But that would mean her birthday is soon, for the day of the Lady's Return is in but a few weeks. If the Bitter Ones should plan their attack for then..."

"When the Lady is most distant from us," said Radvyed grimly, "as well as being Beloved's birthday, the day of the casting of the name curse, and the anniversary of her mother's death."

"Ravens are gathering above the Lady's Forest," said Rue. Arkost strode to the window, although it did not face toward the Forest directly. He opened it, letting in cold air, and peered out into the dusk.

"I do not see them. It is too dark," he said, drawing back and closing the shutters, then the windows and drapes, enfolding them, thought Rue, in comfort and warmth, at least for now.

Beloved stood silent between Rue and Radvyed. Thoughts and memories of change crowded her mind: birth, death; one mother lost, another gained; her recent shift from isolation to inclusion within so many ties and bonds she felt as though she were interlaced in a complex yet nourishing web. Now it seemed the day was coming when those who hated her sought to smother the ones who had accepted her, and she must be among those who found the way to remain alive and free.

"I agree that the day of my mother's death is the most likely day of attack," Beloved said at last, and everyone else, who had been conversing around her, ceased speaking. "As I understand it, my aunt, this Khaladona, blames my mother for my father's ruin. My mother cursed him as she lay dying." Beloved glanced at Rue, who nodded. Besserdech's tower had been full of the news of the dead mistress's last words, heard by the horrified midwife. "It would make sense for Khaladona to seek the strongest time to strike. The solstice, too, favors the followers of the Ice Raven, for winter is his season of power." The others considered these combined factors and found them unencouraging.

"Yet we have strengths she is unaware of," continued Beloved. "The people and their bonds to the land and to us of the royal House. Khaladona will think the Lady weak and uninterested, perhaps. What is the Master's state in winter?"

"The Master," Arkost answered, to Beloved's surprise, for she had thought him closer to the Lady, "is thoughtful in winter. It is then He plans and dreams the works His hands will bring forth in the spring and summer."

She nodded. "Again, Khaladona may see Him as uncaring or sleeping," remarked Beloved. Radvyed stirred and she turned to him. "I recall, Husband, the words of the *seveyati*. The Lady and Master guard Tamtir by giving it to us. Yet I do not believe that They then turn away."

Radvyed smiled at her. "No. They do not turn away, no matter the season."

"The solstice—the Lady's Return—is not for a few weeks, as you said, Your Splendor. We have time then, to ready the people," said Beloved.

Arkost turned to face his daughter-in-law. Radvyed and Gladna were also staring at Beloved. "Ready them?" repeated the king. "How? For what?"

"For whatever may come, Your Splendor," Beloved replied. "But they must be ready, if I am to be the focus of Tamtir's power, to feed that power to me."

Arkost frowned. "And how will they do that?"

"I am not sure," admitted Beloved and she did not lose her composure when the king flung up his arms in exasperation and even Gladna sighed. "I look to Zevedan and Sonza for direction. It would not surprise me if the *zelohni* and the *kamini* were somehow involved."

"Ice, illusions, death," muttered Arkost, dissatisfied. "How to combat them?"

"With fire, truth, life," said Radvyed, "the gifts of the Master and the Lady. We have turned aside death and overcome malice before today—even before our own times. We will do it again."

He took Beloved's hand and smiled at her, saying nothing of his fear for her, nor of his weariness, although it seemed to him that from the moment his mother had first turned pale and weak there had been no tranquility for them. But anxiety and fatigue never made any task easier, and complaining of them never made any load lighter. So Radvyed smiled at his wife and was rewarded with her flushed cheek and the press of her hand in his clasp.

Arkost looked at the young couple, who in the midst of trouble were still able to create a small space of joy, and shook his head. Then he thought, *Aye, and why not? They take on the tasks they have been set with a will. Why not carry your love's smile with you into hardship, to ease what can be eased and to remember there are things besides dread and malevolence in the world?* So thinking, he turned and looked at his own wife, his queen, sitting back in her chair, fingers curled lightly around the ends of the armrests. Gladna felt his gaze on her and looked up. Arkost smiled, a little lopsided, a little rueful. She gave half a laugh and held out her hand to him. He took it in his and took in, too, the ready sparkle in her eye, and all at once, the world showed itself once again to be a place of wonders, perilous but heady.

Chapter Fifty-Four

The temples and halls were consulted. A bardic researcher, working with an eccentric historian who studied the influence of mage clans on foreign kingdoms, discovered an ancient rhyme. The two paused in their argument about the etymology of an archaic word long enough to propose their belief that the verse referred to the Ice Raven's creation during a long-ago winter solstice. The *seveyati*, combing their oldest records, noted warnings against the trickster Ice Raven when walking the starplains the night of the Lady's Return, for he liked to spin illusions that the sun would never rise again and that the stars were erratic and malignant. Nevertheless, the holy ones kept praying and walking the sky leas, gathering what strength and knowledge they could. They noted that the plains were colder, the fields dimmer, than in past roamings.

Beloved suffered dreams of not one white raven, but many. In her nightmares she was an infant, abandoned in the snow, and a whirling mass of blue-eyed birds beat at her with their strong wings and pecked at her with their icy beaks. She screamed but no one heard her. She reached for her power, and found but a frozen trickle. She would then wake, her body knotted and her cheeks wet, with Radvyed curled around her, crooning her name.

Based on these signs and clues, king and Council still reckoned the Lady's Return as the most likely date of attack. Yet even as Tamtir struggled to prepare for an assumed assault on a supposed date, Arkost, Gladna, and everyone else involved in the preparations and decisions understood they were stumbling in the dark. They knew enough to grasp their danger but not enough to comprehend its means or shape. Arkost grew haggard, Gladna grave, Radvyed perturbed, and Beloved strained. Winter settled heavily on the palace, unleavened by the usual cozy gatherings of the solstice season. The darkening days muted hope and dulled conviction.

Radvyed laid down the reports of unseasonable ice storms and frowned. He stood abruptly and paced to the wall map of Tamtir that hung in his study. The prince did not need to look at the depiction of the kingdom to realize that the ice storms, combined with the unusual and damaging incidents of hail, traced the inner borders of the kingdom. Yes, here just south of the Bielna River, which ran almost parallel to Tamtir's northern border, six storms of either ice or hail in the past month—from near the fork of the Bielna and the Kranich, to high in the Vorenta Hills, to the eastern seacoast. It was the same story to the west and south: storms just on the Tamtir side of the extensive Krandin range, in the southern forests. The storms had damaged crops on the northern edge of the Koleben Plain, interfered with trade ships on the coast, hindered fishing on Lake Yuzhenil in the south, and disrupted the trade caravans using the king's highways to the west.

He stared a moment longer at the map, his hands clasped behind his back, then turned and strode back to his desk and leafed through the reports again. Each storm had been intense but circumscribed.

They had all been reported as isolated events, some causing more damage than others. Yet when read one after another, and with the geographical points considered together, it was impossible to ignore the pattern they made.

Radvyed picked up the sheaf of documents and walked to the door adjoining his father's study. After knocking and being bidden to enter, he went in. King Arkost sat at his desk, frowning over a stack of papers.

Everyone in the palace seemed to be frowning more these days, thought Radvyed, as the certainty of a hostile attack combined with the uncertainty of how and when tightened nerves, shortened tempers, and robbed all of needed rest. Only this morning he had comforted Beloved, who had once more woken from a nightmare weeping in his arms. After the first few bad dreams, she would not say anything about them, except that they were sent by the Bitter Ones to torment her. He shook his head briskly to throw off the remembered sense of helplessness and cleared his throat.

Arkost looked up, his brows still drawn. He waved his son to a seat in front of his desk. "Sit, sit. I have this hour received some tidings from the temples that I am not sure how to interpret," the king said, glancing down again at the papers. He looked back up at Radvyed. "Tell me first your news, then I will ask your thoughts on mine." He set down the documents and sat back, giving his attention fully to Radvyed.

The prince held up his stack of sheets. "We are concerned about weather attacks. Therefore, I gathered the reports of storms for the past three months." His father nodded. "Since our return to Tamtir, there have been twenty-four unseasonable or unusual storms in the kingdom. Hail where hail very rarely falls. Ice where it either never strikes, or weeks earlier than anyone looked for it."

The king thoughtfully rubbed his beard. "Twenty-four seems rather more than most years," he agreed.

"All the storms were small in area, but intense in their effects," said Radvyed. "Look." He spread the documents on the desk so his father could see. "Here in Rechnayeg, hail damaged the *zernuka* crop. There is a series of storms across the northern edge of the Koleben Plain."

Arkost riffled through the papers, scanning the headings, which noted the date, location, and nature of each event. He stopped, then went back and leafed through them more slowly. The king had seen the pattern. He looked up and met Radvyed's eyes.

"You see, do you not, Father? They form a loose circle—"

"Yes, yes, I see," said the king. "A loop around Tamtir." He set the papers down and, elbows on the desk, gripped his hands into a single fist, looking away at the far wall. He set his jaw then looked at Radvyed. "I will not let them make it a noose."

Radvyed held his gaze. He, too, was determined to thwart the Bitter Ones' plans. But how to repel such an enemy as this, who attacked and did damage so insidiously that it took weeks to understand there had been an assault?

His father sighed and held up the sheaf of papers he had been perusing when Radvyed came in.

"Here is another front I do not know how to defend," he said heavily. Radvyed raised his eyebrows. What new front could there be?

"You know the *seveyati* undertook to walk the sky leas for any sign of the Ice Raven," said Arkost. Radvyed nodded, a wave of uneasiness washing through him.

"Well," said the king, "it seems they have indeed found such evidence—or at least of the Raven's followers. Sonza writes that seven of the Lady's priestesses were struck senseless while their spirits walked the sunfields." Radvyed took a quick breath, alarmed. He had not thought anything could harm a holy one as they trod the ways of the sun. "They are alive, but cold and unresponsive. They have been transferred to their solars' infirmaries—for this happened to *seveyati* of different temples—to be cared for until they can be recalled to themselves."

"But how—"

The king held up a hand and Radvyed fell silent. "That is not all," said Arkost. "Nine forges report similar cases, Zevedan tells me. Nine priests of the Master stricken while walking the starplains." Arkost stood and paced across the room. "It is unconscionable. It is blasphemous." He turned to look at his son. "And I do not know what to do about it."

Radvyed sat, absorbing the affront to the Lady and Master and the newly revealed vulnerability of their acolytes. And now they faced the daunting challenge of averting further attacks.

"But that is not all," continued the king, passing one hand over his brow. Radvyed braced himself. "Both Sonza and Zevedan plan to keep sending *seveyati* into the spirit realms. They insist they will not cede the sunfields and starplains to the Ice Raven or his followers. Of course, I can do nothing about that decision, either." The king could not command nor gainsay the holy ones in their own sphere of knowledge and authority. He sighed and returned to his desk. Standing, he rapped his knuckles on it lightly, considering. He looked at Radvyed. "What do you think?"

Radvyed shook his head. "It seems plain that somehow these mages are ambushing or overpowering the holy ones in the sky leas. But how to prevent or repel such attacks, if the *seveyati* do not know how..." He opened his hands in a gesture of powerlessness. "I will ask Beloved if she has any ideas. It may be that sorcerers regularly wage such battles."

Arkost nodded and resumed his seat behind his desk. He gestured to the papers Radvyed had brought to him. "Good work finding the different reports and the pattern of events."

Radvyed dipped his chin. "The privy council suggested looking back for just such a pattern," he said, stacking them neatly and standing.

His father snorted. "Yes, yes, I already acknowledged the other day that your wife's council was a good idea. It does not become you to gloat."

Radvyed smiled.

"Talk to *Apara* Zatilina," said Arkost, naming the head of the *strazha*. "Let her know the situation. Ask for any thoughts about defense or resistance. Verify that the affected towns and *mireni* have what they need for recovery." He watched as Radvyed bobbed a shallow bow and turned toward the heir's study.

"Speaking of Beloved," said the king. Radvyed stopped in the doorway and looked back, waiting for his father to continue. "What is she doing today?"

A corner of Radvyed's lips quirked up. "Practicing magic," he said.

"There must be a way!" said Beloved, her stiff posture and raspy voice betraying her frustration. She stared about at the dormant roses surrounding her, as if one might volunteer a solution if she only glared fiercely enough.

She, Rue, and Dris were in the royal rose garden, bundled against the cold. Dris said the frosts had come early this year. The gardener did not need to state the suspected reason. Beloved would bring this piece of information to her husband's attention, in case the king and queen were not already aware of it.

"There is a way. You simply have not found it yet," said Rue. Beloved huffed in annoyance and stalked off a few paces. The two older women watched her patiently.

Beloved came back and stood before the rosebush onto which her own cutting had been grafted. It had taken well, but now the whole plant was withdrawn into its winter sleep. The women had reasoned that the grafted scion might be a possible means for Beloved to access the reservoir of power held by Tamtir. So far, Beloved had not met with any success.

Nevertheless, she closed her eyes and tried again, this time clasping the stem firmly enough that a prickle stung her ungloved palm and released a drop of blood. She reached out with her power and entered the cutting they had carried from the Hidden House. She slipped through its familiar stem and passed the graft join, easing into the cane of the main plant. The rosebush felt sleepy and sluggish. She sank into the cane to where it arched from the cold earth. The warmth of her power helped her flow gently down, down into an anchor root. Here she let her power seep out through several smaller, feeder roots, into the chill soil. Nothing. Nothing but earth, and tiny creatures, and the sleeping, inert roots of nearby plants. Beloved pulled her power back to her, careful to disturb the plant as little as possible. Finally, she released the stem and opened her eyes. Dris bent to reassure herself no harm had come to the rosebush.

"Nothing. Again," said Beloved, moving away and sitting down on a nearby bench. "The rose knew me and was not perturbed by me. I followed the sap path down to the roots and into the earth. But I encounter nothing that holds power."

Rue sat next to her heart-daughter. "Or nothing that you recognize as such." Beloved sat back against the bench and gave Rue an exasperated look.

Dris clapped her hands, getting the others' attention, and turned her eyes upward in bantering imitation of Beloved.

"I did not roll my eyes!" Beloved said on a smothered laugh as she directed the same look at Dris. Her aunt snorted and signed, *Yes, you did.* Rue smiled and Beloved shook her head.

Rue picked up Beloved's hand and turned it over. There was a little blood smeared on the palm. "And the blood did nothing either? Usually you can use it, is that not so?"

Dris came over and looked at Beloved's palm. She took off a glove and touched the small wound, making sure no prickle remained snagged there.

Beloved sighed. "The blood helped me move more freely in the bush, nothing more. I am missing some crucial link."

Dris narrowed her eyes and motioned too quickly for the other women to catch even the basic signs they had been learning. Seeing their incomprehension, Dris took out her pocket slate.

You said power drenches Tamtir, that it is everywhere. Why can you not touch it?

Beloved groaned and put her hands to her face. Dropping them, she said, looking at Dris, "Because the power is so...so diffuse." Beloved held her hands in fists close to her chest, then opened and wiggled her fingers while spreading her hands apart, illustrating her meaning. She continued, speaking and gesturing. "The power is scattered, like individual droplets. I can feel it in the earth, the air. But I cannot gather it and use it. I do not know how to call it to me or join my power with it." Beloved had wrestled with the problem of claiming some piece of the palace or grounds as a sorcerer might, but she was wary of disturbing the native magic that saturated the kingdom. Therefore, she had turned her mind to how to forge a link with or create a conduit to Tamtir's power, so that she could deploy it in the kingdom's defense.

After a few minutes of silence, Rue said, "Maybe neither sap nor blood. Maybe you should try something with fire."

Dris nodded as Rue signed *fire* and left to bring out the portable firepit from the shed where it was kept. As Rue and Beloved watched Dris stride off, Beloved rested her head on Rue's shoulder. Nothing to do but keep trying.

Queen Gladna entered the quiet ward of the infirmary of the largest solar in Zolatar, accompanied by Sonza. The *seveyata* assigned to watch over the patients stood at the queen's approach and bowed, fist to heart. Gladna nodded and walked down the room. The first few beds held the usual patients one expected. Two elderly women, grown old in the Lady's service, sat and played a game of foxes and hounds, the board placed on a table between their beds. Another woman had a full leg cast; she appeared to be sketching, the paper supported by a footed tray set over her lap. Yet another had no obvious injury, but was sleeping, cocooned in blankets. As the queen passed them, the three who were awake greeted her as the attendant had. Gladna smiled, acknowledging them, but continued to the end of the ward, where two eerily still women lay flat on their backs.

Sonza stopped beside Gladna and the two women gazed at the patients. The stricken *seveyati* had no mark on them. Shallow breaths betokened unwholesome lethargy. Their faces were not tranquil, but empty, and they lay as they had been arranged, limbs straight and heavy. They were not dead, they were not asleep, yet they partook of both those states. The effect was uncanny.

Gladna wondered if she had looked like this during her own illness. No wonder her poor Arkost had lost weight and gone grayer. He never said much about the fear that had burdened him during that time. Yet Gladna had noticed the daily easing of tension about his brow when she greeted him in the morning now, whether they woke together or she met him at breakfast.

"Milera was brought here yesterday, Your Splendor," said Sonza, indicating the woman with dark, springy hair. "She is from the solar in Dapelen. They thought it best to bring her to us."

Gladna nodded. Dapelen was a small town just north of Zolatar.

"I think you know Yalena," said Sonza.

Gladna looked at the other woman, whose straight yellow hair lay on her shoulders and chest. It was hard to reconcile the playful, witty woman she knew with this still and silent effigy.

"Did you discuss with your healers what I propose to do?" asked Gladna, turning to Sonza.

"Yes," said Sonza, and she gestured for the attendant to join them. "This is Caleda. She has not yet finished her training at the Healer Hall, but by Lady's Glory will be fully trained." Almost a full healer then, with just the final six months or so of her apprenticeship to fulfill. The infirmary post was probably part of her practicum.

Caleda neared them, her eyes filled with anxious hope. "I have spoken with my senior. She is skeptical that the remedy will be effective, as Your Splendor did not suffer the same malady. You were never completely unresponsive as our sisters are. However, she and the others she spoke with do not believe any harm can come from trying."

The queen smiled. "Indeed." She had not forgotten the resentment and doubt expressed by Selya, the head healer, at that unforgettable

Great Council session. It explained, perhaps, why no senior healers had chosen to be present today. Well, if it worked, the healers would soon know of it, and if it did not, few were here to see Gladna's failure.

Gladna brought to mind Arkost's account of how her own healing had transpired. She loosened the laces of her bodice and drew out the little netted bag that held Beloved's rose. Opening it, she removed the flower. It was still fresh, its deep-red petals velvety, the golden heart exuding a fragrance like no other. The two other women took quick breaths, surprised by its enchanting, indescribable scent.

"Please pull down the blankets and loosen the necks of their nightgowns," said Gladna to the wide-eyed Caleda. The attendant bent over Yalena, who was nearest to her, and uncovered and untied the ribbon at her throat. She gently pulled aside the two sides of the gown.

Gladna knelt by the bed, her knees cushioned by her winter skirts. Sonza and Caleda made small sounds of shock and distress at the queen's uncomfortable and lowly position, which Gladna ignored. Gently she touched Yalena's eyelids with the flower, then her silent lips. She held the rose to the still woman's nostrils, and counted three breaths. Then, nudging the neckline of the nightgown lower, she placed the rose over Yalena's heart. Picking up one unresponsive hand and then the other, Gladna folded them over the rose on the *seveyata*'s chest.

Sonza and Caleda drew a little nearer, gazing at Yalena intently. Silence claimed the ward: the players' game pieces no longer clicked on the board; the artist's pencil no longer scratched on her paper. The air itself seemed to still with breathless waiting.

Gladna could feel her own heartbeat throbbing in her ears, too loud and too quick. Her knees ached. There was no change in the torpid woman. The perfume that arose from the flower seemed to mock the queen and her notions. She had deluded herself that she had seen an avenue for healing that had not occurred to the healers, to the *seveyati*, to Beloved or Dris or Arkost or Radvyed. She had taken time from other needs, she had interrupted the duties of the *seveyati*, in order to indulge a whim. What did she know of either healing or magic? The senior healers had been right not to cater to her foolishness. Gladna wiped the tears that welled, blurring her sight. She had so hoped. But she had been wrong.

Gladna touched the flower, meaning to remove the rose, apologize for her pointless intrusion, and go. Even as Gladna was framing the words to accompany her retreat, Sonza gripped her shoulder. Gladna startled at the unexpected touch from the contained and respectful *seveyata*. The queen glanced up at Sonza. The priestess was not looking at her, but down at the inert woman. Gladna turned back to Yalena, her hand still on the rose.

Was that more color in her cheeks? Did the chest rise and fall more deeply? Had she imagined the twitch of the nose, the flicker of an eyelid? Gladna held her breath, hoping, yet braced for renewed disappointment. Had she just felt the press of the other woman's fingers on her own?

Yalena opened her eyes and blinked once, twice.

Sonza gasped and her grip on Gladna's shoulder tightened. Caleda brought her hands up to her mouth and peered over them, her eyes brimming with tears. Gladna's own sight blurred again, but now with relief and joy.

"Sisters?" said Yalena uncertainly, her voice raspy. She saw the queen and swallowed. "Your Splendor?" She tried to bow where she lay and bring her fist to her heart, but discovered her fingers were tangled with the queen's and moreover, held a rose. The *seveyati* laughed through their tears as the queen and awakened woman sorted themselves out.

Caleda helped adjust the back of the bed so Yalena could sit up and look around.

Glad cries came from the other end of the ward as the game players and the artist saw their sister revived. Yalena seemed surprised to be in the infirmary. She looked about in bewilderment and put a hand to her temple, as if trying to recall the events that brought her there. Her gaze fell on the other bed, where Milera lay.

Gladna scrambled up from her knees and hastened to the other woman, who was still lost in torpor. Milera was younger than Yalena, her springy curls frolicking on the pillow as the woman herself lay still as stone. Gladna knelt by her bed. Again she touched eyelids and lips with the rose; again she let its fragrance be drawn into the quiet lungs. She placed the flower over Milera's heart and arranged the limp hands so they held it.

"If I may suggest, Your Splendor," said Caleda. Gladna looked up at her. The healer gestured to Gladna's eyes. "I...I believe your tears to be part of the spe—part of the remedy."

Her tears? Gladna did not remember Arkost mentioning tears. But she had brushed them away just now, before reaching for the rose where it had lain on Yalena's breast. Gladna nodded, drew two fingers across the wet skin under one eye, and touched them to the flower now resting on Milera's chest.

Sonza, Caleda, and Yalena joined Gladna in watching the inert woman. The far end of the ward quieted. Would the rose remedy work once more? Gladna knotted her fingers together on the edge of the mattress. Had Yalena's awakening been a fluke? How cruel if one woman had been revived while the other remained trapped in languor.

As they watched, hardly daring to breathe, Milera's color warmed, her chest rose on a swift lungful of air, and her eyelids fluttered. The brown eyes opened wide and blinked several times. Milera's hands closed on the flower as she turned her head and saw the women gathered near her bed.

"Who—what—where am I?" she asked through a dry throat. She recognized Sonza and her brows drew together, then her puzzled gaze found the smiling queen and she gasped and made a clumsy obeisance.

"You are safe and well," said Sonza, who did not hide her clogged voice or wet eyes. "In the infirmary of the prime solar in Zolatar."

CHAPTER FIFTY-FIVE

The next day, Beloved listened to Sonza's account of the awakening of the two priestesses. Sonza's perspective added a different dimension to what Beloved had learned about the event from the queen, as the priestess proposed theories of how sorcerers and holy ones traversed the fields of the numinous.

Beloved had not thought about using her power to help the lost *seveyati*. She knew nothing of the spirit-walking they did in the Lady's sunfields and had assumed she was insufficiently holy, not to mention too ignorant, to reach them. When Sonza mentioned the queen's tears, Beloved was even more intrigued, and she determined to think later about this unlooked-for union of her power with that of the royal house. It was another path to pursue in her quest to join her magic with Tamtir's, although she could not see how this new knowledge might be applied to defend the kingdom.

Unfortunately, they could not immediately revive all the stricken holy ones. It was not practical for anyone of the royal house to travel about Tamtir reviving torpid *seveyati*. All efforts must be directed toward discerning the mode and hour of hostilities and devising defenses and counterattacks. It was not clear that the Bitter Ones even planned a cardinal strike. Perhaps, as *Apara* Zatilina had suggested, they proposed to gnaw at the edges of the kingdom, weakening it, as wolves harried a deer. Arkost had pointed out that still suggested a killing stroke.

Beloved agreed that some major attack loomed. The beacon spell seemed to indicate focused rancor. Yet they still did not know how to avert storms or repel whatever else the Bitter Ones might throw at them, whether the scattered attacks continued or a single assault was planned. The mood at the palace for the past weeks had been bleak.

Sonza and Beloved stood outside in the solar's *zelohn*, in the large atrium that formed the center of the temple. An elm, perhaps a century and a half old, held court in the middle of it, with smaller trees gathered about. Loucha and Baleka, who had formed part of the privy council, stood a few respectful paces apart, while Rue and Dris walked among the trees and shrubs. Children ran and played, as it was the midmorning break in the temple's school day. Beloved had come to consult with the *seveyati* about prayers or rituals invoking fire or sap. She thought perhaps if she understood how the Tamtireni called on the Lady's gifts, she might discover how to unite and channel their powers.

It was one of the temple schoolchildren, spinning in a circle while looking at the sky, who first saw the birds. She lost her footing and stumbled, but kept staring up.

"*Seveyata* Sonza!" she cried, pointing overhead.

Beloved and the priestesses all looked up; Rue also turned and raised her eyes. She touched Dris's arm, and the gardener shaded her eyes as she stared upward.

A group of six—no, nine, no, *fifteen* birds—ravens, Beloved realized—swooped, dipping low before soaring again.

"I did not think ravens gathered in such groups," said Loucha, following their flight with her gaze.

Before anyone could answer, the birds wheeled, hovered together for a moment, then shot towards the little group standing in the atrium. The teachers supervising playtime quickly called and gathered the children, hustling them indoors. Other priestesses about their business gasped and shouted, running toward the princess and prime *seveyata* before veering away from the mobbing ravens, arms covering heads and faces.

Beloved saw the extended talons, the buffeting wings, the sharp beaks, and was hurled, open-eyed, into the nightmares that had afflicted her for weeks. All was feathers, screams, claws, and blood. She hunched, cold with horror, knowing there would be no waking from this to her husband's arms.

Arms curved about her head, Beloved cowered, as the ravens ripped at her skin, tore at her hair, pecked at her ribs and fingers and spine. The shrill calls of the birds, the choked sobs of someone nearby, the coppery smell of blood, the cold prickle of fear, the hard beat of wings, the heavy throb of her heartbeat, the sharp agony of lacerations—Beloved was tossed about in a maelstrom of terror and pain.

She heard a high-pitched cry and knew it for Rue's voice.

Sudden fury burned through Beloved, freeing her muscles and clearing her frightened mind. She half straightened from her crouch and peered between her arms so she could watch the birds as they swooped. Her anger rose, hot and focused. Did they think she feared blood? Blood was her element. She smeared the bleeding back of one hand across her mouth and tasted the bright, singing power of it. How dare they come here, in the Lady's own precinct, to harm Beloved's own!

Her rage, an underground river, surged, and she flung out a hand, snapped her fingers, and pointed at a bird. It burst into flame. Fending off birds with her right arm, she snapped and pointed with her left hand, spinning and tracking ravens as they dove and rose and dove again. Swift flames flared and faded until she turned one last circle and there were no more birds to incinerate.

Beloved let her arms drop and stood panting. She looked around. Where were Rue, Dris, the others? Dris got up from the ground. Her aunt had grabbed a straggling child and curled herself around him to shield him from the birds. Her clothes were torn, and there was blood, but the gardener and child were whole. Rue sat up from where she had flung herself on the ground and pushed a straggling lock out of her face. She had made it farther into the trees with the priestesses. Safe. They were all safe. Scratched, dirty, disheveled, but safe. Beloved's shoulders slumped and she passed shaking hands over her face.

Rue and Dris surrounded her, touching her cheeks and stroking her hair. Sonza, Loucha, and Baleka hovered a pace or two back, faces filled with concern and wonder. The child, frightened and awed, ran inside to join his teacher and schoolmates. Beloved could hear the murmur from the onlookers beyond their group, as the *seveyati* marveled and speculated.

After another moment, when Beloved's breathing had calmed and they had all realized no serious injury had been suffered, she said, "Let us go inside."

Beloved and Radvyed argued that night about her leaving the palace precincts while the Bitter Ones threatened Tamtir. Radvyed did not like that the ravens had found her and attacked her in the Lady's own temple. He insisted on inspecting all her scratches—or wounds, as he called them—and tending them himself with healing ointment.

"You must see that it is neither safe nor prudent for you to leave the palace." His voice was edged but his fingers gentle as he daubed some salve near the outside corner of her left eye.

"I need to visit the *zelohni* and *kamini* in the city, in the *mirenzemi*, in workshops and halls to understand better how Tamtir's power knits land and people together. I cannot do that remaining in our chambers," Beloved answered, but she let him turn her head so he could reach a long scratch on her neck. The lacerations were already healing—she was a sorceress, after all—but she thought that caring for her in this way calmed Radvyed. It also reminded her that their disagreement was not born of disgust or indifference on his part, but worry for her well-being.

He set the pot of ointment on the table next to him. Radvyed looked down at his fingers, rubbing them together to rid himself of the last traces of the salve. He lifted his gaze and met Beloved's eyes.

"You are determined to do this. To go out, to visit..." He gestured toward the fireplace with its granite hearthstone, and looked away for a moment, his jaw tightening. "The beacon spell means they can always find you, is it not so? What if another time they send thirty, forty, a hundred birds? What if—"

Beloved leaned forward and kissed him. He let her silence him, but when she drew back, his eyes demanded a reply.

She sighed and took one of his hands, lacing their fingers. Beloved swallowed, then said, "I must do all that I can to protect Tamtir."

Radvyed looked at their hands then back at Beloved's face. He smoothed a strand of hair back from her forehead with his other hand.

"Will you take some of the *strazha* with you?" he asked.

"Yes, if their escort will ease your mind."

He gave a resigned huff.

She smiled faintly, and kissed his knuckles. "Thank you, Husband."
Radvyed arched a brow. "Thank you for setting aside your misgivings.
For finding a way to bear your fears for me."

"Have you no fears, then?"

"Too many." She rested her cheek against the back of his hand. "But
giving them mastery over me has never diminished or banished them."

He turned her knuckles so he could kiss them. "Then you shall
continue my tuition in courage, Beloved."

*Escape, escape, I must escape. I must go, run, flee, there is danger, pressing
danger, danger pursuing me, I must flee—*

"Beloved! Beloved, wake up!"

Caught! Caught, smothered, bound, no, I will not be bound again—

"Beloved! It is your Husband, your Radvyed!"

Lies and bindings, lacerations and danger, betrayal—

*Hot, ready rage rising, building—burn the bonds and fly away
free—*

Coolness clasping one wrist, sweet as mountain water

Air, cool air, I can breathe—what—where—

"I give myself to you. I give all of myself to you."

I know that voice

Still held, still bound, yet the voice steadied her heartbeat, gave space
for the rage and the panic to cool and calm. She paused, flames licking
at her fingers, ready to burn a path to freedom.

"You are my Beloved and I am your Husband," said the voice, low,
slightly breathless, familiar. Beloved rested in it, as it began again,
pledging devotion and fealty. She was held not by chains or briars, but
by sheltering arms.

She opened her eyes.

They were in their bedchamber. The fire burned low and red. In the dimness she could see the shadowy rumples of disarranged blankets on the bed, and pillows tumbled onto the floor. She was in Radvyed's embrace, his chest to her back, and his voice murmured, slow and reassuring, in her ear.

He held her firmly, his arms crossing her torso. He had her arms pinned to her side, but her right hand was open, palm out. She looked down at it. Blue flames, like a flower of fire, flickered on her palm. Beloved took a sharp breath, closed her fingers, and let her hand fall. She sagged against Radvyed. His voice faltered.

"Beloved?" he asked.

"Yes, Husband," she answered, and felt the deep sigh that shuddered through him. He hugged her and nuzzled her neck. She felt a tear, damp against her skin.

Beloved let her head fall back against Radvyed's shoulder. Her eyes prickled and the fire in the hearth blurred and wavered. Cold night air blew in over their heads. They were on the floor, sprawled underneath the open window.

"Can we," she began, then cleared her throat. She was so tired. Radvyed shifted, pulling them up into a more upright sitting position. Beloved tried again. "Can we shut the window and sit by the fire?"

Radvyed hugged her again, then turned her so he could see her eyes. After a moment he kissed her cheek, then they rose to their feet together. Beloved went to encourage the fire while Radvyed closed first the shutters and then the window sash and heavy curtains. He picked up their robes from where they had draped them over a chest earlier in the evening and handed Beloved hers. She put it on, then stood, uncertain, her fingers worrying the lapels.

Radvyed sat in his chair. "Come here, Beloved," he said.

She hesitated, then sat on his lap and turned toward him, placing her arms around his neck.

"Why was the window open?" she asked.

It was a moment before he answered. "Because you opened it," he said.

Beloved swallowed but did not look away from his face.

"I woke because you threw the covers back," he said, "and muttered about needing to leave, to fly, to be free. You leapt out of bed and ran to the window and opened it. I thought you were having one of your nightmares." He looked past her shoulder and swallowed, then returned his gaze to hers before continuing. "You opened the shutters. I came to you, thinking you were dreaming or sleepwalking, and that I would—then you climbed onto the sill, you leaned—" He stopped and pressed his forehead to hers, his breathing unsteady.

Beloved put her hands to his cheeks and waited. At last, he pulled his head back so they could look at each other again. Her hands dropped to his shoulders.

"You were going to throw yourself down," Radvyed said.

Beloved drew in a hard, sudden breath. It was hard to tell whether she trembled or he.

"I pulled you back," said Radvyed, and cleared his throat. "You—you fought me. And then I could feel you swelling with magic, as you did at the Council. And I—you did not seem to know me." His voice broke and he stopped, looking away again and blinking rapidly. Beloved's own eyes welled and her mouth quivered. She pressed her lips together and forced herself to breathe calmly.

Radvyed looked back at her. "I knew not what to do. I remembered when I found you in your garden, that I knew not how to help you then, but the words I said seemed...and then the words we shared in the Tower...I hoped they would help you to know, to remember me, to bring you back..."

"They did," said Beloved. "They did. You did rightly." She brushed back a lock that had fallen in his face, and tightened her hand in his hair, absorbing the warm reality of him. "I had a dream. A nightmare." She furrowed her brow. "No, more than a nightmare. All I knew was the need to flee, to escape." She paused. "That must have been what drove me from the bed to the window."

He nodded. "And then?"

"And then, the danger pursuing me seemed to have caught me, was trapping and binding me, smothering..." She broke off at his stricken expression. "No, Husband, there was no other way! You had to restrain me from harming myself." She waited until he acknowledged her point with a slight dip of his chin.

"I felt then," said Beloved, her chest tight as she thought about what might have happened, "that I must use my pow—my magic to break away." Her voice lowered and her fingers gripped his shoulders. "Fire. Fire. I would burn my way free." She remembered her hand flinging fire at the ravens that very day—no, the day before, surely it was past midnight now. How the flames had devoured them, swift as thought, leaving nothing but dying sparks and drifting ashes.

Radvyed placed his hands over the fingers digging into his shoulders. "But you did not. I am here, whole and unharmed. What stopped you?"

"You," she said. Her voice shook and she rubbed her wet face on her shoulder and sniffled. "You. You stopped me. I heard your voice, telling me I was your Beloved, that you were my Husband. I felt—" Beloved looked at her wrist, where her marriage bracelet gleamed in the fire's light, and traced its links with a finger. "I felt your bracelet, and it was cool and calming. And your voice, I knew your voice, I listened and I—I came back to myself."

Radvyed's embrace tightened.

"This was an attack?" he said after a few minutes. "By the Bitter Ones?"

Beloved thought over the quality of the nightmare that was not a nightmare. It had been uncanny, as if a suggestion had been implanted in her dreaming. The impulse to escape had felt like an intervention from outside of herself, not an upwelling of her own heart. And it had occurred after she had foiled the physical attack at the temple that very day.

"Yes," she said.

Radvyed closed his eyes for a moment then opened them and looked at Beloved, anguish tautening his perfect features and pressing bruises under his eyes. "How can...what am I..." He stopped, unable to speak through a thickened throat. "How can I help you when they assault you in your sleep, where I cannot be? I am no sorcerer. I know nothing of—"

"Be you," Beloved said. She burrowed into his embrace and pushed her face into his neck, trying to get closer. "Be you holding me." And then she let the tears come.

Sonza regretted that it was winter, so the meeting could not be held outside, in the forge's *zelohn*. Instead, they were here at a table in the dark hall of the temple's *kamin*, with the smells of smoke, leather, iron, and sweat hanging, subtle but persistent, in the air. She glanced up at the high, slatted windows that vented the chamber while protecting the interior against the weather. In winter, the Master's servants worked on smaller projects, so the main forge and its bellows were quiet. The hall, like many of the Master's temples, was gloomier than most solars. The fires were always well tended, however, and Sonza sighed at the welcome warmth from the hearth. She looked around the table as a young *seveyat* served hot drinks and small spiced tarts.

Sixteen people, eight servants of the Lady and eight of the Master, had gathered to discuss the troubling attacks upon the *seveyati* as they walked the sky leas. The meeting began with reports detailing each incident. Sonza then related the visit of Queen Gladna to the infirmary at the prime solar. While the revival of Milera and Yalena was welcome news, the tidings that the queen would not go forth to minister to stricken *seveyati* outside of Zolatar was less so. All understood the reasons, but no one knew how long the torpid *seveyati* could exist in their uncanny states without damage or death. It was decided that the stricken holy ones would be conveyed with care to temples in the city, where the queen or another member of the royal house could tend to them with the healing flower.

"This brings us to our next problem," said Zevedan. "How do we shield against such strikes and ambushes in the future? For Sonza and I"—he nodded briefly at the *seveyata*—"have informed His Splendor that we will continue to walk the ways of sun and stars, absorbing their light, tending what is in our charge, and offering ourselves to Lady and Master."

Most murmured in agreement with the decision to continue to walk the sky leas, although one or two shifted uneasily in their seats.

"His Splendor was not happy with our decision, as he feels responsible for all who live within Tamtir," said Sonza, taking up the tale. "He does not know how to protect us as we walk the holy ways." She exchanged glances with Zevedan. *Not happy* did not adequately describe King Arkost's frustration and worry. But when the *seveyati* had pointed out that he could not prevent them from their chosen course, he had made a request.

"His Splendor particularly asks that we *seveyati* mine our lore, searching for prayers or rites that might serve as armor or shield to protect us," said Zevedan. "We have grown complacent, perhaps, in believing no harm could come to us as we traveled the sky leas, and so have let such devotions fade," he added heavily.

"So let us now gather the flowers and fruits of our wisdom," added Sonza, "and see if we may press out a wine of strength or weave some garland of protection." She placed three scrolls on top of the notes about Milera and Yalena's recovery. "For instance, we have found in our archives a prayer invoking the Lady's light as a wall of flame..."

The meeting went on for several more hours, as the *seveyati* considered and discussed and sent for more documents, temple bards, and historians of the holy. Finally, they dispersed to their solars and forges, satisfied with the work they had begun.

Sonza sat in her carriage, wrapped up well against the cold. They were more ready to face attacks, she thought, but still had no way to predict or undermine them. She folded her mittened hands over the document satchel in her lap and sighed. They must continue searching and praying, striving to follow the light, using the tools given them by Lady and Master, and keeping hearts and minds open to insight and instruction. Silently she recited one of the prayers discussed at the meeting. *Lady of Light, hold me in Your flaming heart. Lady of Fire, let your brightness run in my veins...*

Rue worked next to Dris at the long table of the Rose Gardener's stillroom and savored the cool quiet of the place. Its ordered space pleased Rue: the shelves offering vessels, jars, and bottles; the high window that let in the pale winter sun; the large, sturdy worktable in the center of the room; the deep, stone sink set in the wall across from the hearth. Time seemed to flow at a different pace in the stillroom, as though drying flowers or extracting essences required unhurried hands.

Vel stood at the sink, rinsing rose hips in a large bowl of cold water before scooping them out with a ladle and placing them in a colander to drain. The stepstool he stood on rocked slightly as he worked. Water softly splashed against stone.

Rue trimmed the stems from the rose hips heaped in a basket on the table, and then set them in a wooden bowl for Dris, who cut them in half and removed the seeds. The air was filled with the sweet fragrance of the hips. It was pleasant to work at a straightforward task after weeks of guessing and planning and worrying.

The fruit of the roses would be used to make rose hip tea for Beloved to drink. She and Dris had conferred about whether roses other than Beloved's own would be beneficial in the spells to fortify and protect a magic-wielder. They decided that as Beloved was now deeply bound to Tamtir, all the roses of the royal gardens would be effective in her preparations for the assumed confrontation with the Bitter Ones. Petals, as well as rose hips, had been harvested from all the rose plants of the royal garden. Beloved would bathe in their rosewater.

Rue allowed herself this time in the stillroom to not think about the forms the confrontation could take. Their work here would help Beloved in that arduous hour, even if it were only because Rue's fierce love was brewed into the tea and the bathwater. Her hands trembled and her knife almost slipped. She paused to compose herself before returning her attention to her task.

The splashing at the sink stopped. Vel came to stand on Dris's other side, waiting for her to fill another bowl with seeded rose hips. Dris set down the small sharp knife she was using to dig out the seeds and tapped Rue's arm. Rue dropped a newly trimmed hip in the bowl between them and looked at Dris.

Rue watched attentively as Dris signed. As she and Beloved had begun taking lessons at the herald's guild hall in Tikrek, they were able to converse a little in the hand language. Rue caught *Beloved, rose, gift,* and *queen.* She hesitantly imitated a sign she did not know. Dris finger-spelled the word: *refresh.*

"Beloved needs to refresh the rose she gave to the queen?" Rue asked in both speech and sign.

Dris nodded. *Before the solstice. With blood and rosewater. I will tell Beloved, but she has much to think of now.* Dris waited until Rue dipped her head in acknowledgment.

Rue thought back to when the rose was first gathered by Radvyed. How worried she had been, how afraid he would never return, leaving her heart-daughter to perish, wounded and forsaken and beyond Rue's help. And yet he had, he had come and had given Beloved what Rue had never been able to provide: freedom, surcease from pain, a true name, a new life.

Rue set down her knife and clasped Dris's forearm. The gardener looked at her and seeing Rue's face, turned toward her.

"Thank you," said Rue. The words were hard to speak around the lump in her throat. Her fingers felt clumsy and thick as she signed. She swallowed. "Thank you for sending the prince."

Dris laid a rough hand on Rue's and squeezed.

Holding Rue's gaze, Dris slowly replied, *Thank you for caring for my sister's child as your own.*

Rue sniffed and blinked, and Dris's slight smile was soft. They stood a moment, acknowledging the sisterhood sprung from their shared protective love for Beloved. Vel, bored, wandered to the window and jumped in place, trying to see out into the garden.

Dris turned back to the table and bumped her shoulder into Rue's. She tapped her finger on the rim of the bowl between them. Clearly Dris thought they should get back to work.

Rue pulled a handkerchief from her pocket and dabbed her eyes. Something in the scent of the hips was making them water. As she picked up her knife to trim another hip, she heard Vel counting flagstones as he hopped back to the sink. She let the hips' fragrance fill her lungs and bent once more to her task.

She stood barefoot on a dark, wide plain. The high grass, tall as her knees, spread as far as she could see, rippling in the low wind, each blade touched with starlight. She looked up, and the sky was heavy with stars. She had never seen so many. The soft, deep black of the sky, spangled with clusters and constellations and comets, enhanced the brilliance of the Master's handiwork. She drew in a long breath, filling herself with cool, quiet air, then let it go.

Just as she began to allow her thoughts to drift in the black-and-silver tranquility of the night, her gaze was caught by a whirling clot of stars. Were they falling? No, they were approaching her, where she stood, among the suddenly stiff, prickly grasses. The stars hurtled closer, and she saw they were not stars, but birds. Not a cluster, but a flock. Ice-white, blue-clawed, silent as snow falling, they circled her, cold blue eyes marking and assessing their target. Then they spiraled up, hovered, and dove.

Her nightmare in a new iteration. But she was no infant, helpless and vulnerable.

Yet when she reached for her heart of fire, she found only cold coals. She called up her rage, but only gelid terror coursed through her. Her mouth opened to scream, but her throat closed as though blocked with ice. She tried to run, but her feet were frozen to the icy surface of the soil.

The nightmare seized her. Her power was inert and chill as death.

She trembled as the ravens flew around her, close enough to brush her skin with their feathers, for their claws to catch at her hair. She waited for beaks to rip her skin and peck at her eyes, as they had at the solar. Instead, the silent bodies swooped and wove about her. What were they doing? Why did she feel terror when they did not touch her?

And then she understood. Their flight was a dance, a spell, and as the ravens flew cold cords of power unspooled, winding about her. She bit the inside of her cheek until it bled but tasted only the malice of the beacon spell's taint, overwhelming her own power in this place claimed by the Ice Raven's followers.

Its taste was bitter, for the ravens were the instruments of the Bitter Ones, sent to frighten, bind, and destroy her. Already she felt the icy bands drawing tighter, stealing the warmth from her muscles and constricting her ribs. The cords of power felt barbed, as if they physically dug into and dragged at her flesh.

Queen Gladna's words, from long ago they seemed, spun and shifted in her mind.

It is not merely our destruction but our suffering they desire.

Our suffering. Our destruction.

Our suffering they desire.

Desire our suffering.

And in the pain and fear, she found a rasp of mirthless laughter, a grim shred of will, a spiniferous gesture of defiance. Her own bitter, salt seed.

She stiffened her spine and braced her body. No, not wholly frozen, not yet completely conquered. The surprised birds hesitated in their flight, pausing their pattern to hover in a ring above her head. She arched her back, straining as she reached deep into her most painful, hopeless memories: the times her bodily misery, her self-loathing, and her inveterate despair seemed to swallow her. Her unprotected eyes stared up through the circle of ice-white birds to the distant stars beyond. Tears formed and froze and blinded her.

If you desire my suffering, then feast. Feast until you *choke* on it.

From her chest burst a vine, kin to that in whose imprisoning limbs she had spent most of her life. Long coils, thorny and venomous, whipped out, shredding the cold lines of power woven about her. The vine entangled the ravens, snaring their wings and pricking their eyes.

She tumbled backwards, arms outstretched, onto the hard ground. All her anguish and doubt and anger she fed into the vine, thick as her wrist at the base, rising from her chest. Its branches thrashed, snagging feathers and talons. The birds screamed as they struggled in the barbed vine's writhing loops. She watched as her pain and her bitterness destroyed the ravens sent by her enemies. They finally shattered into blue-white flakes and drifted away. She saw the last motes scatter and fade as she lay gasping and spent in the ice-edged grass.

The stars glittered, pale and indistinct. The vine, sapped of strength, shriveled, cracked into dust, and fell about her, bitter ashes.

Her heart slowed. Her breath stilled. Cold settled into her flesh and pressed her to the earth. Victory over the ravens had demanded much. Perhaps everything.

She would not rise again. She should be sad, but she was too weary.

High above, a star caught her dimming eye. It blazed brighter than any she had known. She clung to it with her gaze. A token of unchanging beauty to carry into the final darkness, the eternal cold.

Then a scent filled her head, her lungs, her veins. It was familiar, yet elusive. Comforting, yet invigorating. Healing old wounds and coaxing her most guarded core to open to risk.

Her heart thumped against her ribs. Her limbs prickled and stung.

She opened her eyes, and he was there, holding her as always, the fingers of one hand tangled with hers, as they both held a rose to her breast.

Radvyed only felt the tightness of his chest ease when Beloved blinked, and he could see that she was here with him now, in their bedchamber, body and spirit, no longer dream-walking. His face was wet and his throat dry, and he did not think he would dare to sleep ever again, but she was back, and he was grateful. Her fingers in his were warming, and the blue-gray tint to her skin was fading.

So, too, were the dreadful purple-black marks that had streaked her arms, legs, and torso. They had reminded him of the binding vines under her skin when she had been Hideous. The largest and darkest was the bruise-like stain that had swallowed the scar on her chest.

Beloved lifted her free hand to touch his cheek and hair. He rubbed his head against her fingers, his eyes fixed on her face.

People stirred around them. His mother's voice called for food and drink. His father sat down heavily, causing a chair to creak. Rue hovered, and Dris, too. Radvyed sat up to let them see for themselves that Beloved no longer lay in thrall to the uncanny passivity that had stricken the *seveyati*, although the holy ones had not suffered the welt-like streaks. He groped in his pocket for a handkerchief and wiped the tears from his face.

Beloved smiled at Rue and Dris, and let them touch her face, her hair, her hands, and inspect her limbs. Languor still lingered, and the chill of her paralysis, but she could sit up. A few *damashi* moved quietly about the room, arranging tables with refreshments, lighting a few more candles, and bringing a brazier closer to the bed where Beloved sat propped up against pillows.

The healer on duty at the palace drew near, examined Beloved, and found no injury or illness. He advised food, drink, and rest, and said he would spend what was left of the night in the chamber next door. Arkost dispatched messengers to solar, forge, and healer hall, rescinding earlier demands for immediate attendance and arranging an early-morning meeting. Gladna, at Beloved's insistence, tucked away the rose again in its little netted pouch.

At last everyone had somewhat reassured themselves as to Beloved's well-being, and seated themselves with hot wine and spiced honey-rolls.

Arkost cleared his throat. "Beloved. We know you have been enduring frightening dreams, and we know of the attempt to influence you as you slept a sennight ago."

Beloved nodded.

"Was this another such attack? Or were you—is it possible you were walking the sunfields or the starplains?" asked Arkost.

"For your state was very much like that of the afflicted *seveyati*," said Gladna. "Yet I had not thought you trod the holy ways."

At a faint scratching sound, Radvyed glanced aside and saw that Rue was writing on the slate Beloved kept in their room. He turned back to Beloved, who frowned down into her wine. Her hands shook. Radvyed helped her take a sip then set the cup on the bedside table.

"I do not think that I walked the sky leas," she began, and told them what she had undergone. Radvyed's blood ran cold. From the sharp intakes of breath around him, he was not the only one alarmed by her account. He reached for her hand again, needing to feel its warmth and vitality.

A heavy silence enfolded the chamber, as everyone pondered Beloved's tale.

"Although you defeated these emissaries," said Gladna, "I do not believe the Bitter Ones to be crushed. They have lost a skirmish only."

Dris took the slate from Rue and wrote. Rue read out loud, "Yes, they are testing your strength." Rue looked up. "And looking for weaknesses," she added.

"So far you have repelled them," Arkost said. "Although you have been hard-pressed, I think."

Beloved clutched Radvyed's hand as she released a shaky breath. "Yes." Her brows drew together and her jaw tightened. "But I will not yield."

Radvyed looked at her determined face but said nothing.

Arkost nodded and rubbed his beard. "It is the tenth of the month," he said. "Five more days until the Lady's Return." He crossed his arms and leaned back in his seat. "Do we all still agree that the solstice is a likely date for a major attack?"

"You do not think that driving Beloved to throw herself from a window or assailing her sleep—shadow—dream-self are major attacks?" demanded Radvyed, stumbling over the accurate term for this night's ambush.

Beloved squeezed his hand. Neither of them brought up how close she had come to burning him alive the week before.

Arkost turned to his son. "No, I do not. They mean to destroy Tamtir. Hence the storms, the attacks on our holy ones, even, perhaps, your mother's illness."

Radvyed glanced away, chastened yet not placated.

"The attacks on Beloved are serious and troubling," said Arkost. "But they do not seem to me to be all-out assaults. Beloved's death or incapacity would grievously harm Tamtir and personally weaken us who know and love her." He paused. "Yet I do not know that such would cause Tamtir to fall."

"It may be there will never be such an assault," added Gladna. "It may be that their strategy is a long chain of attacks and strikes that undermine us slowly, until, they believe, we beg mercy of them or turn on one another."

Arkost snorted. Gladna smiled at him.

"I speak only of what may be their plan," she said.

Rue and Dris conferred, bent over the slate. Rue cleared her throat. Everyone turned toward her.

"We still believe," said Rue, indicating herself and Dris, "that the primary attack will come the night of the Lady's Return. For all the reasons we gave before, which have not changed: the significance of the date, the season, and the solstice." Dris nodded her agreement.

"Very well," said Arkost. "Keeping in mind that we may be thoroughly mistaken, we will continue to plan for the Lady's Return as the night of expected assault." He rose, and the others also stood, except for Beloved and Radvyed. "If you can rest, do so. We all need to be strong and alert in the days—and nights—to come."

With that, king and queen, heart-mother and aunt, bestowed loving, if anxious, good nights. The door shut behind them.

Radvyed climbed into the bed next to Beloved and wrapped his arms around her. She turned into him, pressing against him, seeking solace as well as warmth. They lay quiet the rest of the night, but slept no more.

Chapter Fifty-Six

The following afternoon, Arkost, Gladna, Radvyed, and Beloved gathered in the king's study. Notes, maps, and other papers were strewn and stacked untidily at one end of a worktable while the remains of a platter of sandwiches and a cold pot of *chelek* occupied the other. The four of them reviewed once more the preparations for the eve of the Lady's Return.

The people of Tamtir had their part to contribute in *setting the ocean wave into motion*, as Loucha called it. Zevedan, Mesaz, Sonza, and Loucha, with Beloved and Dris, had devised a plan for the waking and harnessing of Tamtir's power. They did not know if it would work. Nevertheless, it constituted their best hope, formed from experience, speculation, and prayer. Beloved explained the adjustments made most recently to the arrangements.

Each household was responsible for their own *zelohn* and *kamin*. On the eve of the winter solstice, beginning at sunset, members of each house would stand within the *zelohn*, as thinly shod as was possible and still avoid frostbite. Others would lay face down on the *kamin*, heart and left hand to the stone. As close contact as possible with earth and stone was urged, but torches and braziers, for heat and light, were permissible, as they would not interfere with the flow of power. If a household was composed of only one resident, that person was to station themselves at either *zelohn* or *kamin*, depending on whether they were more strongly drawn to Lady or Master. No *zelohn* or *kamin* could be left unguarded.

Mireni and those of their bloodlines would attend the common *zelohni* and *kamini* of their districts. Further, the *mireni* in rural areas and elders in towns and villages were to ensure that all in their charge had support by designating additional people to fortify households in need of help. Local associations and guilds had the responsibility of assigning members to protect workshops, halls, and public buildings.

The *seveyati* would mind the *zelohni* and *kamini* of their temples, with the addition of a priest always working at the forge that was at the heart of each temple dedicated to the Master, and a priestess in contact with the tree at the core of each of the Lady's solars.

"And you, Your Splendor," began Beloved, addressing the king. Arkost held up a hand and she stopped.

"Please," said Arkost, "if you would. Please call me Father." He hardly knew why he chose this moment to say this, as they were laying plans and readying themselves to face an unknown attack with an untested defense. Yet he could tell, from the ill-hidden anxiety of his son, of Dris, and of Rue, that Beloved's part would be the most dangerous and uncertain of all. *This, at least, I can offer to this young woman who has known so much loneliness and suffering: she is of our House and line; she is of us; we are her family. If she is about to risk her life, as I believe she is, then let her know that more than Radvyed's love stands with her.*

Beloved stood stock-still, staring at him, and Arkost saw that her eyes were bright with unshed tears; she was trying not to let them fall. When she gained some measure of control, she said, a little huskily, "I thank you for this gift, Father." Her voice cracked on the last word and Arkost remembered that the man who had begotten her was the man who had cursed her to torment within her own flesh. He felt Gladna come to stand beside him, her hand held out to Beloved.

"To me, as well, you are a daughter," the queen said, her voice low and firm. "You have already a heart-mother and I do not seek to usurp her place. But many women find upon marrying, as I did, another mother brought to them as part of their husband's wedding portion. May I be such a one to you. Please call me Gladna." Beloved took the queen's hand and two tears streaked the younger woman's face before she could speak.

"Thank you," Beloved said, still in that voice that was not quite her own. Although she knew that the words the royal couple had spoken to her when she had arrived at the palace on the first day had made her their child, a fact confirmed by the rites of the wedding day, to hear that they chose her, at this moment of uncertainty and danger—it was more than acceptance. Their love was a warm cloak enfolding her, their trust a bracing tonic strengthening her.

Yet the uncertainty and danger had not yet passed and there were plans to discuss. Beloved took the handkerchief offered her by Radvyed and dried her face. She clutched the cloth in her hand as she looked down at the intricately patterned rug and brought her mind back to what she had been saying.

"And so you, Father," Beloved said, stumbling a little over the word, "and you, Gladna"—again a hesitation before she continued—"you are to attend the Master's *kamin* in his Hall in the palace. That is, Father will be the one with heart and hand to the Stone and, Gladna, it is your part to support him as you may."

The older couple looked at Beloved for a long moment. Arkost frowned. He would have greatly preferred an enemy whom he could encounter on a known field with familiar weapons. Gladna, her brows drawn together in perplexity, sought more detailed instruction.

"Help him as I may? How do you think the Stone may be harmed?" asked the queen.

"If I wished to break the Stone and I looked to the Ice Raven, I would freeze it," said Beloved.

"And how am I to stop that?" inquired the king.

Beloved looked at him in surprise. "Why, by keeping it warm," she answered.

"Do you mean by tending the fire in the hearth?" he asked.

Beloved tilted her head before answering. "Yes, the fire will help. But you will keep it from breaking with your own body."

"My heart and my hand," said Arkost.

"Your own life's blood, if need be," said Beloved. "Is that not your oath as well?"

There was a silence while the king considered how he might prevent a magical freeze and the queen wondered whether she would have to cut her own husband's flesh.

Radvyed looked from one to the other, then turned to Beloved. "No. I will be the one to keep the *kamin* warm," he said. "Not my father, not my mother."

Beloved shook her head before he finished speaking. "No, Husband. Your place is with me in the Lady's Glade by her Tree, guarding her *zelohn*. We will stand where we took our oaths to the land. I need you to anchor me, as your—our—father needs your mother anchoring him."

"What do you mean, anchor?" asked Arkost, confused. Beloved turned to him.

"You and I, Father, are the more volatile ones in our marriage pairings. In my studies, I have seen qualities like ours often related to the element of fire." She raised a hand as the king opened his mouth to object. "No, I have thought on this and talked with others as I strive to understand how power shapes itself, how it moves and works here. We know that I am drawn to the Lady, for she is mistress of the fire in all living things: sap and blood. She is the life-giving sun itself. So Sonza and Loucha have taught me. Is it not so?"

Arkost nodded. Gladna and Radvyed were also paying close attention.

"Instead you, Father, are more drawn to the Master," continued Beloved. "At first I was puzzled, for your essence is more akin to flame than to any other elemental category of power I have encountered. It was only after a long talk with Zhelez that I understood that because power manifests itself differently here, I should expect it to be—be *organized* differently." Radvyed put a hand on her arm.

"Beloved," he said, "this is very interesting and no doubt you are opening new realms of thought in the study of comparative magic—but we are not learned in this field." His wife blinked at him, uncomprehending. "Simplify," he said. She flushed, embarrassed.

"I am sorry," Beloved said. "The point is this. The Master also has an aspect of fire: the fire of his forge, the sparks that rise from it, the stars that he sets burning in the night. So you and I are strong, but volatile. We need a tie to the earth. Gladna is that for you: she is close to the earth aspect of the Lady who is the Gardener and holder of all living things, the ground upon which we all stand." Then Beloved turned to Radvyed. "As you are close to the Master's aspect of stone and ore, the bones of earth, which shall endure and hold, for even if they pass through fire and water, they are made stronger than before."

The king, queen, and prince thought about her words. Beloved wished she could have been clearer. At last Arkost sighed.

"I am a simple man," he said. "You tell me to be by the Master's Stone and guard it with heart, hand, and blood, and so I shall. We can delve into deeper matters of why and how when we have leisure, after the Bitter Ones have been defeated."

He felt Gladna's hand in his and smiled down at her. She looked up at him and her raised eyebrow let him know what she thought of his *simple man* talk. *My anchor*, he thought, and laughed.

CHAPTER FIFTY-SEVEN

It was two days before the Lady's Return and Beloved's birthday. Radvyed and Beloved were in their bedchamber. The time-candle showed it was a little before midnight. The quiet seemed to echo with the business of the past days' meetings, consultations, persuasions, messages, and reports. Tempers had flared and cooled, anxieties had risen and been somewhat allayed—at least enough for thought to go forward, and in thought's train, action. *Yet,* thought Radvyed, *all this seems nothing more than talk and worry to give ourselves something to do until that day that we hope we have named correctly as the day of confrontation. In another day and a half we will all be at our posts, every last child of Tamtir, and then we shall see what happens.*

Beloved stood by the fire, staring down into the flames. There was little light in the rest of the room; only a candle or two on a table near the bed. Darkness and cold seemed to reach out from the corners of the room, their long fingers searching for a warm body to dim and chill. Radvyed did not like the cold stretching forth to smother Beloved, so he moved toward her and stood behind her, his back to what seemed the most encroaching, chilly tendrils. She leaned against him, but stayed watching the fire. Radvyed put his arms around her and rested his chin on her shoulder. She laid her hands over his, holding them to her. They had found, in these anxious, talk-filled days, that they were both most comforted by silence like this, their bodies close and warm, their senses alive but calm in the moment. They watched the leap and heard the snap of flames as the dry smoky smell of the wood invited drowsiness, and as the solid warmth of their bodies pressed against each other.

At last Beloved sighed, as if letting the worries of the hour slip from her and into the fire, to be changed into spark and smoke. She stirred and turned in Radvyed's arms and, placing her hands on either side of his face, drew him down for a kiss. After a moment he broke away to murmur in her ear, "Come to bed." So she did.

Chapter Fifty-Eight

Later, when deep sleep had enfolded them both, Beloved found herself walking in a bright mist. She should be afraid, she thought, given her encounter with the white ravens a few nights before. Yet to her own bemusement, she felt no fear. As she walked, the mist burned off in the light of the place she was, and she could see she was walking barefoot in a landscape she did not recognize. There were no trees, nor hills, nor any shape she could name. She would have said that she was walking amid drifts and heaps, even furrows, of snow, except she felt no chill in the air or beneath her bare feet. All was bright white, with shadows of gold and pale blue, and the surface beneath her soles was light and springy. She looked down at herself and saw she was lightly dressed in some white garment that draped and flowed about her. Looking around again, Beloved saw a more intense brightness ahead and knew that was where her feet were carrying her. She gazed about, almost drinking in the quiet brightness. She glanced up, but the searing blue of the sky was too strong for her: strangely, the whiteness of the stuff that was not snow was easier to bear.

As Beloved walked on, the brighter spot resolved itself into the figure of a seated woman, and when Beloved was nearer, she saw that the woman was very tall and generously proportioned, draped in a garment of white, and with face and head veiled in filmy gold. The woman sat, relaxed yet authoritative, in a wide-seated chair of something like alabaster with a short back and armrests. On Her shoulder was a *sozkol* and She held in her lap, with one large and capable hand, a cage that glittered as if cut from diamond. Beloved could not make out from afar what was in the cage. As she drew nearer, the silent, motionless woman commanded all Beloved's attention.

She stopped some paces from the woman. Beloved held out her palms horizontally in front of her at chest height, as she had seen the priestesses of Velaska do, and bowed. She held the position, her dream sense telling her it was not her part to speak first.

Beloved was trembling with holding herself in the unfamiliar pose when she heard a smiling voice, deep and resonant, say, "Rise, child, and be at ease." Beloved straightened, letting her hands fall, and waited. She felt the veiled gaze considering her. The falcon-like *sozkol*, Beloved noticed out of the corner of her eye, turned its head as it perched on the Lady's shoulder.

"So you will stand by My Tree at the hour of danger," said the Lady. It was not a question; She was musing as if to Herself, but Beloved felt she should answer.

"Yes, Lady," she said. The Lady settled back in Her seat and Beloved wondered whether she had been disrespectful.

"No, I take no offense," said the Lady, although Beloved had not spoken aloud. A pause. "Why?" the Lady asked.

Beloved blinked. "I have sworn oaths—" She stopped, for the Lady had held up Her free hand, palm out. Another pause.

"Why?" the Lady asked again, and this time Her voice was stern. Beloved stared at the veiled face. Silence opened between them. In that silence, the Lady's single word seemed to sink deeply inside Beloved, persistent and questing.

Why? Beloved knew oaths could be broken. She was not forced to stand by the Tree—terrible things would happen if she broke the bonds of honor, duty, power, and trust—but she could choose to do so. *Why?*

"I am not my father," Beloved said. The Lady heard her, but She was not yet satisfied.

"Why?" asked the Lady again, and now She was not so much stern as relentless.

Beloved wanted to close her eyes, to look away, even to walk away. The Lady's scrutiny penetrated all veils and walls, burned away pretexts and rote answers. The question resonated within Beloved, demanding the truest answer she could sound from the depths of herself. *Why?* She did not desire to break bonds she had freely undertaken: that was true. She refused to be a destroyer like her father: that was also true. Yet those reasons did not satisfy her any more than they satisfied the Lady.

Beloved began to walk through her memories as though through a forest thick with trees.

She was young, looking up at Rue, and seeing that tired but loving face bent over her... She was standing before a mirror, realizing that the uncanny creature staring back at her was herself, and she watched it splinter into shards as she stared at it, watched her vine-ridden, hideous form shatter and scatter, heard the footsteps as Rue came running at the sound of the silvered glass breaking... The years of trying to undo the name curse... The luring and capture of mages to teach her... The day she mastered the spell that rendered anyone who came near her—except for Rue, except for the princes—invisible... Her realization that she could make the Hidden House a refuge for others, rather than a prison...

The day that Rue had found her bent over a book of cold magic, studying poisons.

It was the one time she had ever seen Rue truly frightened. Rue had known that Beloved was studying how to die. Her heart-mother had wept, first silent tears and then horrible sobs, and had taken Beloved's hideous, wretched, vine-pierced body into her strong arms and had held her tightly, uncaring of thorns or stench, rocking and crying.

"Live, live, live. I love you, my little one, my own. Live," Rue had tried to croon, but her voice was ragged and broken. Her arms, however, had held the wailing monster who was weary of suffering, who had wondered whether death would be a delivery not only for herself but for everyone around her.

This was a memory that Beloved herself had almost forgotten, for its misery and shame hurt her deeply. But now as she remembered Rue's words and her embrace, Beloved saw some beauty in that hour: she saw her heart-mother's deep love for her.

Another memory: herself in the ruined walled garden, a sword in her heart that she could no longer bear. She had lain down to die at last and not even Rue could reach her. And then someone had found her, was holding her, was not letting her slip into the peace of nothingness. "I swear I will marry you," said a hoarse voice in her ear. "I give my heart for yours. I am your husband. You are my wife, my sweetheart, my beloved. Stay, stay, stay," and then her world had been flame and agony, but the grip had not loosened, not even when all pain had cooled and faded, and she had opened her eyes to see Radvyed's startled gaze.

She came to a more recent ordeal: feeding the thorny vine rooted in her heart, filling it with all her bitterness and lonely suffering and rejection, destroying the hostile birds, but also draining her own wound.

The memory left her, and Beloved's wide eyes saw the Lady before her once more.

"I choose to live," said Beloved, her voice raspy but sure. "I choose to hope." If there were another, deeper answer, Beloved did not know where to look for it or how to hear it. The Lady absorbed Beloved's reply in silence, then nodded. The *sozkol* shifted on Her shoulder.

"What is in the cage?" asked the Lady and now Beloved could direct her gaze to the cage held in the Lady's lap. The glitter of it was hard and Beloved squinted. The cage seemed to grow larger as she looked at it. Then she saw.

"It is the Fire Bird," whispered Beloved. Even in the bird's misery—her plumage in disarray, her body cramped—Beloved could see the brilliant feathers: gold, hot blue, orange, crimson, but most of all a burning scarlet that gave off heat. The Fire Bird awkwardly turned her neck so that one dull gold eye stared at Beloved. Then Beloved realized something else. "The cage is made of ice," she said.

"Yes," said the Lady. Beloved looked at the draggled bird, whose prison was so restrictive that she could not spread her wings.

"Is this my father's doing?" asked Beloved.

"Not his alone," said the Lady.

"Why do You not free her?" asked Beloved.

"Why do not you?" replied the Lady. And as Beloved turned her eyes from the Fire Bird to the Lady, she felt herself falling back, or perhaps the Lady was withdrawing, now nothing but a pinpoint of light in a vista of blue and white, and then Beloved felt the mattress beneath her and the blanket on top of her, heard the steady breathing of Radvyed as he slept, and she stared up into the darkness of their bedchamber. She sprawled there as one regrouping after a fall, making sure she was whole and sane. *A dream?* she wondered. *Or a walk among the sunfields, where I truly encountered the Lady Herself?*

Beloved lay next to her husband, who remained distant in sleep, and wrestled with thought until morning.

Chapter Fifty-Nine

Radvyed awoke alone in their bed. His chest constricted for a moment, as he remembered another morning he had woken alone and had found his wife gone, but then he saw a tray with a pot of *chelek* on a table, and the signs that someone had poured herself a cup, and he breathed again. He rolled to his back, stretched, and sat up. *Tomorrow*, he thought. *Tomorrow is the day.* He rose from the bed, poured himself some *chelek*, and went looking for Beloved.

He found her in the privy council room. Stifling a yawn and carrying his cup of *chelek*, he entered the room and walked past the oval table until he joined her at the other end. The blackened sigil of the Ice Raven seemed to hover on the right-hand wall. Despite the horror of the earlier attacks, this Raven was neither threatening nor reassuring. It was simply itself. As Radvyed turned to face the wall Beloved was contemplating, opposite the Ice Raven, he slid his right hand to the small of Beloved's back. Last night the wall had been blank. Today there was a figure of a bird, but this sigil was not the Ice Raven.

"Is this the Fire Bird?" Radvyed asked.

Beloved had one arm wrapped around her waist and her other elbow propped on it as she held her chin. She did not seem disturbed, but pensive. His wife nodded, not yet ready to speak. He studied the Fire Bird. Unlike the other image, this one had not been burned into the wall. Instead—Radvyed bent forward—some dark pigment had been used to delineate it—at first he thought it was black, but then he realized it was a deep red. He straightened. It reminded him of the deep red of her rose, the velvet petals so saturated with color that they gleamed with black undertones. Beloved leaned into him and Radvyed tightened his arm.

"I had a strange dream last night," she said, "and this morning this was on the wall." They both looked at the Fire Bird, which, like the Ice Raven, was shown in flight, her long tail spread and sweeping, her elegant neck curved and proud.

"Come have breakfast," said Radvyed, "and tell me about it."

He listened as she told him her dream. When Beloved had finished, she poured herself another cup of *chelek*. Radvyed said nothing until she began to sip it.

"One thing has become clear to me," he said, and waited for her to look at him, "and that is, you mages do not understand the purpose of sleep, which is *rest*." She put down her cup and stared at him with her mouth open. Radvyed grinned at her and Beloved was surprised into a laugh. He held his hand out and she put hers into it. He closed his hand around her fingers, firm and warm. His face serious, now that he had given her a moment of lightness, he said, "I do not pretend to understand the whole of your dream, but I do know this. The Lady loves us, and when She acts it is for our good. Time will bring a surer understanding."

"Who knows how much more time we have," Beloved answered and sighed. Unknowingly she echoed in her mind Radvyed's earlier thought upon waking: *tomorrow*. She was anxious. Radvyed, she knew, and even the king and queen, she thought, did not doubt that she could draw on the wide sea of power that was Tamtir and use it to protect *zelohn* and *kamin*, people and House. Her husband's confidence was rooted in past deeds she—and they as a couple—had performed. Yet in those feats she had acted from the power that dwelt inside her, as reliable and as intrinsic as her own breath moving in and out of her chest. Strong, difficult spells, yes, but work she knew she was born to do.

This, however, was different. Despite rites and oaths, dreams and promises, Beloved was diffident. She still felt a stranger in Tamtir. She had cast her lot with the kingdom, the people, even the Lady and Master—but she did not yet feel herself of the place, no matter what others said. Her power was not anchored here. Some things took time. Yet she must be ready and able tomorrow.

It was a quiet day. There was activity, but the plans had all been made, the instructions given, the orders sent out. Now was as the time before battle, when soldiers checked weapons and gear, and rested if they could, while commanders looked over troops and plans. Now there was the time to think and double-check and wonder whether their plans would fail or if they had calculated amiss or had mis-named the day. Sonza sent that she had seen in a sun vision the Lady holding a caged bird of flaming scarlet; Zevedan reported seeing the white-winged Ice Raven among the stars, sly and elusive. Too many signs, thought Radvyed, and too little understanding of how to read them.

The day dragged on. Beloved became very quiet and the furnishings of their apartments, to Radvyed's eye, darkened as if with age and wear. Dris came by with a mass of dried rose petals and a jar of mixed rose hips and dried petals. Beloved smiled and took the basket and jar, drawing the scent of the petals in. Before night fell she would bathe in water infused with the petals and would drink rose tea. Radvyed had never smelled such a fragrance from dried flowers before and he wondered what practical magic Dris had performed on them. Dris was worried, he thought, as he noted the tightness around her eyes, a deeper line between her brows. After Beloved assured her aunt that she had refreshed Gladna's rose, the gardener touched her niece's cheek and looked into the younger woman's eyes a moment and left.

Rue's serene presence steadied everyone's nerves. Once when Beloved had left the room for a moment, however, Radvyed saw Rue droop in her chair and cover her eyes with her hand. Before he could move to comfort her, Beloved had returned, and Rue straightened, presenting her usual tranquil face.

Radvyed imagined people all over Tamtir readying themselves for the day to come. Bards and *seveyati* had been charged with explaining and directing. The *mireni*, too, lent their aid and authority, giving weight to the strange-sounding tales of magic and peril. He wondered what the people thought of the danger they had been warned of and the instructions they had been given. How would parents prepare their children without terrifying them?

Radvyed knew Tamtir well, from the royal family's regular Tithings and less structured Visitings and Ridings. As he stood over the maps spread out in his father's study, he could see in his mind's eye each *mirenzem*, each feature of the landscape. To the north flowed the mighty river Bielna, whose waters cut through the northwestern arm of the Krandin Range to pour, wide and white-watered, onto the Koleben Plain. There she spread herself even more, yet curved with stealthy swiftness east, passing between the Vorenta Hills and joining the cold Rasovel Sea. He saw the river ports and towns that drew trade and fish from the river's course and the broad plain south of her, fertile and green. At her meeting with the sea was the northernmost seaport of Tamtir, Konachek; from there the coastline pushed unevenly east into the sea before falling back as it dropped southward. West of Cape Misolen straggled the Sinevy Hills, which looked east to the sea and west to the royal city. A second seaport, Sabreka, was tucked into the southern inner curve of the cape, while the third major and southern-most port, Grozgaven, sat instead at the feet of the eastern peaks of the Krandins.

Radvyed looked at one map, then another, continuing to trace with his gaze all the familiar places of this land bestowed upon his House and his people: the Krandin Range as it left the eastern sea and swept west and north, holding half of Tamtir in its embrace; the dense southern forests; the spurs of the Maliniv and Perset Hills that thrust north from the southern arm of the Krandins; the Kranich River, brown, slow-moving, and generous, easing his way east and south after branching off the Bielna a little way out of the mountains, until he found his home waters in Lake Yuzhenil. The prince thought of the people of Tamtir. Wherever they were, mountain or sea, plain or river, lakeside or city center, tomorrow before the sun glanced over the earth they would all be at their places, with varying degrees of understand-ing, trusting that their valor and loyalty would be protection for their beloved land.

Radvyed touched the maps, naming and calling to mind each fea-ture, touching in spirit the people of each town and holding, as if the very act of bringing them to mind and thinking of them with ten-derness and faith would place them more surely under the protection of the Lady and the Master. He felt he was acting foolishly, but also necessarily, and so he blessed the whole kingdom, league by league, community by community. Beloved, with his parents, entered as his finger brushed the last village, the one near the border where he had stayed when he had first ridden west in search of Hideous and a hidden flower. He raised his head, straightened and smiled tiredly.

Beloved gave him an odd look, but said nothing, merely taking his hand. Hers was cold and Radvyed held it firmly. Then they all four left the study and with some distracted light talk made their way to the family dining hall. *A last meal*, thought Radvyed, then resolutely turned his thoughts to Beloved, and how best to help her in these hours of waiting, whether by talking of small things, going over their plans again, or sharing his silent presence.

It seemed night would never come and then it fell abruptly, the stars thickly strewn in the inky blackness of the sky. The cold deepened with the darkness, sharp and insistent. Everyone knew they should try to sleep in the time before the appointed hour of midnight, but few were able to settle into anything more than an anxious doze. The Eve of the Lady's Return was usually a vigil night, when the people of Tamtir waited to welcome the dawn that heralded the time of greater sunlight. It was a solemn watch before days of feasting and merriment and gratitude, but this time the waiting was tense. Jokes fell flat; tempers were short; children were fretful. The fires in the hearths seemed smaller and feebler; the light shed by candles flickered uncertainly.

After dinner, back in their rooms, Radvyed held Beloved on his lap in the large chair in front of the fireplace, both of them wrapped in a woolen blanket. Her eyes darted often to the time-candle on the mantelpiece. The candle, thought Radvyed as he tried to cuddle his wife's stiff form, seemed to burn both too fast and too slowly. It seemed the hour of attack flew towards them on grim wings; it seemed the hour for action crawled forward on broken knees. *So much depends on guesses, the valor of the moment, the strength of this one woman*, he thought. *When the sun sets tomorrow, what will there be of Tamtir?*

Chapter Sixty

Bells tolled the half hour before midnight. Radvyed and Beloved met Arkost and Gladna in the queen's sitting room. All through the palace were the sounds of people on the move, going to their assigned posts. Dris would be in the rose garden, guarding that *zelohn*. Various *dovoreni* and *damashi* and others resident at the palace, not required at their family's holdings or households, had been appointed to hearths, gardens, and fields. Rue would be in the Lady's Forest. It was only now Radvyed realized that Beloved's heart-mother was perhaps the one person over two years of age in Tamtir who had (as far as he knew) taken no oaths to bind herself to the land and the people. *Too late now*, he thought. *And surely her bond to Beloved is strong enough to include her in whatever protection or spell Beloved musters.*

The meeting of the king, queen, prince, and Beloved was brief. Few words were spoken; there were swift embraces, an exchange of glances, a hand pressed, then no more. The time for thinking, planning, worrying, and calculating had passed. It was time to act.

Arkost and Gladna hastened down to the Master's Hall, using a small, dark, spiraling inner stair. The Hall had never seemed as majestic or as remote as it did this night, thought the queen as she emerged from the ancient stairwell through a low door. The columns vaulted and met, unseen in the darkness, far above their heads. The jewels sparkled in the dimness with the cold, bright light of the stars—indifferent, Gladna thought, to the beating hearts below. The Hall was lit with torches set into the sconces on each column, but the torches seemed overwhelmed this night, serving to emphasize the darkness rather than to dispel it. She gazed down the nave to the Master's *kamin* at the other end. In the fireplace leapt a fire, smaller than usual, but defiant and bright. Her heart eased as she and Arkost, hand in hand, strode down the Hall. It was empty but for them and the flames. Beloved and the Master's *seveyati* had decided it so: every *kamin* and temple forge must be guarded, and no attendants could be spared to support the king and queen.

They stood before the fire, almost on the *kamin* itself. Arkost knelt on the cold stone floor. After removing his gloves, he opened his cloak and the top part of his robe, then loosened the ties at the neck of his linen shirt. Gladna knelt beside him, helping him bare his gray-haired, barrel-like chest. Arkost lay down, the front of his body pressed to the *kamin*, his hands palm down on it. He gave a soft grunt as he settled his weight.

"My love?" said the queen, still kneeling at his side, her hand resting on his back.

"Heart and hand," the king said. "It is not as cold as I had feared." He paused and with one hand seemed to be searching among his garments. He produced a knife, longer than an eating implement, shorter than most weapons. He pushed it towards his wife. Gladna looked down at it. He peered up at her and said, "In case more than heart and hand are required."

She went still for a moment, then said, "Yes, love." She laid her head on his broad back, reaching down a hand to find his. Nothing to do now but wait.

Radvyed and Beloved were joined by Rue at a palace door that opened onto a path leading to the Lady's Forest. They each bore a torch for light; torch stands had been set earlier during the day as part of their preparations. *Not so long ago I walked this path in my wedding garments*, thought Beloved. Now they wore much simpler attire, chosen for warmth and comfort. She had boots that could be easily unlaced, for it was her part to be barefoot as she stood within the Lady's *zelohn*. *The people will be cold tonight*, she thought, and this commonplace discomfort seemed incongruous with the malice that threatened. *Yet it is as real.*

The three moved in silence. It did not seem a moment for light talk and no one had anything of substance to say that had not already been said several times over. *It is almost a relief to have the moment come upon us at last*, thought Beloved. *Soon all will be discovered and decided and done.*

Rue would not be entering the Lady's Glade. She had realized long before the prince that only through Beloved was she herself tied to Tamtir. Yet she had not been ready to bind herself to this place and people. As for oaths to the House—she did not think anyone in Tamtir was more closely bound than she to her heart-daughter. Beloved had expressed concern, but had not been able to bring herself to force Rue to take oaths; nor could she deny the strength of the bond they shared. Beloved had prevailed in her desire that Rue be nearby, however, and within the Lady's Forest. It would have to suffice.

Rue had chosen a spot that had drawn her attention, a little off the path, where a tree of large girth had fallen. Its insides had been hollowed out by decay, but it was so large that a young tree had taken root in a knot in the fallen tree's side. The smaller tree had spread its branches while it grew, so now there was a sheltered bower. When the Forest was in leaf it was particularly lovely; now its slender branches shivered in the cold. Rue did not mind the nakedness of woods in winter. She liked to see the framework of things.

When the three of them drew abreast of the place, Rue stopped. The other two turned towards her. How hard it was not to show her anxiety. Would this be the last time she looked on her heart-daughter's face? But fear would not help Beloved. So Rue kept her face calm and if her gloved hand shook a little as she touched the younger woman's cheek, well, it was cold this night. She had planned to say something, but found she could not. So she gave a half smile, and leaned forward to kiss Beloved, then turned away. *No time to tarry*, Rue told herself. *No time for tears.* She left the path and moved through the brush to her chosen spot. When she reached it, she turned and gave a small wave to the two torchlit figures, obscured by trees, on the path. They waved and resumed their way. Rue watched their torches bobbing towards the Glade and looked about her. She set her torch in its stand, breathed in a deep lungful of chilly air, and prepared to wait.

Beloved and Radvyed continued in silence, walking with care by the flickering torchlight. They could see, now and then, the distant glimmer of other torches among the trees, marking where some of the *seveyati* dedicated to the Lady were preparing to keep watch. Shadows leapt, reached, and receded as they walked, making the world about

Radvyed and Beloved seem both a restricted circle of light and a form-less, boundless darkness. The air was cold and crisp; the leaves crackled and crunched under their feet. At last they came to the Glade.

Beloved had never been in the sacred clearing when it was full dark. It opened before them like a lake of shadow while they stood under the eaves of the trees edging the Glade. Radvyed took a few steps forward, then turned to wait for her. She followed, then paused to look up. The sky was overcast, the cloud cover glowing faintly with light from the hidden young moon. Beloved frowned. The moon, only two days past new, should not be able to cast light strong enough to make the clouds even dimly luminous. Sparks thrown up by the torches swirled and faded, their light quickly extinguished. She drew her gaze back down and saw Radvyed walking ahead towards the circle of the Lady's *zelohn* proper, where they had stood to make their marriage vows. The Tree rose bare-limbed beyond it, its aged form twisted, yet strong and solid. *How many winds, snows, storms, and fair days have you known, Elder?* Beloved thought, and seeing its stark standing figure, was somehow heartened.

Radvyed had reached the *zelohn* and was waiting for her. As Beloved made her way across the dark grass, she let herself admire his beauty by torchlight. Light and shadow touched his face and form with caressing fingers, enhancing his comeliness. Radvyed's steady gaze was on her, patient as he tried to hide his worry. To Beloved, his steadfastness of soul anchored and shone through his remarkable beauty, making his looks something more than delicious to the senses. Then she shook her head a little. *You may contemplate your husband and his qualities to your heart's content later,* she promised herself. *After.* She did not permit herself to think about if there were no *after.*

Beloved walked to Radvyed, carrying her torch's light forward as though it were an amulet against harm. They each set their torches within the stands that had already been placed near the *zelohn*. Then Radvyed knelt before her and began unlacing her boots. Beloved looked down at his bent head and thought how unlike her childhood ideas of a prince he was. He knelt on the cold, hard ground, removing her boots and stockings without any hint that such a task might be beneath him or damaging to his dignity. Radvyed paused after he bared her left foot, rubbing it for a moment, as if trying to protect it from the cold. He set it down and tugged on the laces of her right boot. She switched the hand she rested on his shoulder to keep her balance and looked up at the sky.

Against the unnatural muted glow of the cloud cover Beloved saw dark birds circling. She stilled, alert. At first three, then five, swirling around some invisible center point, then ten, fifteen. Soon she saw more than she could keep count of or estimate, as though there were a point of entry through the clouds that the host of birds were flying through. They did not dive or swoop. One by one they came, faster and faster, the sweep of their high flight circling ever wider, until she could no longer see the dim clouds but only sensed that overhead was a turbulent mass of silent feathered bodies carrying rage and malice. Beloved gripped Radvyed's shoulder as he set down her right foot. Radvyed rose and followed her gaze upward. He swallowed at the ever-widening swirling darkness and looked at her.

"It is the hour," Beloved said, and stepped over the low wall. Autumn grass and flowers had filled the *zelohn* after their marriage ceremony, but now all was brown and dormant. Radvyed followed and stood behind her within the enclosure, loosely clasping his arms about her waist. The ground was cold, so cold. Her toes shrank from contact with it even as she tried to stand strongly, to use the earth to support her. But as the minutes passed, the cold came between her and the ground. Beloved became numb to her connection to the earth.

The chill air crept between her back and Radvyed's chest, making him seem a dumb, stiff form made of cloth rather than warm flesh. Beloved felt panic trying to gain purchase on her thoughts, rising like a howl in her mind. *I cannot. I am nothing. I do not belong. I cannot. I am nothing. I do not belong.* She felt as though the weight of all the *kamini* and *zelohni* of the kingdom pressed upon her, as though the heartbeats of all the brave, frightened Tamtireni throbbed in her skull. Radvyed tightened his arms, bringing his chest closer to her back. She breathed, deeply and slowly.

Beloved shut her eyes and thought, *I can. I will. I am Beloved. I am of Tamtir.* As though she had closed and barred a window, the panic fell back. She knew it lurked, waiting for weakness, watching for an opening.

Beloved's feet became so cold that her legs felt like they ended in stumps rather than feet. She swayed a little and Radvyed steadied her. After some time—it was hard to judge how long—she glanced up: the birds had dispersed, spreading over Tamtir, she guessed. What would they do? How would she counter? She could hardly incinerate such a flock one by one, even if they had been in her orbit. And no heart-rooted vine could engirdle or snare such a far-flung multitude.

When Beloved lowered her gaze, she saw a white wispy fog filtering through the trees surrounding the Glade, chilling the air even more and confusing her sight. The torchlight did not penetrate it. The fog glided forward, feinted, ebbed a little, circled, then crept forward again. Beloved noticed it did not cross the boundary of the *zelohn.* She stared, trying to perceive—*there!*—there was a figure in the fog—it came closer, and she felt the window in her mind blast open and the gleeful panic rush in: *I cannot I am nothing I do not belong I cannot I am nothing I do not belong I cannot....* The fog resolved into an eerie white shade in the form of a tall, cloaked man. His thin lips sneered;

his deep-set eyes glared down at her. Rue and Dris had described him to her. She had seen his image once or twice in books. But Beloved knew him now by his malice and contempt.

It was the ghost of her father, invoked by the followers of the Ice Raven, that master of illusions and attendant of death.

Chapter Sixty-One

Alya lay on the *kamin* of her house, in front of the fireplace. Her heart and hand were pressed to the cold stone. How long she lay there, skin to stone, waiting for some mysterious threat, she did not know. She became aware of a cold white mist slinking across the floor. Before she could make sense of fog in the house and in front of a fire, she saw a shape forming within the mist and coming close to her. Her grandmother, her mother's mother, whom she had loved, and who had died shortly after Alya's marriage to Van. Alya gasped. The ghost spoke.

"Oh, Alya," said Nani, and somehow the face that had always looked on Alya with kindness was hard with anger, even contempt. "How could you leave us to marry that idiot farmer, leave your family, leave *me*?" Alya stared, frightened and confused—Nani had liked Van; she had said so. Now the beloved voice became cold. "I never liked him, that clod, and I never forgave you. I died from shame and a broken heart. *You* killed me!"

Where had this specter come from? Why was she here? Alya trembled where she lay; the *kamin* was icy under her.

"Get up off the floor," snapped her grandmother. "You disgust me, crawling like that."

Alya could not make herself shut her eyes, but she did not obey this Nani who was not Nani. The long-missed voice's haranguing shredded her heart, but they had been told not to move, not to abandon their post. Alya stayed pressed to the sacred stone, her tears wetting the *kamin*, as the ghost with her Nani's face and voice found every tender point of memory, and befouled it.

Outside, Van stood barefoot within the *zelohn*. He felt awkward, for they had been told no tools or weapons would serve against the attack to come. So he stood, shoulders tight, hands clenching and unclenching at his sides, on edge, waiting for he knew not what. Night on his farm had never bothered him, for he did not fear the dark, but tonight he was grateful for the company of a torch set in a low stand by his side. A movement caught his eye and he looked up. Against the eerily dim-lit sky were flung the shadows of birds. As Van watched, some detached from a large flock and circled down to his farm, dark and menacing, as though this were no random flight. He watched them—ravens, they seemed—settle on the roofs of the house and barn, on the fences and gates. He heard the mule kicking at her stall, once, twice. The two cows lowed, fell silent, then called again. The animals were restless, but not panicked. Indeed, he was sure he himself was more unquiet than any of them. He did not move, for the messages from the royal city had been clear: *Do not leave your* zelohni *and* kamini *for any reason.*

The birds were unsettling enough, yet they were but harbingers of the uncanny white fog that crept forward. It advanced toward Van, its shifting shapes as compelling as flames, but nightmarish. He tried to steady his breathing—*nothing to fear here, just some birds and a bit of fog.* He heard a stifled scream from the house—*Alya!*—but before he could react, a shape coalesced in front of him, and he forgot his frightened wife. His elder brother, Shar, dead these forty years, stood before him, arms crossed over his wide chest, a scowl marring his face. Van's weight rocked back on his heels as though his brother had slapped him. *Why is he looking at me like that? How comes he here?*

"So here you are, after forty years of growing fat on what should have been *my* inheritance," said Shar. Had Van ever heard that tone from him before? Van wanted to speak, but his throat closed with shock. The ghost cast a scathing glance around. "Lived here happy, have you, with your silly town wife? Never thinking that everything here should have been *mine*. Never thinking about *me* and how I died. *Pleased* I was gone and out of your way at last."

No, Van wanted to say, *who are you, you are not Shar, my big brother, generous, bold-hearted, the strongest of us all. I think of you often*, he wanted to say, *we all mourned you. I still miss you.* But Van found himself confused and in doubt. Had his brother been like this and he had not known? He had been a youth when Shar had died, cut down in his young manhood in an accident—Van remembered the storm, the river at the ford rising so quickly, and Shar getting down to hold the horse pulling their wagon, the darkness and wildness of the wind and rain, and then his brother disappearing, pulled under...one of the worst memories of Van's life. And here stood Shar, unsmiling, sneering, accusing—*ah, Lady! Show me light!*

The Shar that was unlike Shar smirked at him. "Thought we all loved and cared for one another, did you? I see that Petor got out soon enough, following that sea witch, preferring to live like a lapdog in a stinking fishing village rather than stay another moment here with you and the rest."

No, Van wanted to say, *no*, but ghost-Shar smiled knowingly, and the words froze in Van's throat.

Up in the Sinevy Hills, in a little village with an improbable orchard, the spinster wept as a shade shaped like her father stood before the very shrubs the princess had blessed with her touch. He taunted the crying woman with every unkind word she had ever said, every hard look she had ever given, every unfriendly deed she had ever done. Then the specter of her dead sister drifted from the house to join him. When her father's ghost paused, as if to draw breath, the sister who was not her sister gleefully sneered that the spinster's work was shoddy, the whole village hated her, her husband long since regretted marrying her. The sobbing woman stayed within the *zelohn*, arms crossed over her head as she crouched beneath the blows of scorn and recrimination. Would this night of tears never end?

Not far away, prostrate on the forge's *kamin*, the blacksmith tried to shut his eyes to the scenes being played out before him in the uncanny fog. He saw things he had made break and cause disaster: the metal tongue of a wagon snapping; a scythe slipping and cutting a man's thigh. He saw a horse shod by him kicking a man to the ground and trampling him; saw another horse go lame from his poor work. He saw tools that he had forged used for harm, even to kill: hammers, nails, knives. *Master*, he cried silently, *Master, You know I have always put my best into everything I have made. Master!* But he could not shut his eyes and was soon lost in a maze of pain.

So it was all over the kingdom, whether farm, *mirenzem*, village, city, or temple. First came the ravens, heralds of grief, like eager spectators at a blood sport, settling near wherever people were, watching, waiting. Then came the fog, cold, clammy, cunning, showing to each guardian of *zelohn* and *kamin* what would give them the most pain, what would wound them most with guilt and grief. Part of the horror and the terror was the helplessness—each person unable to close their eyes, to look away, to think of something else, to speak, to banish the figures of relentless misery.

Not even the people of the palace were shielded—indeed, an observer might have said that the avid ravens and the chill fog were most thick at the palace, its gardens, and the woods behind.

Dris stood in the center of the rose garden, alone. She had watched the ravens gathering during the day, but now she understood that those birds were merely local ones unsettled and compelled by some call they did not recognize but could not ignore. She saw the invader ravens coming through an unseen opening in the cloud cover, swirling down, like ink steadily dripped into clear water, the stain of them spreading out, darkening the air, blotting out the young, cloud-dulled moon. The hair on her body, especially at the back of her neck, prickled. Dris no longer paid attention to the cold that had been pinching and scraping at her moments before, for the white fog creeping among the rose plants disturbed her far more. She braced for an attack even as she chastised herself. *They have taken your parents, your sister, your clan, your guardian, and your home from you already. What can they do now?* She watched as the chill mist began to assume a shape she recognized. *Ah, Fire Bird, no,* she cried silently. Dris felt the hot tears on her cold cheeks as her eyes met the angry gaze of Beloved's mother, her lost sister, Amarrasal.

Rue heard but could not see the swirling mass of ravens in flight. The birds did not call out, but the rush of thousands of feathers made its own sound and created its own wind. The trees stirred as they passed. A dozen ravens drifted down among the higher branches of the trees near her and found perches. She did not see them, but she felt their mocking eyes upon her. The torch flickered; its flame shrank. Rue stood still, straining to hear, to see. A white fog began to stalk through the trees towards her. She took a deep breath, refusing to allow herself to panic. *Nothing to fear. Nothing here.* The fog was drawing together at a point on the ground perhaps two paces from where she stood. Something was forming, shaping itself. She leaned closer to see, perhaps already knowing, for her breathing became labored. Her heart stopped; time stilled; the world narrowed. Then her heart throbbed again, kicking at her ribs, beating painfully and too fast. Rue's knees buckled and she crumpled, her palms catching her as she fell forward onto her arms. Kneeling, with sobs too large to escape her chest choking her, she stared at the small baby crying on the ground before her. *My Dulsan!* She crawled towards him and tried to gather him up in her arms. But she could not hold him; her arms closed on nothing. She tried, again and again, until she lay on the ground in despair with her hands outstretched, staring at her dead baby who never ceased wailing for his mother.

No ravens found a way into the Master's Hall, for the doors had been shut and a fire burned in the fireplace, closing off the chimney passage. Yet they gathered outside in the gardens and on the roofs and balconies of the palace. The Hall grew cold, despite the fire, and the fog was heedless of doors. It slunk along the floor to the king and queen at their post. The firelight flickered over the bodies of the man stretched out on the floor and the woman bending over him. Although the fog was silent, something made them look up—perhaps the fire had retreated. Gladna watched the eerie fog advancing towards them from the shadowed length of the Hall and bent protectively over her husband. "Arkost," she said. She felt him shift as he turned his head. Figures walked towards them out of the chill mist. They each saw their own pain take shape before their eyes.

The queen could only make out one form, the smallest, who came to stand before her. Padrenna, her closest childhood friend. They had been distantly related. Padrenna's family lived at Gladna's *mirenzem*, one of the many branches of a large family that shared its houses as served the whole family best. They had been so inseparable that everyone had called the pair of them Padna. They shared tutors, meals, clothes, and a bedroom. They had sworn a blood pact under a midsummer full moon: sisters forever, never to be parted.

But one winter there had been an illness that touched everyone of the *mirenzem*, some with a light hand, some with a heavy. Gladna had lain in the same bed next to her sworn sister, holding her as Padrenna's swollen body shook with relentless coughing. One morning Gladna woke with her friend's cold body in her arms. It had taken three adults to make Gladna let go. Now Padrenna stood in front of the queen. The ghost-girl's hands hung at her sides; her eyes leaked tears. "Did you forget me so soon, sister?" she whispered. "You found love, joy, laughter, though you know I am dust?" Gladna could not reply. She could barely breathe. She heard Arkost groan beneath her. What was he seeing? But the queen could not turn her eyes or free her thoughts from the reproachful figure of Padrenna as her sworn sister pierced her with accusations of shallow-heartedness and betrayal.

Arkost could not see Padrenna. Instead he saw, with terrible clarity, the men, women, and children affected by his own poor decisions, by his lack of wisdom or foresight, by his inability to shield his people from calamity. He saw the faces from the judgments that cost him sleep, cases with little evidence or information to guide him, or in which witnesses were contradictory, or for which there was no good solution: families, even *mirenzemi*, riven by violence and lies. He saw the dead from the year he and the Council had put more royal resources into supporting the Healer Hall, fearing another winter outbreak of fen fever, and instead Tamtir had endured storms that had killed the wheat crop and led to hunger. He saw the broken bodies from the sudden collapse of a bridge in the mountains on market day morning, when traffic was at its busiest. He saw children carried off by flash floods, merchants and sailors lost at sea, people trapped in houses razed by fire. And added to all these, the starved, pleading, wretched faces of the envoys from abroad during the time of the salt curse, begging him to teach them the protection that guarded Tamtir.

Arkost did not turn away. *It is right*, he thought, *that I be made to look on this. This is part of my lot as king.* But, *Master*, he cried, as the people kept coming, silent yet condemning, *You know I have tried!*

And failed, was the answer he read in the ghost faces. *And failed.* After he knew not how long, he became aware of the severe chill of the Stone beneath him. It seemed—*but the Master's own* kamin?—to be contracting, as if with cold.

Dris could make no answer to the terrible accusations shaped by her sister's mouth, hard words accompanied by the ghost's scornful signing: *You are the least of us. You escaped because you are defective, a dud with no ability to command or channel power, a dry and fruitless branch. You are a servant without pride or dignity. You disgrace us. Why do you live when your clan has been destroyed? You think you are someone now, but that is only because she is* my *daughter...* Dris stood before the tirade of contempt and condemnation, knowing this shade was *not* her sister, *not* Amarrasal, but the work of the Bitter Ones. *Not real, not real, not real*, Dris repeated to herself. And yet she wept.

As the people of Tamtir came face-to-face with the specters of their griefs and regrets and fears, an icy snow began to fall, gently, silently, stealthily. Ravens watched as the forms of the people, like statues of sorrow, began to be lost under the clinging, gritty flakes.

Chapter Sixty-Two

In the Lady's Glade, Beloved stood facing the man she had never met but who had sired her. Even in this colorless, insubstantial form he conveyed hatred and distaste for her so forcefully that she had to struggle not to step back from him. But there was Radvyed behind her, steady and firm against her back. Her father stared at her, waiting, she thought, for her to drop her eyes. After what seemed like an eternity, his lip lifted in something between a sneer and a snarl. They had not yet exchanged a single word. He flicked a glance behind her, at her husband, and smirked.

That princeling is your support when you confront Me? She heard the growling voice directly in her head, echoing between her ears: both an attack and a violation. *You tie yourself to an ignorant and bumbling kingdom, a House and a line without power? Stupid and weak.*

"Yet this kingdom resisted your power and this princeling was the means to break it," Beloved replied. She wished she could thrust her thoughts into his brain. But he was a ghost, a shape only: the Bitter Ones' malice made manifest.

Now there was a full snarl. *It does not resist Me now. This entire kingdom is whimpering in misery in front of its dead. It will soon be covered by ice and stand only as a sign that no one crosses Me and triumphs.* Beloved did indeed feel the brush of snow on her cheeks as it fell. Her body was almost wholly numb with cold now. She could no longer feel Radvyed holding her or standing behind her.

"Your salt failed and so will your ice," she said. "Your birds are ash and dust." Was Radvyed there? What was he seeing?

No rosewater now, little princess. No sap, no sun, no fire. The Ice Raven Clan holds the winter sky and so holds you and this foolish little plot of ground you call a kingdom.

"The Lady and the Master hold the sky. The Lady and Master hold Tamtir." Beloved's voice was snatched by an icy flurry and her words were flung away, lost in the cold and dark. She wondered whether drinking the rose hip tea and bathing in the rosewater brewed from the royal roses had had any effect at all.

Now the smirk returned to her shade-sire's face and his arms gestured widely. *And yet the snow falls onto their powerless people, as they grovel on stone and crouch on earth.*

"We are not powerless." She chose the words that her father's sister had spoken. It seemed months ago that Beloved had been woken out of sleep to follow a spell's path and stumble upon a conspiracy.

The specter of her father stared at her, holding her eyes. Then he rocked, forward and back, always holding her gaze with his, until finally his mouth opened and he laughed, at first a single-voiced, croaking sound, but then the sound multiplied, until out of the one mouth came the mirthless laughter of many throats—the taunts of the Bitter Ones. *You are the dregs, the leavings, of the Ice Raven Clan. You will be annihilated and with you every entity bound to you. For you are not even Hideous anymore. You are nothing. I again renounce you. Be no more.*

Beloved felt as though she were held in a fist of ice, a fist that was tightening about her, crushing her with cold and numbness and darkness. The Tree behind her groaned and shrieked. Its limbs were laden with ice; its roots and trunk attacked by cold. Was the Master's Stone close to cracking? Fear clutched at her with frigid, strangling fingers. *You will be annihilated and with you every entity bound to you.* As Beloved stared into the white eyes of her ghost-father, the faces of all those to whom she was bound flashed through her mind: Rue, Radvyed, Dris, Arkost, Gladna, Alya, Van, Namira, Oumyest, Vel, the gardeners, the councilors, the villagers, the *mireni*, the shopkeepers, the *dovoreni,* the scholars, the bards, the *seveyati,* the artisans, the *damashi* and *kuniki*...

The Bitter Ones reached for her through her father's specter. Their spell cramped her body. *Not a fist*, Beloved thought, *but a cage of ice,* and she remembered the Fire Bird on the Lady's lap, wretched in her glittering cage. *Why do You not free her?* Beloved had asked. *Why do not you?* had been the Lady's reply.

Beloved had not answered, because the Lady had released her then, but she would have said: *I have not the power.* But now she thought, *I am in the cage. I am the Fire Bird.*

The Lady and the Master are keepers of flame.

I am accepted of them.

I do not fear ice.

I *do* not *fear ice.*

Beloved sought within her for the center of her power: the embers she kept banked, the sparks she kept contained.

She was not in a sleep-space shaped by the Bitter Ones this night.

She stood on the Lady's sacred earth, with the Master's stars above.

Beloved dropped the veils masking her power, loosed all self-imposed fetters. She let her power flare as it willed and sank into the burning heart of herself.

Her eyes still locked with her father's, Beloved stared, seeking behind the milky color, wanting to reach the Bitter Ones, wherever they were assembled as they cast a spell to overthrow a kingdom.

I am the Fire Bird. I die and I rise and I die and I rise again.

She had had her first death, her first loss of self when she had barely been a self, as a baby. She had lost herself as Hideous, then had made a life as the Lady Generous of the Hidden House. She had become the dying dragon in the garden and had risen as Beloved. They had sought to destroy her again and again: they had attacked her with bespelled birds, driven her into a frenzy of fear and dread, and violated her sleep to weave a lethal spell-net about her soul. Yet she had risen again and again, sustained by Radvyed and the strength, born of suffering endured, that welled in her inmost heart. Now she was stricken with the ice of death, but she would once more rise, rise, *rise*—and live. She was not finished yet.

She stoked and stirred the inextinguishable, restless fire at the core of her. Undomesticated, willful, turbulent—she knew and embraced all its—*her*—volatility, wildness, and ferocity.

Heat radiated from Beloved's heart, through her arms and fingers, down her legs and into her feet, prickling and burning, waking her benumbed limbs. She straightened. As her feet grew warm, she felt the earth beneath them, and she poured her heat down into the Lady's *zelohn*, down into the soil, seeking the Tree's roots.

Beloved saw again Radvyed bending over the maps of Tamtir, his fingers brushing every feature, blessing the realm—every man, woman, and child, every river, hill, and plain. She tasted once more the burst of wine on her tongue at their wedding; she recalled how her mouth had filled with the essence of Tamtir when she bit into the bread. She saw the *sozkol* rising from her hand and the star forged by the wedding bond.

She had still more power within her. Beloved remembered the day of her testimony before the Council when she had realized she could raze the stone palace with her internal fire. She tipped her head back a little, never removing her gaze from the eyes of the ghost in front of her, and urged the fire to grow hotter. No longer embers or sparks now, no longer mere warmth. She spread her feet and dug her toes into the ground softening under her heat. The Tree had stopped groaning. She could hear ice thawing, dripping. She permitted herself a smile as she continued to stare into her ghost-father's face.

He stopped laughing and slitted his eyes. He, too, now held himself in a strong stance and he reached his arms out, fingers spread, toward her. *So you can warm a patch of ground. So what? The Fire Bird has all the power of a plucked chicken. She can give you nothing. You will flame up and die down, like a dry leaf thrown on a coal.*

Beloved's fiery river of power flowed strongly through her, but she knew the ghost was right. Her own power alone was not enough to free the realm. She needed the ocean that Loucha had spoken of. But Beloved merely smiled thinly at the shade of her sire, hoping that if his smirk had seemed insufferable to her earlier, her own would irritate him—*them*—at least as much.

And still she sent her power down, down into the earth. She needed to find the connection with Tamtir's diffuse ocean of magic. She spun out filaments of sorcery, her power searching like roots seeking water. She felt the bond with Radvyed—*not quite it*. She felt the Tree draw up her heat into itself and begin to repel the ice—*good, but not enough*. Through the Tree Beloved touched the growing things in field and forest, garden and *zelohn*, all over Tamtir—yet it was not enough. In winter, green things were sluggish and dormant. It was not enough to break the Bitter Ones' icy grip. They must be overthrown, defeated, banished. There was power to be had, more than enough, if she could but find it and unlock it. Yet she still did not know how.

Her father's chin lifted in triumph. Beloved sensed ravens gathering ever more thickly in the trees. Radvyed's hands were on her hips, his bulk at her back. All at once she had a bird's-eye view of herself, small and foolish, standing in a patch of dirt clear of snow with one bare tree and an ordinary man, while the relentless snow erased everything and everyone else in the realm, and ravens assembled to witness the quiet end of an insignificant kingdom.

Beloved narrowed her eyes. Those were not her thoughts. She snarled into the hateful face of her father and fed her anger into the fire at the heart of her. *I reject your lies, your thoughts, your eyes.* The picture of herself as small and helpless vanished. The snow melted in an ever-widening circle. But she still had not found the key.

Chapter Sixty-Three

Arkost felt the *kamin* beneath him shrinking with cold. He must not let it crack. *If I wanted to destroy the Master's Stone, I would freeze it,* Beloved had said.

How do I guard it?

Keep it warm. Yet here he was prostrate upon it and it was he who was becoming colder, not the *kamin* warmer. The fire in the hearth was retreating; the ghosts were pressing closer. But they did not touch the *kamin.*

What more can I do? Think! He remembered the blade he had given to Gladna earlier that evening. He remembered the day of their coronation, when they had smeared their blood on this very Stone, swearing to guard it with their lives. Beloved thought it was magic, a bond formed in some invisible fashion that he still did not understand. A blood bond. Blood was death, yes, but also life.

"Gladna. Gladna!" He had no voice. Damned chill. Damned ghosts. What was she seeing? The same as he, or some other misery? "Gladna!"

"Yes, Arkost." Her voice rasped. She had been crying.

"The knife. Give me the knife."

Silence. He felt her press closer to his back.

"Give me the knife! The Stone is about to break!"

He felt her fumbling—*she is numb with cold, too*—and then the knife hilt was thrust into his hand. He raised himself a little, bracing himself with his right hand, his palm pressed to the *kamin*. Gladna adjusted herself to support him. Arkost gripped the knife and suddenly thought of the moment in the Council when Beloved had displayed her scar. *Yes, show me the way, daughter.* He pressed the point against his chest and let it sink in just a little. He wanted a shallow gash, not a stab wound. He needed blood. Gritting his teeth, he dragged the knife diagonally across his chest, the cut starting at the right shoulder. It was clumsy—his hand was cold, he was lifting himself off the floor, he could not use his dominant hand—but the knife was sharp. There was blood. He drew the blade clear, dropping it with a gasp, and lay down on the *kamin*, letting his blood flow onto it. Was this what was needed? Was it enough?

Gladna bent over her husband. She had, through great effort, wrenched her eyes from the sight of Padrenna's ghost. *It is what* they *want me to see, and I* will not *obey.* She had overcome herself enough to hand a knife to her husband so that he might cut open his own chest. Was it enough? Was the *kamin* warming at all? Gladna pulled off her gloves awkwardly and put one hand down. She felt the stone slippery with blood. *Golden Lady, give me strength.* The Stone did not seem frozen, but it was cold. Stupid of her not to have felt it before. How could she judge now? She rubbed it with cold fingers and then stopped. Was the Stone *absorbing* the blood? *O Lady.* How much did it need? Would it take all of Arkost's? She felt the *kamin* with both hands. Yes. Yes, the Stone was taking it in.

"Arkost. Arkost!" He was still staring at whatever the mist was showing him. She touched his face, heedless of the blood that was now smeared on her hand. He was growing weak. *No.* There had to be something she could do.

How was the salt broken, then? she heard herself asking Radvyed, not long after he had returned with Beloved. Her son had looked off for a moment, then turned to her.

I have never seen anything like it, Mother. She sprinkled the ground with rosewater and it was healed, reborn. He had laughed in amazement and awe. *She is a lady of great power.*

Yes, thought Gladna, *too easy to forget that, because she does not* look *like a lady of great power.* Her fingers through habit touched her chest where she wore Beloved's rose close to her heart. Realizing what she was doing, she clenched her fingers. *This. I can use this.* She scrabbled at the fastenings of her garments, digging for the little pouch with the rose in it. Beloved had refreshed it, whatever that meant. As Arkost had a few minutes before, Gladna remembered their oaths on their coronation day. She looked around, saw the knife, and snatched it up. So many clothes. Her fingers so chilled. In frustration she cut at her clothing until her chest was exposed. Her fingers closed over the pouch, and she allowed herself a moment to grieve: if this did not work, if it worked but it killed one or both of them... *My life for Tamtir, for Radvyed*, she thought, and entertained grief no more.

Gladna cut the pouch free, and then, still holding the knife, fumbled for the flower inside. Its lovely fragrance escaped and floated free. Gladna's shoulders lost some of their stiffness; unperceived by the queen, the ghosts fell back a little, and the king was now able to shut his eyes. She held the rose, peering at in it the wavering firelight. *Heart of my heart*, she heard Beloved saying. *Now, how best to do this*, Gladna wondered, and remembered Beloved's frustration: how her new daughter regarded them all as stumbling about in the dark, doing great spells while all unaware of the danger and the cost. Suddenly Gladna laughed. *Why stop now? This kingdom rests on a thousand years of fumbling with magic.* She drew the knife across her palm, opening a shallow cut. She held the rose against it, pressing her chest close against her silent husband's back. Remembering the stricken *seveyati*, she wiped the tears from her wet face and rubbed them into the petals. Gladna reached down beside Arkost and laid her bloody palm and the rose against the Stone. *Drink that, thirsty one,* she thought. *And if that is not enough, you will have all my tears.*

Radvyed did not understand what was going on. The sky above the Lady's Glade seemed to be the center from which the strangely silent ravens swirled and dispersed—never good to have great flocks of scavenger birds, of course, but would they attack the people directly, as they had at the solar and in Beloved's dream? He and Beloved stood within the Lady's *zelohn*, facing away from her Tree. He had placed himself behind Beloved, ready to support her if needed, but unsure what might come at them and how to repel whatever it might be. Then the eerie fog had started. He felt Beloved stiffen. Was that a figure, a man stepping out of the fog? Radvyed could not see him clearly. He could not see anything beyond vague shapes and shadows. He tried to wipe his eyes with the gloved fingers of one hand, but his vision remained blurred. What was happening? Beloved spoke, but Radvyed heard only a muffled sound. What was wrong with him? He shook his head, but his vision remained obscured and his hearing obstructed. The cold intensified and he became aware that an icy snow was falling. The Tree behind them groaned. He tried to twist his neck to look over his shoulder at it, but with his blurred vision he could make out little in the weak torchlight. Then he noticed heat coming off Beloved's body. He remembered her fiery anger at the Council and how she had spoken of herself as having an affinity with the Lady through sap and flame. Radvyed hoped it would be enough. He hoped *he* would be enough for whatever she needed this night.

Rue huddled alone in the Forest. She let the snow fall on her, let it cover her up. She knew the baby before her was not her baby, that it was only a ghost. She knew the ravens in the trees were watching her pain, their sleek ink-black feathers blurred by dark and snow. She knew the ghost was sent to torment her. Yet if this was all she could have of her long-lost child—a specter sent by enemies to break her—she would take it, drink in the sight of him, gather to her heart his ear-grating wails, even if it killed her. As she lay there, cold and heartbroken, the ravens' black eyes on her, Death did seem to place a hand on her shoulder. And still she let the ghost of her Dulsan hold her there.

Beloved poured all her power into the earth, seeking, seeking, her magic coursing like water needing to find its level. Where, how, what to do? Should she release flame from her hands, try to disperse the uncanny mist? Should she incinerate the clever beady eyes of the watching birds? Should she—*oh!* The shock was such that she broke eye contact with her father's ghost, and her head was thrown back, her arms flung out to her sides, as though she had been struck by a lightning bolt. Beloved did not know it, but a reaching finger of her power had found the earth beneath the Master's blood-soaked Stone; it forged a link between the Stone's fresh royal blood and the Tree's sleeping sap. All Beloved knew was that she had been scrabbling in a dry land and now she had stumbled upon a geyser, a bursting dam;

she was hit with hundred-foot waves. She was a river, but now she had found the ocean.

Both the king and the queen felt the moment when Beloved's power met that of the Master's Stone, although they, like she, did not know what had happened. Arkost gasped and shuddered, his whole body overcome by a wave of heat that surged into him through his chest, which was pressed to the *kamin* and still seeping blood. Gladna, half crouched, half lying on top of him, her hand holding Beloved's rose against the Stone, felt a similar, shocking tide of heat rising from her palm through her arm. Tears slid out of the corners of her eyes. *She did it. She* did *it.* Neither of them saw the mist melting away, taking with it the figures of their sadness and guilt. But their relief and triumph were short-lived, for the heat that had swept up into their bodies now burned more fiercely. Moments before they had been battling against bone-deep chill; now they found themselves overwhelmed by fire. *Dark Master! Golden Lady!* And then all was flame.

Beloved struggled to channel the overwhelming surge of Tamtir's awakened power. It was not like her own, as different as seawater from fresh. Would it heed her or swallow her? Beloved welcomed it, let it rush up, into her, and asked it: *Be heat, flame. See our enemy.* To her surprise, it recognized her. *Grafted scion,* roared a many-throated voice in her mind. She had no time to wonder at the image of a cut rose with a blood drop at its clipped end. *Yes,* said the voice. *Defend Tamtir.*

She opened herself fully to Tamtir, letting its power surge into and claim her. She became the crucible heart where the blood- and earth-power of Tamtir and its people flooded her and transmuted into irresistible heat, then flowed back into the earth and spread—and spread, and spread. The ravens watching from above could see the circles of melted snow widening, as though Beloved were a pebble dropped into water and the heat she directed into the earth the ripples on the surface.

Beloved herself could no longer think, beyond the necessity of allowing the tide of power to wash into her body, transform into magical heat, and then rush out again. She was blind now, her head back, her ears filled with the clamor of surging power. Her skin crackled, with physical heat or magic or both, she did not know. She only knew she had not yet finished.

Wherever the earth thawed, the mist faded and then disappeared. Rue felt the earth beneath her cheek become warm and then wet with melting snow. She watched as the ghostly form of her baby faded. *Beloved*, she thought, and then let grief swallow her whole.

Dris became aware of something changing—the air? Was it the pale light before dawn? The torches seemed to gain strength, although their flames still danced fitfully. The specter of her sister still sneered at her, but the shape of it was blurred. The mist was lifting, dispersing. Dris did not dare relax or move. Then she found she was just a woman alone, no longer beset by memories or regrets, standing amid the dormant roses as the snow withdrew. Dris slumped, exhausted, and closed her eyes. She felt the wet grit of her tears on her cheeks, but did not wipe it away. *Not yet over*, she thought. *Hold steady and wait.*

Beloved was burning. Her body was snapping, gusting flame, all fixed contours gone, all scaffolding charred dust. And yet she knew, with whatever thought or consciousness still informed the fire that was her body, that it was not yet enough. What more could she do or give?

Radvyed held the blazing body of his lover, consort, and wife. His wedding bracelet burned like a brand on his wrist. To his eyes, slitted against the flames, her shape flickered and changed: doe, lioness, mare, rose, bird, tree, dragon, and yet other shapes that formed and fled before his confused gaze had grasped them. He held on, for that was his only task this day and, he began to think, the only task of his life, to hold to what was most dear—the kingdom, Beloved, hope. *I am the Badger, the Oak, the Mountain. I held her as she dissolved and was remade. I held her when her mother's rage and father's bitterness shattered about us in thunder and lightning. I will hold her now, even if there remains nothing but wind and smoke.* Then he dimly realized, *Yet there is neither.*

Chapter Sixty-Four

F ar above, on Her Seat of Judgment, the Sun Lady's penetrating gaze regards the lands that lie below the cloud furrows of Her sunfields. Night is not dark for Her; distance is not obscurity. Whatever She turns Her gaze upon She sees clearly. She contemplates the kingdom of Tamtir. She sees the malice and wrath of the Bitter Ones, formed and sent as a vast flock of ravens, spreading over the sky just above the kingdom, like an unfurling plume of dark and oily smoke. She watches as their chill mist slinks about the land, calling forth fears, griefs, and regrets, spinning deceits, and molding itself into the shapes of the dead. She sees the people of Tamtir, guarding each *zelohn* and *kamin* despite their cold and their terror and their bewilderment. Her sight touches each one: the aged, the children, those in their prime. In the Hall of the Master She sees the heaped figures of the king and queen on the Stone, lying in their own blood, their bodies caught up in a conflagration of mystical power. Yet they press themselves only more fiercely to the *kamin* beneath them. She sees Dris weeping but on her feet amid the roses; She sees Rue, alone and heartbroken, racked by loss. She sees Beloved, who has made herself a crucible and a conduit for the power of Tamtir—land, people, and House—and who now holds no one shape, but rather is as tongues of flame. And holding her, the young prince who found her and made her of the realm.

A *sozkol*, lithe and swift as a falcon, sits on the Lady's shoulder, awaiting her bidding. On Her knee is still the cage of ice that holds the Fire Bird, her long tail limp, her crest drooping. How long the Golden One watches, how long She ponders, no mere human can say, for what is time to that Lady? She weighs the anguish and the bravery of Tamtir; she notes the king and queen who hold back nothing, not even their own blood; she considers the outpouring of Beloved's essence in the service of her adopted people. She glances at the *sozkol* and it arrows from Her shoulder towards the earth. The Sun Lady calls, *Predun!*

My Lady? replies Her Consort, setting aside His thoughts of making. *How may I serve You?*

The Ice Raven oversteps.

Predun gazes into the night and sees the Ice Raven slipping among the chilly stars, riding the currents of power and darkness. Predun whistles, but the Raven feigns ignorance and soars higher, turns and plummets, pulls up above the clouds and wheels away again among the gems of night. He eludes this snare of shadow and that trap of mist. The Ice Raven gleams with the pride of his unfettered will. When Predun whistles a second time, the Raven divides himself in ever-multiplying fractals, a dizzying storm of white wings, blue eyes, and strong beaks, whirling, evading, bound by no one and nothing.

Predun draws in his net of stars, the infinite web of frozen fire. The net is not confused by illusion; it drags through the realm of night. The Ice Raven catches his wings and tangles his talons in the shadow lines that link the constellations. The Master watches as the Raven twists and struggles, and quiets at last.

He loosens the net and whistles. The white bird alights on Predun's forearm; he looks away from the Master's gaze and shuffles his feet. Then the Ice Raven bows. He holds the bow, wings outspread, head down; he trembles with the strain. The Master frees him with a quiet, *Enough.*

Beloved was dying. *The power is enough; it is I who am failing.* She knew nothing more than the ceaseless, searing blast of power surging through her, up what she had once thought of as her legs, transformed and given purpose and direction in what was once her heart, then rushing back out her former limbs again to warm and defend and save. *My will is all that is left of me. No more strength. Radvyed, Husband...Rue...*

Suddenly she was standing before the Golden Lady's Seat once more. No pain, no effort, no vast power demanding that she channel it or be destroyed. Only light, and clarity, and tranquil thought.

Do you choose to give all for Tamtir? The Lady's voice resonated in Beloved's head, though She did not open her lips. Beloved found herself silently answering thought with thought.

As You know, Lady.

Beloved sensed a faint smile behind the veil. *And do you choose to free the Fire Bird?*

Only tell me what I must do.

Smash the cage.

Beloved struck the cage with her fist. It shattered, scattering shards. Beloved gasped as she felt a sharp pain and looked down. From her chest protruded a splinter of ice. She looked up at the Lady.

Mistress?

But the Lady was gazing at the Fire Bird, who was restored to her full, wide-winged, long-tailed, fire-crested glory. The newly plumed bird turned her head and stared at Beloved. All pain and surprise were forgotten as Beloved gazed back into that bright golden eye, as intense as flame. Beloved groped for the ice splinter in her chest, and felt it melt between her fingers. The Fire Bird trilled a high, wild, triumphant note, then swept her sparking, flame-feathered wings. Beloved was back in the Glade.

She swayed. Radvyed's arms gripped her to him. The ghost of her father was gone.

Had she been on fire before? It was nothing to what she was now. She had been mere flames. Now she was molten rock erupting from the earth, soaring in a fountain to the sky. Beloved had only enough time to be pierced by ecstasy before she knew nothing more.

Chapter Sixty-Five

Alya shook herself, as though coming out of a daze. She looked around. The fire in the hearth was low, but burning. The uncanny mist was gone; she tried to remember, but could not seem to—had her grandmother spoken to her? Yet her Nani was dead. How she missed her still. The *kamin* under her seemed warm. Alya wondered whether the Bitter Ones' attack had happened at all, and if it had, whether it was over.

Outside in the *zelohn*, Van staggered a bit, as though he were recovering from a blow to the face. Where was the mist? Why was he thinking of his dead brother? He scrubbed one cheek with the back of his hand. Had he been crying? He looked down and realized that his feet were warm, although he was standing barefoot within the *zelohn* on the day of the Lady's Return. Where was the snow? As Van tried to puzzle out the events of the night, he heard the clear peals of the bells from the solar in Perikrost. He looked east and saw the first rays of dawn break over the hills. Van stood, unashamed of his tears, as Alya, released from her post at the *kamin* by the bells, came to stand next to him. He gripped her hand in his and watched as the Lady blessed them with the bright rays of Her Return. Never had a sunrise been so lovely, so longed for, so welcome. Alya squeezed his hand. How good to be here, together, in this moment.

Gladna woke from dreams of mist, blood, and fire. *And ghosts, as well?* She was cramped and aching. She raised her head and realized she was sprawled over her husband on the floor of the Master's Hall. She blinked and raised herself, sitting back on her heels. The rise and fall of Arkost's back reassured her that he was still living, although she wondered why she had doubted such a thing. The fire in the Master's Hearth still flickered and sparked. Again, why was she surprised and reassured? One of her hands felt unpleasantly sticky, as though—she raised it and much of her memory of the night before came back when she saw the rose. Her hand had a long shallow cut across the palm. She detached Beloved's rose from the dried blood and stared at it. It was as fresh as the day her son had brought it to her. She brought it to her nose and sniffed. Still it gave off that fragrance, so complex she thought she would never identify all the notes of it, and so healing she already felt her stiff muscles relaxing and her mind calming. She found the pouch, tattered from her hastiness in the night. Gladna wrapped the rose in the remains of the little bag, then tucked it securely in her clothing, as close as she could manage to her skin. She stroked Arkost's back.

Arkost opened his eyes and discovered he was still lying face down on the *kamin* of the Master's Hall. Someone was stroking his back, bringing him back into himself, into this moment. He had been in confused dreams of death, grief, and desperate chances, in which the Master's Stone was cracking from cold and he himself had slashed his own chest to guard it, before he had become nothing but fire...

No, not dreams. "Gladna?" How strange his voice sounded, as if he had been shouting, even screaming, for hours.

The hand on his back stilled. "Yes, my darling."

Arkost gingerly raised himself from his prone position, a little dizzy at first, and sat, careful to stay on the *kamin*, for who knew what their situation was? He looked about. The fire was still alight; the Stone was still whole. His wife, although disheveled, looked composed and tranquil, which for some reason made him grin. He looked down at himself and saw his torn clothing and the dried blood on his chest. He reached out for his wife's hand. She clasped his, wincing, and he realized that she, too, had given blood to the Stone. "We are still here, it seems," he commented.

"Yes," she said, smiling. Before he could say more, they heard the bells from the Lady's solar, then from the Master's forge. First came the "all clear," followed by the complicated music that announced that the Lady had indeed Returned, that the longest, darkest night was over. Their hands tightened.

Arkost swallowed and said, "Let us find the children." They helped each other stand and turned to the door at the end of the Hall, where they could see the first glimmer of day.

Chapter Sixty-Six

The king and queen walked the path to the Lady's Forest, cloaks drawn closely about them against the chill. Dris joined them at a meeting of the ways. She was quiet, but clear-eyed. Gladna wondered how the night had passed for her among the bare, thorny canes of roses, alone, as so many of their people had had to be to bear the hours of cold and fear. Yet although Dris seemed to have undergone some trial, she was as one who has come through hardship battered but whole. *We are all still here*, thought Gladna, then felt fear twist her heart. *I hope.*

In the Forest, Dris glanced aside from the path to where Rue had planned to stand watch. Gladna followed the gardener's gaze. No one. Gladna shivered once, but as Dris was not yet anxious, the queen said nothing. At last they were in the Glade itself. No Radvyed. *Where was he?* Was that a female figure sitting at the foot of the Tree? The Tree that was still whole and standing, its leafless branches reaching up into the morning light.

The three crossed the Glade. As they neared the Tree, Gladna could see Rue sitting at its foot. *O Lady.* Her heart gave a hard, sharp thump and then began beating against her ribs like a bird frantic to escape a cage. *Radvyed, Beloved. What*—yet surely Rue would not be so calm if the daughter of her heart were harmed?

They reached the low wall enclosing the *zelohn*. Rue rose to her feet, although she kept a hand on the Tree. She was not smiling, yet she was not grief-stricken. There was something on the ground, within the *zelohn*. Bodies? Gladna, Arkost, and Dris stilled.

There, on the bare earth, lay Beloved and Radvyed. They were on their sides, curled up and spooned together, Radvyed wrapped around Beloved, one arm across her chest, the other clasped about her waist. Beloved had one hand on the arm that lay over her heart; the other was curled by her cheek, as though she were a sleepy child. They were both naked, not just of clothing, but of all hair as well. The ground beneath them was covered with ash, as though a tiny wildfire had scoured only the area of the *zelohn*. Their nakedness and their baldness made them look defenseless, unearthly, new. As Gladna watched, she saw the breath of first one, then the other, in frosty wisps of air, and perceived the slight movement of their torsos. Her knees went weak and she sank to the ground. *They live.*

"Are they cold? Where are their clothes, their hair?" Gladna wondered.

Arkost asked, "May we touch them?"

Dris made no comment, but she continued to look at the prince and princess, as though they were puzzle pieces she should be able to fit together.

"I have not dared to touch them, even to cover them," said Rue. Her voice was gravelly, not at all her usual supple tones. The king and queen glanced at her, then away. No one had escaped the trials of that night. "When I heard the bells, I came here." Rue's hand trembled on the Tree. "It seemed to me the work of the Lady, or at least they seem under Her protection." Her voice shook on the last word and she paused before continuing. "I thought it best to wait until someone of Tamtir were here—of the royal House, or of the *seveyati*—before doing anything that might disturb them." Arkost and Gladna exchanged glances.

"Well," said the king. "This is nothing that I have prepared for. They do not look in danger, however, for they show no signs of feeling the chill—no blue tinge, no shivering." He paused, still considering the sleeping couple, then said, "Most excellent Rue, may we join you here, as I am sure some *seveyati* will be joining us soon?"

Gladna saw Rue smile a little at the combination of formality and friendliness. Arkost and Gladna walked around the *zelohn*. Rue waited until they had seated themselves before sitting down herself, her back against the Tree. Beloved's heart-mother, who had kept her distance from the Lady and the Master, seemed to draw strength from contact with the Lady's Tree, Gladna noted. *I wonder what she endured last night.*

Dris remained standing where she had first stopped, frowning in thought as she, like the other three, stared at the sleeping figures. They reminded her of something, but of what? Some image tugged at her mind, but she could not bring it fully before her. Her niece and the prince looked so fragile and new, and yet they also seemed more real, more present, more alive, than any who looked on their slumber. More alive, more latently powerful... Dris stilled as the earth vibrated beneath her feet, the deep thrum resonating throughout her body. In her mind's eye a rose hip nestled in a woman's large, cupped palm. The hip split, revealing the seeds within, and then the palm was filled with soil. Tiny, tender, double-leaved stems unfurled from the dark dirt. The vibration ceased and Dris staggered, blinking. She looked around—had that been the flash of a *sozkol*? The others, their gazes still on the sleepers, seemed oblivious.

Again Dris looked at Beloved and Radvyed, naked and vulnerable, enfolded in slumber. *Seeds.* Yes, they were seeds dropped into a hollow of the earth, the secret of life within them, curled and holy and dreaming.

CHAPTER SIXTY-SEVEN

*S*eveyati did arrive soon after: Sonza, Loucha, Zevedan, Mesaz, and others that Dris had not known by name but only by sight. Miramoy, the plump, dark-eyed priestess who served as the Lady's Gardener at the main solar of Zolatar, came and studied the curled bodies of the young royals. She was joined by the tall, wiry *seveyata* who guarded the wildness of the Forest, the Woodswoman, Fera. They circled the *zelohn* and spoke in low voices to each other. To Dris's eye, they were awed and wondering, and who could blame them? Miramoy called to Sonza and Zevedan, as well as to Nizh, the priest who oversaw the extraction of ore from the mines of Tamtir. Known as the Delver, he was quick and bright-eyed as a bird, and careful with both the lives of miners and the body of the earth. The *seveyati* had never seen anything like this before, Dris deduced. *Yet is it surprising that the Lady can surprise us?*

The *seveyati* were not the only ones who had come to the Glade once the temple bells had rung the all clear. *Dovoreni* and councilors came, as well as others from the palace, the city, and the surrounding country. *In fact,* thought Dris, *it is much the same as the day of the wedding, except that everyone is heavy-eyed from lack of sleep, dazed from eerie mist-dreams, and confounded by the sight of the prince and princess, bare as babies, curled up sleeping in the ashes of the Lady's* zelohn. Then *we knew what was happening, and what to do; now we do not.* Dris looked about at everyone standing, talking over the events of the night, and gazing upon the sleepers, whom someone had covered with a blanket. Everyone was dressed as they had been for the night's duty, no one thinking now of rank or proper order. Dris smiled. *I like this—though I do wish I understood more about our two seedlings there.*

It seemed the little knot of *seveyati* had reached a conclusion. They approached the king and queen, who were still sitting at the foot of the Tree, next to Rue. Dris blinked, now seeing in the later light of morning that both Arkost and Gladna appeared to have bloodstains on their rumpled clothing. The royal couple watched the *seveyati* approach. Arkost waved a hand, giving them permission to sit and speak. Dris was not able to see what was being said. It occurred to her that perhaps she should enter the conversation, as the Lady had been so gracious as to enlighten her, an adopted daughter of Tamtir. She did not have her pocket slate, so she looked around, wondering whether—yes, there was Rokena, the herald from the wedding, staring wide-eyed at the bodies within the *zelohn*. Dris kept her gaze steadily on her, and then, sure enough, the other woman felt the weight of Dris's attention and looked around. She spotted Dris and, smiling, began to make her way through the gathering to the gardener.

I have something to say to Their Splendors, said Dris. Rokena nodded, and they worked their way through the crowd to the Tree. Gladna saw them first and waved them closer, inviting the pair to join their little group.

The *seveyati* turned and greeted Dris with restrained friendliness. The Rose Gardener was usually from one of the solars or wildwoods and the priestesses of the Lady were not quite at ease with this outlandish woman who had been chosen instead. However, there was no denying that the palace roses thrived, nor that Dris had been instrumental in the queen's healing when the temples had been given no insight. Thus there was respect but a certain constraint. *And so I uphold the traditions of the clans*, Dris thought, with irony. *No one ever knows what exactly to make of us; we are always a little outside. And we like it that way*, she admitted to herself.

Arkost had noticed her arrival. "Dris," he said, "thank you for joining us. Zevedan has explained what he and the other *seveyati* believe happened last night. Followers of the Ice Raven sought to break Tamtir by a potent and far-reaching spell of grief and guilt. We were all visited by ghosts of loved ones or ones whom we felt we had gravely injured." Arkost paused to let Rokena sign to Dris. The king continued, "It seems that through the mercy of the Lady and the Master, these illusions are now but half-forgotten dreams for us and our people." Another pause. Arkost's eyes lost focus for a moment; his hand tugged at his blood-stained clothes.

He blinked and resumed speaking. "As we all knew, we would only be able to combat the great and complex magic of the Bitter Ones if the princess tapped the power of the people and land of Tamtir and joined it to her own gifts." The king looked over towards the *zelohn*. "She was successful. Zevedan reports that a column of fire was seen from the forge, right here by the Tree." Arkost paused again, and Gladna tucked a hand in his elbow. "The fire, which we believe to have been a manifestation of magic rather than a physical fire, since nothing—almost nothing—is burned here..."

He could not look in the direction of the *zelohn* any longer and instead brought his eyes to Dris's. *Now he understands why Rue and I were anxious. He sees that magic is not a docile tool.* "Suddenly the column of fire became a—" The king turned to Nizh. "What did you call it? The liquid rock that bursts from a mountain?"

"*Lava*," said Nizh, a hand on the back of his neck, wonder in his voice.

"Yes, *lava*," said Arkost. "It appeared to the watchmen of the forge as something more powerful, more substantial, than a column of fire. And this upshooting of *lava* incinerated the ravens that hovered, and drove up through the cloud cover that was smothering us with snowfall. The *seveyati* believe that the *lava* followed the power trail of the Bitter Ones, and either destroyed them or rendered them so weak that we need not fear them."

"For a while, at least," amended Gladna. "Let us learn more before we claim full victory." Arkost shook his head, but did not argue.

"So we greet the new day and the Lady's Return," continued the king. Dris understood that by *we* the king meant all Tamtir and its people, not merely the royal line or he himself. "Yet we know not the fate of the prince and princess," he went on. "It is clear that the power the princess was wielding or channeling or commanding"—the king shook his head to signify he did not understand the workings of magic—"that power did have a physical effect on her, on the prince, and on the Lady's own *zelohn*." Arkost looked directly at Dris. "Any insight is welcome, Rose Gardener."

Dris nodded and answered. Rue gasped, having caught Dris's meaning before the interpreter spoke.

"The Lady showed me they are seeds." This caused no little astonishment among those gathered, especially among the priestesses.

"The *Lady* showed—" began Fera, half incredulous, half offended, but Sonza held up a hand for silence. The head *seveyata* turned to Miramoy and raised her eyebrows. The temple Gardener was staring in the direction of the *zelohn*.

"Yes," said Miramoy, "*yes*, that is what they are. Seeds waiting for spring." She smiled in bemusement at Dris, pleased to have the riddle solved.

"Why would she show Dris and not *you*?" asked Fera, still inclined to belligerence.

"Fera, you know better than most that the Lady has a wild heart and does as She wills," said Sonza. Fera flicked a startled glance at the older priestess, then gave Dris a measuring look. The Woodswoman settled back, watchful but no longer quite so suspicious.

"So, Gardeners," the king said, nodding to both Miramoy and Dris, "how do we tend these precious seedlings? For spring is still far."

Chapter Sixty-Eight

Arkost and Gladna later said that what followed was the longest winter they had ever endured. Radvyed and Beloved were not moved, but were left within the Lady's *zelohn*. At first, the report had spread that the prince and princess were dead, then that they were deathly ill. The city and the palace were caught between joyful relief that the Bitter Ones had been repelled and perhaps even defeated, and sorrow that Tamtir's safety was bought at the price of their prince's and princess's lives. When the *seveyati* and bards and royal heralds spread the word that Radvyed and Beloved were instead in a kind of enchanted sleep—like magic seeds awaiting the Spring to wake—the people of Tamtir did not know what to think.

Miramoy and Dris, after conferring together, reassured the king, queen, and Rue that Beloved and Radvyed would take no harm from remaining in the *zelohn*—indeed they insisted the sleepers should not be moved. The *seveyata* explained that many seeds required cold to stimulate germination. Elm trees, such as the Lady's own, needed two or three months of cold for seeds to quicken. Dris pointed out that a period of dormancy enabled roses to rest and gather strength for spring growth. Perhaps the Lady, ventured Miramoy, had plans for the health of House and kingdom.

"Yes, those children must need rest after such a night," said Queen Gladna with a wondering laugh.

"Her rose was grafted to his, was it not?" asked King Arkost thoughtfully. "It seems in this case the sap may flow both ways, bringing invigoration and renewal."

Rue said nothing, but smiled as she touched her new bracelet of rose-petal beads, made for her by Dris.

The rest of the winter the Tamtireni spent talking over, marveling at, and seeking to understand the events of that sacred solstice night. Many a fireside heard a brother telling a brother of half-remembered ghosts, or witnessed a sister holding a sister from whom she had been too long estranged. The memories of that night were not vivid, but they were tenacious, and the people felt the need to be kinder to one another. Relatives and neighbors seemed to see one another with new eyes, knowing that no one had been spared the pain of that night. So from fear and agony came healing and strength, for the Lady and the Master know Their crafts.

As for the knowledge that the prince and princess were sleeping naked as seeds within the *zelohn*, Tamtir responded in a way that surprised both palace and temple. People began traveling to the Lady's Forest, first those from the city and nearby countryside, then those from farther out, until there was no *mirenzem* or town that had not sent someone. Each pilgrim brought with them a branchlet or cutting from home and laid it over the sleepers within the *zelohn*. No one piece was large, for most carried the gift tucked in their clothing. Trees, shrubs, vines—a bit of every plant that dreamed through winter aboveground was brought, and soon a kind of blanket had been formed over the sleepers. Even the king and queen laid rose branchlets from the palace gardens on them. Only Beloved's and Radvyed's faces, opaque and dreaming, could be seen. They were never alone, for Arkost, Gladna, Dris, Rue, and others of the palace, court, and temples came and would sit or stand by them, not minding the cold, needing their nearness, thinking somehow to shelter the young couple with their presence. And there were always the people themselves, solemn and awed as they took in the evidence of the depth of their prince and princess's commitment to Tamtir. A formal watch was set, both day and night. No one truly feared harm coming to Beloved and Radvyed, but they were precious, and so were guarded by the *strazha* as they slept, vulnerable as newborns.

As the spring equinox, or Tselun, neared, that time of change and new balance, an air of expectation breathed through the land. Tselun was always an important festival and holy day, but this year, it became common belief that it would be the day that the princess and the prince awoke. Arkost and Gladna hoped; Rue and Dris kept watch. The holy ones trusted in the Lady and Master's benevolence, however They chose to exert it.

Mystics from solar and forge believed the Bitter Ones to be dead or drained of power: this was good news, yet it did not dominate the consciousness of Tamtir. The business of the kingdom went forward, seemingly as usual, but an undercurrent of longing and anticipation quickened the awareness of time passing. When the equinox was a fortnight away, Arkost found his attention drifting during Council meetings or petition hearings; Gladna often stopped by windows facing the Lady's Forest and wondered, yearning for the day but also dreading disappointment.

Rue spent more of her days in the Glade, by the Tree and near the *zelohn*. She had no formal duties to distract her. The night of the Lady's Return had marked her. To the surprise of the king and queen, she asked to study at the Lady's solar, to be taught more about the Golden One. The priestesses made her welcome, happy to bring this unaligned woman into the fold. They treated her with kindness, and not only because Rue had royalty's ear as Beloved's heart-mother. Although reserved, Rue gave the impression of having suffered and overcome great hardship; further, she simply seemed lonely. In any case, she had been touched somehow by the Lady—her affinity for the Tree had been noted—so the *seveyati* understood that Rue was entrusted to them by the Sun Lady Herself.

At last the eve of Tselun arrived. Zolatar was full of people for the festival, even more than in other years. Gladna felt that the palace and the city—the whole kingdom—were thrumming with excitement. What would happen on the morrow? Would anything? The Glade was already thick with people who had come to watch the night, to see whether the prince and princess would wake. The *strazha* had been forced to cordon off space for the king and queen, along with those few who could reasonably make a case for having more right than another to be there: Rue, Beloved's heart-mother; Dris, her aunt; Sonza and Zevedan as the leaders of the primary solar and forge of Tamtir.

Finally, the crowd in the Glade settled. The evening's revelry gave way to the night's vigil; voices lowered and laughter quieted as people gathered around their braziers. Children were soothed and tucked into blankets for the night. Excited anticipation of the feast turned to thoughtful pondering of the possibilities of the day to come. Would the prince and princess wake? Would they remain asleep? There had been no foretelling or decree from the *seveyati* or the palace of what the day would bring, only the conviction of the people that the pair would wake.

Arkost sat on his bedroll amid the crowd, near the *zelohn*. He had his knees pulled up, his arms loosely circling them, and his hands locked together. The night was clear and cool. Once, before the events of the Lady's Return, he might have questioned the common sense of the people that tomorrow his son and his son's bride would wake. That was before he had begun to fathom the power residing in Tamtir. Nevertheless, anxiety pricked him. Gladna lay next to him, propped on one elbow, not yet able to sleep. She also gazed at the *zelohn*. The heaped offerings of branches, and more recently, early flowers, obscured the forms of the young couple beneath. A few torches were lit, so that folk might see and not step on one another; the braziers were dull red glows scattered about, their embers slowly dying.

Arkost looked up at the sky. The crescent moon rose in silver-white glory above the trees. The stars hung thick and low, their glittering patterns as fascinating as flame. A different light, a different clarity were the gifts of night. The stars, sparks of light, did not flare and vanish; they remained where the Master had placed them and danced the slow steps He commanded. A man on earth could look up and consider them, those gems of frozen fire, and find a measure of order and peace.

After some time, Arkost brought himself to calm acceptance. If the Lady wished the children to wake, they would. If She intended something other for them, they would not. He looked about. A few others were still wakeful. The *strazha*, of course. He looked at his wife. She had fallen asleep. He touched her hair. A torch guttered and went out. The king lay down and slept.

CHAPTER SIXTY-NINE

Beloved was in the dark. Her eyes were closed. Where was she? Without opening her eyes, she listened to her body. Cool air on her cheek. Hand curled by her face. Some kind of blanket over her—over *them*. In the dark, but not alone. A body curved around her. *Radvyed, Husband.* She held his arm over her chest. His other arm circled her waist. His knees were tucked into the crook of hers. What were they lying on? Sand? She was comfortable, but beginning to feel cramped. No pain, but as though she had slept deeply the whole night in one position. She felt rested. She did not try to pursue her fading dreams. They would return if they were important and right now she was more interested in this moment. Were those birds singing? In their bedchamber? Cool air on her cheek, faint light beyond her closed eyelids. No bed-curtains, no shutters? Where were they? Beloved opened her eyes.

Right in front of her was a low wall, high enough to fill most of her vision. She moved the hand by her cheek, testing the surface Radvyed and she lay on. Softer than sand, than dirt even. She turned her hand the little bit she could. Gray dust. Ashes? She turned her head and looked at her shoulder, then tried to look down her body. Not a blanket, or not only. She and Radvyed were covered with twigs, leaves, flowers? She blinked, but her eyes reported the same sight. She laid her head down again. Yes, those were birds. Yes, that was daylight. Yes, they were outside. Why? How?

Beloved moved experimentally. No aches, no injuries. Just a feeling that a good stretch would be wonderful. She tugged gently at Radvyed's arms. But instead of loosening, his arms tightened. His head pressed against her back, and he muttered, "I will not let go."

Beloved stopped pulling at his arms as memory flooded back. The Bitter Ones. The eve of the Lady's Return. The ravens; the white mist; the specter of her father, challenging her, taunting her. The fire of her own power that she had let free. Her desperate seeking for the means to tap the power of the land and the people and then, she still did not understand how, she had found it. The vastness and ferocity of that bottomless source, for which she became a mere channel, and then the Fire Bird herself had—helped her? Shown her how to be fire and live? And Radvyed, who had sworn never to let her go, come what may. He held her still. She closed her eyes and pressed his arms against her. *Badger, oak, mountain*, she thought.

"Husband," Beloved said, "Radvyed, it is done. Wake, my love." Some sort of commotion was audible from beyond the low wall, up, over, and around them. Beloved was not ready to extend her attention so far yet. "Husband," she repeated, moving a little.

Radvyed became very still, then slowly relaxed his hold. She felt him rubbing his cheek against her back. He moved his head, getting his bearings. Then he tensed again.

"Are we outside?"

"Yes."

"Under a pile of branches and leaves?"

"And flowers."

"Naked?"

She smothered a laugh. "Yes." A longer pause. The commotion was becoming louder, more excited.

"With crowds of people about?"

Beloved laughed outright. Radvyed pressed his face against her, his body shaking, until he uncurled from her all at once and rolled to his back. His movement was accompanied by the rustlings of twigs, leaves, and flowers as they slipped and cascaded about him. An old blanket tangled their legs. She rolled, too, creating her own small, murmurous shedding of branchlets and dry petals. They both lay there, laughing at the unexpected ridiculousness of their situation. They looked up into the astonished faces of the king, the queen, Rue, Dris, Sonza, Zevedan, and others known and unknown to them. This only made Beloved and Radvyed laugh the more. They sat up awkwardly, brushing ashes and twigs from their bodies and hair (for it had grown back as they slept, and was rather unruly; the prince had quite a full, shaggy beard), laughing as they took in each detail of the world they had woken to—or awoken: the blankets hastily thrown about their shoulders by Rue and one of the *strazha*; the crowd of people staring back at them with joy, relief, and astonishment; the sight of each other's disheveled hair and ash-smudged skin.

The queen scrambled over the wall and flung herself at Radvyed, embracing him and weeping; Rue snatched Beloved into her arms, and Beloved held her heart-mother as the older woman shuddered and wet Beloved's cheek with tears. Everyone was crying and laughing. The king entered the *zelohn* and gathered into his arms his wife and their child. After a moment, Arkost raised his head and, pulling both Radvyed and Beloved to their feet (the young couple drew their blankets a little more closely about themselves), showed them to the assembled people.

"Let it be known," King Arkost bellowed in a voice that filled the Glade, "and tell all Tamtir the glad tidings, that Princess Beloved and Prince Radvyed are awake, are whole, and live!" The Glade erupted with cheers, shouts, and sobs of relief. Beloved swayed a little with the surge of the people's power, but steadied almost immediately. After the events of the solstice night, these waves of power no longer overwhelmed her. An impromptu and somewhat ragged circle dance broke out; she thought she heard trumpets carrying the news; messengers on the edge of the clearing turned and ran, sprinting for the stables and their horses.

People pressed toward them. Gladna, Arkost, Rue, and Dris, having had their moment to hold and greet Beloved and Radvyed, fell back a little, so others could see and touch them.

Beloved and Radvyed clutched their blankets and let their subjects and friends assure themselves the young couple were alive and well. The princess and prince occasionally exchanged puzzled glances. This was more emotion than they expected. And the air was softer and warmer than it should be on the day of the Lady's Return. Why had they been covered with branches? How did Radvyed grow such a beard overnight?

Later, the urgency of the people calmed a little, although folk kept coming into the Glade even as others, exhausted by emotion and lack of sleep, packed up their things and started home.

Radvyed leaned toward his mother and asked, "Mother, what is it that we do not know? Why the bed of branches? Why the warm weather? Why—?" He stopped when the queen pulled back to look him in the face with surprise and tenderness.

"My handsome boy," Gladna said, "I see you indeed do not know. This is not the day of the Lady's Return. You and Beloved have been sleeping. Today is Tselun. We rejoice to see you wake from your long sleep."

Chapter Seventy

What followed were days of jubilation and feasting and, for Beloved and Radvyed, of explanations, exclamations, and amazement. The tale of what had happened or what could be understood to have happened that dark night was pieced together in talks with the king and queen, the *seveyati*, the bards, and many others with their own stories and experiences.

Were the Bitter Ones vanquished? The *seveyati* who walked the sky leas said they could find no vestige of them. Beloved, seeking echoes and traces of power, found no threat. The beacon spell no longer rode in her veins; she surmised it had burned away in the final conflagration. The king heard no troubling news from the *strazha* posted at the borders and at the ports. It was concluded that if the Bitter Ones were not gone, they were weakened, in disarray, and no immediate threat.

"We are watchful, as always," said King Arkost, "but no longer on the edge of hostilities."

After the events of the winter, everyone—scholars and *seveyati*, *dovoreni* and *mireni*, masters and merchants of the Council—were willing to entertain, at least, some of Beloved's conjectures about magic and what role it played in the health and unity of Tamtir. The bards composed songs to explain and record the events of that night; no one complained that year about the lack of fresh subjects for song. Tamtir had a new vigor surging through it, not only the land awakening in spring, but the people thinking and knowing and feeling things newly.

Beloved and Radvyed were perplexed and astonished that they had been sleeping on a bed of ashes for months. They listened to Dris's and Miramoy's theories with wondering awe. The princess's and prince's freshly grown hair seemed springier than before to their fingers. Their skin, smooth and whole as a baby's, with no blemishes, scars, or callouses, seemed strange to them: only Beloved's great scar remained, but even that was nothing more than a faint silver line. They were themselves, yet different.

It was not only their bodies and faces that were oddly unfamiliar to them. Their memories of the night of the Lady's Return blurred into the dreams of their months-long slumber. They spoke with each other, recovering what had happened: the ravens, the mist, the ghost of her father. The cold that had gripped the Tree. How Beloved had become shifting shapes of fire in Radvyed's arms, then an uprush of flame so dense and intense it had felt like he had clung to a river of molten rock.

"How did you hold me, Husband?" Beloved marveled.

They were sitting outside, on a little balcony off one of the sitting rooms. The rose garden spread below them; the treetops of the Forest brushed the soft sky. Radvyed looked down at their loosely joined hands and their new wedding bracelets. The old ones had been consumed by sorcerous heat. He played a little with Beloved's fingers before looking up with a shy smile.

"How did you become a column of fire and yet remain yourself?" he asked. Beloved stared at him, then smiled and laughed, shaking her head a little.

"With help," she answered, thinking of the Lady, of the Fire Bird, of Tamtir's ocean of power, of Radvyed himself.

His smile grew. "Yes, just so. With help." And he thought of the Master who forged the stars and shaped flame, of his parents giving blood to the Stone, and of the wife who had offered herself so wholly to protect his kingdom and his people.

They were quiet a while, looking at the vista before them, lost in thought. Then Radvyed laughed to himself. When Beloved looked at him inquiringly, he said, "Do you remember before you discovered the Bitter Ones and their hatred?"

She wrinkled her brow. "What do you mean?"

"We had just returned from the Sinevy Hills."

Beloved nodded.

"You thought then you would never be at home in the palace." Radvyed leaned toward her. "Beloved, will you stay with me and be my princess, my wife, my beloved sorceress?"

Beloved returned his gaze. Her heartbeat still quickened every time she looked at his face of almost unearthly beauty, but she was affected also by her knowledge of him: his steadfastness, his kindness, his occasional diffidence, his love.

"Your parents and your people will not object to a sorceress among them?" she asked, smiling. "They will not suggest that perhaps it would be better if I removed myself beyond the border?"

He laughed. "After this winter, I think no one would say a word if you caused a tree to grow through the ballroom floor or covered the walls with flowers or replaced every furnishing with uncut blocks of stone."

"I think I will keep any changes of furniture or adornment to our rooms." She laced her fingers more closely with his. Her grafting onto the royal House had engendered that solstice night an unprecedented working of power. She had finally claimed Tamtir and her magic had strongly rooted. More importantly, however, Tamtir had claimed her, breath, blood, and bone.

Beloved felt the strength of Radvyed's grip and knew however far she flew or wherever she might wander, she would never be lost or alone. She leaned toward him. Before their lips touched, Beloved said, "I am Beloved of Tamtir. I will stay."

EPILOGUE

In addition to the usual Ridings, Tithings, and Visits of the royal family, Beloved liked to go out from the palace on her own. Not on long journeys, for she did not like to be apart from Radvyed for more than a week or three. But she liked to go out and walk and be among the people. She would go dressed plainly, even humbly, asking for shelter if there were no inns when she desired to rest. Hearth fires burned more brightly and forge fires more fiercely in her presence; after she left a place, it was noticed that the flowers bloomed more profusely and the earth yielded more fruit. The prince would joke about these rambles, saying that the princess had gone out for a spell, so the people came to call her outings Spells. They answered the door more kindly to strangers, "Let them in! Could be the princess, out for a Spell!" So hearths were warmer even when Beloved did not bless them in person.

Radvyed remembered to ask the bard Pevetos to make whole the story of the Tower. Intrigued by what he had learned of the Hidden House, Pevetos went there himself to sing the tale to Starzana of the Kaitiren, the matriarch of the Wanderers. In return, she taught him many songs he did not know. Her people kept the House as Beloved had asked, although some liked to wander still.

Arkost and Gladna sponsored a new discipline of study, the Theory and History of Magic, at the College of Learning. When they had time to spare from their duties, they sometimes went to listen to a lecture at the College or to a discussion conducted at the palace itself.

Dris continued as Rose Gardener and mentored many apprentices in her craft. She wore close to her heart with secret pride an amulet carved with a Fire Bird in flight, grasping a rose, given to her by her niece.

Rue, a year or so after the equinox that saw her heart-daughter wake from sleep, moved out of the palace. Beloved, and indeed the whole royal family, were loth to let her go, but she was firm. Rue felt aimless at the palace; although everyone was kind, she had no work or occupation, and this disturbed her. She opened a small inn with a taproom in the city, for she had come to realize that she liked looking after people. It was named the Rose and Tree. Not many months later, a retired *strazha* sergeant had become a regular there, and after some patient courtship on his part, Rue agreed to marry him. Beloved was glad to see her heart-mother happy in her own home.

Beloved took a palace tower for her own, for study, practice, and solitude. It had a roof-window so she always could see the sky above her. Long-thorned vines wound about it, with dark green leaves that did not fade, and the leaves were starred with translucent white flowers. When Beloved did not mind visitors, an ever-changing stairway would lead them to a carved or perhaps painted door; if she did not wish to be disturbed, any seeking her found themselves following flights of steps that politely returned them to the main floor. She did eventually learn all her names and titles, and even earned a few more, but the one she thought truest was *Beloved*.

Radvyed felt his life was like one of those stories of wonder and adventure that he had loved as a boy, but had always thought were but tales. Yet here he was, having grappled with riddles, curses, ghosts, and mage-fire, a prince with a sorceress bride. When their children came, each cherished, he knew himself blessed beyond his boyhood dreams. With bemusement he heard one day that because of the tales told of him—freeing the princess from her name curse, breaking the Griefstone and the salt, anchoring the princess as she burned with all the fierce power of Tamtir—his people called him Radvyed the Sorcerer. How he laughed.

THE END

Acknowledgments

Many people gave encouragement, help, and insight as I wrote this book. I gratefully acknowledge their support and assistance.

Writers need other writers, or at least I do. Thank you to SPWrites for critiques, advice, and friendship: Bria Burton, Cate Bronson, Seth Hollen, Rachel Printy, and Martin Von Cannon. Thank you also to Shakespeare's Sisters, Best Selling Brains, and the Florida Writers Association, especially the St. Pete chapter, for your support, critiques, and camaraderie.

It can be tricky to be related to a writer, because they may ask you to read their work, and what if you don't like it? Nevertheless, some family members still agreed to read an early version of the story, and I thank them: Frances Walker Fox, Jamie Fox, Mike Fox, Luke Fox, Nick Fox, Julia Gamble, Laura Stadter, Lucia Stadter, Mark Stadter, Paul Stadter, and Philip Stadter.

I am also lucky to have friends who undertook to read an early version. Thank you, Amy Hartsough, B. C. Krygowski, Erika Lietzan, Anna Presler, David Robinson, and Sharon Kennedy Wynne.

After the early versions came the later ones, and I am grateful to those who with patience and generosity read the whole thing all over again: Bria Burton, Frances Walker Fox, Rachel Printy, and Martin Von Cannon.

I apologize if I have forgotten anyone.

I am fortunate in the professionals who worked with me on this book. All errors are my own.

Developmental Editor: Kat Howard

Sensitivity Reader: Jacqueline Wunderlich

Proofreader: Emily Stone

Images for the cover design are from Depositphotos. The creators of the images are:

Castle: FairytaleDesign

Ravens: Idelfoto

Rose: Kesu01

Thorns: kopi.in.ua

Starry sky: Rastan

About the Author

Thank you for reading *Handsome and Hideous*!

For the latest news about my books, sign up for my newsletter at mariafoxwriter.com/newsletter/

If you enjoyed this book, a review or a rating wherever you prefer posting your thoughts about books is very helpful.

Maria Fox writes indoors and birds outdoors. If not writing or birding, Maria is probably crocheting, crosswording, or repelling persistent Florida wildlife from her house.

Her online home is mariafoxwriter.com

She also can sometimes be found on social media:

Bluesky: @mariafoxwriter.bsky.social

Instagram: @mariafoxwriter

Mastodon: @mariafoxwriter@mastodon.social

Spoutible: @mariafoxwriter

9 798998 662812